MU123

Discovering mathematics

BOOK A

Units 1–4

This publication forms part of an Open University course. Details of this and other Open University courses can be obtained from the Student Registration and Enquiry Service, The Open University, PO Box 197, Milton Keynes MK7 6BJ, United Kingdom (tel. +44 (0)845 300 6090, email general-enquiries@open.ac.uk).

Alternatively, you may visit the Open University website at www.open.ac.uk where you can learn more about the wide range of courses and packs offered at all levels by The Open University.

To purchase a selection of Open University course materials visit www.ouw.co.uk, or contact Open University Worldwide, Walton Hall, Milton Keynes MK7 6AA, United Kingdom, for a brochure (tel. +44 (0)1908 858793, fax +44 (0)1908 858787, email ouw-customer-services@open.ac.uk).

The Open University, Walton Hall, Milton Keynes, MK7 6AA.

First published 2010.

Edited, designed and typeset by The Open University, using the Open University TeX System.

Printed in the United Kingdom by Charlesworth Press, Wakefield.

The paper used in this publication is procured from forests independently certified to the level of Forest Stewardship Council (FSC) principles and criteria. Chain of custody certification allows the tracing of this paper back to specific forest-management units (see www.fsc.org).

ISBN 978 1 8487 3021 2

1.1

Contents

Contents

UNIT 1
Starting points

Welcome to MU123!

This unit is the first step on a mathematical journey which will be full of ideas and exploration. Mathematics has a fundamental role in almost every aspect of modern life, from the media and business to science and medicine, and beyond. As mathematics plays such an important part in the world, using mathematics in practical situations is one of the four main themes of the course. You'll see how you can use mathematics in everyday life – for example, how to use it to make sense of the numbers you see in the media, and how to interpret tables of data. And you'll see some more specialised applications of mathematics, such as how mathematics is used in developing route-planning software to help drivers get from one place to another as quickly as possible.

But there's more to mathematics than solving practical problems: the subject is also fascinating in its own right. It can be appreciated for its beauty, and it can surprise, delight and challenge you just as much as subjects like literature and art. Abstract mathematics is the second theme of the course. You'll be introduced to some surprising facts about numbers and number patterns, and you'll learn how it's possible to prove that certain facts hold not just for a few numbers, but for infinitely many. Remarkably, some areas of abstract mathematics that initially seemed to have no practical applications now have important uses: for example, modern-day data encryption relies heavily on an abstract subject known as number theory, as you will see.

The third theme of the course is developing your mathematical skills. You need to be able to work confidently with numbers and other elements of mathematics if you're to be effective in using mathematics in your everyday life, in your workplace or in further courses. You'll learn new mathematical skills in statistics, geometry and trigonometry, and some fundamental skills in algebra, that will open up new possibilities for your future study and career options.

The final theme of the course is mathematical communication. You'll learn how to interpret mathematics that's presented to you, and how to present your mathematics to others so that it can be easily understood. You'll find that the feedback you get from your tutor is particularly helpful in helping you to develop your skills in mathematical communication.

The four themes of the course are interlinked: most parts of the course involve more than one of them. In summary, in MU123 you will develop your mathematical skills and your abilities in mathematical communication by studying both practical and abstract mathematical ideas.

Figure 1 The two sides of the Ishango bone

Mathematics has been used to describe and explain the world for thousands of years. The regular marks engraved on a piece of bone found in Africa, known as the Ishango bone (Figure 1), appear to indicate that people were counting and thinking mathematically over 20 000 years ago. More sophisticated mathematical activities such as measuring size and using money were also adopted by many civilisations thousands of years ago.

Introduction

This book contains the first four of the fourteen units in the course; this first unit introduces you to the main themes of the course and the different teaching materials that are used. It also helps you to revise some basic mathematical skills and to start studying mathematics more effectively.

Section 1 gives you some brief advice on studying the course.

In Sections 2 and 3 you will revise some basic mathematical skills, such as rounding numbers, using your calculator and working with negative numbers, fractions and percentages. Your study of later units will be much easier if you are fluent in these basic skills, so these sections give you an opportunity to practise them and make sure that there are no gaps in your understanding. In these sections you will also see some everyday applications of mathematics, and how the media (newspapers, television, radio and the internet) use numbers.

A particular model of calculator is recommended in the Course Guide.

You will need to keep the Course Guide to hand throughout your study of Sections 2 and 3, as it contains several calculator activities that you will be asked to do. If you are not using the recommended calculator, then you may need your calculator manual as well. If you do not have the Course Guide to hand when you reach these activities, then you can return to them later.

Activities 5, 16 and 20, on pages 15, 33 and 36, respectively, are in the Course Guide.

Section 4 introduces you to abstract mathematics. You will see how two simple ideas – adding odd numbers and folding paper strips – can be developed mathematically, with intriguing results.

The final two sections in this unit will help you to think constructively about your study methods. Section 5 gives advice on doing your course assignments and introduces you to the topic of how to write mathematics so that it can be easily understood by others. Section 6 looks at how you might review and improve your study methods.

1 Studying MU123

This short first section tells you what to expect in the course, and helps you to start planning a method of study that will be effective for you.

1.1 The course units

Each unit of MU123 is structured in a similar way. As well as explanations of the mathematics, there are worked examples to study and activities to do. The worked examples show you how to do the mathematics and how to set out your working, and in the activities you are asked to do some mathematics yourself. The best way to learn mathematics is to practise it, so it is important to work through the activities carefully, and to do as many as you can. There are solutions at the end of each unit, which you can use to check your answers, or to obtain a hint if you are stuck!

'Exercise is the beste instrument in learnyng.'
Robert Recorde (1510–1558), mathematician.

Key facts and strategies are highlighted in pink boxes, so that you can refer to them easily. You will also see blue boxes, like the one on the right, which tell you some of the rich history of mathematics, or contain other interesting items.

Next to some worked examples and activities you will see a computer icon, like the one alongside Activity 1 below. This icon means that you need to use your computer, for example for software and tutorial clips (clips in which tutors explain worked examples).

There are other resources available via your computer, such as the practice quizzes which are online activities that provide further practice, with instant feedback. There are also occasional references to websites that are not part of the course; the computer icon is not used for these.

As you work through each unit you may find it helpful to keep the Handbook to hand. You can use it to look up ideas covered in other units, and you can annotate it with helpful notes and examples.

The first activity asks you to watch the first course video, which introduces you to some of the ideas in the course and gives you a glimpse of what it is like to be a mathematician. It doesn't contain any details that you have to *learn*, so there is no need to take notes – just sit down and enjoy it! If it is not convenient for you to watch the video now, then you can leave it until later, and continue working through the unit. But try to watch the video as soon as possible, as it will help set the scene for studying the unit.

 Video

The video is on the DVD.

Activity 1   *The first course video*

Watch the video 'Welcome to MU123 Discovering mathematics'.

1.2 Studying effectively

Before you start on the mathematics in MU123, it's a good idea to check that you're organised to study effectively, especially if this is your first course with The Open University. This subsection will help you to do that, and there is further advice throughout the course.

Finding time and using it effectively

It is important for you to think about how your study of MU123 will fit in with the rest of your life, and what adjustments you may need to make.

The study planner is on the course website.

Each unit is designed to take about 13 hours of study for an average student: the time that you will need will depend on your mathematical background, and some units may take you longer than others. You will also need to allow some extra time for the assignment questions and other activities such as tutorials. It is important to keep up with the schedule in the study planner as much as possible, or you could find that you have run out of time to study the units needed to complete an assignment before its cut-off date. So try to plan your study times, fitting them in with your other commitments, to make sure that you do not fall behind.

'I can work at home and in my office, and those are the two places I work most. Just anywhere where I've got a pad of paper and a biro ... But if you're sitting waiting in an airport lounge, which for many people would be a very boring experience, for a mathematician it isn't. Get out some paper and have a think about things.'

Timothy Gowers, Professor of Mathematics, University of Cambridge, and Fields medallist.

Some people study late in the evening while others are more alert first thing in the morning. Which are you: a nightingale or a lark – or neither? What is the smallest study period that is likely to be useful to you? Some students find that even a ten-minute burst is enough to try an activity or to keep them going and set them musing, whereas others find that they need at least half an hour for effective study.

If you do not have continuous access to a computer, then it is worth checking which sections, or parts of sections, can be studied without one, and planning ahead accordingly. However, you are advised to study the course material in the order in which it is presented, as in later parts you will often need some of the skills and knowledge covered earlier.

It can take some time to find out what study pattern works best for you, and it's worth thinking about this as you work through this first unit.

Making notes

Some students find that making their own notes in a notebook or on sheets of paper is an invaluable part of their learning process, as putting things in their own words helps them to make sense of ideas and remember them. These notes may include summaries of the main ideas, new terminology and notation, things learned from doing the activities, useful examples or even diagrams summarising the main ideas and how they fit together. Other students use different methods to help them to understand and remember the material, such as highlighting bits of the text, jotting brief notes and questions in the margins, and making annotations in the Handbook.

Whatever you decide about making notes, you are advised to write out your solutions to the activities, and to keep them organised. It can be useful to refer to them when you do assignment questions – particularly if you annotate them with brief notes about anything you first got wrong but then corrected, or found difficult but then resolved. Writing out your solutions in full will also give you useful practice in writing mathematics well. This is a skill that you will need for the assignment questions, and there is advice on it in Section 5.

It is a good idea to think about how to keep track of any non-urgent questions that you want to ask your tutor by phone or at a tutorial. For example, you could make a list in your notes, or stick labels on the edges of relevant pages.

Bal was so delighted with his marginal annotations that he had them published in hardback edition!

Getting help

Remember that you are not alone with the course materials. Your tutor is there to help you with any mathematical problems that you encounter, and he or she can also provide advice on other matters to do with your progress on the course, such as what you should do if you are worried about completing a part of the course in time. You can also discuss the course with other students, for example at tutorials or on the online course forum. They may be able to help you with certain topics, and you may be able to help them too. Trying to explain an idea to someone is often an excellent way of learning – especially if they ask lots of questions! You should also find it interesting and reassuring just to see how other students are studying the course.

If you are stuck on a particular mathematical point, then it's worth spending a few minutes trying to resolve it yourself – if you can, then you are likely to learn from the process, and you should remember what you have learned more easily in future. It may help to look back at the material that led up to that point, and make sure that you fully understand it. But you should not spend a large amount of time puzzling over a particular point without making progress. Many difficulties can be resolved rapidly if you contact your tutor or post a message on the course forum, leaving you more time to get on with the rest of the unit.

EUREKA!

An occasion when you resolve a problem is often called a 'Eureka moment'. The Greek mathematician Archimedes (c. 287–212 BC) was interested in all the mathematical sciences, from geometry and arithmetic to mechanics and astronomy. There is a story that he was in the bath one day when he suddenly realised that the way objects displace water gave the answer to a problem that had been puzzling him – he leapt out of the bath shouting 'Eureka!' ('I have found it!').

Figure 2 An Italian postage stamp celebrating Archimedes

If a problem arises because you are a little rusty on some of the basic mathematical skills that you are expected to have before the start of the course, then you may find it useful to set aside some extra study time and refer to Maths Help. This is an online resource provided by The Open University, which contains help with basic mathematics. There is a link to Maths Help on the course website.

2 Working with numbers

This section and Section 3 will help you to revise and practise some of the basic mathematical and calculator skills that you will need to be able to use fluently in later units. If you have already made sure that you have the basic mathematical skills needed for the course, as recommended in the course description, then you should find most of these two sections straightforward.

Most students find that they need to improve their fluency in at least some of the skills, and sort out small gaps in their knowledge, so it is important that you work through these sections thoroughly, doing the activities and checking your answers against the solutions at the end of the unit. You may not be aware of some of the gaps in your knowledge or skills, so even if you feel confident about a topic you should still try the activities to make sure.

If you feel that you need more practice on a topic than is provided in the printed unit, then visit the website to see whether there are any suitable practice quiz questions. For some topics you may also be able to find further practice in Maths Help. There are references in the margins to tell you which topics are covered in Maths Help, and where.

2.1 Getting the order right

Suppose that you are buying a box of wallpaper paste costing £8, and 12 rolls of wallpaper at £14 each. The calculation for the total cost in £ can be written as

$$8 + 12 \times 14.$$

To work out the cost, you first do the multiplication and then do the addition, which gives the answer £176. You know that you should do the multiplication before the addition because you know the context of the calculation.

But will your calculator do the same? Or will it work from left to right and do the addition first and then the multiplication, to obtain the answer £280? Try it! Type the whole calculation into your calculator and press the '=' key.

You should find that your calculator gives the correct answer of £176. This is because the following convention is used in mathematics.

Order of operations: BIDMAS

Carry out mathematical operations in the following order.

B	brackets
I	indices (powers and roots)
D	divisions $\left.\right\}$ same precedence
M	multiplications
A	additions $\left.\right\}$ same precedence
S	subtractions

When operations have the same precedence, work from left to right.

The BIDMAS rules tell you the order in which to deal with the operations $+$, $-$, $\times$ and $\div$, and also *powers* and *roots*. Remember that to raise a number to a power, you multiply it by itself a specified number of times. For example, 2^3 means three 2s multiplied together:

$$2^3 = 2 \times 2 \times 2.$$

The superscript 3 here is called the power, index or exponent. Roots are revised in Unit 3.

Example 1 reminds you how to use the BIDMAS rules. It also illustrates another feature that you will see throughout the course. Some of the worked examples include lines of green text, marked with icons like ⌬. This text tells you what someone doing the mathematics might be thinking, but wouldn't write down. It should help you to understand how you might do a similar calculation yourself.

2^3 is read as 'two cubed', and 5^2 (in Example 1) is read as 'five squared'. For powers other than 2 or 3, you say 'to the power': for example, 7^4 is read as 'seven to the power four' or 'seven to the four' for short.

The plural of 'index' is 'indices'.

Example 1 *Using the BIDMAS rules*

Work out the answers to the calculations below without using your calculator.

(a) $8 - 2 + 5 - 1$ (b) $5 + 12 \div 4$ (c) 4×5^2 (d) $(5 - 3) \times 4$

For help with the BIDMAS rules, see Maths Help Module 1, Subsections 3.5 and 3.6.

Solution

(a) ⌬ The addition and subtractions have the same precedence, so do them in order from left to right. ⌬

$$8 - 2 + 5 - 1 = 6 + 5 - 1 = 11 - 1 = 10$$

(b) ⌬ Do the division first, then the addition. ⌬

$$5 + 12 \div 4 = 5 + 3 = 8$$

(c) ⌬ Work out the power first, then do the multiplication. ⌬

$$4 \times 5^2 = 4 \times 25 = 100$$

(d) ⌬ Do the calculation in brackets first, then do the multiplication. ⌬

$$(5 - 3) \times 4 = 2 \times 4 = 8$$

Four fours puzzle

A well-known puzzle asks you to use four fours, together with mathematical symbols such as $+$, $-$, $\times$, $\div$ and brackets, to write down a calculation for each of the numbers from 1 to 10. For example,

$$1 = 44 \div 44$$

and

$$3 = (4 + 4 + 4) \div 4.$$

You might like to try the other numbers. (There are answers on the course website.)

Activity 2   *Using the BIDMAS rules*

Work out the answers to the calculations below without using your calculator.

(a) $9 + 7 - 2 - 4$ (b) $2 \times (7 - 4)$ (c) $(3 + 5) \times 3$

(d) $(3 + 4) \times (2 + 3)$ (e) $3^2 + 4^3$

Activity 3   *More BIDMAS*

Check whether each of these calculations is correct. For those that are incorrect, add brackets to make them correct.

(a) $2 \times 5 + 3 = 16$ (b) $3 + 4 \times 7 = 49$ (c) $1 + 2 \times 3 = 7$

(d) $9 - 3 \times 2 = 3$ (e) $2 \times 3 + 3 \times 5 = 60$

Mathematical terms

There are many terms that have specific meanings in mathematics. When the meaning of a term is explained in the course, the term is printed in bold. Important terms and their definitions are also collected together in the Glossary in the Handbook.

Some terms used for calculations are explained below.

Some terms for calculations

The **sum** of two numbers is the result of adding them together.

A **difference** between two numbers is the result of subtracting one from the other. There are two possible answers, depending on which way round you take the numbers, but usually the smaller number is subtracted from the larger.

The **product** of two numbers is the result of multiplying them.

A **quotient** of two numbers is the result of dividing one by the other. There are two possible answers, depending on which way round you take the numbers.

Activity 4   *Sums and differences*

By trying some positive numbers less than 10, can you find the following?

(a) Two numbers with sum 12 and product 32

(b) Two numbers with difference 2 and quotient 2

2.2 Using your calculator

You are expected to use your calculator for most numerical calculations in MU123. You can refer to either the 'Calculator guide' section in the

Course Guide (if you are using the recommended calculator) or your calculator manual to remind yourself which keys to press. Sometimes you may find that it is quicker to do a simple calculation in your head or on paper.

Occasionally you are asked not to use your calculator. This is usually so that you can practise a technique that you will need to use later when you learn algebra.

When you type a calculation into your calculator, it is important to think about the BIDMAS rules, to ensure that the operations are carried out in the order you intend.

In the next activity you will practise the following basic calculator skills.

- Enter calculations correctly, using the number keys, the $+$, $-$, $\times$ and $\div$ keys and the bracket keys.
- Display answers as either decimals or fractions.
- Use the power keys.
- Correct mistakes in entering calculations.

> The manual for the recommended calculator contains much more information than is covered in the Course Guide.

Activity 5 *Getting to know your calculator*

Work through Subsection 4.1 of the Course Guide.

> If you are not using the recommended calculator, then you may need your calculator manual as well as the Course Guide.

2.3 Units of measurement

Many everyday calculations involve measurements of some kind: for example, lengths, times, amounts of money, and so on. In the UK, both the metric and imperial systems of measurements are used. In the metric system, the different units for the same type of quantity are related to each other via powers of ten: for example, 1 metre is the same as 100 (or 10^2) centimetres. In the imperial system, the units are related in different ways: for example, 1 stone is the same as 14 pounds.

> For more help with units, see Maths Help Module 1, Section 2.

This course mostly uses the standard metric system known as the Système Internationale d'Unités (SI units). This system is used by the scientific community generally and is the main system of measurement in nearly every country in the world.

> In the US, 'metre' is spelt as 'meter'.

There are seven base SI units, from which all the other units are derived. The **base units** (and their abbreviations) used most frequently in the course are the metre (m), the kilogram (kg) and the second (s). Prefixes are used to indicate smaller or larger units. For example, millimetres, centimetres, metres and kilometres are all used to measure length. The most common prefixes are shown in Table 1, and there is a more extensive list in the Handbook.

> The metric system was founded in France in the wake of the French Revolution, and work on SI units has been ongoing since the middle of the twentieth century. At the time of writing, the only countries who have not adopted SI units as their sole or primary system of measurement are the United States, Burma (Myanmar) and Liberia.

Table I   Some common prefixes

Prefix	Abbreviation	Meaning	Example
milli	m	a thousandth $\left(\frac{1}{1000}\right)$	1 millimetre (mm) $= \frac{1}{1000}$ metre
centi	c	a hundredth $\left(\frac{1}{100}\right)$	1 centimetre (cm) $= \frac{1}{100}$ metre
kilo	k	a thousand (1000)	1 kilometre (km) $= 1000$ metres

Converting units

Sometimes you need to convert measurements from one unit to another. For example, suppose that you are thinking of installing new kitchen cabinets. If you measure lengths in your kitchen in metres and then find that the dimensions of new kitchen cabinets are given in millimetres, then you will need to convert both sets of measurements to the same units, say millimetres. Or if your answer to a calculation is 0.006 kg, then it will usually be better to convert it to grams, since 6 g is both simpler and easier to imagine.

In much of Europe the decimal point is denoted by a comma rather than a dot, so 0.006 kg would be written as 0,006 kg.

To convert from one unit to another, you should first find how many of the smaller units are equivalent to one of the larger units – if the units are metric, then you can tell this from the prefixes. If you want to convert to the smaller unit, then there will be more of these units so you need to multiply by this number. If you want to convert to the larger unit, then there will be fewer of these units so you need to divide by the number. This is illustrated in the next example.

Example 2   *Converting measurements to different metric units*

(a) Convert 580 cm to m.

(b) Convert 0.65 g to mg.

Solution

(a) To convert to a larger unit, divide.

   There are 100 cm in 1 m, so

$$580\,\text{cm} = (580 \div 100)\,\text{m} = 5.8\,\text{m}.$$

(b) To convert to a smaller unit, multiply.

   There are 1000 mg in 1 g, so

$$0.65\,\text{g} = (0.65 \times 1000)\,\text{mg} = 650\,\text{mg}.$$

Diff between 'mass' and 'weight' explained in page 186 in Unit 4

A few other metric units are commonly used alongside the SI units. The metric tonne (t), which is equivalent to 1000 kg, is often used to measure heavy masses, such as vehicles. The litre (l) is often used to measure volumes, particularly of liquids, even though the SI unit for volume is the cubic metre. One litre is equivalent to 1000 cubic centimetres (cm^3 or cc), so 1000 litres is equivalent to $1\,\text{m}^3$.

There is an SI unit for temperature – the kelvin (K) – but it is mainly used by scientists. In the UK most people use the Celsius scale, which is part of the metric system. Some people still use the non-metric Fahrenheit scale.

Time is also often measured in non-metric units – you have probably never heard of a kilosecond! Seconds (s), minutes (min), hours (h) and days are used, even though this makes conversion calculations more complicated.

Example 3 *Converting units of time*

(a) Convert 2.85 hours into minutes.

(b) Convert 54 hours into days.

Solution

(a) 💬 To convert to a smaller unit, multiply. 💬

There are 60 minutes in 1 hour, so

$$2.85 \text{ hours} = (2.85 \times 60) \text{ minutes}$$
$$= 171 \text{ minutes}.$$

(b) 💬 To convert to a larger unit, divide. 💬

There are 24 hours in a day, so

$$54 \text{ hours} = (54 \div 24) \text{ days}$$
$$= 2.25 \text{ days}.$$

If Example 3(a) had asked for 2.85 hours to be converted into hours *and minutes*, then just the 0.85 hours would need to be converted into minutes:

$$0.85 \text{ hours} = (0.85 \times 60) \text{ minutes} = 51 \text{ minutes}.$$

So 2.85 hours is the same as 2 hours and 51 minutes.

Activity 6 *Converting units*

Make the following conversions.

(a) 6100 m into km   (b) 560 kg into t   (c) 3.45 hours into minutes

(d) 0.35 g into mg   (e) 450 ml into l   (f) 75 cm into m

The UK has embraced metric units rather less enthusiastically than most other countries, and many of its traditional imperial units are still used. If you live in the UK, you may be comfortable with measuring kitchen cabinets in millimetres and buying petrol in litres, for example, but you may think of your height in feet and inches, and your weight in stones and pounds. Most British recipe books give both metric and imperial measurements for ingredients. When following recipes, it is advisable to use one or the other, not mix the two!

In 1969 the UK government set up the Metrication Board, with the aim of ensuring substantial adoption of metric units in the UK by 1975. In particular, it was planned that road sign conversion would take place in 1973. However, in 1970 the conversion programme was put on hold indefinitely, and successive British governments have negotiated with the European Union to opt out of using metric units on road signs.

NASA lost the Mars Climate Orbiter spacecraft in 1999 as a result of an error caused because one team working on the project used imperial units of measurement while another used metric units.

Figure 3 An early metric road sign in the UK, on Barnespool Bridge in London, which was put up for the 1908 Olympic Games. The sign uses 'kilos' as an abbreviation for kilometres.

If you are more familiar with imperial units than metric units, then the rhymes in Figure 4 might help you to remember the approximate sizes of some of the metric units.

Figure 4   Rhymes for metric units

Alternatively, measuring some items in or around your home in metric units may help you to visualise the sizes of the units – most doors are about 2 metres high, for example.

> ### *Using units*
>
> When you answer a question that involves units:
>
> - remember to include units in your answers
> - check whether you are asked to give your answers in particular units.

2.4   Rounding numbers

For help with rounding numbers, see Maths Help Module 2, Section 1.

When you make a measurement, it is sometimes helpful to *round* your answer. For example, if you were measuring the height of a child, then an answer rounded to the nearest centimetre would probably be adequate. If, say, your measurement was as shown in Figure 5 – between 91 cm and 92 cm but closer to 91 cm – then you would round it down to 91 cm. If your measurement was between 91 cm and 92 cm but closer to 92 cm, then you would round it up. The measurement 91.5 is halfway between the two values, so you could round it either way, but it is usual to round up.

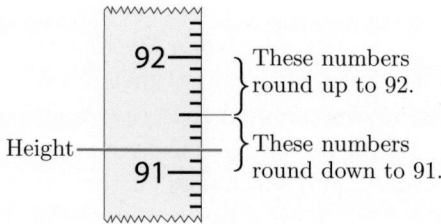

Figure 5   Measuring the height of a child

A (decimal) **digit** is one of the symbols 0, 1, 2, 3, 4, 5, 6, 7, 8, 9.

Another situation where you often need to round numbers is when you are doing calculations, since the answers provided by your calculator can consist of long strings of digits.

Decimal places

Numbers arising from calculations are sometimes rounded to a particular number of **decimal places**. The decimal places are the positions of the digits to the right of the decimal point, as shown in Figure 6. The abbreviation 'd.p.' is often used for 'decimal place(s)'.

For more help with rounding to a number of decimal places, see Maths Help Module 2, Subsection 1.4.

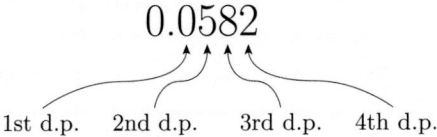

$$0.0582$$

1st d.p.   2nd d.p.   3rd d.p.   4th d.p.

Figure 6   Decimal places

For example, in a calculation involving money, the final answer might be rounded to two decimal places, so that it can be interpreted in pounds and pence.

Once you have decided where to round a number, you should use the following rule to decide whether to round up or down.

> **Strategy**   *To round a number*
>
> Look at the digit immediately after where you want to round.
>
> Round up if this digit is 5 or more, and down otherwise.

When you round a number, you should state how it has been rounded, in brackets after the rounded number. This is shown in the next example.

Example 4   *Rounding to a number of decimal places*

Round the following numbers as indicated.

(a) 0.0582 to three decimal places

(b) 7.056 83 to one decimal place

(c) 2.3971 to two decimal places

A long string of digits is easier to read if there are thin spaces between groups of three digits, as in 12 345 and 0.123 45. (Some texts use commas instead of thin spaces.)

Solution

(a) Look at the digit after the first three decimal places: 0. 058 2. It is 2, which is less than 5, so round down.

0.0582 = 0.058 (to 3 d.p.)

(b) Look at the digit after the first decimal place: 7. 0 56 83. It is 5, which is 5 or more, so round up.

7.056 83 = 7.1 (to 1 d.p.)

(c) Look at the digit after the first two decimal places: 2. 39 71. It is 7, which is is 5 or more, so round up.

2.3971 = 2.40 (to 2 d.p.)

Notice that in Example 4(c), a 0 is included after the 4 to make it clear that the number is rounded to *two* decimal places. You should do likewise when you round numbers yourself.

Activity 7   *Rounding to a number of decimal places*

Round the following numbers as indicated.

(a) 2.2364 to two decimal places

(b) 0.005 47 to three decimal places

(c) 42.598 17 to four decimal places

(d) 7.98 to one decimal place

As an alternative to writing in brackets how you rounded a number, you can replace the equals sign by $\approx$, the 'approximately equals' sign. For example, instead of writing

$$2.3971 = 2.40 \text{ (to 2 d.p.)},$$

you can write

$$2.3971 \approx 2.40.$$

However, it is usually preferable to state the rounding that you used.

You should not write just

$$2.3971 = 2.40,$$

because this is incorrect: the numbers 2.3971 and 2.40 are not equal.

The symbol $\approx$ is read as 'is approximately equal to'.

> There have been a few reports of fraudsters in the US using rounding to become rich. They used computer programs to remove tiny amounts of money from lots of bank accounts, by rounding down to the nearest cent and putting the remaining fractions of cents into other accounts. These small amounts were not noticed as missing from any particular account, but they built up into huge sums of money. This is an example of so-called *salami-slicing* or *penny-shaving* fraud, in which thin slivers of money are removed from many accounts. Modern-day banking systems have built-in checks to prevent this type of fraud.

Significant figures

Another way of specifying where a number should be rounded involves looking at its **significant figures**. The first significant figure of a number is its first non-zero digit (from the left). The next significant figure is the next digit, and so on, as illustrated in Figure 7. Common abbreviations for 'significant figure(s)' are 's.f.' and 'sig. fig.'.

For more help with rounding to a number of significant figures, see Maths Help Module 1, Subsections 1.5 and 1.6.

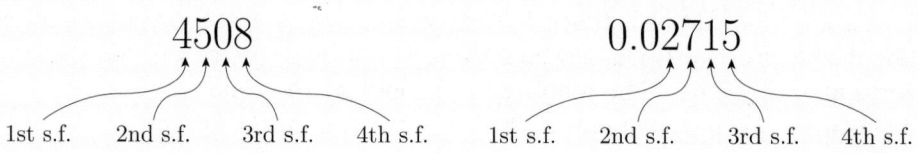

Figure 7 Significant figures

The first significant figure of a number is the most important digit for telling you how big the number is. For example, the digit 4 in the number 4508 in Figure 7 tells you that the number is between four and five thousand, while the digit 2 in the number 0.027 15 tells you that this number is between two hundredths and three hundredths. The second significant figure is the next most important digit for telling you how big the number is, and so on.

The usual '5 or more' rule in the strategy on page 19 is used when rounding to a particular number of significant figures.

Example 5   *Rounding to a number of significant figures*

Round the following numbers as indicated.

(a) 36.9572 to four significant figures

(b) 0.000 349 to one significant figure

(c) 56.0463 to one significant figure

(d) 0.0198 to two significant figures

Solution

(a) Look at the digit after the first four significant figures: 36.95 72. It is 7, which is greater than 5, so round up.

   36.9572 = 36.96 (to 4 s.f.)

(b) Look at the digit after the first significant figure: 0.000 3 49. It is 4, which is less than 5, so round down.

   0.000 349 = 0.0003 (to 1 s.f.)

(c) Look at the digit after the first significant figure: 5 6.0463. It is 6, which is greater than 5, so round up.

   56.0463 = 60 (to 1 s.f.)

(d) Look at the digit after the first two significant figures: 0.0 19 8. It is 8, which is greater than 5, so round up.

   0.0198 = 0.020 (to 2 s.f.)

In Example 5(d) a 0 is included after the 2 to make it clear that the number is rounded to *two* significant figures. You should do likewise when you round numbers yourself.

One or more zeros in a rounded number may be significant figures. For example, the final zero in the number 0.020 in the solution to Example 5(d) is significant: this number is rounded to two significant figures, and the second significant figure just happens to be zero. In contrast, the zero in the number 60 in the solution to Example 5(c) is not significant, as the number is rounded to just one significant figure.

If you are told that a distance is 3700 metres, say, without any information about how the number has been rounded, then you cannot tell whether the zeros are significant. The number 3700 could be the result of rounding 3684 to two significant figures, 3697 to three significant figures, or 3700 to four significant figures, for example. This is one reason why it is important to state how a number has been rounded, as shown in Example 5.

In the first case neither of the zeros is significant, in the second case only the first zero is significant, and in the third case both zeros are significant.

When you see a measurement such as 3700 metres with no information about whether or how the number has been rounded, you can usually assume that any zeros at the end are *not* significant.

Activity 8   *Rounding to a number of significant figures*

Round the following numbers as indicated.

(a) 23 650 to two significant figures

(b) 0.005 47 to one significant figure

(c) 42.598 17 to four significant figures

Other types of rounding

Numbers are also sometimes rounded to the nearest ten, or hundred, or thousand, and so on. For example, if you were writing a report on a concert that had an audience figure of 58 217, then you might choose to round this number to the nearest thousand, to give 58 000, or perhaps to the nearest ten thousand, to give 60 000. The '5 or more' rule is used to decide whether to round up or down. Similarly, you can also round to the nearest metre, or the nearest 10 kilograms, and so on.

Choosing which type of rounding to use

Rounding to a number of significant figures is often the most useful type of rounding to use. For example, the height of a mountain might be usefully quoted as 4559 m to the nearest metre, but if you need to know the height of a woman who is 1.65 m tall then an approximation to the nearest metre is not useful. In each case, however, rounding to three significant figures gives a useful approximation: 4560 m for the height of the mountain and 1.65 m for the height of the woman.

Rounding answers appropriately

Often, the measurements that you have used in a calculation give you an indication of the amount of rounding that you should use for your answer.

For example, the road distance from Paris to Lyon is 465 km. Suppose that you want to convert this distance into miles. You can use the fact that

$$1\,\text{km} = 0.621\,371\,192 \text{ miles (to 9 s.f.).}$$

Multiplying the distance in km by the conversion factor gives the distance in miles as

$$465 \times 0.621\,371\,192 = 288.937\,604\,3.$$

It is inappropriate to leave the answer as 288.937 604 3 miles, as this suggests that the distance has been measured very carefully indeed! The original measurement seems to be given to three significant figures, so your answer should be similarly rounded – to three, or possibly fewer, significant figures. Rounding to three significant figures gives the distance as 289 miles.

To see why this amount of rounding is appropriate, let's consider what the actual distance could be. It was given as 465 km to the nearest kilometre, so it could be anything from 464.5 km up to (but not including) 465.5 km, as shown in Figure 8.

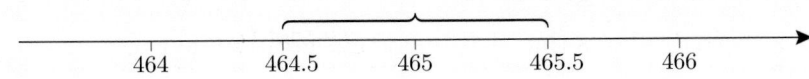

Figure 8 Numbers that round to 465

Now, 464.5 km is equivalent to 288.626 918 7 miles, and 465.5 km is equivalent to 289.248 289 9 miles. Since the actual distance lies between these two values, it is certainly 289 miles when rounded to three significant figures, as you can see from Figure 9. So the amount of rounding was appropriate.

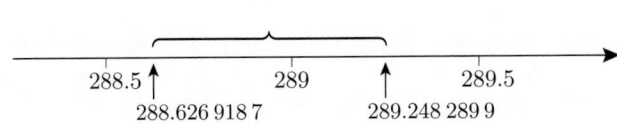

Figure 9 Numbers between 288.626 918 7 and 289.248 289 9

When you are rounding answers, you should round to no more significant figures than the number of significant figures in the least precise number in the calculation. For example, in the calculation above, the measurement and the conversion factor were rounded to three and nine significant figures, respectively, so the answer should be rounded to no more than three significant figures.

Sometimes it is appropriate to round to fewer significant figures than the number of significant figures in the least precise number. A full analysis of rounding is outside the scope of the course, so activities and TMA questions will often state what rounding to use in your answers. Otherwise, rounding to the number of significant figures in the least precise number used should be acceptable. The number of *significant figures* an answer is stated to is known as the **precision** of the answer.

Activity 9 *Rounding an answer appropriately*

In this activity you are asked to convert 465 km into miles again, but this time using the following less precise conversion factor:

   1 km is approximately equal to 0.62 miles.

(a) Do the calculation and round your answer to the nearest mile. Compare your answer to the answer found in the calculation on page 22, and comment on why they are not the same.

(b) Round your answer appropriately.

Rounding at the right time

The next activity shows that it is important not to round too early in a calculation.

Activity 10   *Rounding at different stages of a calculation*

1 km =
0.621 371 192 miles (to 9 s.f.)

Suppose that you want to calculate the length, in miles, of a return journey to a town 36 km away. Use the conversion factor given earlier (repeated in the margin) to carry out the following calculations.

(a) Convert 36 km to miles, and round your answer to the nearest mile. Use this answer to find the total length of the journey.

(b) Convert 36 km to miles. With the unrounded answer still in your calculator display, type '× 2' into your calculator, and press the '=' key to obtain the total length of the journey. Round your answer to the nearest mile.

(c) Comment on which of parts (a) and (b) is the better way of carrying out the calculation.

As you saw in Activity 10, if you do a calculation in two or more steps, and round your answer after one of these steps, then your final answer may be inaccurate. This is known as a **rounding error**.

It was reported in the *New York Times* in 1991 that Tina Lubin, a public servant who dealt with the $14.8 billion payroll for the city government of New York, had 'learned to think of $10 million as a rounding error'!

Whenever you use an earlier answer in a later calculation, you should use all the digits that your calculator provided for the earlier answer, to avoid rounding errors. This is known as 'using full calculator precision'. You may not need all the digits, but it is usually not clear how many digits you do need, so it is simplest to use them all.

If you cannot use a full-calculator-precision number displayed on your calculator immediately, then you can note it down for later, or store it in your calculator's memory. You will be reminded about how to use the memory key on your calculator later in the course.

The symbol '...' is called an *ellipsis* and is used when something has been left out. It is read as 'dot, dot, dot'.

When you use a full-calculator-precision number that has a long string of digits after the decimal point, you do not need to include all the digits in the working that you write down. You can write down just a few of them – usually at least three digits after the decimal point, or at least three significant digits – and use the symbol '...' to show that you have omitted the rest. For example, if your calculator gives you the number 2.478 260 87, and you then use the calculator to multiply this number by 6, then you might write down

$$2.478\ldots \times 6 = 14.869\ldots = 14.87 \text{ (to 4 s.f.).}$$

When you omit some of the digits of a number just before you round it, you should make sure that you have written down enough digits so that someone reading your working can see that the rounding is correct. This is done for the number '14.869...' above.

Considering the context

When you round an answer, it is also important to consider the context. For example, if you are calculating how many cupboards will fit along your kitchen wall and your answer is 7.9, then you should round *down* and buy only seven cupboards, because eight cupboards wouldn't fit! On the other hand, if you are painting your kitchen and need 1.2 tins of paint, then you should round *up* and buy two tins; otherwise you will run out of paint.

The box below summarises the key points about rounding.

> ### Rounding answers
>
> - Use full calculator precision *throughout* calculations, to avoid rounding errors.
> - Round your answer appropriately, taking account of the measurements used and the context.
> - Check that you have followed any instructions on rounding given in a question.

2.5 Checking your answers

When you carry out a calculation, it is helpful to have a rough idea of the expected answer. If your answer is very different from your estimate, then you know to look for a mistake. The mistake could be in your working, or it might have occurred when you used your calculator.

For help with estimating answers, see Maths Help Module 2, Section 2.

One simple way to estimate an answer is to think about the context. For example, if you were totting up a weekly shopping bill for a family of four, then you might expect an answer between £100 and £200. You would be surprised if your answer turned out to be £1500 or £15!

Another way to estimate an answer is to round all the numbers in the calculation – perhaps to one significant figure, or to nearby numbers that are easy to work with – and carry out the calculation with the rounded numbers. It should be possible to do this fairly quickly, either in your head or on a piece of paper, as the next example shows. This type of estimate may not highlight a mistake in your working, as you could make the same mistake when you do the calculation with the rounded numbers. But it will help you to spot mistakes that happen when you use your calculator.

Example 6 *Estimating an answer*

The road distances in kilometres between three places in Scotland are shown overleaf. Suppose that you are planning a round trip in which you start at Edinburgh, visit Perth and Glasgow, and return to Edinburgh, in a minibus whose fuel consumption is 12 kilometres per litre of fuel.

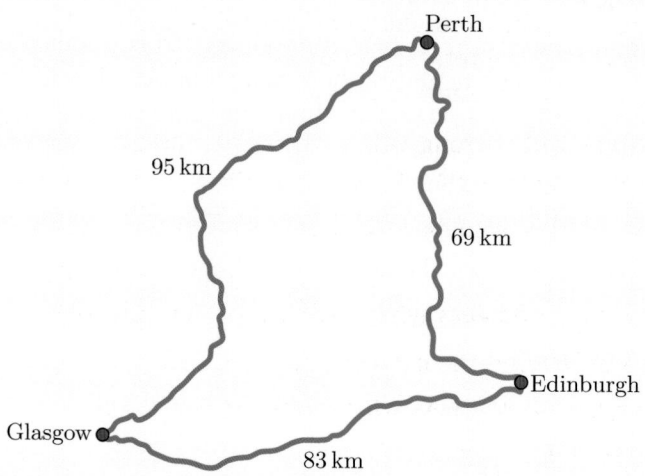

(a) Estimate the amount of fuel needed for the trip.

(b) Use your calculator to work out the amount of fuel needed, to the nearest litre.

Solution

(a) Round the numbers to one significant figure.

An estimate for the total distance in km is

$$70 + 100 + 80 = 250.$$

The minibus can travel about 10 km on 1 litre of fuel, so the amount of fuel needed, in litres, is approximately

$$250 \div 10 = 25.$$

So an estimate for the amount of fuel needed is 25 litres.

(b) The amount of fuel needed, in litres, is

$$(69 + 95 + 83) \div 12 = 21 \text{ (to the nearest whole number).}$$

So the amount of fuel needed is 21 litres, to the nearest litre.

The answer is fairly close to the estimate, so there is no evidence of a mistake.

Checking for calculator mistakes

If your answer to a calculation seems to be wrong (you might know this because you estimated it) and you suspect that you made a mistake when you used your calculator, then the first thing to check is whether you have mistyped something. If the calculation is displayed on your calculator screen, then you should check the numbers and operations carefully, and edit the calculation to correct any errors.

If your calculator does not display calculations, then to check for mistyping you should enter the calculation again.

The next thing to check is whether the calculation you entered was the correct one. You need to think about the BIDMAS rules. For example, if you had intended to carry out the calculation in Example 6(b), and had typed

$$69 + 95 + 83 \div 12,$$

then you would have obtained the wrong answer, because your calculator would do the division before the additions. You need to include the brackets, as in the solution above.

If you still cannot find a mistake, then you can try breaking the calculation into simpler steps. For example, to do the calculation in Example 6, you could first work out the total distance, which is 247 km, and then divide 247 by 12 to find the amount of fuel in litres.

For help with checking answers, see Maths Help Module 2, Section 3.

If nothing seems to be wrong with the way you used your calculator, then you may need to check your estimate, or refine it – *it* could be the problem!

Here is a summary of some key points to check when using your calculator.

> ### Checking your answers when using your calculator
>
> - Have you entered the calculation correctly?
> - Have you used brackets where needed?
> - Is the answer reasonable? Think about the context or work out an estimate.

Activity 11   *Spotting errors in a calculation*

A craftswoman makes handmade jewellery boxes. It takes her 2 hours and 30 minutes to make each box, and 1 hour and 45 minutes to apply the decoration. She works for 7.5 hours each day. Suppose that you need to know how many working days it would take the craftswoman to make and decorate 48 jewellery boxes.

(a) Estimate the number of days needed.

(b) A student typed the calculation shown below into a calculator, and concluded that the number of days needed is 12. Try to identify the two mistakes.

(c) Use your calculator to find how many days are needed, and round your answer appropriately.

In this section you have revised some basic skills in working with numbers; you will need to use these skills frequently throughout the rest of the course.

3 Negative numbers and fractions

Negative numbers, fractions and percentages (which can be thought of as a type of fraction) occur frequently in both everyday and abstract mathematics. In this section you will revise some basic skills with these types of numbers and see some everyday applications of these skills.

3.1 Negative numbers

For help with negative numbers, see Maths Help Module 1, Subsections 1.9 and 1.10.

You are probably familiar with negative numbers in the context of temperatures. For example, the minus sign in '$-5°C$' indicates a temperature five degrees below zero. Negative numbers are also used to represent debt.

An **integer** is any one of the numbers
$\ldots, -3, -2, -1, 0, 1, 2, 3, \ldots$.

You can think of all numbers as lying on a line, called the **number line**. Figure 10 shows part of the number line, with the positions of the integers marked. The positive numbers are to the right of zero, and the negative numbers are to the left. Zero itself is neither positive nor negative.

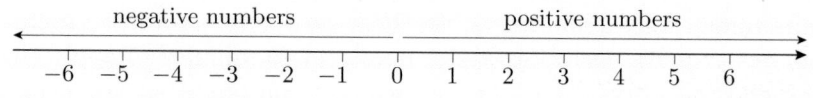

Figure 10 The number line

The number -1 is read as 'minus 1' or 'negative 1'.

The numbers on the number line get bigger as you go from left to right. For example, the number -1 is greater than the number -3, since -1 lies further to the right. You may find it helpful to use Figure 10 when you do the next activity.

Activity 12 *Comparing temperatures*

The noon temperatures on six consecutive winter days are given in the table below.

Sunday	Monday	Tuesday	Wednesday	Thursday	Friday
$-3°C$	$-6°C$	$-2°C$	$2°C$	$0°C$	$-4°C$

On which days was the noon temperature lower than on Sunday?

Higher or lower?

In 2007 a lottery scratchcard game was withdrawn, within a week of being launched, because players could not understand the negative numbers involved. To win a prize, players had to scratch away a window to reveal a temperature lower than the temperature shown on the card. As the game had a winter theme, the displayed temperature was usually negative. Many players thought that -3 was lower than -4, for example, and complained to the lottery company when they thought they had won a prize but were told that they had not.

You will often need to use negative numbers in MU123. The rest of this subsection reminds you how to add, subtract, multiply and divide them.

Adding and subtracting negative numbers

No matter what number you start with – whether it is positive, negative or zero – if you want to add a *positive* number to it then you move along the number line to the right. For example,

$$-2 + 5 = 3,$$

as illustrated in Figure 11.

See Maths Help Module 1, Subsections 3.16–3.19.

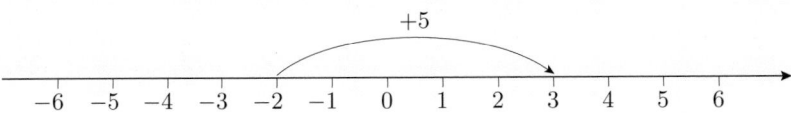

Figure 11   Adding a positive number

Similarly, to subtract a *positive* number you move along the number line to the left. For example,

$$-1 - 4 = -5,$$

as illustrated in Figure 12.

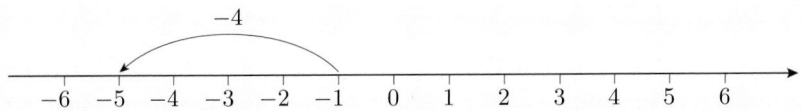

Figure 12   Subtracting a positive number

Activity 13   *Adding and subtracting positive numbers*

Work out the following calculations without using your calculator.

(a) $-6 + 2$ (b) $-1 + 3$ (c) $2 - 7$ (d) $-3 - 4$ (e) $5 - 7 - 2$

To add and subtract *negative* numbers, use the rules in the box below.

> **Adding and subtracting negative numbers**
>
> Adding a negative number is the same as subtracting the corresponding positive number.
>
> Subtracting a negative number is the same as adding the corresponding positive number.

The next example illustrates these rules. There is a tutorial clip for this example, as indicated by the icon in the margin. If you find the example difficult to follow, try watching the clip. The clip also discusses the reasons behind the rules.

Notice that some of the negative numbers in this example are enclosed in brackets. This is because no two of the mathematical symbols $+$, $-$, $\times$ and $\div$ should be written next to each other, as that would look confusing. So if you want to show that you are adding -2 to 4, for example, then you should put brackets around '-2' and write $4 + (-2)$, not $4 + -2$.

 Tutorial clip

Example 7   *Adding and subtracting negative numbers*

Work out the following calculations without using your calculator.

(a) $-3 + (-6)$ (b) $4 + (-2)$ (c) $0 - (-6)$

(d) $1 - (-2)$ (e) $-2 - (-3)$

Solution

To *add* a negative number, *subtract* the corresponding positive number.

(a) $-3 + (-6) = -3 - 6 = -9$

(b) $4 + (-2) = 4 - 2 = 2$

To *subtract* a negative number, *add* the corresponding positive number.

(c) $0 - (-6) = 0 + 6 = 6$

(d) $1 - (-2) = 1 + 2 = 3$

(e) $-2 - (-3) = -2 + 3 = 1$

Activity 14   *Adding and subtracting negative numbers*

Work out the following calculations without using your calculator.

(a) $2 + (-7)$ (b) $-8 + (-5)$ (c) $1 - (-3)$ (d) $-6 - (-9)$

(e) $-4 - (-4)$ (f) $3 - (-2) + (-4)$ (g) $7 + (-6) - 3$

So far, adding and subtracting zero has not been mentioned. As you would expect, this has no effect on the number you start with: for example

$$-4 + 0 = -4 \quad \text{and} \quad 3 - 0 = 3.$$

Multiplying and dividing negative numbers

For help with multiplying and dividing negative numbers, see Maths Help Module 1, Subsections 3.20–3.22.

Now let's look at how to multiply and divide negative numbers. First consider the multiplication $3 \times (-2)$. This means 'three lots of -2', so

$$3 \times (-2) = (-2) + (-2) + (-2)$$
$$= -2 - 2 - 2$$
$$= -6.$$

The order in which you multiply numbers doesn't matter, so the calculation above also tells you that

$$(-2) \times 3 = -6.$$

This example illustrates the first rule in the box below.

Multiplying and dividing negative numbers

When two numbers are multiplied or divided:

- if the signs are *different*, then the answer is *negative*
- if the signs are *the same*, then the answer is *positive*.

The parts of the numbers other than the signs are just multiplied or divided in the usual way. The next example illustrates these rules. Its tutorial clip explains the calculations in more detail, and also contains more explanation of the rules.

The following table might help you to remember these rules:

	+	−
+	+	−
−	−	+

For example, if you want to multiply a positive number by a negative number, look for the entry corresponding to the row and column headings + and −, respectively: the entry is −, so the answer is negative.

Example 8   *Multiplying and dividing negative numbers*

 Tutorial clip

Work out the following calculations without using your calculator.

(a) $(-5) \times 6$ (b) $9 \div (-3)$ (c) $(-3) \times (-7)$

(d) $(-70) \div (-10)$ (e) $(-2) \times 3 \times (-4)$

Solution

(a) A negative times a positive (different signs) gives a negative.

$(-5) \times 6 = -30$

(b) A positive divided by a negative (different signs) gives a negative.

$9 \div (-3) = -3$

(c) A negative times a negative (same signs) gives a positive.

$(-3) \times (-7) = 21$

(d) A negative divided by a negative (same signs) gives a positive.

$(-70) \div (-10) = 7$

(e) Do the multiplications one at a time. In the first multiplication, a negative times a positive gives a negative. Then this negative, times a negative, gives a positive.

$(-2) \times 3 \times (-4) = (-6) \times (-4) = 24$

Activity 15   *Multiplying and dividing negative numbers*

Work out the following calculations without using your calculator.

(a) $5 \times (-3)$ (b) $(-2) \times (-4)$ (c) $6 \times (-10)$ (d) $25 \div (-5)$

(e) $(-49) \div (-7)$ (f) $(-36) \div 12$ (g) $(-2) \times (-5) \times (-4)$

A minus indicating a negative in a calculation has the same precedence as subtraction in the BIDMAS rules. For example, in the calculation -3^2, the power is dealt with first, so the answer is -9. The calculation does not mean the square of -3, so the answer is not $(-3) \times (-3) = 9$.

Despite their importance in modern-day mathematics, negative numbers were rejected by some British mathematicians as late as the eighteenth century. Francis Maseres (1731–1824) wrote that they 'darken the very whole doctrines of the equations and make dark of the things which are in their nature excessively obvious and simple'.

However, over a thousand years earlier, the Indian mathematician Brahmagupta (598–670) wrote down the rules for adding, subtracting, multiplying and dividing negative numbers, in terms of debt (negative numbers) and fortune (positive numbers).

The result of multiplying any number (whether positive, negative or zero) by zero is zero. For example,

$$4 \times 0 = 0, \quad 0 \times (-3) = 0, \quad 0 \times 0 = 0.$$

However, no number can be divided by zero. For example,

$$-3 \div 0$$

has no meaning. (This is because the answer to this calculation would have to be a number such that if you multiplied it by zero you would get -3, and there is no such number.)

On the other hand, the result of dividing zero by any non-zero number is zero. For example,

$$0 \div (-3) = 0.$$

Brahmagupta was also the first known person to write down rules for doing arithmetic with the number zero, though later medieval mathematicians remained confused about how a symbol used to represent the concept of nothing could itself be a number.

The best way to become confident with operations on negative numbers – as with all topics in mathematics – is to practise.

Practise, practise, practise!

Throughout your studies in mathematics, try as many activities as you can. You may *think* that you understand the mathematics you are reading, but you need to try it yourself to be sure. The more you practise, the more confident and fluent you will become, and the better you will remember how to do the mathematics when it comes up again. Each unit of the course contains plenty of practice activities, both within the text and in the practice quizzes.

Negative numbers on your calculator

Another way to practise calculations involving negative numbers is to make up some examples of your own and check your answers on your calculator. The next activity reminds you how to use your calculator for negative number calculations.

Activity 16 *Using your calculator for negative numbers*

Work through Subsection 4.2 of the Course Guide.

3.2 Fractions

Although decimal numbers are used in many everyday situations, there are occasions when fractions are appropriate. For example, in 2002 it was reported that the populations of four-fifths of the bird species, half of the plant species and a third of the insect species on arable farmland in Great Britain had declined. The fractions here make it clear that the populations of most of the bird species had declined, but that the insect species had fared better.

Fractions are also important in mathematics, particularly in algebra. In this subsection you will revise how to work with fractions, and you will see some everyday uses of them.

A **fraction** is a number that describes the relationship between part of something and the whole. For example, the disc in Figure 13 is divided into five equal parts, of which three are shaded. To express this, we write that $\frac{3}{5}$ (three-fifths) of the disc is shaded. The fraction $\frac{3}{5}$ can also be written as 3/5.

The top number in a fraction is called the **numerator** and the bottom number is called the **denominator**. So the fraction $\frac{3}{5}$ has numerator 3 and denominator 5.

Fractions can be converted to decimal form by dividing the numerator by the denominator. For example,

$$\tfrac{3}{5} = 3 \div 5 = 0.6 \quad \text{and} \quad \tfrac{2}{11} = 2 \div 11 = 0.181\,818\,18\ldots.$$

However, it is usually best not to convert fractions to decimals, but to leave them as they are. This is especially true for a fraction that does not have a short exact decimal form, such as $\frac{2}{11}$.

Equivalent fractions

Each fraction can be written in many different, but **equivalent**, forms. For example, $\frac{1}{2}$ is the same as $\frac{2}{4}$, $\frac{3}{6}$ and $\frac{4}{8}$, as you can see from Figure 14. You can use the following method to convert between different forms of a fraction.

> #### To find a fraction equivalent to a given fraction
>
> Multiply or divide the numerator and denominator by the same non-zero number.

For example,

$$\frac{5}{6} = \frac{5 \times 4}{6 \times 4} = \frac{20}{24} \quad \text{and} \quad \frac{25}{50} = \frac{25 \div 5}{50 \div 5} = \frac{5}{10}.$$

For help with fractions, see Maths Help Module 1, Subsection 1.7.

Source: Robinson, R.A. and Sutherland, W.J. (2002) 'Post-war changes in arable farming and biodiversity in Great Britain', *Journal of Applied Ecology*, vol. 39, pp. 157–76.

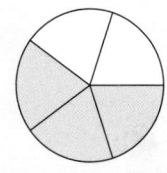

Figure 13 $\frac{3}{5}$ of a disc

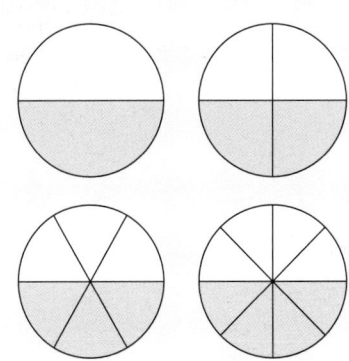

Figure 14 $\frac{1}{2} = \frac{2}{4} = \frac{3}{6} = \frac{4}{8}$

Simplifying fractions

When you divide the top and bottom of a fraction by a whole number larger than 1, you get an equivalent fraction with a smaller numerator and denominator. This is known as **cancelling** the fraction. When a fraction has been cancelled to give the smallest possible numerator and denominator (but still whole numbers), it is said to be in its **simplest form** or **lowest terms**.

For help with simplifying fractions, see Maths Help Module 1, Subsection 1.8.

For example, the fraction $\frac{24}{30}$ can be cancelled by dividing top and bottom by 6. This calculation would normally be set out as follows:

$$\frac{\overset{4}{\cancel{24}}}{\underset{5}{\cancel{30}}} = \frac{4}{5}.$$

The fraction $\frac{4}{5}$ is in its simplest form because there is no whole number that divides exactly into both 4 and 5.

Cancelling can be carried out in stages. For example, to cancel $\frac{24}{30}$ you could divide top and bottom first by 2, and then by 3:

$$\frac{\overset{\overset{4}{\cancel{12}}}{\cancel{24}}}{\underset{\underset{5}{\cancel{15}}}{\cancel{30}}} = \frac{4}{5}.$$

Activity 17   *Writing fractions in their simplest forms*

(a) Express each of the following fractions in its simplest form, without using your calculator.

   (i) $\frac{7}{21}$ (ii) $\frac{48}{72}$ (iii) $\frac{35}{105}$

(b) In a survey of 1200 students, 720 said that they have a part-time job. What fraction of the students is this? Give your answer in its simplest form.

Fractions (and percentages, which are discussed in Section 3.3) are often used in media headlines because of their impact. For example, if a media article were to be written about the survey in Activity 17(b), then it might have the headline 'Three-fifths of students have part-time jobs'. This would have more impact than '720 out of 1200 students questioned have part-time jobs'.

However, the fractions and percentages in headlines can sometimes be misleading. When you read a headline that involves a fraction or a percentage of a group of people, it is worth reading the article to see whether it includes the answers to the following questions.

• How many people were included in the survey?

• Are the people in the survey representative of the overall population?

For example, you might not be impressed by the headline 'Three-fifths of students have part-time jobs' if you found that it was based on interviewing five students in a supermarket, and three of them were working on the tills!

Mixed numbers and improper fractions

A **proper fraction** is a fraction in which the numerator is smaller than the denominator, such as $\frac{2}{3}$.

A number that consists of a whole number plus a proper fraction is called a **mixed number**. For example, the mixed number $1\frac{2}{3}$ is illustrated in Figure 15. Each mixed number can also be written as an **improper fraction** – a fraction in which the numerator is larger than the denominator. For example, you can see from Figure 16 that $1\frac{2}{3}$ contains five thirds altogether, so it is the same as $\frac{5}{3}$. An improper fraction is also known as a **top-heavy fraction**.

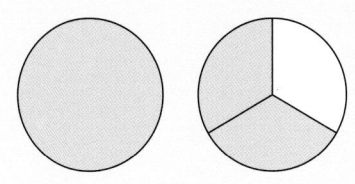

Figure 15   The mixed number $1\frac{2}{3}$

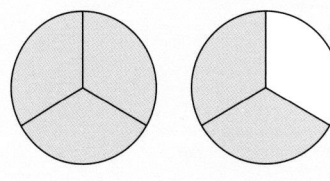

Figure 16   The improper fraction $\frac{5}{3} = 1\frac{2}{3}$

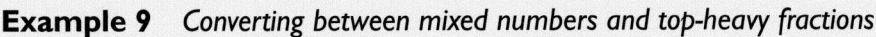

Example 9   *Converting between mixed numbers and top-heavy fractions*

(a) Write $2\frac{5}{8}$ as a top-heavy fraction.

(b) Write $\frac{13}{4}$ as a mixed number.

Solution

(a) There are eight eighths in one whole, so $2\frac{5}{8}$ can be written as two lots of eight eighths plus five more eighths.

$$2\frac{5}{8} = \frac{2 \times 8 + 5}{8} = \frac{21}{8}$$

(b) Divide 4 into 13. The answer is 3, remainder 1.

$$\frac{13}{4} = 3\frac{1}{4}$$

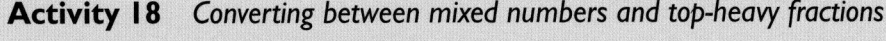

Activity 18   *Converting between mixed numbers and top-heavy fractions*

(a) Write $5\frac{2}{3}$ as a top-heavy fraction.

(b) Write $\frac{18}{5}$ as a mixed number.

Fractions of quantities

Sometimes you need to calculate fractions of quantities. For example, if you have a recipe that serves eight people, and you want to make it for three people or thirty people, say, then you have to scale the quantities of the ingredients. The next example shows you two ways of doing this. The second method involves fractions and is slightly quicker.

Example 10   *Scaling a recipe*

A recipe for eight people specifies 750 g of strawberries. What quantity of strawberries would be needed for three people?

Solution

First method

 Work out the quantity of strawberries needed for one person. Use this to find the quantity of strawberries needed for three people.

The quantity of strawberries needed for one person is

$$750\,\text{g} \div 8 = 93.75\,\text{g}.$$

Of course, instead of working out the correct quantity of strawberries for three people, you could just halve the quantity for eight people and serve bigger portions!

So the quantity of strawberries needed for three people is

$$3 \times 93.75\,\text{g} = 281.25\,\text{g} = 280\,\text{g} \ (\text{to 2 s.f.}).$$

Second method

Find the fraction of the original quantity that is needed, and use this to calculate the quantity of strawberries needed.

Three-eighths of the original quantity is required. So the quantity of strawberries needed for three people is

$$\tfrac{3}{8} \times 750\,\text{g} = 3 \div 8 \times 750\,\text{g} = 281.25\,\text{g} = 280\,\text{g} \ (\text{to 2 s.f.}).$$

In Example 10, the answer to a question was calculated in two different ways. There are often many different ways to solve a problem, so you may sometimes find that you have used a method different from one used in the unit or suggested by someone else. As long as your reasoning and answer are correct, this doesn't usually matter. However, it is a good idea to look at any model solution provided, as it may suggest an alternative and possibly quicker method that you could use to solve a similar problem in the future.

Activity 19   *Calculating fractions of quantities*

(a) Work out the following fractions of quantities.

   (i) $\tfrac{4}{5}$ of 60 ml   (ii) $\tfrac{5}{8}$ of 20 kg

(b) A recipe for potato curry for 6 people uses 900 g of potatoes. If you are making the curry for 20 people, what quantity of potatoes do you need?

In theory you can scale any recipe to cater for a group of any size, but in practice you may wish to adjust your answers a little. It is important that you have enough food for everyone, but you may also wish to minimise waste and cost. The larger the group of diners, the more likely it is that a few people will eat only small portions or none at all, so caterers often use guidelines such as the following:

> Allow 150 g of potatoes per person for up to 10 people; for more than 10 people, allow 125 g per person.

In general, when you are using mathematics to make practical decisions, it is important to think about whether your calculations are appropriate for the situation.

Fractions on your calculator

In the next activity you will use your calculator to carry out calculations involving fractions.

Activity 20   *Using your calculator for fractions*

Work through Subsection 4.3 of the Course Guide.

3.3   Percentages

You may have noticed that relatively few types of fraction are used in the media – the only types commonly used are halves, thirds, quarters, and perhaps fifths or eighths. You don't usually come across fractions like $\frac{9}{20}$ or $\frac{37}{54}$, because fractions like these are difficult to visualise and compare. Instead, **percentages** are often used.

For help with percentages, see Maths Help Module 3, Subsection 3.1.

A percentage is a fraction with a denominator of 100. It is often written using the percent symbol %.

e.g. $\frac{25}{100} = 25\%$

This subsection reminds you of some basic techniques for calculating with percentages, and shows you how they can be used to make comparisons and describe changes. It also shows you how some of the numbers and percentages quoted in the media might have been manipulated to portray an author's point of view, or to make a news story seem more dramatic than it really is.

The term 'per cent' means 'per 100'. So, for example, if the packaging of a cake tells you that 20% of the cake is fat, then it means that $\frac{20}{100}$ (or $\frac{1}{5}$) of the cake is fat.

The symbol % is read as 'per cent'.

A percentage can be converted to a fraction or a decimal. To do this, you first write the percentage in the form of a fraction with denominator 100, then you simplify this to get a fraction, or divide out to get a decimal. For example,

For help with these conversions, see Maths Help Module 3, Subsection 3.2.

$$45\% = \frac{45}{100} = \frac{9}{20}$$

and

$$45\% = \frac{45}{100} = 45 \div 100 = 0.45.$$

Similarly,

$$100\% = \frac{100}{100} = 1.$$

To convert the other way – from a fraction or decimal to a percentage – you just need to multiply by 100%. Because 100% = 1, this does not change the value of the fraction or decimal; it just allows it to be written as a percentage. For example,

$$\tfrac{2}{5} = \tfrac{2}{5} \times 100\% = 40\%$$

and

$$0.015 = 0.015 \times 100\% = 1.5\%.$$

Activity 21   *Converting between percentages, fractions and decimals*

(a) Complete the following table.

Percentage	Decimal	Fraction
60%		
		$\frac{7}{8}$
	1.35	

(b) Convert 3.8% to a decimal.

It is often helpful to express one number as a percentage of another. This is done by expressing the first number as a fraction of the second number, and then converting the fraction to a percentage, by multiplying by 100%. This is summarised in the box below.

> **Strategy**   *To express a number as a percentage of another number*
>
> Calculate
> $$\frac{\text{first number}}{\text{second number}} \times 100\%.$$

Example 11   *Expressing a number as a percentage of another number*

In a survey of 1500 mature students, 465 agreed with the statement that higher education is vital for getting a new career. What percentage of the group is this?

Solution

💭 Write down the fraction and convert it to a percentage. 💭

The fraction of students who agreed with the statement is
$$\frac{465}{1500}.$$
So the percentage of students who agreed with the statement is
$$\frac{465}{1500} \times 100\% = 31\%.$$

Activity 22   *Expressing a number as a percentage of another number*

In the survey in Example 11, 420 of the 1500 mature students said that their main reason for going to university was the potential to earn more money. What percentage of the group is this?

Using percentages to make comparisons

One advantage of using percentages rather than fractions is that they are easy to compare. For example, if you were informed that $\frac{7}{9}$ of the pupils in a year group at a school attained the nationally expected standard in English, while $\frac{3}{4}$ of the year group attained the nationally expected standard in mathematics, then you might not be able to tell immediately which subject had the better performance. On the other hand, if you were informed that 78% and 75% of the year group attained the expected levels in English and mathematics, respectively, then you would know immediately that the performance in English is slightly better.

In the example above there is only one group – a year group at a school – but percentages also make it easy to compare figures for different groups. For example, if you were told that 121 pupils from a year group at one school and 86 pupils from the corresponding year group at another school had achieved a certain standard, then you could not tell which school had performed better because the year group at one school might have many more pupils than the year group at the other school. To compare the performance of the two schools, you need to calculate the percentage of pupils at each school who achieved the standard.

A comparison which takes account of underlying numbers in this way is called a **relative comparison**. Here the comparison is relative to the numbers of pupils in the year groups at the two schools. If no account is taken of the underlying numbers – for example, if you just compare the numbers of pupils achieving the standard – then the comparison is known as an **absolute comparison**.

Activity 23   *Making a relative comparison*

Some fictional results from two English schools in 2009 are given in the table below.

	Number of pupils tested	Number of pupils achieving five or more GCSEs at grades C and above
School A	194	121
School B	130	86

Calculate, for each school, the percentage of pupils who achieved five or more GCSEs at grades C and above. Which school had the better performance, on this measure?

Even when it is clear that a relative comparison is fairer than an absolute one, it is not always clear what the comparison should be *relative to*. For example, the relative comparison in Activity 23 shows which of the two schools had the better performance, but it certainly does not show which school had the better teaching. It might be that the pupils at one of the schools tended to have poorer skills when they started at the school than the pupils at the other school. A fair relative comparison would need to take figures for this issue, and probably others, into account. This is why school league tables do not always provide a good way to compare schools. 'Value-added' measures of performance, which take into account the attainment of the pupils at the time when they start at the school, are better, but it is difficult to devise a truly fair method of comparison.

Well done, Freddy! You've improved 100% since last term! But as for you, Johnny, I'm afraid you've only managed a 4% improvement!

You might like to watch out for examples of absolute and relative comparisons in the media, as different viewpoints can be put forward depending on the comparison used. For example, an article reporting that a police force had solved fewer crimes one year than it had solved in the previous year might lead you to think that the crime-solving peformance of the force had deteriorated. However, if it turned out that fewer crimes were reported in the second year than in the first, then a relative comparision might show that the crime-solving performance of the force had improved. When you read a media report it is worth thinking about what the viewpoint of the author might be, and whether the figures could be analysed in a different way. We'll return to this topic at the end of this section.

Percentages of quantities

Sometimes you need to work out a percentage of a quantity. For example, at the time of writing, if you buy a house in the UK costing £300 000, then you have to pay 3% of this cost in stamp duty. Calculations like this can be worked out using the strategy below.

Stamp duty is a tax on land and property transactions in the UK.

Strategy   *To calculate a percentage of a quantity*

Change the percentage to a fraction or a decimal, and multiply by the quantity.

Example 12   *Calculating a percentage of a quantity*

What is 3% of £300 000?

Solution

$$3\% \text{ of } £300\,000 = \tfrac{3}{100} \times £300\,000 = £9000.$$

Activity 24   *Calculating percentages of quantities*

(a) Work out the following.

   (i) 30% of 150 g   (ii) 110% of 70 ml   (iii) 0.5% of £220

(b) To sell an item, an internet auction site charges a fee of £1.50 for the insertion of an advertisement, together with fees of 9% of the first £30 of the selling price and 5% of the remainder of the selling price. If you use the site to sell an item for £75, what is the total fee that you pay?

Percentage increases and decreases

For help with percentage increases and decreases, see Maths Help Module 3, Subsections 3.3–3.5.

Another common use of percentages is in indicating how quantities have changed. For example, the depreciation in the value of a car during a year, and the change in house prices from one month to the next, can both be conveniently described by percentages.

A percentage increase or decrease is calculated by expressing the increase or decrease as a fraction of the original value, and then converting the fraction to a percentage, by multiplying by 100%. This is summarised in the box below.

Strategy   *To calculate a percentage increase or decrease*

Calculate

$$\frac{\text{actual increase or decrease}}{\text{original value}} \times 100\%.$$

Example 13   *Calculating a percentage increase*

Last year 1450 students enrolled on a mathematics course. This year 1870 students have enrolled. What is the percentage increase in the number of students?

Solution

The actual increase is $1870 - 1450 = 420$.

So the increase as a percentage of the original number is

$$\frac{420}{1450} \times 100\% = 29\% \text{ (to 2 s.f.)}.$$

Hence there is a 29% increase in the number of students.

Activity 25   *Calculating a percentage decrease*

The number of complaints received by a customer services department has fallen from 145 to 125 over the last month. What is the percentage decrease?

Often you know about a percentage increase or decrease in the value of something, and you want to work out the new value. For example, if an item you want to buy is priced at £599 and the shop is advertising a '15% off day', then you might want to calculate the reduced price. There are two main ways of working out the new value that results from a percentage increase or decrease. The next example shows you both methods.

Example 14   *Calculating a value resulting from a percentage decrease*

A computer originally priced at £599 is reduced by 15% in a sale. What is the new price?

Solution

First method

Calculate the decrease in price and subtract it from the original price.

The decrease in price is

15% of £599 = $0.15 \times £599 = £89.85$.

So the reduced price is

£599 − £89.85 = £509.15.

Second method

Use the fact that you have to pay 100% − 15% of the original price.

The reduced price is $100\% - 15\% = 85\%$ of the original price. So the reduced price is

85% of £599 = $0.85 \times £599 = £509.15$.

When you use the second method to calculate the result of a percentage *increase*, you have to multiply the original value by a percentage greater than 100%, as illustrated in the next example.

Example 15   *Calculating a value resulting from a percentage increase*

The rent on a flat is £800 per month and is to be raised by 5%. What is the new rent?

Solution

The new rent is $100\% + 5\% = 105\%$ of the original rent. So the new rent is

$$105\% \text{ of } £800 = 1.05 \times £800 = £840.$$

Activity 26   *Calculating values resulting from percentage changes*

(a) Work out the new price of a car if the original price was £15 400 and the price has been reduced by 20%.

(b) If a weekly wage of £360 is increased by 2.5%, what is the new weekly wage?

(c) If a barrel of oil costs $90 and the price rises by 100%, what is the new price?

You may have found part (c) of Activity 26 quite surprising: if something increases by 100%, then it doubles. You can also work out that if something increases by 200% then it triples, and if something increases by 300% then it quadruples, and so on.

Here is another example that you might find surprising. From the third quarter of 2005 to the third quarter of 2007, the average price of a house in the UK rose from £165 000 to £200 000. The actual increase was £200 000 − £165 000 = £35 000, so the percentage increase was

$$\frac{35\,000}{165\,000} \times 100\% = 21\% \text{ (to 2 s.f.).}$$

By the fourth quarter of 2008, the average house price had fallen back to about £165 000 again. This is a percentage decrease of

$$\frac{35\,000}{200\,000} \times 100\% = 18\% \text{ (to 2 s.f.).}$$

So the average house price rose by 21%, but had to fall by only 18% to get back to the original value! This is because the rise started from a smaller value than the fall did.

In 2008, the UK government reduced the rate of value added tax (VAT) from 17.5% to 15%, in response to the economic situation at the time. Many people thought that this meant prices should drop by 2.5%, but in fact the reduction was smaller: only about 2.1%. To see why, consider an item that cost £100 exclusive of VAT. When the VAT rate was 17.5%, the item cost £117.50, and when the VAT rate was 15%, it cost £115. So the VAT cut caused the price to decrease by £2.50 from an original price of £117.50, and hence the percentage decrease was

$$\frac{2.5}{117.5} \times 100\% = 2.1\% \text{ (to 2 s.f.)}.$$

Many shops had to put up notices explaining the perceived discrepancy. Some of the notices included worked examples like the one above!

Making sense of numbers in the media

The final activity in this section asks you to use some of the techniques that you've met to make sense of two fictitious newspaper cuttings. Although both cuttings use the same data, their conclusions appear contradictory.

Table 2 shows the total UK government spending in England and the amount spent on public order, in 2002–3 and 2006–7.

Table 2 UK government spending in England (£ billion)

	2002–3	2006–7
Total expenditure	274.2	359.2
Public order and safety	18.7	23.7

Source: www.hm-treasury.gov.uk

The public order category includes spending on the police, fire services, law courts, prisons and associated research.

A billion (bn) is a thousand million.

The two cuttings below illustrate how the figures in Table 2 can provide evidence for either praise or criticism of the government's spending on public order in England, depending on how the numbers are manipulated. To understand the numbers in the cuttings, you also need to know that the population of England was about 50 million in 2007.

Spending on public order rises by 27% in 4 years

Government spending on public order rose from £18.7 billion in 2002 to £23.7 billion in 2006. This increase of £5 billion represents an extra £100 spent on public order for every man, woman and child throughout England.

PUBLIC ORDER SERVICES LOSE OUT BY £800 MILLION

In 2002, out of every £1 it spent, the government spent a miserly 6.8p on public order. By 2006, it had fallen to 6.6p – a drop of 3%. Based on 2006 government spending figures, this represents a loss to law and order of almost £800 million.

Figure 17 Two fictional newspaper articles based on the data in Table 2

Activity 27 *Checking the figures*

(a) Explain how the figures of 27% and £100 in the cutting on the left of Figure 17 were derived.

(b) For each of 2002–3 and 2006–7, calculate the percentage of total expenditure that was spent on public order. Check that these percentages correspond to the amounts of 6.8p and 6.6p in the cutting on the right of Figure 17.

(c) How much would the government have spent on public order in 2006–7 if it had spent the same percentage of total expenditure as in 2002–3? Give your answer to three significant figures.

(d) Use your rounded answer to part (c) to explain how the figure of £800 million in the second cutting has been derived.

(e) What criticisms could you make of each article?

In this subsection you have revised some of the ways that percentages are used, and met the idea of absolute and relative comparisons. You have also seen how percentages and other numbers can be used in the media to promote particular points of view. You may read media articles more critically in future!

4 Thinking mathematically

'I really think that solving a mathematical puzzle is a little bit like trying to find *who done it* in a murder mystery.'

Marcus du Sautoy, Professor of Mathematics, University of Oxford.

In the previous two sections, you concentrated on practical mathematics and the sorts of calculations that you can do to describe or understand everyday situations. In this section you will explore some mathematical ideas that are interesting in their own right. These ideas come from a branch of mathematics known as pure mathematics. This is mathematics that does not necessarily have practical applications, but is studied because it is interesting and intriguing, and often beautiful.

4.1 An odd pattern

This first subsection invites you to think about a mathematical problem that arises from curiosity about numbers. First, here are the names given to various special types of numbers.

The usual counting numbers

$$1, 2, 3, 4, \ldots$$

are called the **natural numbers** (or positive integers).

Each natural number is either even or odd. The **even** natural numbers,

$$2, 4, 6, 8, \ldots,$$

are those that can be divided by 2 exactly; that is, an even number can be divided 'evenly' into two parts. For example,

$$8 \div 2 = 4.$$

The **odd** natural numbers,

$$1, 3, 5, 7, \ldots,$$

are those that cannot be divided by 2 exactly; that is, when an odd number is divided by 2, there is 1 left over. For example,

$$7 \div 2 = 3 \text{ remainder } 1.$$

There might be an odd number of socks in your sock drawer!

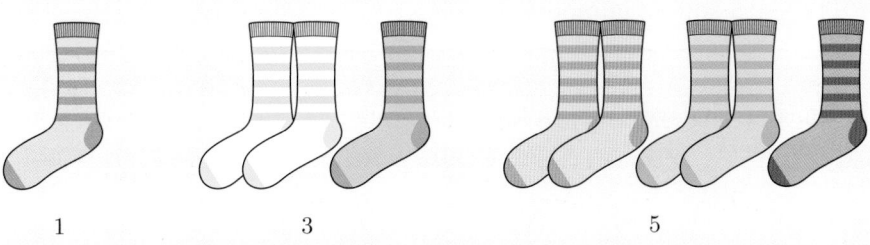

Figure 18 Odd socks

It is not just the *positive* integers that are either even or odd. For example, 0, -2 and -4 are even numbers, and -1 and -3 are odd numbers. However, this subsection is about positive integers, so, for example, 'the first four odd numbers' means the first four positive ones: 1, 3, 5 and 7.

The **square numbers**

$$1, 4, 9, 16, \ldots$$

are obtained by multiplying each natural number by itself:

$$1 = 1 \times 1 = 1^2,$$
$$4 = 2 \times 2 = 2^2,$$
$$9 = 3 \times 3 = 3^2,$$
$$16 = 4 \times 4 = 4^2,$$

and so on. The square numbers can be represented as patterns of dots arranged as squares, as shown in Figure 19. These patterns explain why multiplying a number by itself is called *squaring*.

Figure 19 The first five square numbers as patterns of dots

Perhaps you hadn't thought of representing numbers as patterns of dots before, but you will see shortly that this can be helpful in discovering properties of numbers.

Activity 28   *Types of numbers*

Write down the following numbers.

(a) The sixth natural number

(b) The sixth even number

(c) The sixth odd number

(d) The sixth square number

Houses are not always numbered with odd numbers on one side of the street and even numbers on the other. In remote parts of Australia they are sometimes numbered according to their distance from a junction, so house 265 is 2650 metres from the junction, for example. Houses may also be numbered according to when they were built: 1 for the first house, 2 for the second, and so on. The numbering system used may depend on what information it is important to convey!

Now imagine that you are walking down one side of a street, looking at the house numbers $1, 3, 5, \ldots$. What happens if you add these numbers up?

Activity 29   *Adding odd numbers*

(a) Complete the following table of sums of odd numbers.

How many odd numbers	Sum
1	$1 = 1$
2	$1 + 3 = 4$
3	$1 + 3 + 5 =$
4	$1 + 3 + 5 + 7 =$
5	$1 + 3 + 5 + 7 + 9 =$
6	$1 + 3 + 5 + 7 + 9 + 11 =$

(b) What do you notice about these sums?

In Activity 29 you might have spotted a rather surprising result. The sums look familiar – they are all square numbers. Moreover, each sum is the square of the number of odd numbers that are added. It looks as if adding consecutive odd numbers starting from 1 *always* results in the square of the number of odd numbers that are added. At this stage, this statement is a **conjecture** – an informed guess about what might be true, from considering a few cases. So far, there is not enough information to conclude that what we have observed will always happen, no matter how many odd numbers are added.

If we use the letter n to represent any natural number, then the conjecture can be expressed in the following neat way.

Conjecture

If you add up the first n odd numbers, then the sum is always n^2.

To develop more confidence in this conjecture, you can check that it works for cases you haven't tried. According to the conjecture, when you add the first seven odd numbers the answer should be 7^2, which is 49. Checking this sum gives $1 + 3 + 5 + 7 + 9 + 11 + 13$, which is indeed equal to 49.

At this point, it seems increasingly likely that the conjecture is true, and you can check it for many natural numbers n. But no amount of checking of individual cases can prove that it is true for *all* natural numbers n. However, it turns out that we can prove this by considering patterns of dots.

You have seen that the square numbers can be represented as square patterns of dots. What about the odd numbers? One way to represent them is as L-shaped patterns of dots. Figure 20 shows the first four odd numbers represented in this way.

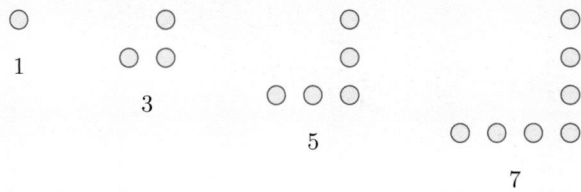

Figure 20 L-shaped patterns for 1, 3, 5 and 7

Let's consider the sum of these four odd numbers. It is $1 + 3 + 5 + 7 = 16$, and you know that this number of dots can be arranged in the square pattern shown in Figure 21.

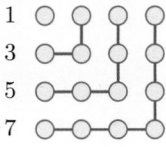

Figure 21 The 4×4 square

Now, a good question is: can you combine the four L-shaped patterns of dots to make the square pattern? Figure 22 shows how this can be done – the lines show the four separate L-shaped patterns.

Figure 22 Four odd numbers make a 4×4 square

This picture is very suggestive and you are surely itching to add to it the next L-shaped pattern of 9 dots and so make a 5×5 square! This is shown in Figure 23.

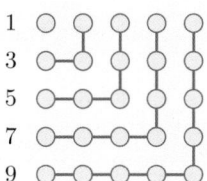

Figure 23   Five odd numbers make a 5×5 square

You can make larger and larger squares of dots by adding larger and larger L-shaped patterns of dots. At each stage you add on the next odd number of dots, and the result is the next square number. So, if you put together the first n of the L-shaped patterns of dots, where n is a natural number, then the result is a square of n^2 dots. This is shown in Figure 25.

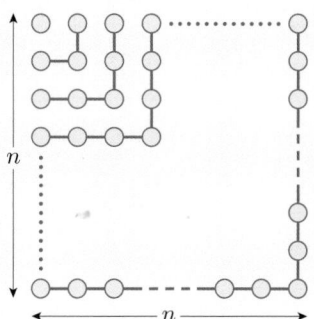

Figure 25 n odd numbers make an $n \times n$ square

Because you can do this for *any* natural number n, you can see that the conjecture is true. That is, the sum of the first n odd numbers is always n^2. So the conjecture has now been proved.

A mathematical statement that has been proved is called a **theorem** or a **result**. So we now have the following result.

> **Result**
>
> If you add up the first n odd numbers, then the sum is always n^2.

'The mathematician's patterns, like the painter's or the poet's, must be beautiful; the ideas, like the colours or the words, must fit together in a harmonious way. Beauty is the first test: there is no permanent place in the world for ugly mathematics.'

G.H. Hardy, in
A Mathematician's Apology,
Cambridge University Press, 1940.

Figure 24   G.H. Hardy (1877–1947)

Activity 30   *Using the result*

Use the result above to find the sum of the first 100 odd numbers.

BEGIN HERE ↓

Such is the power of mathematics – it is certainly easier to use the result than to add 100 numbers!

In this subsection a result about adding odd numbers was proved using geometric reasoning. However, for many results there is no geometric proof. Instead, mathematicians often use *algebra*. You will learn about algebra later in the course, and in Unit 9 you will see an algebraic proof of a formula for adding up sequences of numbers.

4.2 From folding to fractals

In this subsection, you will see how recognising a pattern that arises from simply folding a strip of paper leads to some surprising and far-reaching ideas.

In the video that you watched in Activity 1, you saw a strip of paper being folded in half repeatedly. The strip was partially unfolded after each fold, and the patterns that were seen by looking at the strip edge-on are shown in Figure 26.

Origami, the ancient art of paper folding, has many practical applications, from the design of solar panels on satellites and space telescopes to modelling the performance of airbags.

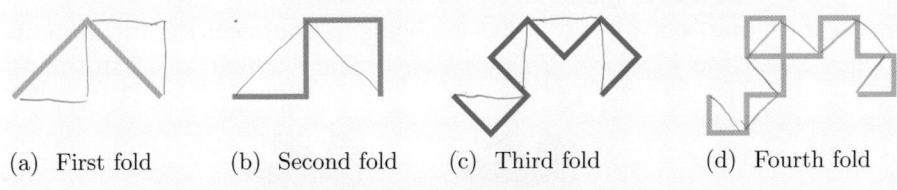

(a) First fold   (b) Second fold   (c) Third fold   (d) Fourth fold

Figure 26   Folds in a strip of paper

It is difficult to fold a piece of paper in half more than about six or seven times, even if you start with a long strip. For a long time it was thought that the limit was eight folds, but twelve folds have now been achieved. So only a few patterns can be generated by physically folding a paper strip.

However, by thinking mathematically you can generate the pattern that corresponds to as many folds as you like! If you think carefully about the patterns in Figure 26 (and quite a bit of thought is needed), you can see that to get from one pattern to the next you replace each line in the old pattern by two new lines at right angles to each other – this is what happens when you make a new fold. The two new lines are either to the right or to the left of the old line: the first pair of new lines is to the right, the next pair to the left, and so on. This is illustrated in Figure 27.

If you want to try folding a strip of paper yourself to produce the patterns in Figure 26, then you need to be careful to always fold the strip the 'same way', or you will obtain different patterns. There are instructions for folding the strip on the course website.

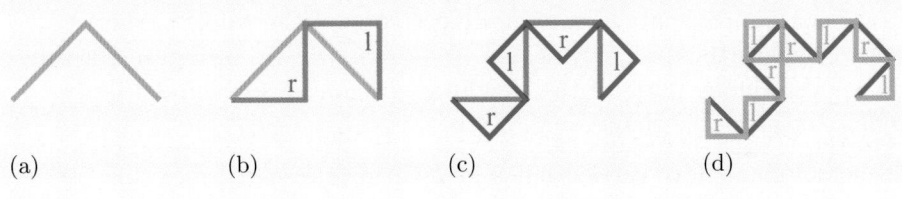

(a)   (b)   (c)   (d)

Figure 27   How to get each edge pattern from the one before

You can use this process to find the next few patterns. The first ten patterns are shown in Figure 28.

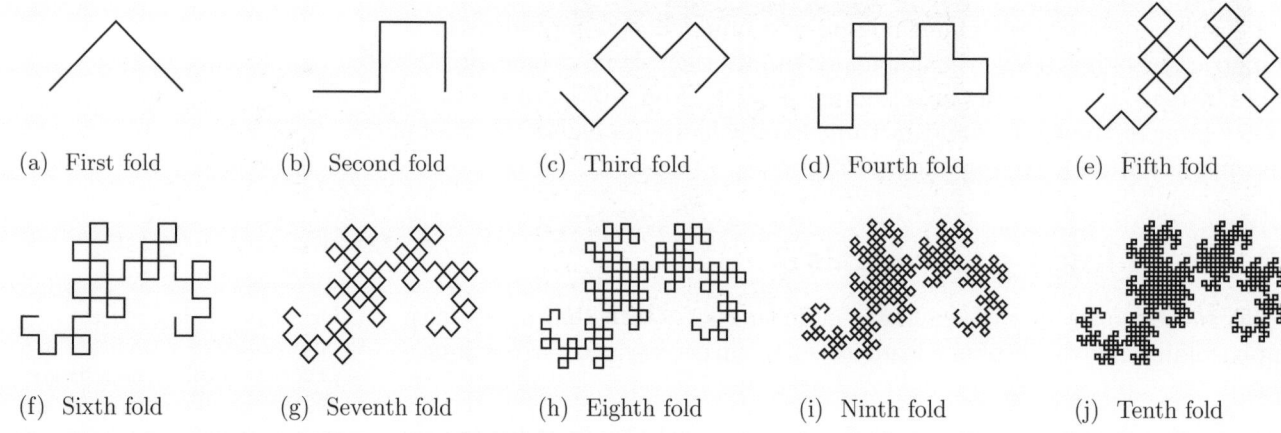

(a) First fold   (b) Second fold   (c) Third fold   (d) Fourth fold   (e) Fifth fold

(f) Sixth fold   (g) Seventh fold   (h) Eighth fold   (i) Ninth fold   (j) Tenth fold

Figure 28   The first ten patterns

Infinite means endless and without limit.

The Heighway dragon is sometimes called the *Jurassic Park dragon*, as it was printed in copies of Michael Crichton's novel *Jurassic Park*. It is also sometimes known as the *Harter–Heighway dragon*, or even just the *dragon curve*. It was first investigated by NASA physicists John Heighway, William Harter and Bruce Banks and was described by Martin Gardner in *Scientific American* in 1967.

From a mathematical point of view, the pattern can be developed to correspond to *infinitely* many folds, when, amazingly, it is no longer a collection of lines, but forms a filled-in shape, as shown in Figure 29. This shape is called the *Heighway dragon*, and it is an example of a **fractal**.

Figure 29   The pattern after infinitely many folds

'As to the word *fractal*, I coined it on some precisely datable evening in the winter of 1975, from a very concrete Latin adjective, fractus, which denoted a stone's shape after it was hit very hard.'

Benoit Mandelbrot, quoted in Hargittai, I. and Laurent, T.C. (eds) (2002) *Symmetry 2000*, pp. 133–41, Portland Press.

The word 'fractal' was coined by the French mathematician Benoit Mandelbrot to describe a shape that is irregular at all scales, no matter how closely you look. Many fractals can be split into parts, each of which is (at least approximately) a reduced-size copy of the whole shape. A shape that has this property is said to be *self-similar*. In Figure 29, you can see that many parts of the Heighway dragon have a shape that is similar to the whole shape.

Mathematicians have carried out a great deal of research into the properties of fractals in recent years. Fractals are also used in many practical situations, from modelling internet traffic and fluctuations in world stock markets, to medical research. They also abound in nature, for example in the structure of clouds and snowflakes, and in the patterns of lightning. Our own bodies contain a myriad of self-similar fractal systems: for instance, our circulatory systems have this structure – the branching of tiny capillaries is similar to the branching of major arteries and veins. Some more examples of self-similar shapes are shown in Figure 30.

(a) (b) (c)

Figure 30 Self-similarity in (a) a human lung, (b) Romanesco broccoli and (c) a fern

Isn't it surprising that a shape as curly as the Heighway dragon arises naturally from straight lines and right angles? Another surprising fact is that, despite the rough shape of the Heighway dragon, you can cover a flat surface with Heighway-dragon-shaped 'tiles', with no gaps or overlaps! In fact this can be done in several different ways, two of which are shown in Figure 31.

Figure 31 Heighway dragon tilings

In this section you have seen some surprising patterns emerge from simple beginnings – adding odd numbers and folding paper. In the first example you saw how by thinking mathematically – representing numbers as patterns of dots – you could prove that a property was true for any number of odd numbers, not just for those you had checked. In the second example you saw how by thinking about a pattern mathematically you could extend it beyond what is possible physically, with intriguing results. These examples illustrate just a little of the power and beauty of the kind of mathematics that fascinates many mathematicians. You can look for mathematics in all kinds of situations: asking yourself the tantalising question 'What would happen if ...?' is often a good way to start!

'Now let me explain a wonderful thing: the more mathematics you learn, the more opportunities you will find for asking new questions.'

Ian Stewart, Professor of Mathematics, University of Warwick (2006) in *Letters to a young mathematician*, New York, Basic Books.

5 Preparing your assignments

There are two kinds of assignments in MU123: interactive computer-marked assignments (iCMAs) and tutor-marked assignments (TMAs). This section helps you to prepare for these assignments and gives you some advice on how to tackle them. The instructions for submitting your assignments are on the course website.

The first subsection helps you to review your progress on the course so far, and the second subsection provides some suggestions for how to approach the iCMAs. The final subsection is based around a sample TMA question. It provides some guidelines to help you to write the kind of clearly explained answers that your tutor will be looking for. Learning how to express your mathematics well, so that a reader can easily understand it, is an important part of learning mathematics.

Figure 32 A French postage stamp celebrating Galois

Evariste Galois (1811–1832) was a brilliant young mathematician who died in a duel at the age of 20. He spent some of his final hours editing his mathematical manuscripts and writing a summary of his discoveries. It took mathematicians many years to understand his notes, but they now form the basis of a branch of advanced mathematics called Galois theory. A moral of his story is that you should write down your ideas in good time, and explain them clearly, so they can be easily understood by others. Another moral is to avoid duelling!

When should you start your assignment questions?

Most students find that it is best to start each assignment question fairly soon after studying the course material on which the question is based. For example, you might find it helpful to do each assignment question immediately after studying the relevant section or sections in the unit. This allows you to focus closely on the topics and may alert you to the need to re-read some sections. Alternatively, you might prefer to work through the whole of each unit before tackling the assignment questions on the unit. This has the advantage that you might find some questions on the earlier parts of a unit easier when you have studied the whole unit. Also, if you leave a short gap between studying the material relevant to an assignment question and attempting the question, then you should find that you are better able to remember key ideas, since the more times you use a concept or technique, the better you remember it. This should make your study of future units and courses easier.

It is usually not a good idea to defer starting an assignment until close to the cut-off date. This is because you may need time to revise some topics or contact your tutor with questions, and you are unlikely to be able to produce your best work if you are under time pressure. Also, something unexpected may happen near the cut-off date, so you should allow some contingency time.

If you are an experienced student, then you have probably already paused to take stock of your progress, whether formally or not. It is a good idea to do this every so often.

5.1 Reviewing your progress

Before you start on the assignment questions for a unit, it is a good idea to spend a few moments thinking about the progress that you have made while studying the unit. You should check whether there are any topics that you need help with, or any topics on which you need more practice. If you sort out any problems, then you should find it easier to do the assignment questions, and you will also find it easier to understand the material in the later units.

In the next activity you are asked to look back over your work on this unit and use the practice quiz to help you to assess your progress. The practice quizzes for each unit can be accessed from the course website, along with other resources for each unit – you may have tried some of the questions earlier in the unit. The quizzes are similar in style to the iCMA questions, so you can also use them to familiarise yourself with the process of answering iCMA questions before you attempt the first iCMA.

Practice quiz

Activity 31 *Checking your progress*

(a) Are you confident about the mathematical skills covered in this unit? Look back at your answers to the activities, and any notes you made, to identify where you might need more practice. You might like to complete the table below, to help you to organise your thoughts.

Topic	Confident	Need more practice	Unhappy with this topic
BIDMAS	✓		
Using your calculator	✓		
Units of measurement	✓		
Rounding	✓		
Checking answers	✓		
Negative numbers	✓		
Fractions	✓		
Percentages	✓		

(b) Try the practice quiz questions on this unit if you have not already done so, to check your understanding of the topics above.

(c) If you are still not confident in some areas, then plan what you will do to improve your understanding and skills. You may need to allow some extra time to work through some topics in Maths Help, or to try some more practice quiz questions. If you are not sure of the best way forward, then contact your tutor for advice.

5.2 iCMA questions

When you do the iCMA questions on a unit, you should have the unit and any notes that you made to hand, as you will probably find it helpful to consult them. You will also need a pen or pencil, paper and your calculator.

Make sure that you read each question carefully, so that you understand what is required before you start to work out your answer. You do not have to complete all the questions in an iCMA in one session: you can answer a few questions at a time, in any order, and save your answers. You can change your answers in later sessions if you wish, before submitting the iCMA.

Once you have completed the questions in an iCMA, it is a good idea to read through the questions again, to check that you are happy with your answers and that you have answered as many questions as you can.

iCMA

There are more details about iCMAs in the Course Guide (in the 'Study guide' and the 'Technology guide' sections).

Activity 32   *Answering iCMA questions*

Find the first iCMA on the course website. Follow the instructions given there and try some of the questions. Complete as many of the questions as you can before the cut-off date.

If you find a lot of questions in the first iCMA difficult, then you may need to seek advice from your tutor.

5.3   TMA questions

TMAs are more substantial pieces of work than iCMAs. They allow your tutor to assess how you present and explain your mathematical ideas, as well as the accuracy of your mathematics. An example of part of a TMA question is shown below.

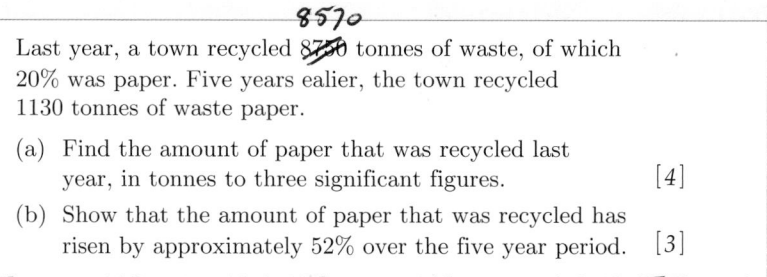

Last year, a town recycled ~~8750~~ 8570 tonnes of waste, of which 20% was paper. Five years ealier, the town recycled 1130 tonnes of waste paper.

(a)   Find the amount of paper that was recycled last year, in tonnes to three significant figures.   [4]

(b)   Show that the amount of paper that was recycled has risen by approximately 52% over the five year period.   [3]

Figure 33   Part of a typical TMA question

TMA questions are usually similar to activities in the units, but they include marks for the question parts, in square brackets at the right-hand side. Usually, the more marks a question part is worth, the more substantial your solution should be.

If you are not sure how to do part of a TMA question, then look back through the unit and any notes that you made, to remind yourself of the methods that you could use. For example, for part (a) of the question above you could look back at Subsection 3.3, which is about percentages, and in particular at Example 12 on page 40, which illustrates how to calculate a percentage of a quantity. If looking back through the unit does not help, and you are stuck, then contact your tutor.

Once you have decided what method seems appropriate for a question part, you need to write out a full and clear solution for your tutor. You may find it helpful to write a rough version first.

The TMA solutions shown in this section are in a handwritten style. You can type or handwrite your TMA solutions, as you prefer.

Here is an example of a solution to part (a) of the question above that would be awarded full marks by a tutor. The solution has been annotated to show the key steps.

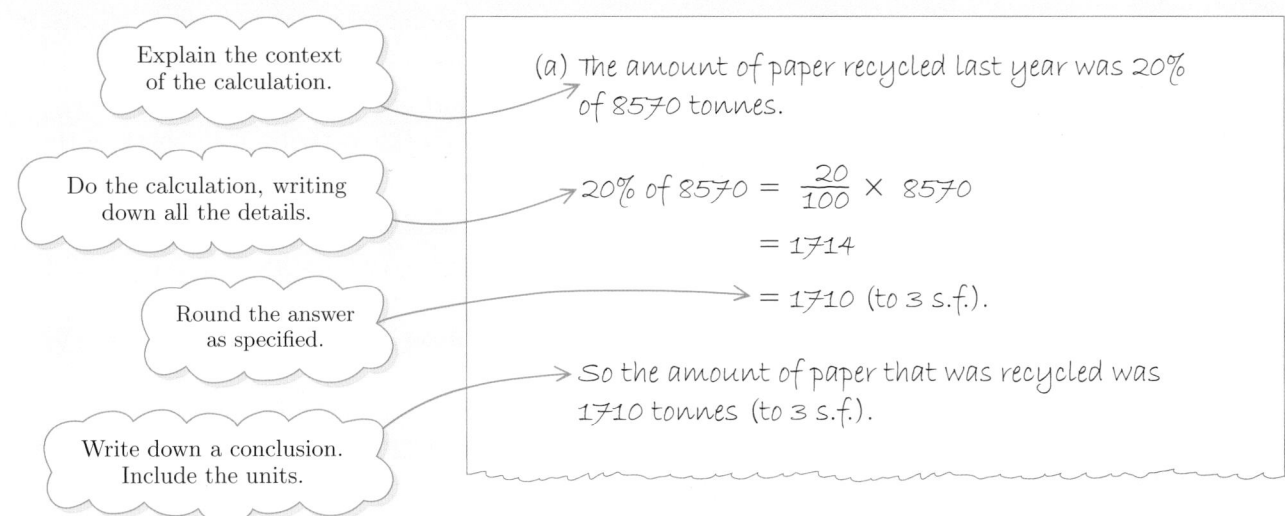

Figure 34 An annotated solution to a typical TMA question

Notice that the solution has been written in sentences, and the final sentence gives a clear conclusion in the context of the question, and includes the appropriate units. This means that anyone reading the solution can easily understand it.

There is always more than one way to write a solution. Here is an alternative solution to the same question part, which would be equally acceptable.

> (a) The amount of paper recycled last year was
> 20 percent of 8570 t = 0.2 × 8570 t
> = 1714 t
> = 1710 t (to 3 s.f.).

Figure 35 An alternative solution to the TMA question

In this second solution, the explanation and details of the calculation, and the conclusion, are all given in one sentence. You may be able to do this for a short calculation, but you must make sure that the sentence makes sense and that the answer at the end of the sentence includes the appropriate units.

If you are not sure how much explanation or detail you need to include in your solution to a TMA question, then use the worked examples in the units as a guide. Remember that the green thinks text is not part of the solutions, but all the other words *are* part of them, and your solutions should include similar amounts of explanation and working.

In the next activity you are asked to write out a solution to part (b) of the TMA question. This question part actually gives you the answer, 52%, and asks you to *show* how it can be worked out. Because of this, none of the marks for this question part will be for the final answer – all three marks will be for working and explanation.

When you are doing a question that gives you the answer, you should not use the given answer in your working. Just work it out as usual, and then check that your answer matches the one given in the question.

Activity 33 *Writing a good solution*

Try to write out a good solution to part (b) of the TMA question on page 54. Then look at the comments on this activity in the back of the unit.

Activity 34 *Improving a solution*

Here is an incorrect and poorly explained solution to parts (a) and (b) of the TMA question.

> (a) $8570 = 0.2 \times 8570 = 1714$
>
> (b) $1714 - 1130 = 584 = \dfrac{584}{1714} = .34$

Write down some suggestions for how the solution could be improved. Then look at the comments on this activity in the back of the unit.

Although the solution in Activity 34 could be significantly improved, it does show some understanding of how the question could be answered and so it would be awarded some marks.

There are several other things to notice about this solution. First, equals signs are used incorrectly, which is another reason why the solution is difficult to follow. Whenever you use an equals sign, whatever is on the left of the equals sign must be equal to whatever is on the right. So it is wrong to write

$$8570 = 0.2 \times 8570,$$

as in the solution, because the number on the left, 8570, is not equal to the calculation on the right, 0.2×8570.

Activity 35 *Using equals signs correctly*

Can you spot two other places in the solution in Activity 34 where equals signs have been used incorrectly?

For help with reading and writing mathematics, and approaches to problem solving, see Maths Help Module 6.

Another thing to notice about the solution in Activity 34 is that its author should have spotted that the answer to part (b) is wrong, because the correct answer, 52%, is given in the question. It is always worth thinking about whether your answer is likely to be correct. You can often do this even when the answer is not given in the question. For example, if you were doing part (a) of the TMA question and you obtained the answer 17 100 tonnes, say, for the amount of paper recycled last year, then you might have spotted that this answer is too large. You could spot this by considering the context: 17 100 tonnes is more than the total amount of waste recycled. Alternatively you could have estimated that the correct answer is approximately 20% of 10 000 tonnes, which is 2000 tonnes.

Notice that although the author of the solution wrote down the wrong fraction in part (b), he or she went on to evaluate it correctly as 0.34. If you make a mistake but your calculations following the mistake are correct, then you may be awarded marks for these calculations even though your final answer is incorrect. These marks are known as 'follow-through marks'. Your tutor may use the abbreviation 'F.T.' to indicate follow-through marks or reasoning.

The incorrect solution in Activity 34 illustrates why it is so important to explain your solutions clearly. It is important that your tutor can follow your working, and also that you yourself can follow it if you look over it some time later. If you use mathematics in your workplace, then it is also important that you write down clearly explained solutions for your colleagues.

When you have written out your solution to a TMA question, you should read through the question again, to make sure that you have answered all the parts and given all your answers in the required form. Then read over your solution again, to make sure that your explanations make sense. It can be helpful to do this after a break – you might be surprised to find that what you have written down does not quite say what you meant it to.

Some guidelines for writing good mathematics are summarised below.

Things to remember when writing your own mathematics

- Write in sentences, explaining your reasoning step by step.
- Use link words like 'so' to make your solution easier to read.
- Start each new idea on a new line.
- Use notation correctly, especially equals signs.
- Include units where appropriate.
- Give a conclusion, in the appropriate context.
- Read through what you have written to check that it makes sense.

You have seen that if a question part starts with the word 'show', then the answer is given in the question, and all the marks are for explanation and working. Table 3 gives some similar words that you might see in TMA questions, and explains what sorts of answers are expected.

Table 3 Instructions in mathematics questions

Instruction	Explanation
find, determine, calculate, work out	You need to give both an answer and the details of how the answer is worked out. Some of the marks are for the answer, and some are for explanation and working.
show, verify, check	The answer is given to you, and you need to give the details of how it is worked out. All of the marks are for explanation and working.
write down, state, list	You need to give only an answer; no explanation or working is required. All of the marks are for the answer. This is usually because the answer can be found without doing any working.

Explanation and working are nearly always required in your solution to a TMA question, so if in doubt, include them!

 TMA

Activity 36   *Answering the TMA questions for Unit 1*

If you have not already done so, find and read the document on the course website that gives you information about submitting TMAs – it is in the same place as the TMAs. Then open the first TMA and prepare your solutions to the questions on Unit 1. Keep your solutions safe until you have completed the other questions in the TMA.

The box below summarises the main steps that you should follow when doing TMA questions.

> ### Preparing solutions to TMA questions
>
> - Start each question well before the cut-off date.
> - Read the questions carefully, noting all the instructions – for example, you may be asked to use a particular method, or round an answer in a particular way.
> - If you are stuck, look back at similar examples and activities in the unit.
> - Contact your tutor if you need help.
> - Write your solutions clearly, giving all the details of your working and explaining it carefully.
> - Check that your answers seem reasonable.
> - Read the questions and your solutions again, to make sure that you have answered all the parts and followed all the instructions.

6 Reviewing your study methods

This unit is a little different from the other units in the course, as it aims to introduce the course and check that you are well prepared to study it. Now that you have worked through the unit, you should know how the different course components (such as the tutorial clips, practice quizzes, videos and assignments) can help your learning, and you should have improved your fluency in some essential mathematical skills, including using your calculator.

You have been encouraged to think about your studying, and to make changes to improve it, if necessary. Before you go on to the next unit, it's worth spending a few minutes reviewing how your studying of this unit has gone, to see whether there are any changes that it would be helpful to make to your study methods in future.

- Did you manage to find enough time to complete the unit in the period allocated on the study planner? If not, do you need to rearrange or give up some other activities to make more time, or do you need to try to make better use of the time you have allocated for studying? For example, a greater number of shorter study sessions or studying at a different time of the day may be more effective.

- Can you remember the ideas that you have studied? You do not have to remember everything in the unit, but you will need to use some of the techniques and ideas in later parts of the course. The most important ideas are the ones covered in the practice quizzes and assignment questions. Learning actively, by doing the activities and perhaps making some form of notes, will help your understanding and your ability to apply and remember these ideas.

- Can you quickly find any information that you need? For example, if you want to check what 'improper fraction' means, or revise how to round appropriately, then where would you look first – the unit, the book's index, your notes, the glossary in the Handbook, or the summary pages in the Handbook? Try to get to know what information is contained in different sources, and try to keep your notes organised, so that you can easily find information that you need.

At the end of each unit there is a learning checklist, which you can use to make sure that you have acquired the main skills and knowledge taught in the unit. If there are some skills that you do not feel confident about, then you may need to spend more time on them. However, if doing this will use up some of the time that you have allocated for the next unit, then you should contact your tutor to discuss how to proceed, as it is also important to keep up with the schedule in the study planner.

As well as helping you prepare to study the rest of the course, this unit has also introduced some practical applications of mathematics – for example, it has shown you how to critically assess some types of numerical information in the media. It has also offered you a taste of the power and beauty of abstract mathematics. Mathematics really is everywhere, and in MU123 you will have plenty of opportunities to discover this for yourself!

Learning checklist

After studying this unit, you should be able to:

- find and use the main components of the course, including tutorial clips, practice quizzes, videos and assignments
- plan how you will use your study time effectively
- carry out mathematical operations such as $+$, $-$, $\times$ and $\div$ in the correct order, using the BIDMAS rules
- use your calculator effectively
- understand and use some SI units
- round numbers appropriately to a number of decimal places or significant figures
- check calculations by estimating answers
- understand and use negative numbers, fractions and percentages
- start to critically analyse numerical information in the media
- understand the difference between relative and absolute comparisons
- start to investigate mathematical patterns, make conjectures and appreciate the idea of proof
- start to write mathematics well, using appropriate notation
- review your learning progress and make changes to improve your study methods
- prepare your answers to iCMA and TMA questions.

Solutions and comments on Activities

Activity 2

(a) $9 + 7 - 2 - 4 = 16 - 2 - 4 = 14 - 4 = 10$

(b) $2 \times (7 - 4) = 2 \times 3 = 6$

(c) $(3 + 5) \times 3 = 8 \times 3 = 24$

(d) $(3 + 4) \times (2 + 3) = 7 \times 5 = 35$

(e) $3^2 + 4^3 = 3 \times 3 + 4 \times 4 \times 4 = 9 + 64 = 73$

Activity 3

(a) The calculation is incorrect. A correct calculation is $2 \times (5 + 3) = 16$.

(b) The calculation is incorrect. A correct calculation is $(3 + 4) \times 7 = 49$.

(c) The calculation is correct.

(d) The calculation is correct.

(e) The calculation is incorrect. A correct calculation is $2 \times (3 + 3) \times 5 = 60$.

Activity 4

(a) The numbers are 4 and 8. Their sum is $4 + 8 = 12$ and their product is $4 \times 8 = 32$.
(If you didn't spot the answer quickly, then you could have found it by systematically listing the pairs of whole numbers with sum 12 until you found the pair with product 32.)

(b) The numbers are 2 and 4. Their difference is $4 - 2 = 2$ and their quotient is $4 \div 2 = 2$.

Activity 6

(a) There are 1000 m in 1 km, so
$$6100\,\text{m} = (6100 \div 1000)\,\text{km} = 6.1\,\text{km}.$$

(b) There are 1000 kg in 1 t, so
$$560\,\text{kg} = (560 \div 1000)\,\text{t} = 0.56\,\text{t}.$$

(c) There are 60 minutes in 1 hour, so
$$\begin{aligned} 3.45\,\text{hours} &= (3.45 \times 60)\,\text{minutes} \\ &= 207\,\text{minutes}. \end{aligned}$$

(d) There are 1000 mg in 1 g, so
$$0.35\,\text{g} = (0.35 \times 1000)\,\text{mg} = 350\,\text{mg}.$$

(e) There are 1000 ml in 1 l, so
$$450\,\text{ml} = (450 \div 1000)\,\text{l} = 0.45\,\text{l}.$$

(f) There are 100 cm in 1 m, so
$$75\,\text{cm} = (75 \div 100)\,\text{m} = 0.75\,\text{m}.$$

Activity 7

(a) $2.2364 = 2.24$ (to 2 d.p.)

(b) $0.005\,47 = 0.005$ (to 3 d.p.)

(c) $42.598\,17 = 42.5982$ (to 4 d.p.)

(d) $7.98 = 8.0$ (to 1 d.p.)

(In part (d), the 0 after the decimal point should be included to show that the number has been rounded to one decimal place.)

Activity 8

(a) $23\,650 = 24\,000$ (to 2 s.f.)

(b) $0.005\,47 = 0.005$ (to 1 s.f.)

(c) $42.598\,17 = 42.60$ (to 4 s.f.)

(In part (c), the 0 after the 6 should be included to show that the number has been rounded to four significant figures.)

Activity 9

(a) Using the given conversion factor gives the distance in miles as
$$465 \times 0.62 = 288.3.$$
Rounding to the nearest mile gives the answer 288 miles. This is inaccurate, since we know from the calculation on page 22 that the correct answer to the nearest mile is 289 miles. The conversion factor used in this activity is not precise enough to give an answer correct to the nearest mile.

(b) Rounding to two significant figures gives the answer 290 miles.

(The answer is rounded to two significant figures because two is the number of significant figures in the least precise number used in the calculation. The answer found here agrees with the answer found in the calculation before the activity, 289 miles, because $289 = 290$ (to 2 s.f.).)

Activity 10

(a) The distance, in miles, to the town is $36 \times 0.621\,371\,192$. The answer displayed on the calculator is $22.369\,362\,91$, which rounds to 22 (to the nearest mile). Multiplying by 2 gives
$$2 \times 22 = 44.$$
So the total distance is calculated as 44 miles.

(b) As in part (a), the distance, in miles, to the town is displayed on the calculator as $22.369\,362\,91$. Multiplying by 2 gives
$$\begin{aligned} 2 \times 22.369\,362\,91 &= 44.738\,725\,82 \\ &= 45\ (\text{to the nearest mile}). \end{aligned}$$
So the total distance is 45 miles.

(c) The answer in part (b) is more accurate. In part (a), rounding too early led to an inaccurate final answer.

Activity 11

(a) Each jewellery box takes about 4 hours to make and decorate. A working day is about 8 hours, so about two jewellery boxes can be completed in a working day. So it would take about 24 days to complete 48 jewellery boxes.

(b) The student's first mistake was to forget to include brackets around '2.30 + 1.45'. So the calculator will first multiply 1.45 by 48, then divide by 7.5, and then add 2.30, which is not what the student intended.

The student's other mistake was to assume that if you add 2 hours and 30 minutes to 1 hour and 45 minutes then the total number of hours is $2.30 + 1.45$. This is not correct, since 2 hours and 30 minutes is 2.5 hours, not 2.30 hours, and 1 hour and 45 minutes is 1.75 hours, not 1.45 hours.

(c) The time needed to make and decorate a jewellery box is

2 hours and 30 minutes + 1 hour and 45 minutes

$\qquad = 4$ hours and 15 minutes

$\qquad = 4.25$ hours.

Thus the number of days needed to make and decorate 48 jewellery boxes is

$\qquad 4.25 \times 48 \div 7.5 = 27.2$.

This number has to be rounded up, because all 48 boxes must be finished. So 28 days are needed.

(This answer, unlike the student's, is fairly close to the estimate found in part (a).)

Activity 12

The numbers -6 and -4 lie to the left of -3 on the number line, and the numbers -2, 2 and 0 lie to the right of -3. So the noon temperature was lower on Monday and Friday.

Activity 13

(a) $-6 + 2 = -4$

(b) $-1 + 3 = 2$

(c) $2 - 7 = -5$

(d) $-3 - 4 = -7$

(e) $5 - 7 - 2 = -2 - 2 = -4$

Activity 14

(a) $2 + (-7) = 2 - 7 = -5$

(b) $-8 + (-5) = -8 - 5 = -13$

(c) $1 - (-3) = 1 + 3 = 4$

(d) $-6 - (-9) = -6 + 9 = 3$

(e) $-4 - (-4) = -4 + 4 = 0$

(f) $3 - (-2) + (-4) = 3 + 2 - 4 = 5 - 4 = 1$

(g) $7 + (-6) - 3 = 7 - 6 - 3 = 1 - 3 = -2$

Activity 15

(a) $5 \times (-3) = -15$

(b) $(-2) \times (-4) = 8$

(c) $6 \times (-10) = -60$

(d) $25 \div (-5) = -5$

(e) $(-49) \div (-7) = 7$

(f) $(-36) \div 12 = -3$

(g) $(-2) \times (-5) \times (-4) = 10 \times (-4) = -40$

Activity 17

(a) (i) $\frac{7}{21} = \frac{1}{3}$

(ii) $\frac{48}{72} = \frac{2}{3}$

(iii) $\frac{35}{105} = \frac{1}{3}$

(b) The fraction of the group is

$\frac{720}{1200} = \frac{3}{5}$.

(You might have cancelled the fraction like this:

$$\frac{\overset{\overset{3}{\cancel{9}}}{\cancel{72}}\,\cancel{720}}{\underset{\underset{5}{\cancel{15}}}{\cancel{120}}\,\cancel{1200}} = \frac{3}{5}\, .$$

But there are many different ways to cancel it.)

Activity 18

(a) $5\frac{2}{3} = \dfrac{5 \times 3 + 2}{3} = \dfrac{17}{3}$

(b) $\frac{18}{5} = 3\frac{3}{5}$

Activity 19

(a) (i) $\frac{4}{5}$ of $60\,\text{ml} = \frac{4}{5} \times 60\,\text{ml}$

$\qquad\qquad = 4 \div 5 \times 60\,\text{ml}$

$\qquad\qquad = 48\,\text{ml}$

(ii) $\frac{5}{8}$ of $20\,\text{kg} = \frac{5}{8} \times 20\,\text{kg}$

$\qquad\qquad = 5 \div 8 \times 20\,\text{kg}$

$\qquad\qquad = 12.5\,\text{kg}$

(b) The quantity of potatoes needed is

$\frac{20}{6} \times 900\,\text{g} = 20 \div 6 \times 900\,\text{g}$

$\qquad\qquad = 3000\,\text{g}$

$\qquad\qquad = 3\,\text{kg}$.

Activity 21

(a) The conversions are

$$60\% = \frac{60}{100} = 0.6,$$
$$60\% = \frac{60}{100} = \frac{3}{5},$$
$$\frac{7}{8} = \frac{7}{8} \times 100\% = 7 \div 8 \times 100\% = 87.5\%,$$
$$\frac{7}{8} = 7 \div 8 = 0.875,$$
$$1.35 = 1.35 \times 100\% = 135\%,$$
$$1.35 = 135\% = \frac{135}{100} = \frac{27}{20} = 1\frac{7}{20}.$$

So the completed table is as follows.

Percentage	Decimal	Fraction
60%	0.6	$\frac{3}{5}$
87.5%	0.875	$\frac{7}{8}$
135%	1.35	$\frac{27}{20}$

(b) $3.8\% = \dfrac{3.8}{100} = 0.038$

Activity 22

The fraction of students is

$$\frac{420}{1500}.$$

So the percentage of students is

$$\frac{420}{1500} \times 100\% = 28\%.$$

Activity 23

The percentage of pupils at School A who achieved the standard is

$$\frac{121}{194} \times 100\% = 62.4\% \text{ (to 1 d.p.).}$$

The percentage of pupils at School B who achieved the standard is

$$\frac{86}{130} \times 100\% = 66.2\% \text{ (to 1 d.p.).}$$

So School B had the better performance.

Activity 24

(a) (i) 30% of $150\,\text{g} = \frac{30}{100} \times 150\,\text{g}$
$$= 0.3 \times 150\,\text{g}$$
$$= 45\,\text{g}$$

(ii) 110% of $70\,\text{ml} = \frac{110}{100} \times 70\,\text{ml}$
$$= 1.1 \times 70\,\text{ml}$$
$$= 77\,\text{ml}$$

(iii) 0.5% of $£220 = \frac{0.5}{100} \times £220$
$$= 0.005 \times £220$$
$$= £1.10$$

(b) The fee paid on the first £30 of the selling price is

$$9\% \text{ of } £30 = \frac{9}{100} \times £30 = £2.70.$$

The remainder of the selling price is £75 − £30 = £45, and the fee paid on this amount is

$$5\% \text{ of } £45 = \frac{5}{100} \times £45 = £2.25.$$

The total fee is the insertion fee plus the two fees above, which is

$$£1.50 + £2.70 + £2.25 = £6.45.$$

Activity 25

The actual decrease is $145 - 125 = 20$.

So the decrease as a percentage of the original number is

$$\frac{20}{145} \times 100\% = 14\% \text{ (to 2 s.f.).}$$

Hence there is a 14% decrease in the number of complaints.

Activity 26

(a) The new price is $100\% - 20\% = 80\%$ of the original price. So the new price is

$$80\% \text{ of } £15\,400 = 0.8 \times £15\,400 = £12\,320.$$

(b) The new wage is $100\% + 2.5\% = 102.5\%$ of the original wage. So the new price is

$$102.5\% \text{ of } £360 = 1.025 \times £360 = £369.$$

(c) The new price is $100\% + 100\% = 200\%$ of the original price. So the new price is

$$200\% \text{ of } \$90 = 2 \times \$90 = \$180.$$

Activity 27

(a) Government spending rose from £18.7 billion (or bn) to £23.7 bn, which is an increase of £5 bn, as stated in the article. So the percentage increase is

$$\frac{5}{18.7} \times 100\% = 27\% \text{ (to 2 s.f.)}.$$

This explains the figure of 27% in the headline of the cutting on the left.

Since the actual increase in spending was £5 bn, and there were about 50 million people in England in 2007, the increase in spending per person was approximately

$$\frac{£5 \text{ bn}}{50 \text{ million}} = \frac{£5000 \text{ million}}{50 \text{ million}}$$
$$= \frac{£5000}{50}$$
$$= £100.$$

This explains the figure of £100 in the headline of the cutting on the left.

(b) The percentage of total expenditure that was spent on public order in 2002–3 was

$$\frac{18.7}{274.2} \times 100\% = 6.8\% \text{ (to 2 s.f.)}.$$

The percentage of total expenditure that was spent on public order in 2006–7 was

$$\frac{23.7}{359.2} \times 100\% = 6.6\% \text{ (to 2 s.f.)}.$$

These percentages correspond to the amounts of 6.8p and 6.6p in the second cutting, because 6.8% of £1 is 6.8p and 6.6% of £1 is 6.6p.

(c) The percentage of total expenditure spent on public order in 2002–3 was approximately 6.8%, or more precisely, 6.819 83...%. If this percentage of total expenditure had been spent on public order in 2006–7, then the spending on public order would have been

$$6.819\,83\ldots\% \text{ of } £359.2 \text{ bn}$$
$$= \frac{6.819\,83\ldots}{100} \times £359.2 \text{ bn}$$
$$= 0.068\,198\,3\ldots \times £359.2 \text{ bn}$$
$$= £24.5 \text{ bn (to 3 s.f.)}.$$

(d) The difference between the amount in part (c) and the amount that the government actually spent on public order in 2006–7 is

$$£24.5 \text{ bn} - £23.7 \text{ bn} = £0.8 \text{ bn} = £800 \text{ million}.$$

This explains how the figure of £800 million was worked out.

(e) The first article, on the left-hand side, emphasises the *absolute* increase in the amount spent, but ignores the fact that prices will have risen over the four-year period as well. So some of the extra £5 bn would be spent just maintaining the level of support that the public received in 2002. The key question here is what new support is being provided for the public – and neither that, nor the amount spent on new support, is stated in the article.

By using a relative comparison, the second article ignores the fact that there was a significant absolute increase in spending on public order, and in total spending. It is not helpful to be told that the percentage of total expenditure that is spent on public order has dropped. That might have been caused by, for example, large increases in spending on health and education, without any loss to spending on public order. A smaller percentage of a larger amount may still be larger than a larger percentage of a smaller amount! The percentage spent has dropped, but again the key question is what effect has that had on the services provided – has there been an overall increase or decrease in those?

Activity 28

(a) The first six natural numbers are 1, 2, 3, 4, 5, 6, so the sixth natural number is 6.

(b) The first six even numbers are 2, 4, 6, 8, 10, 12, so the sixth even number is 12.

(c) The first six odd numbers are 1, 3, 5, 7, 9, 11, so the sixth odd number is 11.

(d) The first six square numbers are 1, 4, 9, 16, 25, 36, so the sixth square number is 36.

Activity 29

(a) The completed table is as follows.

How many odd numbers	Sum
1	$1 = 1$
2	$1 + 3 = 4$
3	$1 + 3 + 5 = 9$
4	$1 + 3 + 5 + 7 = 16$
5	$1 + 3 + 5 + 7 + 9 = 25$
6	$1 + 3 + 5 + 7 + 9 + 11 = 36$

(b) All the sums are square numbers – in fact, each sum is the square of the number of odd numbers that are added.

Activity 30

By the result stated before the activity, the sum of the first 100 odd numbers is $100^2 = 10\,000$.

Activity 31

If you have any concerns about your responses to this activity, then contact your tutor for advice.

Activity 33

Here is an example of a solution to part (b) that would be awarded full marks.

(b) The percentage rise is

$$\frac{\text{actual rise}}{\text{original amount}} \times 100\%$$

$$= \frac{1714 - 1130}{1130} \times 100\%$$

$$= 52\% \text{ (to 2 s.f.)}.$$

Hence the amount of paper recycled has risen by about 52%, as required.

Did you remember to explain your calculation in words, and to write in sentences? And did you remember to use the *unrounded* value 1714 from part (a), not the rounded value 1710? If you used the rounded value, then you will have obtained the answer 51%, which is not the answer given in the question.

Activity 34

See how many of the following possible improvements you spotted – but don't worry if you didn't spot them all! The author of the solution could:

- explain the calculations in words and write in sentences

- include a conclusion for each question part, stating the answer clearly in the context of the question

- include the units in part (a)

- round the answer to part (a) to three significant figures, as requested in the question

- check the answer to part (b) against the given answer of 52%, and try to find the mistake

- correct the mistake – the amount of paper recycled five years ago was 1130 tonnes, not 1714 tonnes, so the increase as a fraction of the amount five years ago is $\frac{584}{1130}$, not $\frac{584}{1714}$

- write .34 as 0.34 – a decimal point should have a digit on each side to make it easy to read – it's easy to mistake .34 for 34

- write 0.34 as the percentage 34%, since the question referred to the percentage rise

- use equals signs correctly – see the text following the activity.

Activity 35

The equals sign in

$$584 = \frac{584}{1714}$$

is used incorrectly. The fraction on the right-hand side is not equal to 584.

The equals sign in

$$\frac{584}{1714} = .34$$

is also used incorrectly. The fraction on the left is not *exactly* equal to 0.34, so the author of the solution should have either used the approximately equals sign or included the rounding precision. That is, he or she should have written either

$$\frac{584}{1714} \approx 0.34$$

or

$$\frac{584}{1714} = 0.34 \text{ (to 2 s.f.)}.$$

(The equals sign in

$$1714 - 1130 = 584$$

is correctly used, but it would be better to explain this calculation in a sentence, such as: 'The increase in the amount of paper recycled is $1714\,\text{t} - 1130\,\text{t} = 584\,\text{t}$.' Then a linking word such as 'So' could be used to introduce the next line of the calculation.)

Mathematical models

Introduction

This unit is primarily concerned with a central theme of the course – how you can use mathematics to help investigate and solve practical problems.

The unit starts with an everyday problem – how do you decide when to set off on a certain journey, in order to reach your destination by a particular time? In Section 1, we consider how to make a rough estimate of the journey time. This section uses some simple mathematical ideas and, at the same time, introduces a general strategy for tackling problems by creating a **mathematical model**.

The aims of a mathematical model are to:

- describe the important features of a real situation mathematically – for example, by using numbers, formulas or graphs

- allow you to make predictions about the situation.

For example, such models can be used to predict traffic flows on roads or to investigate the likely impact of changes to speed limits on sections of motorway. However, a model does simplify the real situation, and emphasises certain aspects of it (such as the speed of a vehicle) and ignores others (such as the weather conditions). Even so, the results from models are often useful in practice, since in many cases an approximate answer is perfectly adequate.

"Assuming, of course, that a woodchuck could chuck wood."

In Section 2, we look at two models that are used to advise motorists on the gap they should leave on the road between their car and the vehicle ahead, and in particular we look at how these models take account of different features of the situation. This section illustrates the fact that problems can be approached in different ways, such as numerically, graphically or through general relationships such as formulas. It also highlights the importance of communicating mathematical ideas in an appropriate way for a wide audience.

Section 3 concentrates on the use of formulas and shows how these can be written concisely. This is an important section because formulas are frequently used in models and also because the skills and terminology covered here form a foundation for the rest of the course. So you are advised to work through the examples, activities and practice quizzes for this section carefully.

Section 4 introduces the use of inequalities, which can be used to specify some of the restrictions and limits on models concisely. Finally, Section 5 provides some advice on how you can improve your mathematics and on how to use the feedback you will receive on your assignments.

Activity 19 on page 96 is in the Course Guide.

Some of the activities in this unit involve the use of your calculator. Instructions for using your calculator are provided in the Course Guide.

I Planning a journey

1.1 Clarifying the question

Often, the first step in tackling a practical problem is to decide what questions you need to ask. For example, consider the problem of getting to the right place at the right time, which arises in many everyday activities such as going to work or to an appointment, on holiday or just meeting friends. Here a key question is: when should you set off?

The answer to this question may depend on several factors, such as what kind of transport is available in the area, which route you decide to take and how fast you can travel.

This section is based on the following scenario. Suppose that two students want to travel from Great Malvern in Worcestershire to Milton Keynes in Buckinghamshire to attend an Open Day at The Open University (Figure 1). If they decide to travel by car and want to arrive by 10:30 am, at what time should they set off?

"YOU AND YOUR SCENIC ROUTES!"

You may also want to consider other factors when planning a journey, such as the amount of pollution produced or which is the most scenic route!

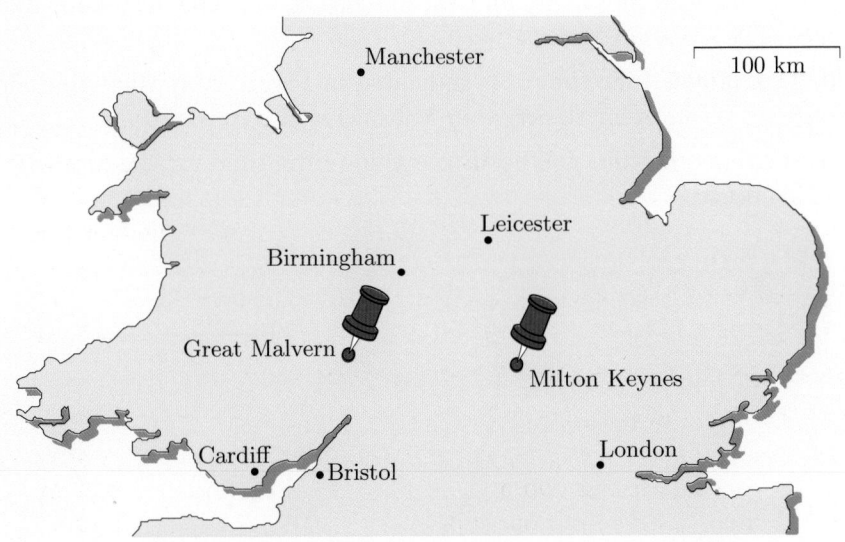

Figure I The start and finish of the journey

One way of tackling this problem is to use a route-planning system, known as a *route planner*, on a website or a satellite navigation device (satnav) to suggest a route and estimate the journey time. Here are some estimates for the time for the car journey between Great Malvern and Milton Keynes, provided by different route planners using various routes:

> 1 h 36 min, 1 h 58 min, 2 h 3 min, 2 h 5 min, 2 h 8 min, 2 h 19 min,
> 2 h 21 min, 2 h 33 min, 2 h 48 min, 3 h 19 min.

You can see that the estimated times vary substantially, with the longest time being more than twice the shortest time! However, most of the times are bunched 'in the middle', so it seems likely that these estimates are the most reliable. You'll see in this section how to make your own estimate for the journey time along a particular route, and you'll consider some of the factors that may affect this estimate.

There are links to some route planners on the course website, so that you can see if there is a similar variation in times for a journey of your own choice.

First, consider the questions in the following activity.

Activity 1 *Preliminary questions*

(a) Why might the route planners estimate different times for the journey?

(b) From Figure 1, the distance in a straight line between Great Malvern and Milton Keynes appears to be just over 100 kilometres. Assuming that the car travels about 50 kilometres in an hour, what is an estimate for the journey time? Do you think this estimate is good enough for planning the time to set off?

How can you obtain an estimate that is more realistic than the one in part (b) of Activity 1?

As with many problems, it helps to consider a simpler version first. There are many possible routes that the students could take, but to see what's involved in calculating the time, let's concentrate here on one particular route.

You can see some information about how to choose the quickest route by watching the video, at the end of this section.

Suppose that the students decide to take the route from Great Malvern to Milton Keynes indicated by a thick pink line on the map in Figure 2. This route uses the M40 motorway and various principal roads, also known as A-roads. The question is now:

> If the students take the route indicated in Figure 2, at what time must they set off in order to arrive in Milton Keynes by 10:30 am?

To answer this question, you need to estimate the time for the journey along this route.

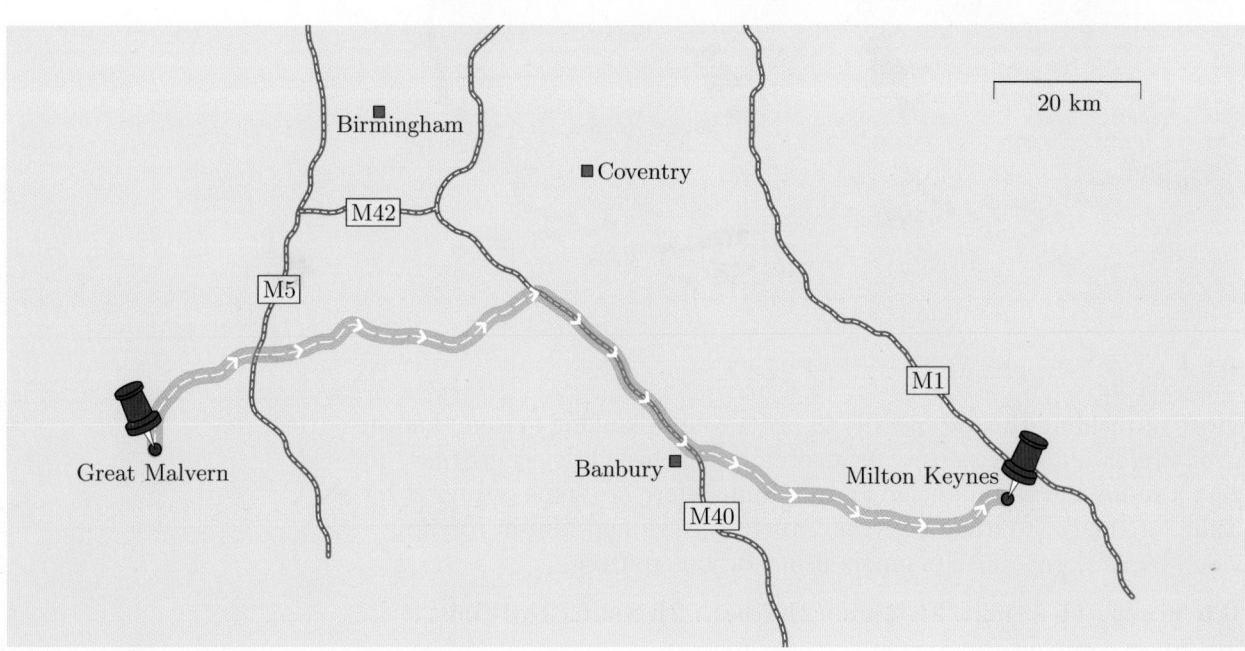

Figure 2 The route for the journey

The time for the journey depends on at least two factors: the *road distance* between Great Malvern and Milton Keynes, and the *speeds* at which the car can travel on different types of roads.

These two factors are discussed in the next two subsections.

1.2   Estimating distances

This subsection is about using maps to find distances. A **map scale** indicates how to determine distances on the ground from distances on a map. On the map in Figure 2 there is a line drawn at the top right to show the map scale graphically. This line indicates that a distance of 2 centimetres on the map represents 20 kilometres on the ground. Thus, by measuring a distance on the map in centimetres and using the map scale, you can obtain the corresponding distance on the ground.

For practice with scale diagrams, see Maths Help Module 5, Subsection 1.1.

Distances on the map can be measured by hand by laying a piece of string approximately along a route and then measuring the string, or by using an *opisometer*, an instrument with a small wheel for measuring distances on maps.

The map scale in Figure 2 can be stated in words as '2 cm represents 20 km', which is equivalent to writing '1 cm represents 10 km'. This means that to find the ground distance in kilometres, you multiply the map distance in centimetres by 10.

Map scales are often written in the form '1 cm = 10 km', but such a statement is incorrect mathematically because a length of 1 centimetre is not equal to a length of 10 kilometres!

Activity 2   *Estimating the distance from a map*

(a) On the map, the distance along the route from Great Malvern to Milton Keynes is 13.8 cm, and the distance along the motorway section of the route is 3 cm (to the nearest mm). What are the corresponding ground distances, in kilometres?

(b) Apart from the section on the motorway, the rest of the route is on principal roads. Use your answers to part (a) to find the distance on the principal roads, in kilometres.

(c) What distance on the map represents 25 km on the ground?

On the map in Figure 2, we interpreted the scale as '1 cm represents 10 km'. Map scales can be written in other forms, so you need to be familiar with these alternatives too. Often, the scale of a map is given as, say, 1 : 500 000 or 1/500 000, which is read as 'one to five hundred thousand'. This means that any distance measured on the map represents 500 000 times that distance on the ground. For example, 1 cm on the map represents 500 000 cm on the ground, 1 mm on the map represents 500 000 mm on the ground, and so on. The number 500 000 is called the **scale factor** of the map.

This type of expression for a map scale is called a representative fraction.

The next example shows how to convert between the two methods of giving a map scale.

Example 1   *Converting map scales*

(a) A map scale is given in words as '1 cm represents 20 km'. What is the scale factor?

(b) A map scale is given as 1 : 250 000. Express this map scale in the form '1 cm represents ?? km'.

Solution

(a) Here, 1 cm on the map represents 20 km on the ground.

   Convert 20 km to centimetres, by using $1\,\text{km} = 1000\,\text{m}$ and $1\,\text{m} = 100\,\text{cm}$.

   Now,

   $$20\,\text{km} = (20 \times 1000)\,\text{m}$$
   $$= 20\,000\,\text{m}$$
   $$= (20\,000 \times 100)\,\text{cm}$$
   $$= 2\,000\,000\,\text{cm}.$$

   So, 1 cm on the map represents 2 000 000 cm on the ground. That is, the map scale is 1 : 2 000 000, so the scale factor is 2 000 000.

(b) Here, 1 cm on the map represents 250 000 cm on the ground.

   Convert 250 000 cm to kilometres.

   Now,

   $$250\,000\,\text{cm} = (250\,000 \div 100)\,\text{m}$$
   $$= 2500\,\text{m}$$
   $$= (2500 \div 1000)\,\text{km}$$
   $$= 2.5\,\text{km}.$$

   So the map scale is '1 cm represents 2.5 km'.

For details of SI units, see Unit 1, Subsection 2.3 or Maths Help Module 1, Section 2.

Here are some similar conversions for you to try.

Activity 3   *Converting map scales*

(a) A map scale is given as '1 cm represents 10 km'. What is the scale factor?

(b) A map scale is given as 1 : 500 000. Express this map scale in the form '1 cm represents ?? km'.

The next example shows you how to use a scale factor to work out the length of a journey from its distance on a map, and also to work out the map distance if you know the ground distance.

Example 2   *Using a map scale*

The scale of a map is 1 : 250 000.

(a) The distance on the map between two places is 7.5 cm. What is the corresponding distance on the ground? Give your answer to two significant figures.

(b) The distance on the ground between two places is 58.4 km. What is the corresponding distance on the map? Give your answer to three significant figures.

Solution

(a) A measurement of 1 cm on the map represents 250 000 cm on the ground. So a map distance of 7.5 cm represents a ground distance of $(7.5 \times 250\,000)$ cm. Now,

$$(7.5 \times 250\,000)\,\text{cm} = 1\,875\,000\,\text{cm}$$
$$= (1\,875\,000 \div 100 \div 1000)\,\text{km}$$
$$= 18.75\,\text{km}$$
$$= 19\,\text{km (to 2 s.f.)}.$$

Alternatively, the map scale 1 : 250 000 can be expressed as '1 cm represents 2.5 km', so a map distance of 7.5 cm represents a ground distance of

See Example 1(b).

$$(7.5 \times 2.5)\,\text{km} = 18.75\,\text{km} = 19\,\text{km (to 2 s.f.)}.$$

(b) The scale factor is 250 000, so the ground distance of 58.4 km is represented by a map distance of $58.4 \div 250\,000$ km. Now,

$$(58.4 \div 250\,000)\,\text{km} = 0.000\,233\,6\,\text{km}$$
$$= (0.000\,233\,6 \times 1000 \times 100)\,\text{cm}$$
$$= 23.36\,\text{cm}$$
$$= 23.4\,\text{cm (to 3 s.f.)}.$$

Alternatively, the map scale 1 : 250 000 can be expressed as '1 cm represents 2.5 km', so a ground distance of 58.4 km is represented by a map distance of

$$(58.4 \div 2.5)\,\text{cm} = 23.36\,\text{cm} = 23.4\,\text{cm (to 3 s.f.)}.$$

Figure 3 summarises the process of converting map distances to ground distances, and vice versa. Here are some similar questions for you to try.

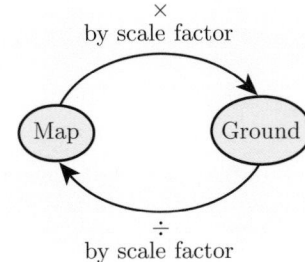

Activity 4   Using map scales

Consider a map with scale 1 : 50 000.

(a) The distance between two towns on the map is 3.4 cm. What is the distance between them on the ground?

(b) The distance along a road is 7.85 km. What is the corresponding distance on the map?

Figure 3   Using a scale factor to convert between ground and map distances

In Activity 2, you made some progress on answering the question about what time the students should set off. You now have an estimate of the distance for both the motorway section (30 km) and the principal road section (108 km) of the route. You have also seen how to calculate ground distances if you are given the scale factor of the map.

To find the time that the journey is likely to take, the next step is to consider the speeds at which you can expect to travel on the different types of roads.

1.3   Understanding speed

This subsection is about the concept of **speed**. The speed of an object indicates how far it travels in a particular period of time. For example, if you are travelling at a constant speed and you cover 40 kilometres in 1 hour, then your speed is 40 kilometres per hour. This speed can also be written as 40 km/h.

'km/h' is read as 'kilometres per hour'.

Therefore

in 1 hour you cover $(40 \times 1)\,\text{km} = 40\,\text{km}$;
in 2 hours you cover $(40 \times 2)\,\text{km} = 80\,\text{km}$;
in 3 hours you cover $(40 \times 3)\,\text{km} = 120\,\text{km}$;
and so on.

Speed can be measured in other units as well: for example, metres per second or miles per hour. These are all examples of **compound units**, since they involve more than one basic unit of measurement.

In practice, you will not be able to travel at a constant speed for a whole journey, as you sometimes have to slow down, speed up or even stop to deal with the traffic and road conditions. Instead, the *average speed* for a journey is used in calculations.

The **average speed** for a journey is calculated using the formula below.

$$\text{average speed} = \frac{\text{distance travelled}}{\text{time taken}}$$

This formula is often written more concisely as

$$\text{average speed} = \frac{\text{distance}}{\text{time}} \quad \text{or} \quad \text{speed} = \frac{\text{distance}}{\text{time}}.$$

With formulas such as this one, where the units are not specified, you can work out the unit used to measure the speed from the units for the distance and the time.

For example, suppose that the distance is measured in metres (m) and the time is measured in seconds (s). To work out the unit for the average speed, substitute these units into the formula above.

Since $\text{average speed} = \dfrac{\text{distance}}{\text{time}}$, the unit for the speed is $\dfrac{\text{m}}{\text{s}}$.

This unit is usually written as m/s and read as 'metres per second'.

Example 3   *Finding an average speed*

Suppose that a car travels a distance of 75 km in 45 minutes on a motorway. What is its average speed? Give your answer in km/h.

Solution

First method

💭 Use the formula to find the average speed in km/min and then convert to km/h. 💭

The distance is 75 km and the time is 45 min. So, by the formula,

$$\text{average speed} = \frac{75}{45}\ \text{km/min} = 1.666\ldots\ \text{km/min}.$$

💭 Now convert this answer to km/h by multiplying the full calculator value for the distance travelled in 1 minute by the number of minutes in an hour. 💭

There are 60 minutes in an hour, so

$$\text{average speed} = (1.666\ldots \times 60)\,\text{km/h} = 100\,\text{km/h}.$$

Second method

💭 Convert the time to hours and then find the average speed in km/h. 💭

First, 45 minutes is $\frac{3}{4}$ of an hour, that is, 0.75 h. So, by the formula,

$$\text{average speed} = \frac{75}{0.75}\,\text{km/h} = 100\,\text{km/h}.$$

Here are some similar examples for you to try.

Activity 5   *Finding average speeds*

Find the average speeds for the following journeys, rounding your answers to two significant figures. Give your answers to parts (a) and (b) in km/h, and your answer to part (c) in m/s.

(a) A journey of 425 km on the motorway that takes 4 hours

(b) A 30 km journey through a city that takes 1 hour 25 minutes

(c) A 100 m sprint that takes 14 seconds

1.4   Finding the time

In Activity 2, you calculated that the route from Great Malvern to Milton Keynes includes 30 km on the M40 motorway and 108 km on principal roads. To find the time required for each part of the journey, you need to use values for the average speeds on each type of road. The average speed of a car on a road depends on many factors, such as how busy the road is, the speed limits, and if there are any delays such as road works.

For the current purpose, you should use the following cautious assumptions about average speeds on these types of roads:

- average speed on principal roads: 50 km/h
- average speed on motorways: 100 km/h.

There are two methods of calculating the time for a journey if you know the distance and the average speed.

Strategy   *To find the time, given the distance and the speed*

First method

Find the time to travel 1 km and then find the time to travel the whole distance.

Second method

Use the formula

$$\text{time} = \frac{\text{distance}}{\text{average speed}}.$$

This is a version of the formula

$$\text{average speed} = \frac{\text{distance}}{\text{time}}$$

given in Subsection 1.3.

The unit of speed used in this formula is the one that involves the distance unit and the time unit; for example, if the distance is in kilometres and the time is in hours, then the speed should be measured in km/h.

The next example applies both methods to find the time for the motorway section of the students' journey from Great Malvern to Milton Keynes.

Example 4 *Calculating the time on the motorway*

Find the time for a journey of 30 km at an average speed of 100 km/h. Give your answer in minutes.

Solution

First method

The average speed is 100 km/h, so 1 km is travelled in $\frac{1}{100}$ h.

Hence, to travel 30 km, it takes $30 \times \frac{1}{100}$ h $= 0.3$ h. Since there are 60 minutes in 1 hour,

$$0.3\,\text{h} = (0.3 \times 60)\,\text{min} = 18\,\text{min}.$$

Second method

By the formula, the time is

$$\frac{30}{100}\,\text{h} = 0.3\,\text{h}.$$

Multiplying by 60 to convert the time into minutes gives 18 min, as before.

Another way to solve Example 4 is to use the informal method shown in the cartoon in the margin. This is possible here because the numbers in the calculation are easy to work with. Even if the numbers are more complicated, you can obtain a rough estimate of the answer by rounding the numbers in the calculation and then using an informal method of this type.

The next activity involves finding the time for the principal roads section of the journey from Great Malvern to Milton Keynes.

> If the speed is 100km/h, it takes 60 mins to travel 100km, so 6 mins to travel 10km. 30km would take 3 lots of 6 mins - that's 18 mins.

Activity 6 *Calculating the time on the principal roads*

(a) Use both of the methods above to find the time for a journey of 108 km at an average speed of 50 km/h. Which method do you prefer?

(b) Use your answer to part (a) and the time found in Example 4 to calculate the total journey time from Great Malvern to Milton Keynes. Round your answer to the nearest 10 minutes.

1.5 Checking and interpreting your results

The solution to Activity 6 suggests that the students' total journey time from Great Malvern to Milton Keynes can be estimated to be about $2\frac{1}{2}$ hours. However, it is a good idea to carry out a couple of further checks to ensure that the answer is reasonable and that it answers the question asked.

Is your answer reasonable?

An important step in solving any problem is to check whether your answer makes sense in the context of the problem and in particular whether it is realistic and roughly what you expected. In this case, you might have compared the answer with other journeys that you had made along similar roads under similar conditions. For example, it usually takes about an hour to travel from Great Malvern to Birmingham – a distance of 70 km, with quite a large section on the M5 motorway. So you might expect a journey of about 140 km to take about 2 hours, and to take longer if it is mostly on principal roads rather than on motorways. This estimate agrees quite well with the journey time obtained earlier.

If you had obtained an answer of say 25 minutes (or 25 hours!) for the whole journey, then the answer *would* have been unreasonable. It might indicate a mistake in the calculations or an unrealistic assumption somewhere – in either case, it would be wise to go back and check both the mathematics and the assumptions made.

In this problem, assumptions were made for average speeds on different types of road. However, traffic conditions vary, and you might expect speeds to be lower during the morning and evening rush hours than during other parts of the day. So, if you need a more accurate estimate of the time, then you may wish to change some of the assumptions for the speed.

To see the effect of modifying the assumed speeds, work through the following activity.

Activity 7   *Changing the assumptions*

The speed limits for cars are 112 km/h on the motorway and 96 km/h on principal roads. The table below shows the times, to the nearest minute, for the 30 km motorway section and the 108 km principal roads part, for different speeds.

These are approximate values; the exact speed limits are 70 mph and 60 mph.

Motorway (30 km)			
Speed in km/h	80	100	112
Time taken in minutes	23	18	16
Principal roads (108 km)			
Speed in km/h	40	50	96
Time taken in minutes	162	130	68

(a) Based on the values in the table, what is the shortest time for the whole journey if the speed limits are observed? Do you think that this time can be achieved?

(b) If the average speed on the motorway drops from 100 km/h to 80 km/h, how much longer does the journey take? If the average speed on the principal roads drops from 50 km/h to 40 km/h, how much longer does the journey take?

(c) Based on these calculations, would you make any changes to the time allowed for the journey?

The table in Activity 7 shows that, for the range of average speeds considered, the journey time for this route can vary from 1 hour 24 minutes to 3 hours 5 minutes. This range is similar to the times predicted by the route planners in Subsection 1.1! Making realistic assumptions about the speeds at which you can travel on different roads is important in order to predict reasonable journey times.

Answering the question asked

The question that we are trying to answer is: 'What time should the students set off in order to arrive in Milton Keynes by 10:30 am if they travel by the route in Figure 2?'

If we assume that the average speeds are 100 km/h on the motorway and 50 km/h on the other roads, then the journey time is predicted to be approximately 2 hours 30 minutes. So, to arrive at the destination by 10:30 am, the starting time should be 8:00 am.

However, in practice it would probably be better to allow some extra time in case there are any unexpected delays or the assumptions for the average speed were too high. As you saw in Activity 7, a change in the average speed for the longer, slower part of the journey could affect the time considerably. There may also be other considerations, such as allowing time for parking.

So the final conclusion may be to allow an extra 30 minutes and leave at 7:30 am, perhaps with a further suggestion to take some work to do, in case the journey goes very smoothly!

1.6 Route planners and models

The assumptions made in this section about distances on roads and possible average speeds, together with the methods and formulas for calculating the predicted times taken, form the elements of a mathematical model, usually called simply a model. Changing the assumptions made or the formulas used would result in a different model.

You have seen that the assumptions that you make about the average speeds on different types of road can have a large effect on the time predicted for the journey. This may account for some of the discrepancies in the times predicted by the route planners – they have used different models with different assumptions. Some route planners may have taken account of factors such as the time of day, how congested the roads are, whether there are any current roadworks, and so on, and others may have used a simple model like ours, ignoring some or all of these factors.

However, remember that we considered only one particular route that seemed to be reasonably direct and made use of principal roads and the M40 motorway. Many other routes could have been taken, and different routes are likely to take different times. Even if you decide that your main priority is to go on the quickest route, different planners may still suggest different routes, depending on which roads they have included in their model.

To decide on suitable routes, a route planner computer program stores a network of roads, and a time for travelling along each section of a road is determined from a suitable model. An **algorithm** – a set of instructions to solve a problem step by step – is then used to check the distances and times of all the possible routes systematically and select the shortest or quickest, as appropriate.

In the next activity you are asked to view a video clip in which experts from the Department of Transport talk about how a certain route planner, called Transport Direct (Figure 4), was developed. The experts discuss the assumptions they made, some aspects of the algorithms used, and how they update the models to take account of user feedback and improved **data**. The word data means facts or statistics, so in this case the new data might include the addition of new roads to the maps or more up-to-date estimates of the travel speeds.

Note that 'data' refers to more than one item, so it is a plural noun.

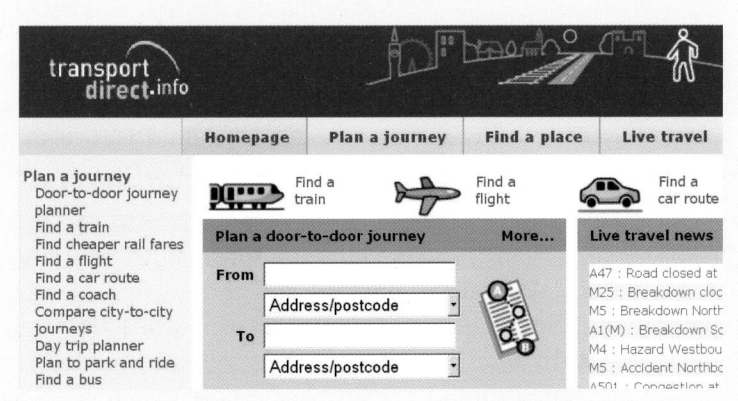

Transport Direct is a government-funded route planner that aims to cover *all* forms of transport within the UK.

Figure 4 The Transport Direct route planner

Activity 8 *Looking at models and algorithms*

 Video

Watch the video for Unit 2. As you do so, jot down some notes to answer the following questions.

The video is on the DVD.

(a) What information can you obtain from the website?

(b) Where are the data for the model obtained? How frequently are they updated? What data can the users provide themselves?

(c) Which time intervals and which roads are included in the model for a particular journey?

(d) How are the routes determined?

(e) How is the planner improved?

The video illustrates various points about using mathematics to solve problems.

- The mathematicians had identified several key problems to solve after discussions with users.

- They use a wide range of different sources of reliable data, obtained from government departments and reputable organisations, which they update frequently. They also include data provided by users.

- Some simplifications and assumptions had to be made so that key problems can be solved quickly enough while users of the website wait.

- The mathematical model is continually being refined and updated to provide more reliable predictions.

" HERE'S THE PROBLEM. OUR G.P.S. SYSTEM
IS IN KILOMETERS, NOT MILES. "

Note that the estimate from a
satnav device is updated
regularly as you travel.
However, you can't rely on
satnav predictions everywhere!

Dijkstra's algorithm

The algorithm used in the Transport Direct route planner was
developed in 1959 by a Dutch computer scientist, Edsger Dijkstra. In
the algorithm, places are represented by dots, and the lines
connecting the dots show the time (or distance) between the two
places. The algorithm then systematically searches for the shortest
time or shortest distance between two points on the diagram.

So what is the best way to estimate the time for a journey – should you
make your own estimate as we have done here, making assumptions about
average speeds based on your own experience, or should you rely on a more
sophisticated route planner, on a website or on a satnav device?

The answer to that question may depend on how accurate you need the
estimate to be and whether a rough estimate obtained from a quick
calculation will suffice. Whichever method you choose, you may now be
more aware of how different factors can affect the journey time, such as
average speeds along different sections of roads, which can change
dramatically at different times of the day or on different days. If you
decide to use a route planner, perhaps the best advice is to monitor how
well the predictions for the journey times match reality in your case, and to
choose a route planner that gives the most reliable results. Although route
planners give predicted times to the nearest minute, they are unlikely to be
this accurate in practice because road conditions are so changeable.

1.7   The modelling cycle

If you look back at the way we tackled the question of estimating the
journey time, then you can see that the problem was broken down into a
series of steps.

First, we posed the question: 'What time should the students set off in
order to arrive in Milton Keynes by 10:30 am?' We then clarified the
problem and saw that it depended on a different question: 'How long will
the journey take?'

Next, the problem was simplified by considering just one route.

Then we collected some data (the distances along different parts of the
route) and made some assumptions (the average speeds on the motorway
and on principal roads). These assumptions made the problem simpler and
easier to solve.

We were then able to describe the method of solution mathematically (for
example, with a formula) and carry out calculations to find an answer.

Before making final predictions, we considered whether this answer was
realistic, and rounded the answer appropriately so that it made sense
within the context of the problem. We also investigated changing the
assumptions to see how sensitive the journey times were to variations in
average speeds.

For some problems, if the conclusions do not seem reasonable, then more extensive changes to the model may be needed. For example, we could have taken the time of day into account and assumed slower average speeds if the journey was during the rush hour.

The types of steps used appear in many problems, and the list of these steps is called the **modelling cycle**. This may seem a rather grand name, but these steps can be applied to more complicated problems, as you saw in the development of the route planner on the video.

This strategy for solving real-world problems is summarised in Figure 5, which indicates why it is called a modelling 'cycle'.

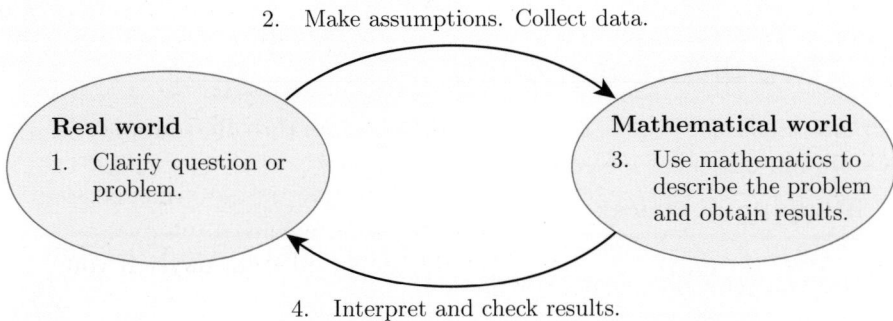

2.   Make assumptions. Collect data.

Real world
1.   Clarify question or problem.

Mathematical world
3.   Use mathematics to describe the problem and obtain results.

4.   Interpret and check results.

Figure 5   The modelling cycle

There are four main steps in the modelling cycle.

The modelling cycle

1.   Describe the problem concisely so that you are clear about what you are trying to do. In real life, and particularly if you are working within a team, this may involve discussing the problem with others.

2.   Make assumptions to simplify the problem, so that you retain the essential features but will be able to describe it mathematically. At this stage, it is also useful to sort out what you already know about the problem, by collecting data and other information.

3.   Describe the problem mathematically using numbers, formulas or graphs, and use these to obtain new results.

4.   Consider what these new results mean practically, and check that the predictions seem reasonable. If the predictions do not match reality, then you may need to refine the assumptions, collect further information and go round the cycle again. Your conclusions are only as good as the data you have used and the assumptions you have made!

Sometimes variants of this cycle are used. For example, in the video, the second stage is split into two parts: making assumptions and then collecting data.

This modelling cycle can be used as a framework for solving many practical problems involving both basic and advanced mathematical skills.

2 Investigating vehicle stopping distances

A common cause of road accidents is drivers failing to leave an adequate gap between their vehicle and the vehicle in front, so the Highway Code includes recommendations for these gaps, at different speeds and in a variety of weather conditions. These recommendations are derived from two different mathematical models. This section compares these two models. It also discusses what each model takes into account, and how the information from the models has been presented so that it can be understood and used by the intended audience.

2.1 Two different models

Section 126 of the Highway Code (2007) contains the following information on stopping distances for cars.

Stopping distances

Drive at a speed that will allow you to stop well within the distance you can see to be clear. You should:

- leave enough space between you and the vehicle in front so that you can pull up safely if it suddenly slows down or stops – the safe rule is never to get closer than the overall stopping distance (see Figure 6)

To apply this two-second rule: when the vehicle in front passes a landmark, count for two seconds; if you pass the landmark before the end of this time, then the gap is too small.

- allow at least a two-second gap between you and the vehicle in front on roads carrying faster-moving traffic and in tunnels where visibility is reduced – the gap should be at least doubled on wet roads and increased still further on icy roads.

Elsewhere in the Highway Code it states: 'In wet weather stopping distances will be at least double those required for stopping on dry roads.'

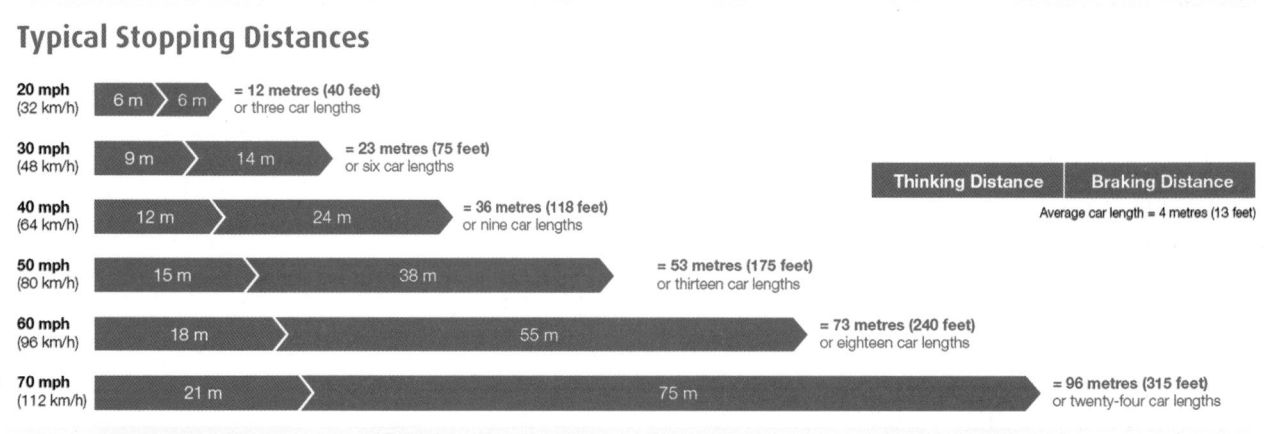

Typical Stopping Distances

Speed	Thinking Distance	Braking Distance	Total
20 mph (32 km/h)	6 m	6 m	= 12 metres (40 feet) or three car lengths
30 mph (48 km/h)	9 m	14 m	= 23 metres (75 feet) or six car lengths
40 mph (64 km/h)	12 m	24 m	= 36 metres (118 feet) or nine car lengths
50 mph (80 km/h)	15 m	38 m	= 53 metres (175 feet) or thirteen car lengths
60 mph (96 km/h)	18 m	55 m	= 73 metres (240 feet) or eighteen car lengths
70 mph (112 km/h)	21 m	75 m	= 96 metres (315 feet) or twenty-four car lengths

Average car length = 4 metres (13 feet)

Figure 6 Typical stopping distances, as stated in Section 126 of the Highway Code (2007)

Notice that the Highway Code stresses that the driver should ensure that they can stop the car safely, whatever the road conditions. Then it provides some guidance on the distances and times that the driver should allow between their vehicle and the one in front, when travelling at different speeds. Two different recommendations are made, based on different models.

- The *distance model* suggests that a safe distance between your vehicle and the one in front is the distance given by the typical stopping distances chart (Figure 6). The stopping distances are presented both as a chart and as numerical measurements.

- The *time model* suggests that a safe distance between your vehicle and the one in front is the distance given by the two-second rule.

Activity 9   *Looking at the Highway Code*

(a) The Highway Code includes both the 'typical stopping distances' chart and the 'two-second rule'. Why do you think both methods have been included?

(b) Which features of the 'typical stopping distances' chart do you think make it easy for people to use? Are there any features that make it difficult to use?

(c) Can you think of any other methods of informing drivers of suitable gaps between cars?

(d) The speeds in the chart are given in both mph and km/h. Use the fact that 1 mile is approximately 1.609 kilometres to check that 40 mph is 64 km/h to the nearest integer.

mph means 'miles per hour'.

Activity 9 was about different ways of presenting ideas that involve mathematics, and it showed the importance of considering whether the intended audience will find the information easy to understand. In particular, you saw how useful a chart can be.

2.2   The distance model and the modelling cycle

This subsection considers how the distance model used in the Highway Code might have been developed, by following the four stages of the modelling cycle.

Stage 1: Clarify the question

Both models have been constructed in order to answer the question:

'What gap between vehicles should be recommended for drivers travelling at different speeds?'

Stage 2: Make assumptions and collect data

The distance model is based on typical stopping distances at various speeds. It has been assumed that the stopping distance is determined by two factors:

- the thinking distance (the distance travelled from when the driver first sees a hazard until he or she applies the brakes)

- the braking distance (the distance travelled from when the brakes are first applied to the point when the vehicle stops).

Each of these distances is determined by the speed.

In this model, a reaction time of $\frac{2}{3}$ of a second has been assumed.

Experiments can be carried out to test the reaction times of drivers, and these experiments would probably produce a range of possible times, depending on the individual and their state of alertness. From the data collected, it is possible to determine a typical reaction time.

Braking distances can be based on experiments with cars or by relying on data obtained from car manufacturers.

This model ignores other features of the situation such as the road surface, the make and weight of the car, the weather conditions and the tiredness of the driver.

Stage 3: Use mathematics to obtain results

Having collected the data and made some assumptions, the next stage is to use some mathematics, in this case working out the distances by using formulas.

While the driver is 'thinking', the car is likely to be travelling at a constant speed. If you know the speed of a vehicle and the time during which it travels at that speed, then you can calculate the distance it travels. For example, if a vehicle travels at $30\,\text{m/s}$ for 2 seconds, then it travels a distance of 60 m. In general, if an object moves for a certain period of time, then the distance it covers in this time is given by the following formula.

This is another version of the formula
$$\text{average speed} = \frac{\text{distance}}{\text{time}}$$
given in Subsection 1.3.

$$\text{distance} = \text{average speed} \times \text{time}$$

The braking distances can be related to the speed by using the data collected to derive a more complicated formula; you will meet formulas of this type later in the course. Roughly speaking, the effect of the formula is that if the speed doubles, then the braking distance quadruples.

Once a formula has been obtained for both the thinking distance and the braking distance, the total stopping distance can be found by adding these two distances together. Using this formula for different speeds gives the results shown in the chart in Figure 6.

Stage 4: Interpret and check the results

The distance model could be checked with reality by, for example, observing whether drivers manage to stop their vehicles within the 'typical stopping distance' and also whether collisions occur less frequently when drivers keep this gap between their vehicle and the next.

Now that you have seen how the distance model might have been developed, the next subsection considers how the recommendations of the distance model compare with those of the time model.

2.3 Comparing the models

In Subsection 2.1 you saw two methods, given by different mathematical models, for choosing an appropriate gap between your car and the car in front. How do these models compare with each other?

The distance model recommends gaps between vehicles at various speeds, so you can compare this model to the time model by calculating the gaps between vehicles at the same speeds when the two-second rule is observed. So we need to calculate these gaps.

Gaps for the time model

You can calculate the gap between cars given by the two-second rule by substituting the time of two seconds and the relevant speed into the formula 'distance = speed × time'. Since the units have to match when you substitute into a formula, the speed must be measured in a unit whose 'time part' is seconds – for example, m/s or km/s. To make a comparison with the distance model possible, we want the answer to be in metres. Therefore the speed used in the formula must be expressed in m/s. However, the speeds that we need to consider – those in Figure 6 – are expressed in mph and km/h.

The example below shows how to convert km/h to m/s by breaking the problem down into smaller steps.

A similar approach was used in Example 3, and you can use this approach whenever you need to convert between compound units.

Example 5   *Converting km/h into m/s*

Convert 32 km/h to m/s. Give your answer to three significant figures.

Solution

A speed of 32 km/h means that in 1 hour the car travels 32 km, that is,

$$32 \times 1000\,\text{m} = 32\,000\,\text{m}.$$

Since there are 60 minutes in an hour and 60 seconds in each minute, there are $60 \times 60 = 3600$ seconds in an hour.

So the car travels 32 000 m in 3600 seconds.

Therefore in 1 second, the car travels

$$\frac{32\,000}{3600}\,\text{m} = 8.888\ldots\,\text{m}.$$

So 32 km/h is 8.89 m/s (to 3 s.f.).

Once the speed is measured in m/s, you can substitute it, and the time 2 seconds, into the formula

$$\text{distance} = \text{speed} \times \text{time}$$

to calculate the gap in metres between vehicles given by the time model. For example, if the speed is 32 km/h, that is, 8.888 . . . m/s, then

$$\text{distance} = 8.888\ldots \times 2\,\text{m}$$
$$= 17.777\ldots\,\text{m}.$$

The two-second gap for the speed 32 km/h is therefore 18 m to the nearest whole number.

Activity 10   *Converting the time model*

(a) Convert 80 km/h to m/s and write the value in the table below, rounding your answer to two decimal places.

The speeds listed in this table are the ones in Figure 6, the 'typical stopping distances' chart.

Vehicle gaps at different speeds

Speed in km/h	Speed in m/s	Time model gap in m	Distance model gap in m
32	8.89	18	12
48	13.33	27	23
64	17.78	36	36
80	22·22 ✓	44	53
96	26.67	53	73
112	31.11	62	96

(b) Fill in the column for the gaps for the time model, rounding your answers to the nearest whole number.

Drawing a graph

Since the suggested gaps between cars are now measured in metres for both models, we can compare the results for the two models directly. Although it is possible to compare the results by looking at the data in the table in the solution to Activity 10, a **graph** can be helpful. This has the advantage of illustrating overall features, which may not be so clear from the numerical data.

For help with graphs, see Maths Help Module 5, Subsection 3.4.

In the next activity you are asked to plot the gaps for the two models on a graph. To help you do that, here are some guidelines for drawing graphs and also an example to remind you how to read values from a graph.

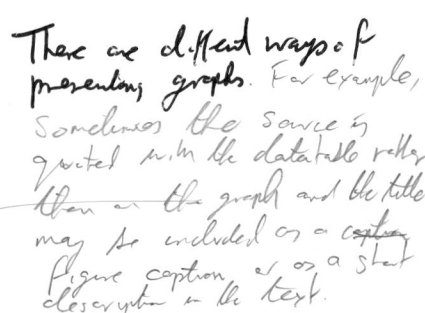

A graph of 'y against x' means that y is on the vertical axis and x is on the horizontal axis.

Tips for drawing a graph or chart based on data

- Include a clear title and the source of the data.
- Label the axes with the names of the quantities and the units.
- Mark the scales clearly, choosing scales that are easy to interpret and that make good use of the space available.

Figure 7 illustrates these points. This is a graph of speed measured in m/s plotted against speed measured in km/h, based on the data given for this conversion in the table in Activity 10. This kind of graph is known as a **conversion graph** because you can use it to convert from one unit to another.

The main features of the graph in Figure 7 have been annotated. The graph has been drawn by choosing the **horizontal axis** to represent the speed in km/h and the **vertical axis** to represent the speed in m/s. The horizontal scale has been marked at intervals of 10 km/h and the vertical scale at intervals of 5 m/s. These scales have been chosen so that it is easy to plot points and read off values.

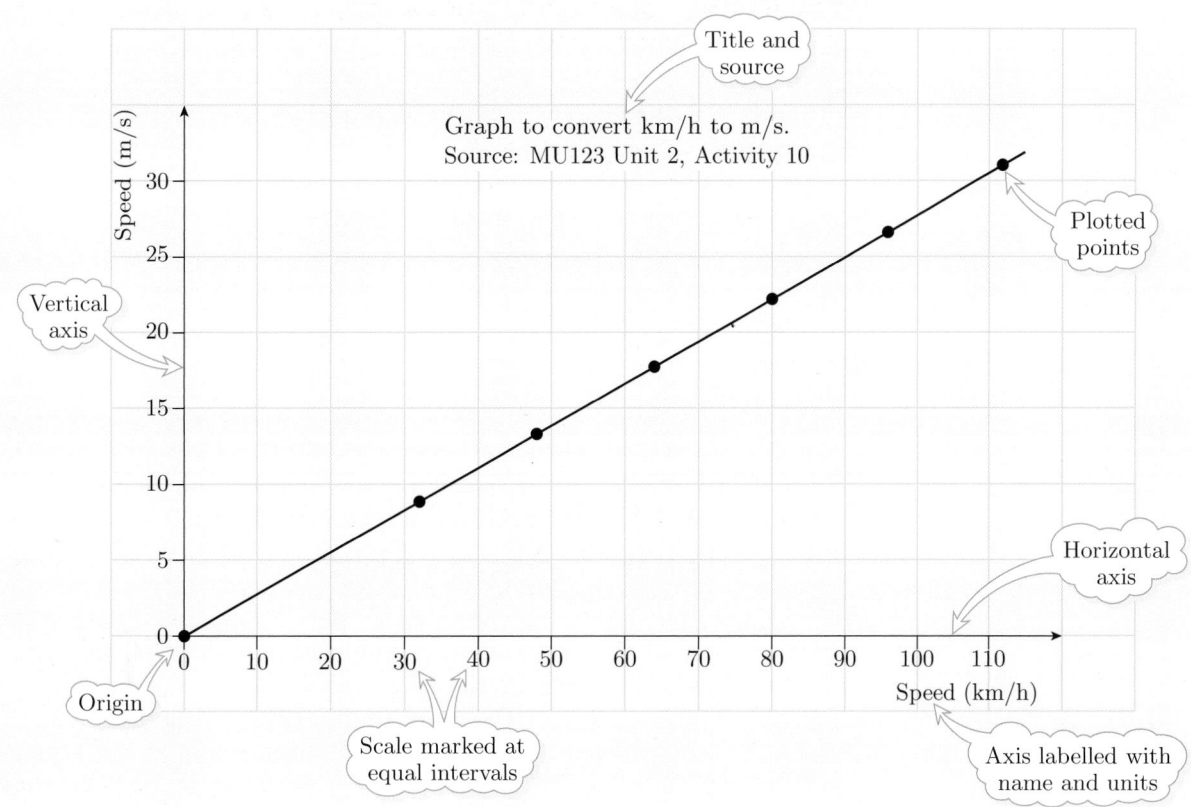

Figure 7 A conversion graph

Note that it is not always necessary to draw an axis all the way to zero. For example, if all the values on the vertical axis are between 52 and 70, then the points are more spaced out and clearer if part of the vertical axis is omitted. If the axis scale does not start at zero, then this should be indicated either by drawing two angled parallel lines, as shown in Figure 8, or by starting the vertical scale at 50.

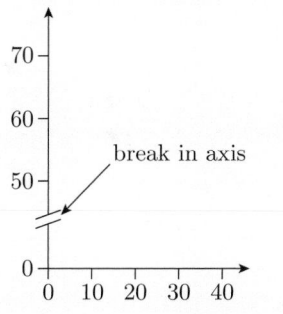

Figure 8 Showing a break in the vertical axis

Each pair of values from the table has been plotted on the graph in Figure 7. For example, the point representing the pair of values $(32, 8.89)$ has been plotted opposite 32 on the horizontal axis and opposite 8.89 on the vertical axis. The first value of the pair, in this case 32, is known as the **horizontal coordinate** and represents the distance the point is to the right of 0 on the horizontal axis. The second value in the pair, 8.89, is known as the **vertical coordinate** and represents the distance the point is above 0 on the vertical axis. We say that the coordinates of the point are $(32, 8.89)$. The point with coordinates $(0, 0)$ is called the **origin**.

You can use either dots, as shown in Figure 7, or small crosses to mark points on a graph. Crosses are often easier to use, particularly for hand-drawn graphs, as they mark points precisely and are clearly visible. The points in Figure 7 are joined by a straight line that passes through the origin.

Interpreting the graph

You can use the graph on the previous page to convert speeds measured in km/h to m/s and vice versa, as illustrated in the next example.

Example 6 *Converting speeds*

Use the graph in Figure 7 to make the following conversions.

(a) Convert 75 km/h to m/s.

(b) Convert 5 m/s to km/h.

Solution

(a) Find 75 on the 'Speed (km/h)' axis, draw a line vertically up to the graph and then draw another line horizontally across to the 'Speed (m/s)' axis, as shown by the short red dashes on the graph in Figure 9. Read off the number on the vertical axis.

   A speed of 75 km/h is approximately 21 m/s.

(b) Find 5 on the 'Speed (m/s)' axis, draw a line horizontally across to the graph and then draw another line vertically down to the 'Speed (km/h)' axis, as shown by the long blue dashes on the graph in Figure 9. Read off the number on the horizontal axis.

   A speed of 5 m/s is approximately 18 km/h.

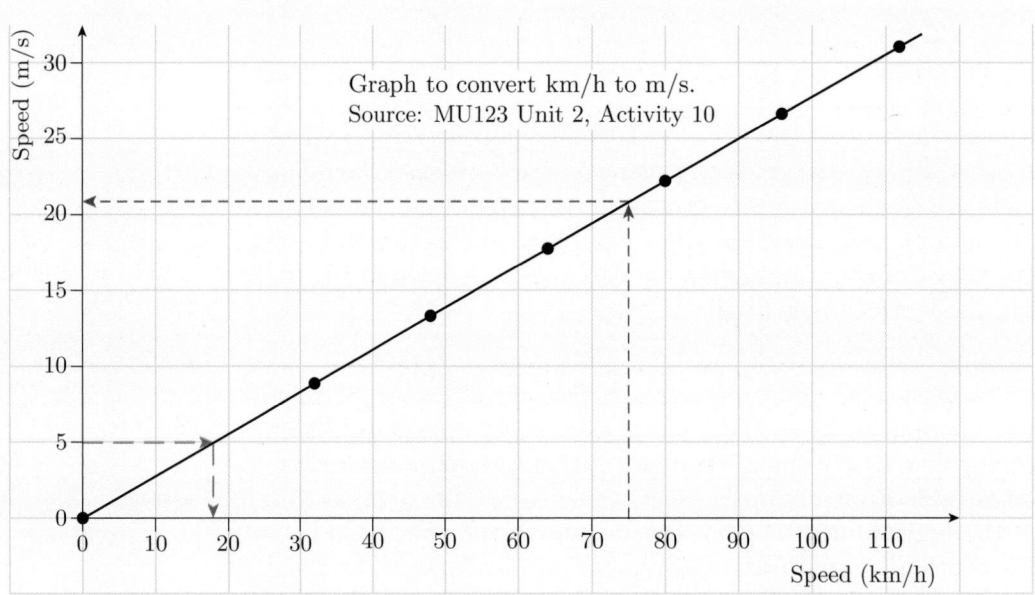

Figure 9 Converting speeds

Here is a similar activity.

Activity 11 *Converting speeds*

Use the graph in Figure 9 to make the following conversions.

(a) Convert 90 km/h to m/s.

(b) Convert 7.5 m/s to km/h.

Now try the next activity, which involves drawing a graph to represent the two models for the gap between vehicles, and then comparing the results.

Activity 12 *Using a graph to compare models*

You will need graph paper for this activity.

(a) Draw a graph to show the recommended gaps for the *distance model*. The vertical axis should show the distance (in metres) and the horizontal axis the speed (in m/s). Start by plotting 6 points, each representing the length of the gap in the distance model for a particular speed, as given in the table in the solution to Activity 10. Then join these points with a smooth curve.

(b) On the same axes, plot the points for the *time model* and join the points with a straight line.

(c) What gaps do the two graphs give for a speed of 25 m/s?

(d) Use the two graphs to explain how the gaps given by the two models are different.

In Activity 12 the vertical axis represented the gap in metres and the horizontal axis represented the speed in m/s. So this is a graph of 'gap *against* speed'.

2.4 Developing the models further

The actual stopping distances for a particular vehicle and driver are likely to depend on many factors, such as the braking efficiency of the car, the road surface, the slope of the road, the weather conditions and the depth of tread on the tyres. One of the most significant factors could be the time that it takes the driver to react to a hazard. If the driver is not alert or is distracted in some way, then the thinking distance could increase substantially, making the overall stopping distance much greater than that suggested by the models in the Highway Code.

The Royal Society for the Prevention of Accidents has developed a computer simulation that allows people to see the effect on their stopping distance of drink driving, using a mobile phone, driving in wet conditions, and so on.

Taking account of these additional factors would involve going around the modelling cycle again, making new assumptions such as increasing the thinking time, developing the mathematical description to include these new assumptions and checking how the new model matches reality.

As noted earlier in the section, it may not be easy to remember or visualise the recommended stopping distances, so a rule that is easier to apply is desirable. A rule based on counting the number of seconds between your car and the one in front is certainly easier to apply, but the question then is: what should the time period be? Recall from Activity 12 that for speeds up to about 18 m/s (or 40 mph), the time model (based on the two-second rule) gives the longer gap, whereas at speeds greater than this, the distance model gives the longer gap. The Highway Code recommends a gap of *at least* two seconds in faster moving traffic.

To make a rule based on time that produced similar gaps to those of the distance model at typical motorway speeds, the time interval would have to be about three seconds. However, a three-second rule would produce much larger gaps than the distance model at lower speeds. So a more realistic time model may be to allow a two-second gap for speeds of up to 18 m/s (or 40 mph) and a three-second gap for speeds greater than 18 m/s (or 40 mph).

This time model is an approximation to the distance model, which is not perfect but can be considered to be sufficiently accurate and more practical.

To summarise this section, you have seen two mathematical models that are used in a practical context, and how the modelling cycle could have been used to develop one of these models. You have also seen the importance of thinking carefully about presenting mathematical information to other people in a form that they can understand easily, whether in a numerical or graphical form or by using formulas. Sometimes a graph or chart can convey information more effectively than text and enable you to extract information that would be difficult to obtain in other ways. Being aware that you can tackle problems in different ways, whether by drawing a graph or diagram, or by looking at some particular numerical cases, as you did in Section 4 of Unit 1, is an important aspect of learning how to solve problems.

3 Using formulas

3.1 From words to letters

Solving a problem in mathematics often involves using a formula. For example, a formula was used in Section 1 to calculate the time for a journey, given the distance and the average speed. Formulas are used extensively in everyday life; for example, to do temperature conversions, and to calculate utility bills and car-parking charges.

Although some formulas are easy to remember when expressed in words, most formulas are written in a more concise form. This is particularly true when they are used in computer programs or spreadsheets, or when they are more complicated. This section explains how to write formulas concisely. It also introduces some conventions used in formulas.

Figure 10 Road sign indicating a 'no through road'

Abbreviations such as h for hours and km for kilometres also make your writing more concise.

In everyday life, many things are represented by symbols; for example, a symbol like a **T** on a road sign, as shown in Figure 10, warns of 'no through road', and the symbol **P** on a map often indicates a car park. Symbols are concise – they save writing out a whole word or sentence and consequently they make it possible to see key information more clearly. In mathematics, you are already familiar with some symbols, such as $\sqrt{}$ and $\div$. In this subsection, you'll see how letters can be used to represent the different quantities in a formula.

In Section 2, the 'word formula'

$$\text{distance} = \text{average speed} \times \text{time}$$

was used to estimate the distance travelled by a car. If we use the letters

s to represent the average speed,
t to represent the time taken,
d to represent the distance travelled,

then this word formula can be written more concisely as the 'letter formula'

$$d = s \times t.$$

If letters are used instead of words in a formula, then it is essential to say what quantities the letters represent.

Using a formula

The letters in a formula stand for numbers that are related in the way given by the formula. Thus you can think of a formula as a way of summarising a calculation process. For example, the formula $d = s \times t$ represents the process:

> To find the value of d, take the value of s and multiply it by the value of t.

When you use a formula, you replace the letters to the right of the equals sign (in the above case, s and t) by numbers, and then carry out the calculation to find the value of the letter to the left (in this case, d).

This process is known as **substituting** values into the formula.

For example, suppose that a bus travels at an average speed of 50 km/h for 1.2 hours, and we want to find the distance that it has travelled.

Rather than using the word formula to find the distance, we can use the more concise formula $d = s \times t$, where d, s and t are defined as before.

Replacing s by 50 and t by 1.2 gives

$$d = 50 \times 1.2 = 60.$$

Hence the distance travelled is 60 km.

We have used particular values of s and t here, but we could easily use the formula again with different values of s and t. Since the values of s, t and d can vary and represent different numbers in different scenarios, they are known as *variables*. In general, any letter that can represent different numbers is called a **variable**.

So a **formula** is an equation in which one variable, called the **subject** of the formula, appears by itself on the left-hand side of the equation and only the other variables appear on the right-hand side. Thus a formula enables you to calculate the value of the subject when you know the values of the other variables. For example, $d = s \times t$ is a formula whose subject is d, because d is the only variable on the left-hand side and you can use this equation to find d if you know the values of s and t.

However, note that the word 'formula' is used rather loosely in mathematics; for example, we sometimes say that

$$s \times t$$

is 'a formula for d'.

In many formulas the variables represent measurements, and it is important to check that the values you substitute are measured in appropriate units.

Formulas with set units

With some formulas the units are already set and cannot be changed. For example, an approximate formula to convert distances in miles to kilometres is $K = 1.6 \times M$, where M is the distance in miles and K is the distance in kilometres, and no other units can be used in this formula. Before you substitute in a formula like this, you must check that the information that you use is expressed in the correct units, and make any conversions. This process is shown in the next example.

Some formulas do not involve units. For example, you saw in Section 4 of Unit 1 that the formula for the nth square number is n^2.

Example 7 *Substituting a value into a formula*

€ is the symbol for euros.

A European car hire company charges €50 per day for the hire of a small car, plus a booking fee of €20. So, the total cost of hiring the car is given by the formula

$$T = 50 \times n + 20,$$

where T is the total cost in € and n is the number of days for which the car is hired.

How much does it cost to hire the car for 2 weeks?

Solution

💭 Check that the given information is in the correct units. 💭

In the formula, the hire time n is measured in *days*, so first convert 2 weeks into days.

There are 7 days in 1 week, so in 2 weeks there are 2×7 days $= 14$ days. Hence $n = 14$.

💭 Substitute and do the calculation. 💭

Substituting $n = 14$ into the formula gives

$$\begin{aligned} T &= 50 \times 14 + 20 \\ &= 700 + 20 \\ &= 720. \end{aligned}$$

💭 State the conclusion, including the correct units. 💭

Hence the cost of hiring the car for 2 weeks is €720.

Here is a similar type of substitution for you to try.

Activity 13 *Substituting a value into a formula*

The length of material needed to make a cushion cover is given by

$$L = 3 \times w + 5,$$

where L is the length of material in cm and w is the width of the cushion in cm. What length of material is needed to make a cover for a cushion of width $0.4\,\text{m}$?

Once you have substituted numbers into a formula, you perform the calculation by using the usual rules of arithmetic. The mnemonic BIDMAS helps you to remember the order of operations:

See Unit 1, Subsection 2.1.

Brackets, then **I**ndices (powers and roots), then **D**ivisions and **M**ultiplications, then **A**dditions and **S**ubtractions.

Here is another example of using a formula.

Example 8 *Calculating the time to walk uphill*

Naismith's Rule estimates that the time taken for a walk up a hill is given by the formula

$$T = \frac{D}{5} + \frac{H}{600},$$

where

T is the time for the walk in hours,
D is the horizontal distance walked in kilometres,
H is the height climbed in metres.

(a) Estimate how long a walk will take if the horizontal distance is 20 km and the height is 1200 m.

(b) Why might you need to allow longer than this estimate?

Solution

(a) Check that the given information is in the correct units.

In this case, the horizontal distance is 20 km and the height climbed is 1200 m. The units here are those specified for the formula, so no conversion is needed.

Substitute and do the calculation.

Substituting $D = 20$ and $H = 1200$ into the formula gives

$$T = \frac{20}{5} + \frac{1200}{600} = 4 + 2 = 6.$$

State the conclusion, including the correct units.

Hence Naismith's Rule predicts a 6-hour walk.

(b) You may need to allow longer than 6 hours to accommodate rest breaks, or because the terrain is difficult, the walkers are unfit or the weather is bad.

Here is a similar substitution for you to try.

Activity 14 *Using Naismith's Rule*

Use Naismith's Rule to estimate the time for a walk in which the horizontal distance is 5000 m and the height is 500 m.

In the next activity, the variable m has no units, so the problem of converting units does not arise.

Activity 15 *Using formulas*

(a) The *mean m* of five numbers a, b, c, d and e is given by the formula

$$m = \frac{a+b+c+d+e}{5}.$$

In a hedgerow survey, the numbers of tree and shrub species in five 30-yard sections of a hedge were found to be 4, 5, 6, 4 and 4. What is the mean number of species in a 30-yard section?

William Naismith was a Scottish climber who, in 1892, developed a rule for estimating walking times. His original rule has since been updated for the metric system.

The rule is based on the assumptions that someone can walk at a speed of 5 km/h on flat ground and also needs to allow an extra minute to climb a height of 10 metres.

The mean is a type of average. You will meet the mean again in Unit 4.

In 1974, Dr Max Hooper obtained data on trees and shrubs from 227 English hedges, whose ages he knew from written records. From these data, he derived a formula to estimate the age of a hedge.

(b) The age of an English hedge can be estimated by using *Hooper's Rule*:

$$A = 110 \times m + 30,$$

where A is the age in years and m is the mean number of tree and shrub species in a 30-yard section.

Use Hooper's Rule to estimate the age of the hedge in part (a) to the nearest hundred years.

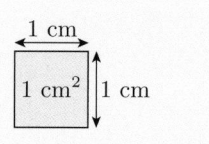

Figure 11   A square whose sides are 1 cm long has an area of 1 square centimetre, or $1\,\text{cm}^2$

Formulas for which you can choose the units

The formula for the area of a rectangle is $A = l \times w$, where A is the area, l is the length and w is the width. Here the units for measuring the rectangle have not been specified, so you can choose which units to use, as long as these units are consistent. So if you measure the length of the rectangle in centimetres, then the width should also be measured in centimetres, and the area in square centimetres; if you measure the length in kilometres, then the width should also be measured in kilometres, and the area in square kilometres.

For example, if the length of a rectangle is 3 m and the width is 0.5 m, then the area is

$$3 \times 0.5\,\text{m}^2 = 1.5\,\text{m}^2.$$

If the units given are not consistent with each other, then you should convert the measurements into appropriate units before substituting them into the formula. For example, if the measurement for the width is given as 50 cm instead of 0.5 m, then you should convert this measurement into 0.5 m and proceed as before, or convert the length of 3 m into 300 cm and obtain the area in square centimetres.

Similarly, in the formula $d = s \times t$, mentioned earlier, the units should be consistent; if the units for the speed are km/h, then the units for the time are h and the units for the distance are km.

Example 9   *Substituting values into a formula*

A car travels at an average speed of 95 km/h. Use the formula

$$d = s \times t$$

to find the distance the car travels in each of the following times.

(a) 2.5 hours   (b) 40 minutes

Give your answers to two significant figures.

Solution

(a) If the unit for speed is km/h and the unit for time is hours, then the distance is in km, so no conversions are required.

When $s = 95$ and $t = 2.5$,

$$d = 95 \times 2.5 = 237.5.$$

So the distance travelled is 240 km (to 2 s.f.).

(b) First, convert the given time into hours. Since

$$40\,\text{min} = \frac{40}{60}\,\text{h} = 0.666\ldots\,\text{h},$$

the time is $0.666\ldots$ h.

When $s = 95$ and $t = 0.666\ldots$,

$$d = 95 \times 0.666\ldots = 63.33\ldots\,.$$

So the distance travelled is $63\,\text{km}$ (to 2 s.f.).

Here are some problems of this type for you to try.

Activity 16 *Substituting values into a formula*

(a) The volume V of a rectangular box is given by

$$V = l \times w \times h,$$

where l is the length, w is the width and h is the height of the box. What is the volume of a box that measures $1.5\,\text{m}$ by $2\,\text{m}$ by $75\,\text{cm}$?

(b) The average speed s of a vehicle is given by the formula $s = d/t$, where d is the distance travelled and t is the time taken. What is the average speed of a coach that travels $80\,\text{km}$ in 1 hour 15 minutes?

One way to help check the consistency of units is to substitute the values for the variables together with their units into the formula. For example, in the area formula $A = l \times w$, the calculation given earlier to find the area of a rectangle with length $3\,\text{m}$ and width $50\,\text{cm}$ could have been written as

$$\begin{aligned} A &= 3\,\text{m} \times 0.5\,\text{m} \\ &= (3 \times 0.5)\,\text{m}^2 \\ &= 1.5\,\text{m}^2, \end{aligned}$$

which shows that the answer is in square metres. If the width had been substituted as $50\,\text{cm}$ instead of $0.5\,\text{m}$, then including the units would have alerted you to the problem, as shown in Figure 12 below.

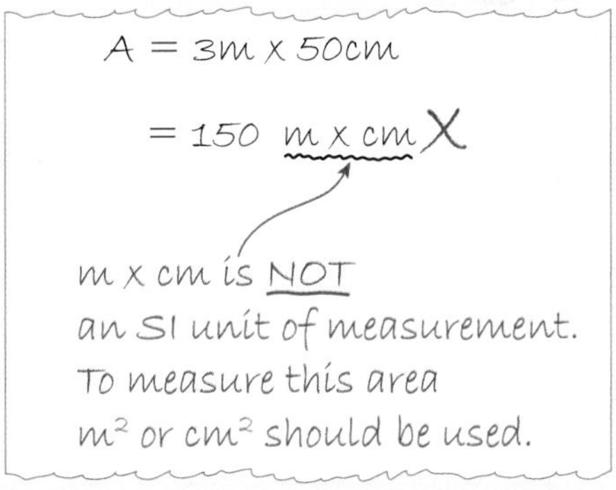

Figure 12 Incorrect use of units in a solution to the area problem

Similarly, the calculation in Example 9(a) could be written as

$$\begin{aligned} d &= 95\,\text{km/h} \times 2.5\,\text{h} \\ &= (95 \times 2.5)\,\text{km} \\ &= 237.5\,\text{km}. \end{aligned}$$

Here, dividing the unit km by the unit h and then multiplying it by h leaves the unit km unchanged.

3.2 Writing formulas concisely

Formulas containing a lot of mathematical symbols can look quite complicated. To make them more concise, multiplication signs are usually omitted.

For example,

> the formula $d = s \times t$ is usually written as $d = st$;
>
> the formula $A = 110 \times m + 30$ is usually written as $A = 110m + 30$.

However, when you substitute numerical values into a formula, you usually have to put the multiplication signs back in, to make the meaning clear. So $3 \times y$ can be written as $3y$, but 3×2 cannot be written as 32.

Another way to write some formulas is to use power notation. For example:

> w^2 means $w \times w$ and is read as 'w squared';
>
> x^3 means $x \times x \times x$ and is read as 'x cubed';
>
> y^4 means $y \times y \times y \times y$ and is read as 'y to the power 4' or 'y to the 4';
>
> and so on.

You should try to write the multiplication sign $\times$ and the letter x in different ways, so they don't get mixed up!

One way to check that you understand what a given formula means is to try describing in words how to *use* the formula.

For example, this is how to use Hooper's Rule, $A = 110m + 30$:

> To find the value of A, multiply the value of m by 110 and then add 30.

Activity 17   *Describing formulas*

Describe in words how to use the following formulas, starting each description with: 'To find the value of ...'.

Then in each case work out the value of the subject when $a = 2$ and $b = 5$.

In these formulas, the variables do not represent any particular quantities and there are no units specified.

(a) $Q = 4a - 5$ (b) $R = \dfrac{a}{3b}$ (c) $P = a^2 + b^2$

Conventions for writing formulas

There are several conventions that are usually followed when writing formulas concisely.

- In products, numbers are usually written first; for example, the formula $K = 1.6 \times M$, or equivalently $K = M \times 1.6$, is written concisely as

  $$K = 1.6M.$$

  Similarly, $(2a + b) \times 3$ is written concisely as $3(2a + b)$. However, $(2a + b)c$ and $c(2a + b)$ are both acceptable ways of writing $(2a + b) \times c$.

In some formulas, however, there are reasons why the variables are not written in alphabetical order.

- In products, letters are often written in alphabetical order; for example, $d = s \times t$, or equivalently $d = t \times s$, is usually written as

  $$d = st.$$

- Finally, divisions are usually written in the form of a fraction; for

Another acceptable form is
$s = d/t$.

  example, $s = d \div t$ is written as $s = \dfrac{d}{t}$ and read as 's equals d over t'.

Here are some examples for you to try.

Activity 18 *Writing formulas concisely*

(a) Write each of the following formulas concisely.

   (i) $M = v \times w$ (ii) $A = \frac{1}{2} \times b \times h$ (iii) $V = p \times r \times r \times h$

(b) Write the following formulas with the multiplication signs put back in.

   (i) $C = 2pr$ (ii) $V = l^3$

   (iii) $s = ut + \frac{1}{2}at^2$ (iv) $A = \frac{1}{2}h(a + b)$

(c) Rewrite the following formulas so that they follow the usual conventions.

   (i) $P = (a + b)2$ (ii) $I = TRP \div 100$

Note that in MU123 texts, and other printed materials, units are printed in normal type, whereas variables are printed in italics. This helps to distinguish between, say, the distance 5 metres, which is printed as 5 m, and the expression $5 \times m$ (that is, 5 times the variable m), which is printed concisely as $5m$. When handwritten, these look identical and the meaning is obtained from the context. This is one reason why units are usually not included in mathematical calculations that involve variables.

The example below uses a formula written in concise form. There is a tutorial clip of this example on the website that you may like to watch.

Example 10 *Estimating the volume of a log*

Tutorial clip

Foresters can estimate the volume of a log of wood by using the formula

$$V = \frac{LD^2}{4\pi},$$

where V is the volume of the log in cubic metres, L is the length of the log in metres, D is the distance around the middle of the log in metres, and π is approximately 3.141 59.

Your calculator should have a key for the number π. The symbol π is the Greek letter pi, read as 'pie'.

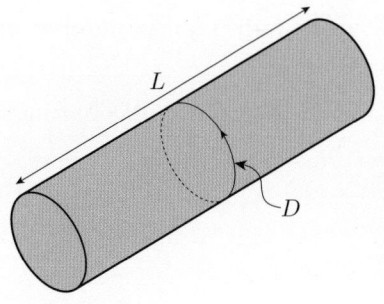

Estimate the volume of a log that is 1.5 m long and 92 cm around the middle, giving your answer to two significant figures.

Solution

Check that the given information is in the correct units.

The length is 1.5 m, so $L = 1.5$. The distance around the middle is 92 cm, but the formula requires the measurement in metres. Since $92\,\text{cm} = (92 \div 100)\,\text{m} = 0.92\,\text{m}$, we have $D = 0.92$.

Substitute and do the calculation.

Substituting $L = 1.5$ and $D = 0.92$ into the formula $V = \dfrac{LD^2}{4\pi}$ gives

$$V = \frac{1.5 \times 0.92^2}{4 \times 3.141\,59\ldots} = \frac{1.2696}{12.566\ldots} = 0.101\ldots\,.$$

State the conclusion, including the correct units.

Hence the volume of the log is $0.10\,\text{m}^3$ (to 2 s.f.).

In the example above, the steps in the calculation were included so that you can see the order in which these steps are carried out. However, as the calculation for V is done using your calculator, it is acceptable to write down the calculation step more briefly like this:

$$V = \frac{1.5 \times 0.92^2}{4\pi} = 0.10 \text{ (to 2 s.f.).}$$

Several different calculator sequences can be used to calculate the final answer, and some of these sequences involve using the memory and other function keys on your calculator. The next activity explains these key sequences in more detail.

Activity 19   Doing longer calculations using your calculator

---

Work through Subsection 4.4 of the Course Guide.

Now try substituting values in some more formulas.

Activity 20   Using letter formulas

(a) The monthly cost of using a phone consists of a fixed monthly charge plus charges for daytime calls. The cost can be calculated using the formula

$$C = 20 + 0.25n,$$

where C is the cost in £, and n is the number of minutes of daytime calls during the month.

What is the phone bill if 94 minutes of daytime calls have been made during the month?

Strictly, the units for BMI are kg/m^2. However, BMIs are usually quoted without units.

(b) A person's *body mass index* (BMI) is given by the formula

$$I = \frac{M}{H^2},$$

where I is their BMI, M is their mass in kilograms, and H is their height in metres.

If I is 25 or greater, then the person is classed as overweight.

A woman has a mass of $72\,\text{kg}$ and a height of $164\,\text{cm}$. Is she overweight?

(c) If you've been on a long car journey with children, then you've probably heard the question: 'Are we nearly there yet?' The following formula has been suggested to estimate the time it will take before this question is asked:

$$T = \frac{1 + 15A}{0.25C^2},$$

where T is the time in minutes, A is the number of activities the children have, and C is the number of children in the car.

If there are 3 children in a car and they have 6 activities, then how long does the formula predict it will be before the question is asked?

> A formula like this was suggested in 2006 by Dwight Barkley, a mathematics professor at the University of Warwick, as a fun exercise for families to think about when going on holiday.

Substituting negative numbers

So far you have substituted only positive numbers into formulas.

When you replace a letter by a negative number, it is usually helpful to include the number in brackets to avoid confusion. Here is an example.

Example 11   *Substituting a negative number*

Consider the formula $A = c^2 - 5c + 3$.

Find the value of A when $c = -2$.

Solution

Putting brackets around -2 and substituting it for c gives

$$\begin{aligned}
A &= (-2)^2 - 5(-2) + 3 \\
&= (-2) \times (-2) - (-10) + 3 \\
&= 4 + 10 + 3 \\
&= 17.
\end{aligned}$$

> An explanation of these steps is given after the example.

In the solution to Example 11, the number -2 has been enclosed in brackets when it is substituted to ensure that the minus sign is not separated from the 2 by mistake. This makes it clear that $(-2)^2$ has to be evaluated as follows:

$$(-2)^2 = (-2) \times (-2) = 4.$$

If the brackets had been omitted here, then this part of the calculation might have been done *incorrectly* as $-2^2 = -2 \times 2 = -(2 \times 2) = -4$.

In the second occurrence of -2 in this solution,

$$-5(-2) \quad \text{was replaced by} \quad -(-10) \quad \text{and then by} \quad +10.$$

To understand these steps, first remember that

$$5(-2) = 5 \times (-2) = -10.$$

> See Unit 1, Subsection 3.1, for the rules for multiplying negative numbers.

Then remember that in the calculation above $-(-10)$ means 'subtract minus 10', and subtracting the negative number -10 is the same as adding the corresponding positive number 10. So in this calculation, $-(-10)$ is the same as $+10$.

However, if the variable being substituted appears first in the calculation on its own, then no brackets are required. For example, if $A = C + 3$ and $C = -2$, then $A = -2 + 3 = 1$.

Sometimes when you are substituting into a formula you have to find the negative of a number. This is the number that is produced by putting a minus sign in front of the number. For example, consider the formula $y = -x$, which means 'to find y, take the negative of x'. If $x = 3$, for example, then $y = -3$. But what happens when x is a negative number?

For example, substituting $x = -2$ into the formula gives $y = -(-2)$.

So what does $-(-2)$ mean?

A negative number can be thought of as the result of a subtraction from zero. For example, $-3 = 0 - 3$. In the same way, $-(-2)$ can be thought of as the subtraction $0 - (-2)$, which is 2. So replacing $-(-2)$ by 2 gives $y = 2$.

In the same way,

$$-(-3) = 3, \quad -(-20) = 20, \quad -(-10.5) = 10.5, \quad -(-\tfrac{3}{5}) = \tfrac{3}{5}.$$

In general, a negative sign in front of a number changes its sign.

Activity 21 *Substituting a negative number*

(a) Consider the formula $G = 6 + a - a^2$. Find the value of G when $a = -4$.

(b) Consider the formula $y = -x + 4$. Find the value of y when $x = -9$.

(c) Consider the formula $v = \dfrac{u - 2}{1.2}$. Find the value of v when $u = -1$.

(d) To convert a temperature from Celsius to Fahrenheit, you can use the formula

$$f = 1.8c + 32,$$

where f is the temperature in degrees Fahrenheit, and c is the temperature in degrees Celsius.

Use this formula to work out the Fahrenheit equivalent of $-10°C$.

Gabriel Daniel Fahrenheit (1686–1736) was the inventor of the mercury thermometer. For the zero point of his temperature scale, he used the lowest measurable temperature that he could reach in his laboratory. He did this so that no everyday temperature would have a negative value.

3.3 Constructing your own formulas

There are many well-known formulas that you can use to solve problems, but sometimes you need to find your own formula. In this subsection you will see how to construct some formulas, and there are further examples throughout the course. You can construct a formula by following the three steps below.

- *First, identify the subject of the formula and the other variables, and their units of measurement.*

  This means that you have to decide the purpose of the formula and what the formula depends on.

For example, suppose that you want to find a formula for the length of a return journey from one place to another (A to B), in terms of the distance between the two places.

Let's call the length of the return journey R, and the distance between the two points d, as illustrated in Figure 13. Both R and d are measured in kilometres. You can choose any letters, but formulas are often easier to remember if the letters remind you of the quantities. Also, it is a good idea not to pick letters such as o and l that could be confused with other symbols such as 0 and 1.

- *Next, find the relationship between the variables.*

Here, you need to think about how to work out R from d.

The length of the return journey R is twice the distance between the two places, that is, two lots of d, which can be written as $2d$.

So the formula is $R = 2d$.

- *Finally, write down all the details of the formula.*

  The formula is $R = 2d$, where R is the length of the return journey in km, and d is the distance between the two points in km.

  Alternatively, and more concisely:

  The length of the return journey R km is given in terms of the distance d km by the formula $R = 2d$.

Note that you should never include units in a formula. For example, it would be incorrect to write the formula as $R = 2d$ km. However, when you use a formula, you need to include the units in your conclusion.

Here is a slightly more complicated example.

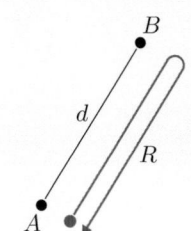

Figure 13 Identifying the subject and variables of a formula

Example 12 *Finding a formula – driving to work*

(a) During a working week, Anya drives from home to her office and back five times, and she also makes a number of trips from her office to head office and back. Her office is 12 miles from her home and 7 miles from the head office.

   Find a formula for d, where d is the total number of miles that Anya drives in a week when she makes n trips to head office.

(b) Use your formula to find the distance driven by Anya in a week when she makes 3 trips to head office.

Solution

(a) Draw a diagram if it helps you to understand the situation. Then tackle the problem step by step, by considering separately the return journeys from her home to the office and from the office to the head office.

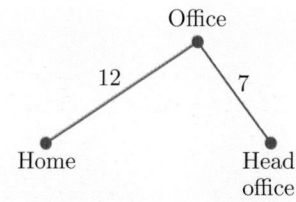

The distance in miles that Anya drives from her home to her office and back is $12 \times 2 = 24$. So in 5 days, the distance in miles that she drives from her home to her office and back is $5 \times 24 = 120$.

The length of the return journey from the office to the head office is 2×7 miles $= 14$ miles. So the distance she drives to the head office and back in n trips is n lots of 14, that is, $14n$ miles.

💭 The total distance in miles that she drives is the sum of the total distance she travels between home and the office, and the total distance between head office and the office. 💭

Remember that the unit 'miles' is *not* included in the formula.

Hence a formula for d is

$$d = 120 + 14n,$$

where d is the distance in miles, and n is the number of trips from the office to the head office.

(b) Substituting $n = 3$ into the formula in part (a) gives

$$d = 120 + 14 \times 3 = 120 + 42 = 162.$$

Include the unit 'miles' in the conclusion.

So the distance is 162 miles.

You can try finding some formulas yourself in the next activity. If you find the relationship between the variables hard to spot, then try some particular numbers first as that might help you to identify the operations involved. For example, in Example 12 you could have asked yourself how to calculate the total distance if the number of trips to head office is 1, 2, 5, and so on.

Looking at some particular numbers often helps you to get a feel for a problem, as you saw in Section 4 of Unit 1.

Then think about which parts of these calculations stay the same and which change. That might help you to discover that the length of the return journey from home to the office is always 120 miles and that this distance always needs to be added to the distance for the trips to the head office and back. Drawing a diagram might help too.

Activity 22 *Finding formulas*

(a) Write down a formula for the total distance, d km, travelled on a journey if m km are travelled on the motorway and p km are travelled on principal roads.

(b) A car can travel 15 km on 1 litre of fuel. Write down a formula for the distance D km the car can travel on f litres of fuel.

(c) A car-hire business has 60 cars, and r cars have been rented out. Write down a formula for the number of cars, N, that are still available to hire.

(d) To estimate the time of a journey through a town, a mathematical model is modified by adding an allowance for the time spent at junctions. From a survey, it is found that allowing 2 minutes extra for each junction is a realistic adjustment. Write down a formula for T, the *extra* time in minutes needed for a journey that goes through J junctions in the town.

The next example shows how checking some particular numbers can help you to spot a pattern that leads to a formula.

 Tutorial clip

---

Example 13 *Finding a formula – the car ferry*

A car ferry can transport both cars and vans. A van requires a space of 9 m, and a car requires a space of 5 m. Find a formula for the length L required for c cars and v vans.

Solution

Consider the space needed for the cars first, and try some particular numbers to start with.

1 car needs a space of 5 m, so 2 cars need $2 \times 5\,\text{m} = 10\,\text{m}$, 3 cars need $3 \times 5\,\text{m} = 15\,\text{m}$, and so on.

So to find the space needed for c cars, c lots of 5 metres are needed, that is, a distance of $5c$ metres.

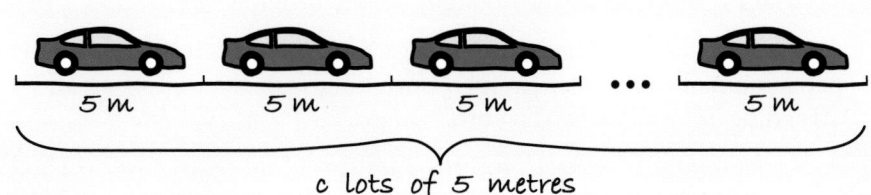

Drawing a diagram may help!

Similarly for the vans.

1 van needs a space of 9 m, so 2 vans need $2 \times 9\,\text{m}$, 3 vans need $3 \times 9\,\text{m}$, and so on.

So the space needed for v vans is $v \times 9$ metres, that is, $9v$ metres.

To find the total length, add the distance for the cars and the distance for the vans together.

So a formula for L is $L = 5c + 9v$, where L is the total length in metres, c is the number of cars, and v is the number of vans.

(As a check, work out the length for, say, 2 cars and 3 vans without using the formula:

the length is $2 \times 5\,\text{m} + 3 \times 9\,\text{m} = 10\,\text{m} + 27\,\text{m} = 37\,\text{m}.$

If you substitute $c = 2$ and $v = 3$ into the formula, then you obtain the same answer.)

If you get a different answer at this stage, then you should go back and check the steps that you used to develop the formula.

The strategy box below summarises the key points for writing down formulas.

Strategy *Finding formulas*

1. Identify the subject of the formula and the other variables, and their units of measurement. If possible, choose letters for the variables that remind you of the context.

2. Find the relationship between the variables.

3. Write down all the details of the formula, defining the variables and stating their units (if appropriate).

(It is a good idea to try particular numbers first to suggest what the formula is like, and then to check that your formula works.)

Here are some formulas for you to find.

Activity 23 *Finding more formulas*

(a) A theatre charges £25 for each adult ticket and £15 for each child ticket, plus an additional booking fee of £5 for each order.

    (i)   Write down a formula for the total cost C in £, if a adult tickets are bought in one order.

    (ii) Write down a formula for the total cost T in £, if a adult tickets and c child tickets are bought in one order.

(b) A children's after-school club charges a registration fee of £20 and £8 per session. Find a formula for P, where £P is the cost of a child attending n sessions at the club.

(c) A furniture manufacturer requires 3 metres of fabric to cover each chair and uses a roll of fabric containing r metres to cover n chairs. Find a formula for s, where s metres is the length of fabric left on the roll.

The next activity asks you to spend a few moments thinking about what you have learned in this section and planning what you should do next.

Activity 24 *Ready to move on?*

This section has introduced you to the ideas in the table on the next page. For each idea, spend a few moments reviewing how you got on by asking yourself the following four questions.

- Did you understand the explanation in the text and any worked examples?

- Did you manage to complete the activities successfully?

- Do you feel confident with this idea?

- Have you been able to complete the associated assignment questions?

If your answer to any of these questions is 'No', then plan what you are going to do in order to sort out your difficulties, bearing in mind your time commitments. For example, the quickest way of sorting out a negative answer to the first question is probably to contact your tutor, if you have not already done so. Make a note of the examples, sections of the text or activities that you don't understand so that you can mention these to your tutor. If you have understood the text and managed to do the activities, but still don't feel confident, then you may like to plan some time to work through the practice quizzes on the website, or use some other resources. Or you may decide to discuss the ideas with other people (perhaps in a tutorial or forum) or watch the tutorial clips again.

Topic	Understood topic	Completed activities	Confident with idea	Completed assignment	What to do next
Substituting in formulas					
Writing formulas concisely					
Using a letter formula					
Units in formulas					
Constructing formulas					

There are no comments on this activity.

4 Inequalities

In Section 3, you considered variables and formulas. This section considers some notation that can be used for describing the range of possible values that a variable can take. This notation is useful both when setting up a model, in order to describe known restrictions on the variables, and when stating your conclusions. For example, the restrictions on a variable that represents the speed of a car might be that it is greater than or equal to zero and less than or equal to the speed limit that applies.

In this situation, when there is a particular number that provides a restriction, or limitation, on the value of a variable, we call the number a **limit**. This section introduces a shorthand way of describing such restrictions.

Stating your conclusions to a problem may also involve comparing your answer with a particular number and seeing whether it is greater than or less than that number. For example, in Activity 12 the time model gave a larger gap than the distance model for speeds *less than* 18 m/s, and in Activity 20 you calculated the body mass index and then checked to see if it was 25 or *greater* in order to determine if the person was overweight.

4.1 Notation for working with inequalities

If two numbers are not equal, then there is an *inequality* between them. The nature of this inequality can be expressed by using the phrases 'less than' and 'greater than' or the inequality signs $<$ and $>$.

If a number lies to the left of another number on the number line, then it is said to be **less than** ~~than~~ the other number. For example, -5 lies to the left of -2, as shown in Figure 14, so -5 is less than -2. This statement can be written more concisely by using the inequality sign $<$ for 'less than':

$$-5 < -2.$$

It is read as 'minus five is less than minus two'.

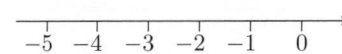

Figure 14 Part of the number line

If a number lies to the right of another number on the number line, then it is said to be **greater than** the other number. For example, -1 lies to the right of -3, so -1 is greater than -3. This statement can be written using the inequality sign $>$ for 'greater than':

$$-1 > -3.$$

It is read as 'minus one is greater than minus three'.

The inequality sign always points towards the smaller of the two numbers; for example, $2 < 3$ and $4 > 3$.

Any statement involving inequality signs is called an **inequality**. Each inequality can be written in two different ways. For example, 4 is greater than 2, so you can write

$$4 > 2,$$

but also 2 is less than 4, so you can write

$$2 < 4.$$

Each way of writing an inequality is obtained from the other by swapping the numbers and reversing the inequality sign. This is called reversing the inequality.

As well as the two inequality signs introduced above, there are two other inequality signs, $\leq$ and $\geq$. The four **inequality signs** and their meanings are given in the following box.

The alternative notations
$$\leqslant \quad \text{for} \quad \leq$$
and
$$\geqslant \quad \text{for} \quad \geq$$
are also used.

> **Inequality signs**
>
> $<$ is less than
> $\leq$ is less than or equal to
> $>$ is greater than
> $\geq$ is greater than or equal to

Inequalities using the signs $<$ and $>$ are often called **strict inequalities** since they do not allow equality.

Here are some examples of correct inequalities:

- $1 < 1.5$, because 1 is less than 1.5.
- $1 \leq 1.5$, because 1 is less than or equal to 1.5 (it is 'less than' 1.5).
- $1 \leq 1$, because 1 is less than or equal to 1 (it is 'equal to' 1).

It may seem strange to write $1 \leq 1.5$ and $1 \leq 1$, when the more precise statements $1 < 1.5$ and $1 = 1$ can be made, and you would not usually write the former statements. The inequality signs $\leq$ and $\geq$ are useful, however, for specifying the range of values that a variable can take, as in the following example.

Example 14   *Specifying the range of a variable*

Suppose that the speed of a car on a UK motorway is s km/h. Write down two inequalities that specify the range of possible legal values of s.

Solution

💬 First, decide what you want to say in words. 💬

The speed must be greater than or equal to zero and should be less than or equal to the speed limit on a UK motorway, that is, 112 km/h (70 mph).

💬 Replace the words by the appropriate inequalities. 💬

So the two inequalities are

$$s \geq 0 \quad \text{and} \quad s \leq 112.$$

Most inequalities that you will meet involve variables. A value of the variable for which the inequality is true is said to **satisfy** the inequality. For example, the number 100 satisfies both the inequalities in Example 14.

4.2 Illustrating inequalities on a number line

An inequality can be represented on a number line by marking the section of the number line where the inequality is true. A section of the number line without any gaps is known as an **interval**. For example, the straight line above the number line in Figure 15 shows the interval consisting of all the numbers less than or equal to 112, so it illustrates the inequality $s \leq 112$. The small solid circle at the limit 112 indicates that 112 is contained in the interval and is a possible value for s. The diagram shows that the possible values for s lie to the left of or exactly on 112.

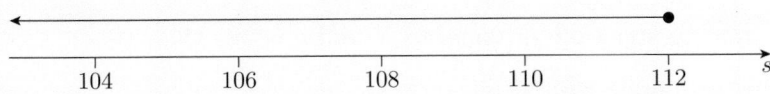

Figure 15   The interval where $s \leq 112$

A strict inequality can be represented on a number line by using a small empty circle at the limit. For example, Figure 16 illustrates the strict inequality $u > 4$. The possible values for u lie to the right of 4.

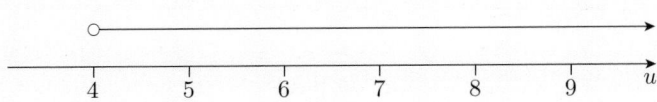

Figure 16   The inequality $u > 4$

Activity 25   *Using inequality signs*

(a) Put the correct sign ($<$ or $>$) in each of the boxes below.

   (i) $12 \,\square\, 3$ (ii) $-5 \,\square\, 3$ (iii) $-2.5 \,\square\, -4.5$

(b) Use number lines to represent each of the following inequalities.

   (i) $a \geq -3$ (ii) $b < 6$ (iii) $c \leq -2.5$

(c) Reverse each of the inequalities in parts (a) and (b).

Sometimes, two inequalities can be combined to make a **double inequality**, as the next example shows.

Tutorial clip

Example 15   *Using a double inequality*

A child who is 5 years or older but not yet 16 is eligible for a child fare on the train. Children under 5 travel free. Suppose that a represents the age of a child in years.

(a) Draw a number line to illustrate the ages eligible for a child fare.

(b) Give a double inequality to describe the age restriction for child fares. Which whole numbers satisfy this inequality?

Solution

(a) Mark the limits at 5 and 16 on the number line first, and then join the limits with a line.

The ages of children who are eligible for a child fare are shown on the number line in Figure 17.

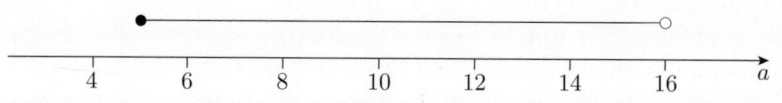

Figure 17 Child fares

(b) The restrictions on the age for a child fare are

  a is greater than or equal to 5, and a is less than 16.

Using inequality signs,

  $a \geq 5$ and $a < 16$.

Now, $a \geq 5$ can be written as $5 \leq a$.

Therefore the inequalities are

  $5 \leq a$ and $a < 16$.

These two inequalities can be combined as the double inequality

  $5 \leq a < 16$.

The whole numbers that satisfy this inequality are

  $5, 6, 7, 8, 9, 10, 11, 12, 13, 14, 15$.

The double inequality $5 \leq a < 16$ is read as

  '5 is less than or equal to a, which is less than 16',

or as

  'a is greater than or equal to 5, and less than 16'.

Here are some similar examples for you to try.

Activity 26 *Restricting variables*

A person's body mass index is denoted by the variable I. The person is classed as

underweight   if I is less than 18.5,
healthy weight   if I is 18.5 or more, but less than 25,
overweight   if I is 25 or more, but less than 30,
obese   if I is 30 or more.

Express each of these four statements as an inequality (single or double), and illustrate each of them as an interval on a number line.

Inequalities can also be used to illustrate the range of possible numbers that round to a particular value.

The number line in Figure 18 shows the values that round to 7.5 when rounded to one decimal place.

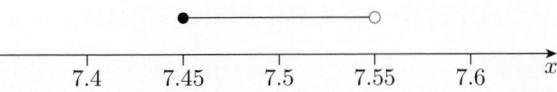

Figure 18 Numbers that round to 7.5

These are the numbers that lie between 7.45 and 7.55, including 7.45 but not 7.55. So the double inequality that gives these numbers is

$7.45 \leq x < 7.55.$

Activity 27 *Describing ranges of numbers*

(a) Illustrate each of the following double inequalities on a number line.

(i) $-2 \leq c \leq 2$ (ii) $-1 < b < 6$ (iii) $-4 < x \leq -1$

(b) Suppose that a variable N can take any value that is a positive whole number. What values of N satisfy the inequality $2 < N \leq 6$?

(c) Write down inequalities to describe the following intervals.

(i)

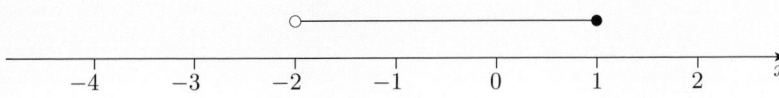

(ii)

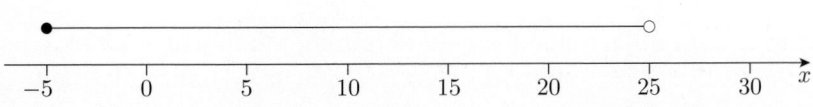

(d) On a number line, show the numbers x that round to 6 when rounded to the nearest whole number. Write down a double inequality that describes these numbers.

This section should have helped you to develop your skills in using inequalities to describe restrictions on variables. You will meet inequalities again in Unit 7.

5 Improving your mathematics

This final section considers several aspects of studying mathematics that you may find helpful. The section is quite short and contains some ideas that you may like to consider throughout your study. Subsection 5.1 looks back at the ways in which you have been solving problems, and suggests a few general strategies that you can use for any mathematical question and that you may find helpful in the future. Subsection 5.2 summarises some advice from students on how to read mathematics, and finally Subsection 5.3 suggests how you can use the feedback you receive on your assignments to improve your work. You may like to come back to this section when you receive your first marked iCMA and TMA.

5.1 Some problem-solving strategies

In this unit you have seen how some everyday problems can be investigated by using mathematics. One way of tackling such real-life problems is to use the modelling cycle. In fact, the steps in the modelling cycle are fairly similar to those that you use when you tackle any mathematics problem, whether it is a practical problem or something more abstract, as summarised in the box below.

You used some numerical examples in Unit 1 when investigating the sums of odd numbers and in Section 3 of this unit when constructing your own formulas.

> ### Tips for tackling mathematics problems
>
> - Check you understand the problem – and if you are not sure, talk to people (your tutor, fellow students, friends) until you do.
>
> - Collect information that will help you to solve it – this may be data, but it can also include techniques that you have used before that may help in this case too. What do you want to find out, and what do you know already?
>
> - Simplify the problem if you can – this may include trying some numerical examples first or breaking the problem down into smaller achievable steps.
>
> - Carry out the mathematics. Remember, there are often several different ways of tackling a problem, including numerically and graphically, which may give different insights. Drawing a diagram often helps too.
>
> - Check that your answers are reasonable and rounded appropriately.

Drawing a diagram is a good way of obtaining a different view of a problem. In this unit, you used diagrams to help with formulas and inequalities. Diagrams can also be used as part of your notes, to help you to connect different ideas together and to remember key ideas for later problems.

Figure 19 shows an example of a diagram that is very useful for remembering the following formulas:

$$\text{speed} = \frac{\text{distance}}{\text{time}}, \quad \text{time} = \frac{\text{distance}}{\text{speed}}, \quad \text{distance} = \text{speed} \times \text{time}.$$

You may already be able to remember these formulas – if not, using the diagram in Figure 19 might help.

To use this diagram to give the right formula, you should decide which quantity you need on the left-hand side of the formula, and cover up that quantity. Then look at the position of the remaining two quantities. For example, if you cover up 'speed', then you are left with 'distance' over 'time'. The other two formulas work in a similar way.

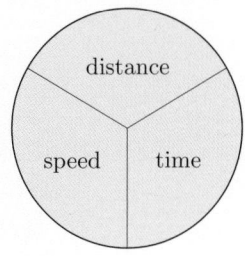

Figure 19 Remembering formulas

5.2 Reading mathematics

Reading mathematics is a different skill from more general reading because you need to concentrate on each word and symbol, learning and using new vocabulary and notation as you go. This means that it takes longer, and you may sometimes feel stuck if you cannot see how to get from one line to the next. For difficult sections, you may find it helpful to annotate the text by including some extra working to explain the steps or notation.

The cartoons below offer advice on how to cope with some of these difficulties.

5.3 Using feedback

Throughout Units 1 and 2 you have been encouraged to assess your progress and to try some of the practice quizzes. So you probably have a fairly good idea of how you are getting on with the course, and you may already be making changes to improve your studying.

Doing the assignments will help you to consolidate the main ideas and provide further evidence of your progress. If you have not already done so, then it's a good idea to try the iCMA and TMA questions for this unit before starting the next unit.

You will receive marks and feedback on the iCMAs and TMAs that you submit. This subsection outlines the kind of feedback you will receive and how to use it. When you receive your feedback, it may be tempting to just look at your overall score and then carry on with the work you are currently studying. However, to gain full benefit from each assignment, you should spend some time, say 20–30 minutes, looking in detail at the feedback you receive. This feedback may suggest how you can improve your solutions, which would help you with later assignments and other parts of the course.

You may find that it is more productive to consider the feedback some time later. Immediately after receiving your score, you may be feeling thrilled with your score or disappointed by it, or even frustrated by any mistakes you made!

iCMA feedback

The feedback on the iCMAs will contain some notes on correct solutions and references to the parts of units where you can find further information or examples. For each question that you answered incorrectly, you should study the solution provided and check that you understand it, particularly where it differs from your solution. Can you see why your answer is incorrect? You may like to try a similar example from the practice quizzes to make sure that you understand the ideas, or if you are still having difficulties, contact your tutor for help. When you have worked through the feedback, spend a few moments thinking about whether you need to make any changes to the way you tackle iCMA questions in the future.

- Do you need to try more practice quiz questions before attempting each iCMA?

- Do you need to allow yourself more time to complete each iCMA?

- Would it be better to tackle iCMA questions as you work through each section of a unit or to work on them only after you have completed each unit?

TMA feedback

The feedback that your tutor provides on your TMAs will be tailored to your solutions, and it may include praise on work you have done well or suggestions for alternative techniques that you may find helpful in the future, as well as constructive comments to help you improve your mathematics and the way you present it. The form attached to your TMA will highlight the main points that you should try to address before you submit your next TMA. It's a good idea to make use of this general advice straight away as you work on the units, so that these ideas will be familiar to you when you tackle the next TMA. For example, your tutor may have commented on how you have explained your solutions, and you can practise improving your skills in this area as you work on the activities in the units.

More detailed comments on your solutions may be provided on your script. You should check through these comments carefully, making sure that you understand them and that you would be able to tackle a similar question successfully in the future, if required to do so. Do you understand why you have lost marks (if any)? If there are any comments or lost marks that you do not understand, contact your tutor.

It is worth making a note of the main points that you need to remember for the next TMA. If you have printed out the assignments, then you may like to write these comments directly on the next TMA. Alternatively, you could highlight the relevant statements on the TMA form or make some more formal notes. It is important to find a helpful way of recording these comments so that you can refer to them easily when you tackle the next TMA.

Activity 28 *Improving your mathematics*

This final activity asks you to spend a few minutes considering any changes that you intend to make to the way you study MU123. (You may like to return to part (b) when you have received the feedback on your TMA.)

(a) Subsection 5.2 gave some advice on reading mathematics. Which parts of this advice have you tried already? Which parts do you intend to try?

(b) Based on your work on the assignments and the feedback that you have received, what changes do you intend to make in the preparation of your next assignments? Even relatively simple things such as allowing a bit more time to check through your assignment when you have finished the questions may help to improve your work.

(c) Do you need to make any changes to the amount of time you have for studying or your study sessions?

There are no comments on this activity.

Learning checklist

After studying this unit, you should be able to:

- use a map scale to estimate distances
- use formulas relating speed, distance and time
- understand how the modelling cycle can be used to solve problems
- appreciate that mathematical models simplify reality, take account of some features, and ignore others
- appreciate that mathematical ideas can be communicated in different ways (for example, numerically or graphically) and the best way to communicate them may depend on the intended audience
- draw and interpret graphs
- use formulas and find your own formulas to describe simple situations
- understand some conventions for writing formulas
- use inequality signs to describe limits and intervals
- review your studying and make changes to improve it.

Solutions and comments on Activities

Activity 1

(a) The route planners may have used different routes or made different assumptions for the speed of the car, the traffic conditions at different times of day or the starting and finishing points of the journey.

(b) The car will travel 50 km in the first hour and then another 50 km in the next hour, making 100 km overall. So the journey will take about 2 hours. This estimate is probably not good enough as it takes no account of the actual distances along the roads between Great Malvern and Milton Keynes or the speeds at which cars tend to travel on different types of roads.

Activity 2

(a) Since 1 cm represents 10 km, the distance along the whole route is
$$(13.8 \times 10)\,\text{km} = 138\,\text{km},$$
and the distance along the motorway is
$$(3 \times 10)\,\text{km} = 30\,\text{km}.$$

(b) The total distance along the route is 138 km, and the distance along the motorway is 30 km. So the distance along the principal roads is
$$(138 - 30)\,\text{km} = 108\,\text{km}.$$

(c) Since 1 cm represents 10 km, the map distance is
$$(25 \div 10)\,\text{cm} = 2.5\,\text{cm}.$$

Activity 3

(a) Here, 1 cm on the map represents 10 km on the ground. Now,
$$\begin{aligned} 10\,\text{km} &= (10 \times 1000)\,\text{m} \\ &= (10\,000 \times 100)\,\text{cm} \\ &= 1\,000\,000\,\text{cm}. \end{aligned}$$
Thus the map scale is 1 : 1 000 000, so the scale factor is 1 000 000.

(b) Here, 1 cm on the map represents 500 000 cm on the ground. Now,
$$\begin{aligned} 500\,000\,\text{cm} &= (500\,000 \div 100)\,\text{m} \\ &= (5000 \div 1000)\,\text{km} \\ &= 5\,\text{km}. \end{aligned}$$
So the map scale is '1 cm represents 5 km'.

Activity 4

(a) The map scale is 1 : 50 000. So a map distance of 3.4 cm represents a ground distance of $3.4 \times 50\,000\,\text{cm} = 170\,000\,\text{cm}$. Now,
$$\begin{aligned} 170\,000\,\text{cm} &= (170\,000 \div 100)\,\text{m} \\ &= 1700\,\text{m} \\ &= (1700 \div 1000)\,\text{km} \\ &= 1.7\,\text{km}. \end{aligned}$$
So the distance between the two towns is 1.7 km.

(b) The map scale is 1 : 50 000. So a ground distance of 7.85 km is represented by a map distance of $7.85 \div 50\,000\,\text{km}$. Now,
$$\begin{aligned} (7.85 \div 50\,000)\,\text{km} &= 0.000\,157\,\text{km} \\ &= (0.000\,157 \times 1000 \times 100)\,\text{cm} \\ &= 15.7\,\text{cm}. \end{aligned}$$
So the map distance is 15.7 cm.

Activity 5

(a) By the formula, the average speed is
$$\frac{425}{4}\,\text{km/h} = 106.25\,\text{km/h} = 110\,\text{km/h} \ (\text{to 2 s.f.}).$$

(b) **First method**

The journey takes $(60 + 25)$ minutes = 85 minutes. So, by the formula, the average speed is
$$\frac{30}{85}\,\text{km/min}.$$
Now we convert this answer to km/h. The distance covered in 1 minute is $\dfrac{30}{85}$ km, so the distance covered in 1 hour is $60 \times \dfrac{30}{85}$ km. So the average speed is
$$\begin{aligned} \frac{60 \times 30}{85}\,\text{km/h} &= 21.17\ldots\,\text{km/h} \\ &= 21\,\text{km/h} \ (\text{to 2 s.f.}). \end{aligned}$$
(Note that keeping the average speed as a fraction here avoids dealing with an awkward decimal.)

Second method

The time 85 minutes is $85/60$ hours $= 1.416\,66\ldots$ hours. So, by the formula, the average speed is
$$\begin{aligned} \frac{30}{1.416\,66\ldots}\,\text{km/h} &= 21.17\ldots\,\text{km/h} \\ &= 21\,\text{km/h} \ (\text{to 2 s.f.}). \end{aligned}$$

(c) By the formula, the average speed is
$$\frac{100}{14}\,\text{m/s} = 7.14\ldots\,\text{m/s} = 7.1\,\text{m/s} \ (\text{to 2 s.f.}).$$

Activity 6

(a) First method

The average speed is 50 km/h, so 1 km is travelled in 1/50 h.

Hence, to travel 108 km, it takes $108/50\,\text{h} = 2.16\,\text{h}$. Since there are 60 minutes in 1 hour,

$$0.16\,\text{h} = (0.16 \times 60)\,\text{min} = 9.6\,\text{min} \approx 10\,\text{min}.$$

So the journey takes 2 h 10 min to the nearest minute.

Second method

By the formula, the time is

$$\frac{108}{50}\,\text{h} = 2.16\,\text{h},$$

that is, 2 h 10 min to the nearest minute, as before.

Which method you prefer is a personal choice – what is important is finding a method that you can use easily, quickly and without making mistakes.

(b) The time for the motorway section was calculated in Example 4 as 0.3 h, so the total journey time is

$$2.16\,\text{h} + 0.3\,\text{h} = 2.46\,\text{h} \approx 2\,\text{h}\,28\,\text{min},$$

that is, 2 h 30 min to the nearest 10 minutes.

Activity 7

Motorway (30 km)			
Speed in km/h	80	100	112
Time taken in minutes	23	18	16
Principal roads (108 km)			
Speed in km/h	40	50	96
Time taken in minutes	162	130	68

(a) The shortest journey times for the motorway and principal roads sections are approximately 16 minutes and 68 minutes, respectively, giving a total time of approximately 1 hour 24 minutes. This time cannot be achieved, since it is necessary to slow down or even stop at times during the journey, for example at junctions.

(b) If the average speed on the motorway drops from 100 km/h to 80 km/h, then the time increases by 5 minutes. So there is not much change in the overall time. This is because the distance on the motorway is quite short. If the average speed on the principal roads drops from 50 km/h to 40 km/h, then the time increases by 32 minutes.

(c) The journey time is quite sensitive to changes in the average speed, so it would probably be wise to allow some extra time for the journey.

Activity 8

Some points about Transport Direct are listed below – don't worry if your comments are slightly different.

(a) The website contains information on journeys by train, plane, coach and car, the latest travel news, parking places, and the carbon footprint of proposed journeys.

(b) The data on the road network are obtained from the Ordnance Survey, and the data on the journey times come from the Highways Agency. The journey time data are obtained from automatic number plate recognition (ANPR) systems, induction loops in the road and floating vehicle data.

The Ordnance Survey data are updated every six weeks, but the journey time data are updated only annually, so journey times are calculated using data from the corresponding journeys a year ago.

The user inputs the details of the required journey, including the origin and the destination, the start time and the date, and can also include details about their car.

(c) The model considers the journey times of traffic on roads at 15-minute intervals throughout each day and at 21 different types of day (for example, holidays, weekdays and weekends). Allowances are also made for junctions. The routes include roads on the main road network and then 'clouds' of roads around the starting point and destination.

(d) A route is obtained by using a computer algorithm that systematically searches through all possible routes using roads either on the main road network or in the 'clouds'.

(e) The planner is improved by taking account of user feedback, updating the data and gathering new data, for example from local authorities.

Activity 9

(a) The information given in the 'typical stopping distances' chart shows the effect of the thinking and braking distances, and provides detailed information on these distances, both in metres and as car lengths, to make it easier to visualise. However, it may be difficult to estimate the distances on the road, especially at higher speeds. By comparison, the 'two-second rule' is easier to remember and to use. Including both models gives users a choice of ways to check the gap.

(b) Picturing the distance in car lengths should make the distances easier to visualise. Also, splitting the stopping distance into thinking and braking distances indicates that as the speed increases, the braking distance increases rapidly – roughly, it quadruples each time the speed is doubled. Displaying the total distance as a chart also emphasises the lengths of the gaps that should be left between cars. This is not so apparent from the two-second rule. The chart is clear, but remembering the information it contains may be difficult.

(c) An alternative approach is to paint chevrons on the road and advise drivers to keep at least two chevrons apart; this has been tried on sections of some UK motorways. However, this method doesn't take account of different road conditions or types of vehicle.

(d) At 40 mph, you travel 40 miles in 1 hour, that is, a distance of

$$40 \times 1.609 \, \text{km} = 64.36 \, \text{km}.$$

So 40 mph is 64 km/h to the nearest integer.

Activity 10

(a) As in Example 5, the speed 80 km/h is

$$\frac{80 \times 1000}{60 \times 60} \, \text{m/s} = \frac{80\,000}{3600} \, \text{m/s}$$
$$= 22.22 \, \text{m/s (to 2 d.p.)}.$$

(b) In each case, the length in metres of the gap in the time model is twice the speed in m/s.

Speed in km/h	Speed in m/s	Time model gap in m	Distance model gap in m
32	8.89	18	12
48	13.33	27	23
64	17.78	36	36
80	22.22	44	53
96	26.67	53	73
112	31.11	62	96

Activity 11

(a) A speed of 90 km/h is approximately 25 m/s.

(b) A speed of 7.5 m/s is approximately 27 km/h.

Activity 12

(a) The graph is shown below.

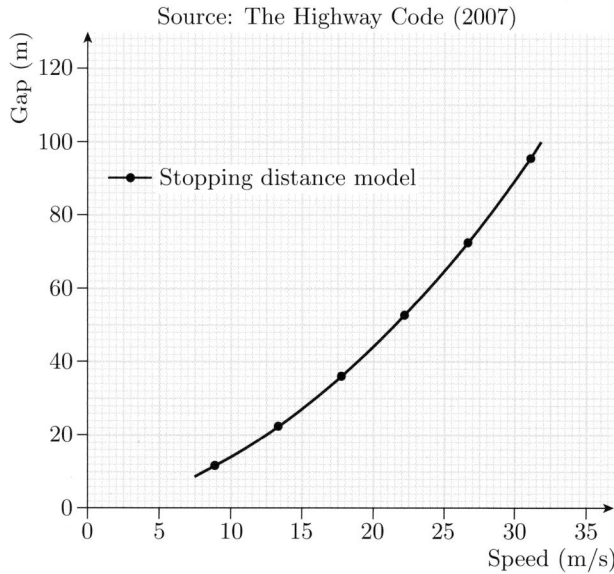

Recommended gaps between cars travelling at different speeds
Source: The Highway Code (2007)

Check that you have included the title and source of the data and that you have labelled the axes with their titles, units and scales. The points should be joined with a smooth curve.

(b) The line is plotted below.

Recommended gaps between cars travelling at different speeds
Source: The Highway Code (2007)

(c) At 25 m/s, the time model gives a gap of 50 m and the distance model gives a gap of about 65 m.

(d) The distance model gives the smaller gap up to a speed of about $18\,\text{m/s}$. At speeds greater than $18\,\text{m/s}$, the time model gives the smaller gap, and the discrepancy between this model and the distance model increases quite rapidly as the speed increases. Notice that the distance model graph is not a straight line.

Activity 13

In the formula, the width w of the material is measured in cm, so first convert $0.4\,\text{m}$ to cm, to give $w = (100 \times 0.4)\,\text{cm} = 40\,\text{cm}$. Substituting $w = 40$ into the formula for L gives

$$L = 3 \times 40 + 5 = 125.$$

So $125\,\text{cm}$, or $1.25\,\text{m}$, of material is needed.

Activity 14

In the formula the horizontal distance is measured in km. Now $5000\,\text{m} = (5000/1000)\,\text{km} = 5\,\text{km}$, so $D = 5$ and $H = 500$. Substituting D and H into the formula for T gives

$$T = \frac{5}{5} + \frac{500}{600} = 1\tfrac{5}{6}.$$

Hence the estimate for the time is $1\tfrac{5}{6}$ hours, or 1 hour 50 minutes.

Activity 15

(a) When $a = 4$, $b = 5$, $c = 6$, $d = 4$ and $e = 4$,

$$m = \frac{4 + 5 + 6 + 4 + 4}{5} = \frac{23}{5} = 4.6.$$

So the mean number of species is 4.6.

(b) When $m = 4.6$,

$$A = 110 \times 4.6 + 30 = 506 + 30 = 536.$$

So, to the nearest hundred years, the hedge is 500 years old.

Activity 16

(a) If the length, width and height are measured in metres, then the volume is in cubic metres. First convert the given height into metres. Since

$$75\,\text{cm} = \frac{75}{100}\,\text{m} = 0.75\,\text{m},$$

the height is $0.75\,\text{m}$.

When $l = 1.5$, $w = 2$ and $h = 0.75$,

$$V = 1.5 \times 2 \times 0.75 = 2.25.$$

So the volume is $2.25\,\text{m}^3$.

(b) If the unit for distance is km and the unit for time is hours, then the unit for speed is km/h. So first convert the given time into hours. Since

$$75\,\text{min} = \frac{75}{60}\,\text{h} = 1.25\,\text{h},$$

the time is $1.25\,\text{h}$.

When $d = 80$ and $t = 1.25$,

$$s = \frac{80}{1.25} = 64.$$

So the average speed is $64\,\text{km/h}$.

Activity 17

(a) To find the value of Q, multiply a by 4 and then subtract 5.

Substituting $a = 2$ gives

$$Q = 4 \times 2 - 5 = 8 - 5 = 3.$$

(b) To find the value of R, divide a by the product of 3 and b.

Substituting $a = 2$ and $b = 5$ gives

$$R = \frac{2}{3 \times 5} = \frac{2}{15}.$$

(c) To find the value of P, square a and square b, and then add the answers together.

Substituting $a = 2$ and $b = 5$ gives

$$P = 2^2 + 5^2 = 4 + 25 = 29.$$

Activity 18

(a) **(i)** $M = vw$

(ii) $A = \tfrac{1}{2}bh$ or $A = \dfrac{bh}{2}$

(iii) $V = hpr^2$

(b) **(i)** $C = 2 \times p \times r$

(ii) $V = l \times l \times l$

(iii) $s = u \times t + \tfrac{1}{2} \times a \times t \times t$

(iv) $A = \tfrac{1}{2} \times h \times (a + b)$

(c) **(i)** $P = 2(a + b)$

(ii) $I = \dfrac{PRT}{100}$

Activity 20

(a) When $n = 94$,

$$C = 20 + 0.25 \times 94 = 20 + 23.5 = 43.5.$$

Hence the phone bill is £43.50.

(b) The formula requires the height in metres, so we calculate

$$164\,\text{cm} = (164 \div 100)\,\text{m} = 1.64\,\text{m}.$$

When $M = 72$ and $H = 1.64$,

$$I = \frac{72}{1.64^2} = \frac{72}{2.6896} = 26.8 \text{ (to 3 s.f.)}.$$

Since I is greater than 25, the woman is classed as being overweight according to her BMI.

(c) When $A = 6$ and $C = 3$,
$$T = \frac{1 + 15 \times 6}{0.25 \times 3^2} = \frac{91}{2.25}$$
$$= 40 \text{ (to the nearest minute)}.$$
So the formula predicts that it takes 40 minutes before the children ask if they are nearly there yet. (This prediction would certainly have to be tested to check if it is reasonable!)

Activity 21

(a) When $a = -4$,
$$G = 6 + (-4) - (-4)^2 = 6 - 4 - 16 = -14.$$

(b) When $x = -9$,
$$y = -(-9) + 4 = 9 + 4 = 13.$$

(c) When $u = -1$,
$$v = \frac{-1 - 2}{1.2} = \frac{-3}{1.2} = -2.5.$$

(d) When $c = -10$,
$$f = 1.8 \times (-10) + 32 = -18 + 32 = 14.$$
Hence $-10°C$ is equivalent to $14°F$.

Activity 22

(a) The formula is $d = m + p$, where d is the total distance in km, m is the distance in km on the motorway, and p is the distance in km on principal roads.

(b) The formula is $D = 15f$, where D is the distance in km, and f is the number of litres of fuel.

(c) The formula is $N = 60 - r$, where N is the number of cars available for hire, and r is the number of cars rented out.

(d) The formula is $T = 2J$, where T is the extra time in minutes, and J is the number of junctions.

Activity 23

(a) **(i)** The total cost is

booking fee + cost of tickets.

If one ticket costs £25, then a tickets cost a lots of £25, that is, £25a.

So the formula is $C = 5 + 25a$, where C is the total cost in £, and a is the number of adults.

(ii) The total cost is

booking fee + cost of adult tickets
    + cost of child tickets.

The cost of a adult tickets is £25a, and the cost of c child tickets is £15c.

So the formula is $T = 5 + 25a + 15c$, where T is the total cost in £, a is the number of adult

tickets, and c is the number of child tickets.

(b) The total cost is

registration fee + cost of sessions.

If one session costs £8, then n sessions cost n lots of £8, that is, £8n.

So the formula is $P = 20 + 8n$, where P is the total cost in £, and n is the number of sessions.

(c) The amount of fabric left is

length of roll − length needed for chairs.

If one chair requires 3 metres, then n chairs require $3n$ metres.

So the formula is $s = r - 3n$, where s is the amount of fabric left in metres, and n is the number of chairs.

Activity 25

(a) **(i)** $12 > 3$ **(ii)** $-5 < 3$

(iii) $-2.5 > -4.5$

(b) **(i)**

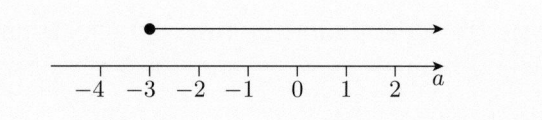

(ii)

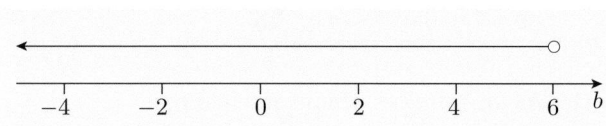

(iii)

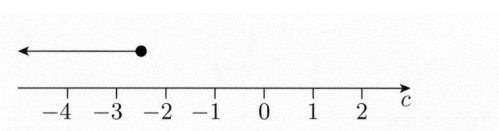

(c) $3 < 12$, $3 > -5$, $-4.5 < -2.5$; $-3 \leq a$, $6 > b$, $-2.5 \geq c$.

Activity 26

The inequalities are as follows:

underweight	$I < 18.5$,
healthy weight	$18.5 \leq I < 25$,
overweight	$25 \leq I < 30$,
obese	$I \geq 30$.

These inequalities are each illustrated in the following figure.

$I < 18.5$

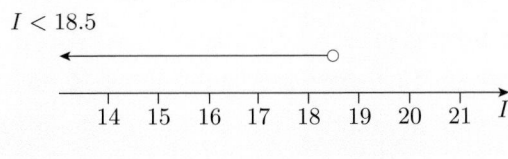

$18.5 \leq I < 25$

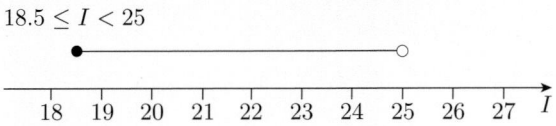

$25 \leq I < 30$

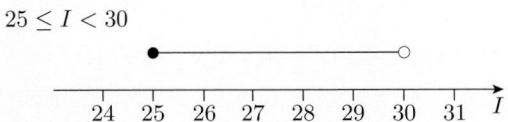

$I \geq 30$

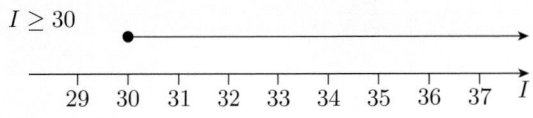

Activity 27

(a) (i)

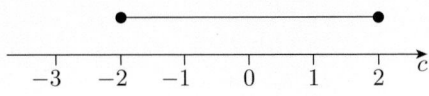

(ii)

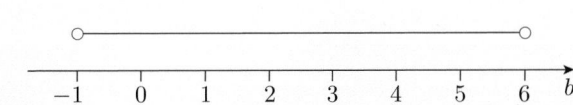

(iii)

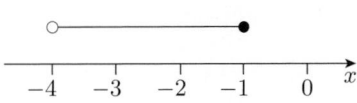

(b) The interval for N is shown below.

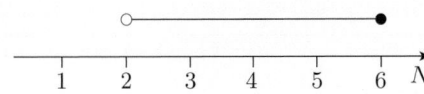

The whole numbers that lie within this interval are 3, 4, 5 and 6.

(c) (i) $-2 < x \leq 1$ **(ii)** $-5 \leq x < 25$

(d)

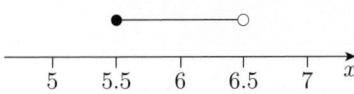

The double inequality for these numbers is
$$5.5 \leq x < 6.5.$$

Numbers

Introduction

This unit is all about numbers. You use numbers in many different ways every day; for example, you might use them to tell the time, look for a particular page in a book, find the price of an item that you want to buy, check your bank balance or make a measurement. You probably don't think about the numbers themselves, and the interesting properties that they have, but these properties have fascinated many people for thousands of years. This unit will give you just a glimpse of the many properties of numbers.

In particular, you will learn about some properties of prime numbers, and about different types of numbers, such as rational and irrational numbers, and how they differ from each other.

Numbers are of course an important part of mathematics, and it is essential that you are able to work with them confidently and perform calculations with them, both by hand and by using your calculator. These skills will underpin much of your later work in the course, so this unit also gives you an opportunity to revise and practise some of your skills in working with numbers, and to learn some new number skills. If you are a little rusty on some of the basic number skills, such as adding fractions, then you may find that you need more detail than is provided in this unit. If so, then you should find it helpful to consult Maths Help via the link on the course website.

In the final section of the unit, you will look at how numbers in the context of *ratio* are useful in all sorts of everyday situations. In particular, you will learn about *aspect ratio*, which provides a way to describe the shapes of rectangles. Many forms of media involve rectangular shapes; for example, computer and television screens, photographs, printed pages and video pictures are all usually rectangular. Aspect ratio is important in determining, for example, how well different shapes of rectangular picture fit on different shapes of rectangular screen.

The calculator section of the Course Guide is needed for two of the activities in this unit. If you do not have the Course Guide to hand when you reach these activities, then you can omit them and return to them later.

> 'Why are numbers beautiful? It's like asking why is Beethoven's Ninth Symphony beautiful. If you don't see why, someone can't tell you. I know numbers are beautiful. If they aren't beautiful, nothing is.'
>
> Paul Erdös (1913–1996), Hungarian mathematician.
>
> Paul Erdös was one of the most unusual and prolific mathematicians in history. He travelled constantly, living out of a suitcase, and collaborated with other mathematicians wherever he went.

> Activities 27 and 35, on pages 148 and 159, respectively, are in the Course Guide.

1 Natural numbers

As you saw in Unit 1, the **integers** are the numbers

$$\ldots,\ -3,\ -2,\ -1,\ 0,\ 1,\ 2,\ 3,\ \ldots.$$

This section is about the **positive integers**,

$$1,\ 2,\ 3,\ \ldots,$$

which are also known as the **natural numbers**.

The natural numbers are the first numbers that people learn about, and you might think of them as rather uninteresting. In fact, they have many intriguing properties that continue to fascinate mathematicians, and are an important part of the branch of mathematics known as number theory. Their properties also have many important applications in the real world.

1.1 Multiples

When you use a cash machine to withdraw money, it gives you options for the amount of money that it will dispense. The options might be

£20, £30, £40, £50, £100, £200.

These amounts are all *multiples* of £10. Most UK cash machines dispense only multiples of £10, because they contain only £10 and £20 notes.

In general, a **multiple** of a natural number is the result of multiplying it by a natural number. For example, the multiples of 6 are 6, 12, 18, 24, 30, and so on, because

$1 \times 6 = 6$,

$2 \times 6 = 12$,

$3 \times 6 = 18$,

and so on.

Another way to think of the multiples of 6 is that they are the numbers into which 6 divides exactly. For example, 324 is a multiple of 6 because

$324 \div 6 = 54$, and 54 is a whole number,

but 472 is a not a multiple of 6 because

$472 \div 6 = 78.666\ldots$, which is not a whole number.

$1 \times 6 = 6$
$2 \times 6 = 12$
$3 \times 6 = 18$
$4 \times 6 = 24$
$5 \times 6 = 30$
$6 \times 6 = 36$
$7 \times 6 = 42$
$8 \times 6 = 48$
$9 \times 6 = 54$
$10 \times 6 = 60$

Figure I The first ten multiples of six are the answers in the six times table

The numbers $0, -6, -12, \ldots$ can also be considered to be multiples of 6. However, this section is all about *positive* integers; so, for example, 'the first four multiples of 6' means the first four positive multiples: $6, 12, 18$ and 24.

Activity I *Multiples of natural numbers*

(a) Write down the first five multiples of 7.

(b) The tickets for an event cost £11 each, and all the ticket money is put in a cash box that is initially empty. After the event, the cash box is found to contain £4183. Is this a correct amount?

Common multiples

Look at these lists of the first few multiples of 6 and 8:

multiples of 6: 6, 12, 18, 24, 30, 36, 42, 48, 54, 60, ... ,

multiples of 8: 8, 16, 24, 32, 40, 48, 56, 64, 72, 80, ...

Notice that the number 24 appears in both lists. We say that it is a *common* multiple of 6 and 8. There are other common multiples of 6 and 8: the number 48 also appears in both lists, and if the lists were extended, then you would see that other numbers, for example 72, 96 and 120, also appear in both lists. In fact there are infinitely many common multiples of 6 and 8. The common multiple 24 is special, however, as it is the smallest. We say that it is the *lowest common multiple* of 6 and 8.

These ideas are summarised in the box below.

A **common multiple** of two or more numbers is a number that is a multiple of all of them. The **lowest common multiple (LCM)** of two or more numbers is the smallest number that is a multiple of all of them. An alternative name for lowest common multiple is **least common multiple**.

In the box on the previous page, 'number' means 'natural number'. We often use the word 'number' in this way when we are discussing the natural numbers.

Activity 2 *Finding lowest common multiples*

(a) Write down the first four multiples of each of the numbers 2, 3, 4, 6 and 8. Use your answers to find the lowest common multiple of each of the following pairs of numbers.

   (i) 2 and 3   (ii) 4 and 6   (iii) 4 and 8

(b) Find the lowest common multiple of 2, 3 and 8.

Activity 3 *Sharing chocolates*

(a) A confectionery manufacturer wants to produce a box of chocolates that can be shared evenly among the people in any group of four or fewer people. What is the smallest number of chocolates that can be in the box?

(b) If the manufacturer wanted the box to contain more chocolates than this, what would be the next suitable number of chocolates?

1.2 Factors

A natural number that divides exactly into a second natural number is called a **factor** or **divisor** of the second number. For example, 2 is a factor of 10, since 2 divides exactly into 10.

Factors are closely related to multiples, since '2 is a factor of 10' means the same as '10 is a multiple of 2'. Another way of saying the same thing is '10 is **divisible** by 2'.

Every natural number greater than 1 has at least two factors, itself and 1, but most numbers have more factors than this. For example, the number 10 has four factors: 1, 2, 5 and 10.

The factors of a number can be arranged into **factor pairs**, where the two factors in each pair multiply together to give the number. For example, the factor pairs of 10 are

   $1, 10$ (since $1 \times 10 = 10$),
   $2, 5$ (since $2 \times 5 = 10$).

You can use the idea of factor pairs to help you find all the factors of a number. Here is the strategy – you might like to think about why it works.

Strategy *To find the factors of a number*

- Try the numbers $1, 2, 3, 4, \ldots$ in turn. Whenever you find a factor, write down the other factor in the factor pair.

- Stop when you get a factor pair that you have already.

The following example illustrates this strategy.

Example 1   *Finding the factors of a number*

Find all the factors of 28.

Solution

The first factor pair of a number is always 1 and the number.

The first factor pair is 1, 28.

Try 2.

The next factor pair is 2, 14.

Try 3: it's not a factor. Try 4.

The next factor pair is 4, 7.

Try 5: it's not a factor. Try 6: it's not a factor. Try 7: this gives the factor pair 7, 4, which is already found, so stop. To finish, list the factors in increasing order.

The factors of 28 are 1, 2, 4, 7, 14 and 28.

Activity 4   *Finding the factors of a number*

Find all the factors of the following numbers.

(a) 20   (b) 24   (c) 45

Because the factors of a number form pairs, most numbers have an even number of factors. The only exceptions are the square numbers, each of which has an odd number of factors. This is because one of the factors of a square number pairs with itself. For example, the square number 25 has three factors: the factor pair 1, 25, and the factor 5, which pairs with itself.

Remember that a *square number* is the result of multiplying a whole number by itself. For example, 25 is a square number because $25 = 5 \times 5$.

The tests in the box below can be useful when you are trying to find the factors of a number. They give you a quick way to tell whether a given number is divisible by 2, 3, 5 or 9.

Divisibility tests

A number is divisible by

- 2 if it ends in 0, 2, 4, 6 or 8
- 3 if its digits add up to a multiple of 3
- 5 if it ends in 0 or 5
- 9 if its digits add up to a multiple of 9.

If a number does not satisfy a test above, then it is not divisible by the specified number.

You may see an explanation of why the tests for divisibility by 3 and 9 work if you go on to take further mathematics courses.

Activity 5   *Testing for divisibility*

(a) Is 621 divisible by 3?

(b) Is 273 divisible by 9?

Common factors

Look at these lists of the factors of 12 and 18:

> factors of 12: 1, 2, 3, 4, 6, 12;
> factors of 18: 1, 2, 3, 6, 9, 18.

The numbers that appear in both lists are called the *common* factors of 12 and 18. So the common factors of 12 and 18 are 1, 2, 3 and 6. The largest common factor of 12 and 18 is 6, and this is usually called the *highest* common factor. These ideas are summarised in the box below.

A **common factor** of two or more numbers is a number that is a factor of all of them. The **highest common factor** (**HCF**) of two or more numbers is the *largest* number that is a factor of all of them. An alternative name for highest common factor is **greatest common divisor** (**GCD**).

Activity 6 *Finding highest common factors*

Use the solution to Activity 4, and the lists of factors of 12 and 18 given above, to list the common factors of each of the following sets of numbers. Hence write down the highest common factor of each set of numbers.

(a) 20 and 24   (b) 12 and 24   (c) 18, 20 and 24

Highest common factors can be useful when you are cancelling fractions. When you want to cancel a fraction down to its simplest form, you need to divide top and bottom by the highest common factor of the numerator and denominator. For example, consider the fraction $\frac{24}{30}$. Dividing top and bottom by 6, the highest common factor of 24 and 30, gives $\frac{4}{5}$. Because 6 is the *highest* common factor of 24 and 30, the numerator and denominator of the simplified fraction have no common factors, other than 1, so the fraction is in its simplest form.

It doesn't matter if you don't immediately spot the highest common factor of the numerator and denominator of a fraction – you can always cancel the fraction down in stages, in the way shown in Unit 1.

There is a quicker way to find highest common factors than the method that you have seen in this subsection. It involves *prime numbers*, which you will learn about in the next subsection.

1.3 Prime numbers

You have seen that every natural number greater than 1 has at least two factors, itself and 1. A natural number that has *exactly* two factors is called a **prime number**, or just a **prime**. For example, 3 is a prime number since its only factors are 1 and 3, but 4 is not a prime number because its factors are 1, 2 and 4. The number 1 is *not* a prime number, as it has only one factor, namely 1. Here are the first 25 prime numbers.

The prime numbers under 100

2, 3, 5, 7, 11, 13, 17, 19, 23, 29, 31, 37, 41, 43, 47, 53, 59, 61, 67, 71, 73, 79, 83, 89, 97

The prime numbers are the 'building blocks' of all the natural numbers, in a sense that you will learn about in the next subsection.

There is a simple algorithm for finding all the prime numbers up to a certain number, which is attributed to the Greek mathematician Eratosthenes (c. 276 BC – c. 197 BC), and known as the *Sieve of Eratosthenes*. Eratosthenes was a librarian at the famous library at Alexandria.

The algorithm works well provided that the certain number is not too large, and modified forms of it are still used by mathematicians today. The course website has a link to a website demonstrating the Sieve of Eratosthenes.

Eratosthenes was a man of many talents: he was a mathematician, geographer, historian and literary critic. He was the first person to make a good measurement of the circumference of the Earth, and he came up with the idea of the leap year, which stops the calendar drifting out of step with the seasons.

Activity 7 *Last digits of prime numbers*

Every prime number except 2 and 5 ends in 1, 3, 7 or 9. Can you explain why?

Prime numbers play a central role in both abstract and real-world mathematics. In the real world, prime numbers are often used in encryption systems that are used to protect confidential information when it is transmitted electronically. Encryption involves turning such information into an unrecognisable form so that it cannot be understood until it is turned back into its original form.

Mathematicians have proved many theorems about prime numbers, and they are still working to prove many conjectures. In the next activity you are asked to investigate some properties of prime numbers. This activity will give you a taste of the area of mathematics known as number theory.

Activity 8 *Investigating prime numbers*

(a) The following table lists all the odd prime numbers under 30. Complete the second row to give the remainder when each prime number is divided by 4.

Of course, the only *even* prime number is 2!

Prime number	3	5	7	11	13	17	19	23	29
Remainder	3	1	3						

(b) Some prime numbers can be written as the sum of two square numbers: for example, $29 = 25 + 4$. Complete the following table with ticks and crosses to indicate whether each prime number can be written as the sum of two square numbers.

Prime number	3	5	7	11	13	17	19	23	29
Sum of two squares?		✓			✓	✓			✓

(c) By comparing the completed tables from parts (a) and (b), make a conjecture about which odd prime numbers can be written as the sum of two square numbers. Try to obtain more evidence for your conjecture by considering one or two slightly larger prime numbers.

You will learn more about Euclid in Unit 8.

There are infinitely many prime numbers – this was proved more than 2000 years ago by the Greek mathematician Euclid. Despite this, it is difficult to identify very large prime numbers.

Thousands of prime number enthusiasts throughout the world are interested in breaking the record for the largest known prime number. Most of them search for Mersenne primes – primes of the form $2^n - 1$ for some natural number n. For example, 7 and 31 are Mersenne primes because $7 = 2^3 - 1$ and $31 = 2^5 - 1$.

At the time of writing, forty-seven Mersenne primes are known. The latest three of these were discovered in August and September 2008 and June 2009, and the discoverer of the earliest of these three primes won a \$100 000 prize for the first Mersenne prime with more than ten million digits. This prime number was found using software provided by the *Great Internet Mersenne Prime Search*, a scheme in which enthusiasts can download free software that uses the spare processing power of their computers.

At the time of writing, a \$3000 prize is available for each new Mersenne prime discovered, and there is a \$150 000 prize for the first Mersenne prime with more than 100 million digits.

Mersenne primes are named after the French mathematician Marin Mersenne (1588–1648), who investigated them. It can be proved that if $2^n - 1$ is prime, then n must be prime.

Figure 2   Marin Mersenne

The course website has a link to a website where you can find out the latest news about prime numbers.

It would be easy to find prime numbers if they formed some sort of regular pattern, but they do not. The Swiss mathematician Leonhard Euler (1707–1783) wrote: 'Mathematicians have tried in vain to this day to discover some order in the sequence of prime numbers, and we have reason to believe that it is a mystery into which the mind will never penetrate.'

1.4 Prime factors

A natural number greater than 1 that is not a prime number is called a **composite number**. The first few composite numbers are

  4, 6, 8, 9, 10, 12, 14, 15, ...

Unlike a prime number, a composite number can be written as a product of two factors, neither of which is 1. For example,

  $360 = 20 \times 18.$

Composite numbers can often be written as products of even more factors. For example, the number 360 can be broken down into a product of more factors in the following way. The factors 20 and 18 are themselves composite, so they can also be written as products of two factors, neither of which is 1. For example,

  $20 = 4 \times 5 \quad \text{and} \quad 18 = 3 \times 6.$

So 360 can be written as a product of *four* factors, none of which is 1:

  $360 = 4 \times 5 \times 3 \times 6.$

The process here can be set out as a **factor tree**, as shown in Figure 3.

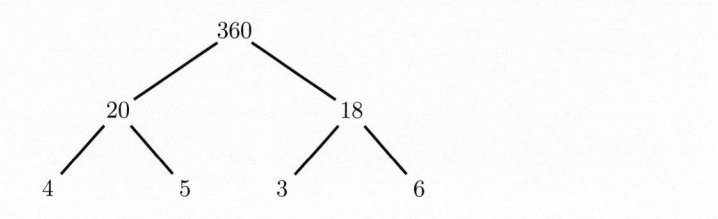

Figure 3   A factor tree for 360

You can continue the process until all the numbers at the ends of the tree are prime numbers. The result is shown in Figure 4, with the prime numbers circled.

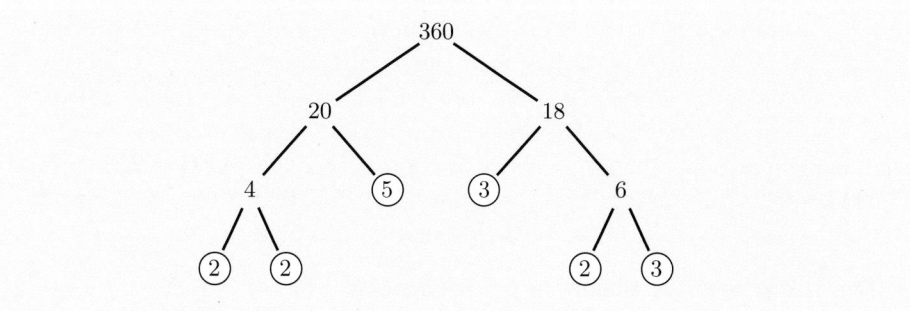

Figure 4   A completed factor tree for 360

It follows from Figure 4 that

$360 = 2 \times 2 \times 5 \times 3 \times 2 \times 3.$

Writing the factors in increasing order gives

$360 = 2 \times 2 \times 2 \times 3 \times 3 \times 5.$

And writing $2 \times 2 \times 2$ as 2^3 and 3×3 as 3^2 gives the simpler form

$360 = 2^3 \times 3^2 \times 5.$

Here the number 360 is written as a product of prime factors. You can use a process similar to the one above to write any composite number as a product of prime factors.

The process of writing a natural number as a product of factors greater than 1 (whether prime or not) is called **factorisation**. The factorisation above was started by writing $360 = 20 \times 18$, but it could also have been started by writing $360 = 10 \times 36$, or $360 = 9 \times 40$, for example. And there are different ways to proceed with the numbers further down the factor tree, too. Figure 5 shows a different factor tree for 360.

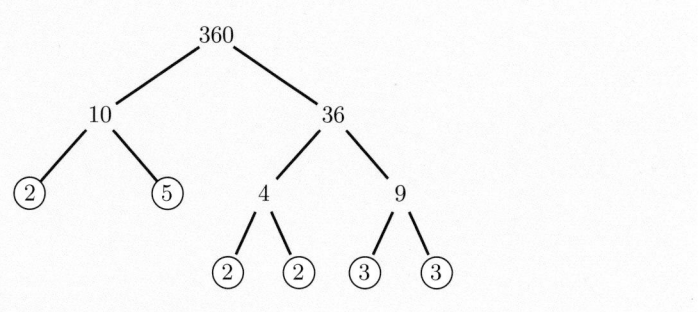

Figure 5   Another factor tree for 360

This second factor tree gives the same result:

$$360 = 2^3 \times 3^2 \times 5.$$

Activity 9 *Using a factor tree*

(a) Use a factor tree to write the number 300 as a product of prime factors.

(b) Repeat part (a) using a different factor tree.

In Activity 9 you should have obtained the same answer in parts (a) and (b). That is, you should have obtained the same prime factors, and the same number of each of the prime factors.

In fact, no matter how you factorise a composite number into a product of prime factors, you will always obtain the same answer (except that you can usually change the order of the factors – for example, you could write $15 = 3 \times 5$ or $15 = 5 \times 3$). It can be proved that this is true for *every* composite number, an important result known as the *fundamental theorem of arithmetic*.

A version of the fundamental theorem of arithmetic appears in Euclid's *Elements* (c. 300 BC). The first rigorous proof was given by the German mathematician Carl Friedrich Gauss (1777–1855) in his famous treatise *Disquisitiones Arithmeticae*, published in 1801.

The fundamental theorem of arithmetic

Every natural number greater than 1 can be written as a product of prime numbers in just one way (except that the order of the primes in the product can be changed).

For a natural number that is prime, the 'product' is just the number itself.

The **prime factorisation** of a natural number is the product of prime factors that is equal to it. Here are the prime factorisations of the numbers from 2 to 10:

$$
\begin{array}{lll}
2 = 2, & 3 = 3, & 4 = 2^2, \\
5 = 5, & 6 = 2 \times 3, & 7 = 7, \\
8 = 2^3, & 9 = 3^2, & 10 = 2 \times 5.
\end{array}
$$

The fundamental theorem of arithmetic is the reason why the prime numbers can be thought of as the building blocks of the natural numbers.

When you want to write a number as a product of prime factors, it is sometimes helpful to be systematic. Start by writing the number as

the smallest possible prime × a number,

and do the same with each composite number in the factor tree. If you do this for the number 252, then you obtain the factor tree in Figure 7. So $252 = 2^2 \times 3^2 \times 7$.

Figure 6 Carl Friedrich Gauss in 1803

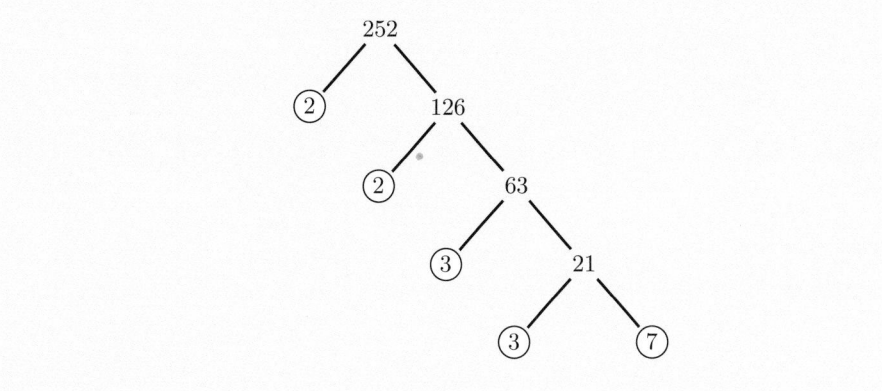

Figure 7 A systematic factor tree for 252

With this systematic method, at each level of the factor tree you get a prime factor and a composite factor, until the final level when you get two prime factors. At each stage 'the smallest possible prime' is the same as, or bigger than, the previous prime factor.

You don't need to set out the working as a factor tree – you might prefer to set it out like this:

$$252 = 2 \times 126$$
$$= 2 \times 2 \times 63$$
$$= 2 \times 2 \times 3 \times 21$$
$$= 2 \times 2 \times 3 \times 3 \times 7$$
$$= 2^2 \times 3^2 \times 7.$$

Activity 10 *Factorising numbers into products of primes*

Write each of the following numbers as a product of prime factors.

(a) 72   (b) 855   (c) 1000   (d) 847

The method suggested above for finding the prime factorisation of a number works well if the prime factors are fairly small, but it is time-consuming if they are large. For example, the prime factorisation of the number 899 is 29×31, so to find this factorisation you would have to test each prime number from 2 to 29 to see whether it is a factor of 899.

Despite much research, no one has managed to find a quick method for finding large prime factors of a number. So multiplying two large prime numbers together is a process that is quick to carry out but slow to reverse. For example, you could quickly multiply the primes 29 and 31 to obtain the answer 899, but if you were given the number 899 and asked to find the prime factors, then it would take you much longer!

A computer can multiply two 150-digit prime numbers in seconds, but if a suitable computer program were given the result, then it would probably not be able to find the two prime factors within a human lifetime. Mathematicians have found a clever way to exploit this fact to design secure encryption systems. With the advent of internet banking and online purchasing, the security of personal information such as account details and credit card numbers has become an essential field of computer science. It is number theory that underpins these computer security systems.

 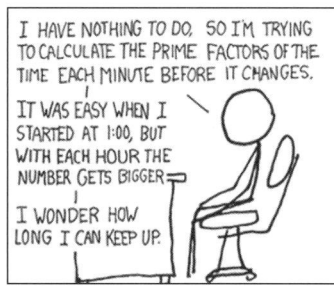  

You can use prime factorisations to help you find the lowest common multiples and highest common factors of sets of numbers.

Example 2 *Using prime factorisations to find LCMs and HCFs*

Find the lowest common multiple and highest common factor of 84 and 280.

Solution

Write out the prime factorisations, with a column for each different prime.

$$84 = 2^2 \times 3 \quad \times 7$$
$$280 = 2^3 \quad \times 5 \times 7$$

To find the LCM, multiply together the *highest* power of the prime in each column.

The LCM of 84 and 280 is

$$2^3 \times 3 \times 5 \times 7 = 840.$$

To find the HCF, multiply together the *lowest* power of the prime in each column, considering only the primes that occur in all the rows.

The HCF of 84 and 280 is

$$2^2 \times 7 = 28.$$

$$84 = 2^2 \times \text{\textcircled{3}} \quad \times \text{\textcircled{7}}$$

$$280 = \text{\textcircled{2^3}} \quad \times \text{\textcircled{5}} \times 7$$

$$84 = \text{\textcircled{2^2}} \times 3 \quad \times \text{\textcircled{7}}$$

$$280 = 2^3 \quad \times 5 \times 7$$

The methods used in Example 2 are summarised below.

Strategy *To find the LCM or HCF of two or more numbers*

- Find the prime factorisations of the numbers.
- To find the LCM, multiply together the highest power of each prime factor occurring in any of the numbers.
- To find the HCF, multiply together the lowest power of each prime factor common to all the numbers.

Activity 11 *Using prime factorisations to find LCMs and HCFs*

Use prime factorisations to find the lowest common multiple and highest common factor of each of the following sets of numbers.

(a) 18 and 30   (b) 9, 18 and 30

The next activity illustrates a method that can be useful when you want to find the lowest common multiple or highest common factor of just two numbers, which are fairly small.

Activity 12 *Finding LCMs and HCFs of two numbers*

In the diagram below, one circle contains all the prime factors of 84, and the other circle contains all the prime factors of 280. The common prime factors of 84 and 280 are in the overlap of the two circles.

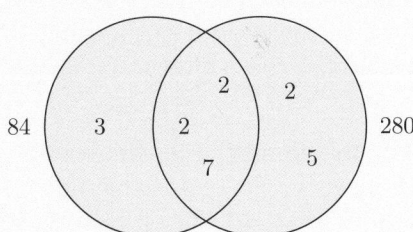

(a) Can you explain how you could use this diagram to find the lowest common multiple and highest common factor of 84 and 280? (In Example 2 a different method was used to determine that the LCM is 840 and the HCF is 28.)

(b) Check your answer to Activity 11(a) by drawing a similar diagram for 18 and 30 and using it to find the lowest common multiple and highest common factor of these numbers.

1.5 Powers

In the previous subsection you worked with powers of prime numbers. This subsection is all about powers.

As you know, 'raising a number to a power' means multiplying the number by itself a specified number of times. For example, raising 2 to the power 3 gives

$$2^3 = 2 \times 2 \times 2.$$

Here the number 2 is called the **base number** or just **base**, and the superscript 3 is called the **power**, **index** or **exponent**. The word 'power' is also used to refer to the *result* of raising a number to a power – for example, we say that 2^3 is a **power** of 2. When we write expressions like 2^3, we say that we are using **index form** or **index notation**.

The **square** and **cube** of a number are the results of raising it to the powers 2 and 3, respectively. For example, the square of 2 is $2^2 = 4$, and the cube of 2 is $2^3 = 8$. (Remember that, for example, 2^2 is read as 'two squared' and 2^3 is read as 'two cubed'. The power 2^5 is read as 'two to the power five' or 'two to the five'. Other indices are read in a similar way to 2^5.)

Standard large numbers like a billion and a trillion can be conveniently described in index form. You can see from the following table that it is easier to look at the index than to count the number of zeros!

As you saw in Unit 1, the plural of 'index' in this context is 'indices'. The word 'index' has several different meanings in English – confusingly, some have plural 'indices', while others have plural 'indexes'! For example, there are *indexes* at the backs of the course books.

Sometimes you may hear 2^5 read as 'two to the fifth', which is short for 'two to the fifth power'. This is potentially confusing, as it could be interpreted as $2^{1/5}$, but the meaning is normally clear from the context.

Table 1 Standard large numbers

Name	Number	Number in index form
million	1 000 000	10^6
billion (UK and US)	1 000 000 000	10^9
trillion (UK and US)	1 000 000 000 000	10^{12}

The word 'billion' meant 10^{12} rather than 10^9 in the UK until 1974, when the British government decided to switch to the American meaning to avoid confusion in financial markets. Similarly, the word 'trillion' has traditionally meant 10^{18} in the UK, but there has recently been a switch to the American meaning, 10^{12}. Many European countries still use these alternative meanings of 'billion' and 'trillion'.

A *googol* is 10^{100}, but this number is of limited use, as it is greater than the number of atoms in the observable universe! The word was invented by a child, nine-year-old Milton Sirotta, in 1938. He was asked by his uncle, the American mathematician Edward Kasner (1878–1955), what name he would give to a really large number. The word 'googol' gave rise, via a playful misspelling, to the name of the internet search engine Google.

The next few pages describe some basic rules for carrying out calculations with numbers written in index form. It is worth getting to know these rules, as they will be useful later.

Multiplying numbers in index form

The superscript notation for powers was introduced by the French philosopher and mathematician René Descartes (1596–1650). It was Descartes who wrote the famous philosophical statement *'Cogito ergo sum'*, commonly interpreted in English as 'I think, therefore I am'.

Sometimes you need to multiply numbers in index form. For example, suppose that you want to multiply 10^2 by 10^3. You can do this as follows:

$$10^2 \times 10^3 = (10 \times 10) \times (10 \times 10 \times 10) = 10^5.$$

You can see that the total number of 10s multiplied together is the sum of the indices, $2 + 3 = 5$. In general we have the following fact.

To multiply numbers in index form that have the same base number, add the indices:

$$a^m \times a^n = a^{m+n}.$$

Example 3 *Multiplying powers*

Write each of the following products concisely in index form.

(a) $3^4 \times 3^5$ (b) 5×5^9 (c) $2^4 \times 3^7$

(d) $2^3 \times 7 \times 2^2 \times 7^2$ (e) 9×3^5

Solution

(a) $3^4 \times 3^5 = 3^{4+5} = 3^9$

(b) Multiplying 5^9 by 5 increases the index by 1, because the number 5 is the same as 5^1.

$$5 \times 5^9 = 5^{1+9} = 5^{10}$$

(c) The product $2^4 \times 3^7$ cannot be written any more concisely, as the base numbers are different.

(d) $2^3 \times 7 \times 2^2 \times 7^2 = 2^{3+2} \times 7^{1+2} = 2^5 \times 7^3$

(e) The base numbers are different, but they can be made the same.
$$9 \times 3^5 = 3^2 \times 3^5 = 3^{2+5} = 3^7$$

Activity 13   *Multiplying powers*

(a) Write each of the following products concisely in index form.

   (i) $3^4 \times 3^3$ (ii) $7^2 \times 7$ (iii) $10^2 \times 10^3 \times 10^4$

   (iv) $3^4 \times 5^{12}$ (v) 8×2^5 (vi) 9×3

(b) Use the facts that $294 = 2 \times 3 \times 7^2$ and $441 = 3^2 \times 7^2$ to find the prime factorisation of 294×441.

Activity 14   *Making an estimate by multiplying powers*

Make an estimate to check the claim made on page 132 that a googol (10^{100}) is greater than the number of atoms in the observable universe. To make your estimate, assume that all the atoms in the universe are hydrogen atoms (it is thought that hydrogen atoms account for about 90% of the mass of the universe), and use the following very rough approximations.

   The number of hydrogen atoms in a kilogram is about 10^{27}.
   The mass of a star and its planets is about 10^{30} kg.
   The number of stars in a galaxy is about 10^{12}.
   The number of galaxies in the observable universe is about 10^{11}.

Dividing numbers in index form

Suppose that you want to divide 10^5 by 10^2. You can do this as follows:

$$10^5 \div 10^2 = \frac{10^5}{10^2} = \frac{10 \times 10 \times 10 \times 10 \times 10}{10 \times 10}.$$

If you now divide both top and bottom of the fraction by 10, and then by 10 again, you obtain

$$\frac{\cancel{10} \times \cancel{10} \times 10 \times 10 \times 10}{\cancel{10} \times \cancel{10}} = 10 \times 10 \times 10 = 10^3.$$

You can see that the final number of 10s multiplied together is the difference of the indices, $5 - 2 = 3$.

In general we have the following fact.

> To divide numbers in index form that have the same base number, subtract the indices:
> $$\frac{a^m}{a^n} = a^{m-n}.$$

Activity 15 *Dividing powers*

(a) Write each of the following quotients concisely in index form.

(i) $7^6 \div 7^2$ (ii) $\dfrac{2^{16}}{2^8}$ (iii) $\dfrac{5^{21}}{3^5}$ (iv) $\dfrac{3^7}{3}$

(b) Use the facts that $3456 = 2^7 \times 3^3$ and $12 = 2^2 \times 3$ to find the prime factorisation of $3456 \div 12$.

Raising a number in index form to a power

Suppose that you want to find $(10^2)^3$, the cube of 10^2. To raise any number to the power 3, you multiply three 'copies' of the number together. So

$$(10^2)^3 = 10^2 \times 10^2 \times 10^2 = (10 \times 10) \times (10 \times 10) \times (10 \times 10) = 10^6.$$

The total number of 10s multiplied together is the product of the indices, $2 \times 3 = 6$. In general we have the following fact.

> To raise a number in index form to a power, multiply the indices:
> $$(a^m)^n = a^{mn}.$$

Activity 16 *Raising numbers in index form to powers*

Write each of the following numbers concisely in index form.

(a) $(5^2)^4$ (b) $(7^3)^2$ (c) $(3^5)^3 \times 3^2$ (d) $\dfrac{(2^5)^2}{2^2}$ (e) $\left(\dfrac{2^5}{2^2}\right)^2$

Raising a product or quotient to a power

There are two more facts that are often useful when you are working with powers. Notice that

$$\begin{aligned}
(2 \times 10)^3 &= (2 \times 10) \times (2 \times 10) \times (2 \times 10) \\
&= 2 \times 2 \times 2 \times 10 \times 10 \times 10 \\
&= 2^3 \times 10^3.
\end{aligned}$$

This is an example of the first fact in the box below. The second fact is similar, but it applies to quotients rather than products.

> A power of a product is the same as a product of powers;
> a power of a quotient is the same as a quotient of powers:
> $$(a \times b)^n = a^n \times b^n; \qquad \left(\dfrac{a}{b}\right)^n = \dfrac{a^n}{b^n}.$$

Activity 17 *Finding powers of products and quotients*

(a) (i) Use the fact that $21 = 3 \times 7$ to find the prime factorisation of 21^4.

(ii) Use the fact that $24 = 2^3 \times 3$ to find the prime factorisation of 24^3.

(b) Express the following numbers as fractions in their simplest form without using your calculator.

(i) $\left(\dfrac{2}{7}\right)^2$ (ii) $\left(\dfrac{3}{4}\right)^3$

Raising negative numbers to powers

So far you have worked with natural numbers raised to powers. Other numbers, such as negative numbers, can also be raised to powers. For example,

$$(-2)^2 = (-2) \times (-2) = 4$$

and

$$(-2)^3 = (-2) \times (-2) \times (-2) = 4 \times (-2) = -8.$$

Remember that a negative number times a negative number is a positive number, and a negative number times a positive number is a negative number.

Activity 18 *Calculating powers of negative numbers*

Calculate the following powers.

(a) $(-3)^2$ (b) $(-3)^3$ (c) $(-2)^4$ (d) $(-1)^4$ (e) $(-1)^5$

In calculations like those in Activity 18, every pair of negative numbers multiplies together to give a positive number. So you can see that

* a negative number raised to an even power is positive,

* a negative number raised to an odd power is negative.

In this subsection you have seen five rules that you can use when you are working with numbers in index form. These rules apply to powers of any type of number, including negative numbers and numbers that are not whole. They are known as **index laws**, and they are summarised in the box below. You will meet four other index laws later in the unit.

> **Some index laws**
>
> $a^m \times a^n = a^{m+n}$ $\qquad \dfrac{a^m}{a^n} = a^{m-n}$
>
> $(a^m)^n = a^{mn}$
>
> $(a \times b)^n = a^n \times b^n$ $\qquad \left(\dfrac{a}{b}\right)^n = \dfrac{a^n}{b^n}$

2 Rational numbers

Many numbers besides the natural numbers are needed for everyday mathematics. This section is about the *rational numbers*, which include the natural numbers and many of the other numbers that you are used to working with.

2.1   What is a rational number?

A **rational number** is a number that can be written in the form
$$\frac{\text{integer}}{\text{integer}},$$
that is, as an integer divided by an integer.

Remember that the *integers* are
$$\ldots, -3, -2, -1, 0, 1, 2, 3, \ldots.$$

The following numbers can be written in this form.

- *Any fraction*
  Fractions such as $\frac{3}{4}$ and $\frac{11}{2}$ are already written in the form above and so they are rational numbers.

- *Any mixed number*
  Mixed numbers like $5\frac{1}{3}$ can be written as top-heavy fractions, so they are rational numbers. For example, $5\frac{1}{3} = \frac{16}{3}$.

- *Any whole number*
  For example, $7 = \frac{7}{1}$ and $0 = \frac{0}{1}$.

Remember that *infinite* means 'endless, without limit'; *finite* is the opposite of infinite.

- *Any decimal number with a finite number of digits after the decimal point*
  For example,
  $$0.23 = \frac{23}{100} \quad \text{and} \quad 41.2058 = \frac{412\,058}{10\,000}.$$

- *Some decimal numbers with infinitely many digits after the decimal point*
  For example,
  $$0.333\,333\ldots = \tfrac{1}{3}.$$

- *The negative of any of the numbers above*
  For example,
  $$-4 = \frac{-4}{1} \quad \text{and} \quad -\frac{3}{4} = \frac{-3}{4}.$$

Perhaps you are now wondering whether there are any numbers that are not rational numbers! Well, some decimal numbers with infinitely many digits after the decimal point are not rational numbers. But nearly every number that you use in a real-world application of mathematics is a rational number.

The rest of this subsection is about the decimal forms of rational numbers. In particular, you will find out exactly which numbers with infinitely many digits after the decimal point are rational numbers.

Rational numbers as decimals

Every rational number can be written as a decimal. To do this, you divide the integer on the top of the fraction by the integer on the bottom. For example,
$$\tfrac{5}{8} = 5 \div 8 = 0.625.$$

When you find a decimal in this way, there are two possibilities for the outcome. You might get a decimal number that has only a finite number of digits after the decimal point. This is called a **terminating decimal**. For example, the decimal form 0.625 of $\frac{5}{8}$ is terminating – it has only three digits after the decimal point. Alternatively, you might get a decimal number with a block of one or more digits after the decimal point that repeats indefinitely. For example,

$$\frac{2}{3} = 0.666\,666\ldots$$

and

$$\frac{7}{54} = 0.1\underline{296}\,\underline{296}\,\underline{296}\,\underline{296}\,\underline{296}\ldots.$$

A decimal like this is called a **recurring decimal**.

There are two alternative notations for indicating a recurring decimal. You can either put a dot above the first and last digit of the repeating block, or you can put a line above the whole repeating block. For example,

$$\frac{2}{3} = 0.\dot{6} = 0.\overline{6}$$

and

$$\frac{7}{54} = 0.1\dot{2}9\dot{6} = 0.1\overline{296}.$$

If you would like to know why you always get either a terminating or recurring decimal when you write a rational number as a decimal, then take a look at the document explaining this on the course website. You need to think about long division!

So every rational number, when written in decimal form, is a terminating or recurring decimal. But is the reverse true? That is, is every terminating or recurring decimal a rational number?

Certainly, every *terminating* decimal is a rational number, since it can be written in the form of an integer divided by an integer, as you saw at the beginning of this subsection. It is less obvious that every *recurring* decimal is a rational number, but in fact this is true as well.

So another way to think of the rational numbers is as follows.

> The rational numbers are the decimal numbers that are terminating or recurring.

Now consider the number below – it has an infinite number of digits after the decimal point, and they follow a pattern of larger and larger blocks of 0s separated by individual 1s:

0.010 010 001 000 010 000 01 . . . .

This number is not a terminating decimal and it is not a recurring decimal, as it does not have a *fixed number* of digits that keep repeating. So it is not a rational number! You will learn more about numbers that are not rational in the next section. First, however, it is important to make sure that you are proficient with arithmetical operations on fractions. In the next few subsections you can revise and practise these operations, and learn more about powers.

Of course, if you use your calculator to divide the integer on the top of a fraction by the integer on the bottom, then you will only be able to see the first few digits of the answer. You can obtain more digits by carrying out long division by hand or by using mathematical software. However, the number of digits on your calculator is adequate for most practical purposes.

We know that the first sentence here is true, but that doesn't mean that we know that the reverse is true. Every poodle is a dog, but not every dog is a poodle!

If you go on to study further mathematics courses, then you may learn how to convert recurring decimals to fractions. It is done using basic algebra.

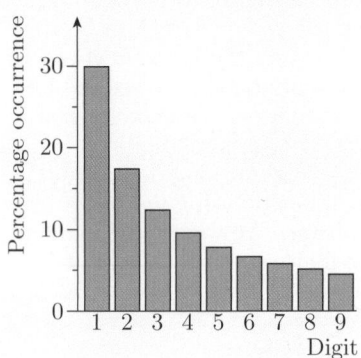

Figure 8　The percentage occurrences of $1, 2, \ldots, 9$ as the first digits of numbers in a table of data

One situation where numbers occur in the real world is in tables of data, such as the prices of stocks and shares, sports statistics, the populations of towns, utility bills, and so on. You might expect that if you were to investigate the first digits of the numbers in such a table then you would find that each of the possible digits $1, 2, \ldots, 9$ occurs equally often. Surprisingly, this is usually not the case. In fact, the digit 1 tends to occur about 30.1% of the time, the digit 2 about 17.6% of the time, and the larger digits less and less frequently, up to the digit 9, which tends to occur about 4.6% of the time. The chart in Figure 8 illustrates how often each digit tends to occur.

This phenomenon was investigated in the 1930s by the American physicist Frank Benford (1883–1948). He analysed thousands of tables of data, and found a mathematical formula that predicts the percentage occurrences of each digit. This formula is known as *Benford's law*. The first rigorous mathematical explanation of it was provided in 1995. Benford's law has been successfully applied to fraud detection, since tables of invented data usually do not have this property.

2.2　Adding and subtracting fractions

You saw in the previous subsection that every rational number can be expressed as a fraction. It is important that you are able to add, subtract, multiply and divide fractions, not only by using your calculator, but also on paper.

One reason for this is that it is useful to be able to do arithmetic with simple fractions without having to resort to your calculator. Another reason is that you will need to use these techniques when you learn algebra later in the course, and you cannot use your calculator for fractions that contain letters! This subsection, and the next, give you a chance to practise these techniques.

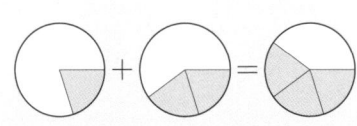

Figure 9　$\frac{1}{5} + \frac{2}{5} = \frac{3}{5}$

First let's look at adding and subtracting fractions. Remember that you can add or subtract fractions only if they are of the same type – that is, if they have the same denominator.

For example, if one-fifth of a pizza is eaten and then another two-fifths of the pizza is eaten, then altogether three-fifths of the pizza has been eaten (Figure 9):

$$\frac{1}{5} + \frac{2}{5} = \frac{3}{5}.$$

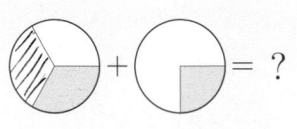

Figure 10　$\frac{2}{3} + \frac{1}{4} = ?$

If fractions are not of the same type, then you cannot add or subtract them directly. For example, if two-thirds of a pizza is eaten and then another quarter of the pizza is eaten, then it is not so clear what fraction of the pizza has been eaten. You cannot carry out the following addition directly (Figure 10):

$$\frac{2}{3} + \frac{1}{4}.$$

In this situation, you need to change the fractions into equivalent fractions of the same type – that is, you need to write them with a **common denominator**. Here you can change the fractions into twelfths (Figure 11):

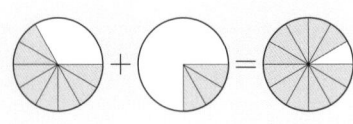

Figure 11　$\frac{8}{12} + \frac{3}{12} = \frac{11}{12}$

$$\frac{2}{3} + \frac{1}{4} = \frac{8}{12} + \frac{3}{12} = \frac{11}{12}.$$

So eleven-twelfths of the pizza has been eaten.

Remember that to find a fraction equivalent to a particular fraction, you multiply (or divide) top and bottom of the fraction by the same number. For example,

$$\frac{2}{3} = \frac{2 \times 4}{3 \times 4} = \frac{8}{12} \quad \text{and} \quad \frac{1}{4} = \frac{1 \times 3}{4 \times 3} = \frac{3}{12}.$$

The next example illustrates some more things to remember when you add and subtract fractions. You should find it helpful to watch the tutorial clip, and there is more detail on fraction calculations in Maths Help.

For advice on adding and subtracting fractions, see Maths Help Module 1, Subsections 3.10–3.11.

Example 4 *Adding and subtracting fractions*

 Tutorial clip

Carry out the following fraction additions and subtractions.

(a) $\frac{3}{8} + \frac{1}{8}$ (b) $\frac{4}{9} + \frac{5}{6}$ (c) $\frac{6}{7} - \frac{2}{3}$ (d) $1\frac{2}{3} + 4\frac{1}{2}$

Solution

(a) The denominators are the same, so add the numerators. Write the answer in its simplest form, by cancelling.

$$\frac{3}{8} + \frac{1}{8} = \frac{4}{8} = \frac{\overset{1}{\cancel{4}}}{\underset{2}{\cancel{8}}} = \frac{1}{2}$$

(b) Make the denominators the same. Write each fraction with denominator 18.

$$\frac{4}{9} + \frac{5}{6} = \frac{8}{18} + \frac{15}{18} = \frac{23}{18} = 1\frac{5}{18}$$

The answer $\frac{23}{18}$ cannot be simplified by cancelling. You can write it as the mixed number $1\frac{5}{18}$ or just leave it as $\frac{23}{18}$.

Some advice on how to choose the common denominator is given after the strategy box below.

(c) Write each fraction with denominator 21.

$$\frac{6}{7} - \frac{2}{3} = \frac{18}{21} - \frac{14}{21} = \frac{4}{21}$$

(d) Add the integer parts of the mixed numbers together, and add the fractional parts together, separately.

$$1\frac{2}{3} + 4\frac{1}{2} = 1 + 4 + \frac{2}{3} + \frac{1}{2} = 5 + \frac{4}{6} + \frac{3}{6} = 5 + \frac{7}{6} = 5 + 1\frac{1}{6} = 6\frac{1}{6}$$

Here is the strategy that was used in Example 4.

I've got lots of fraction calculations to do tonight!

> **Strategy** *To add or subtract fractions*
>
> - Make sure that the denominators are the same. (You may need to write each fraction as an appropriate equivalent fraction.)
> - Add or subtract the numerators.
> - Write the answer in its simplest form.

The trickiest part of adding and subtracting fractions is making the denominators the same. How do you decide what the common denominator should be?

For example, the calculation $\frac{4}{9} + \frac{5}{6}$ in Example 4(b) was carried out by writing each fraction with denominator 18, but how was the number 18 chosen?

The number chosen has to be a common multiple of 9 and 6, because you must be able to get it by multiplying the denominator 9 by something, and also by multiplying the denominator 6 by something.

One way to obtain a common multiple of 6 and 9 is just to multiply them together.

Any common multiple of 9 and 6 will do, but if you want to keep the numbers in the calculation as small as possible, and keep the cancelling of the answer to a minimum, then the best number to choose is the *lowest* common multiple of 9 and 6, which is 18.

Once you have chosen 18, then since $18 = 2 \times 9$ and $18 = 3 \times 6$, you have to multiply the numerator and denominator of the first and second fractions by 2 and 3, respectively, as done in Example 4(b).

Here are some fraction additions and subtractions for you to try.

Activity 19 *Adding and subtracting fractions*

(a) Carry out the following fraction additions and subtractions without using your calculator.

(i) $\frac{2}{9} + \frac{4}{9}$ (ii) $\frac{7}{8} + \frac{9}{24}$ (iii) $\frac{11}{14} - \frac{3}{14}$ (iv) $\frac{5}{6} - \frac{1}{4}$

(v) $2\frac{1}{7} + 4\frac{2}{7}$ (vi) $3\frac{3}{4} - 1\frac{1}{5}$ (vii) $\frac{1}{2} + \frac{1}{3} + \frac{1}{4}$

(b) At the time of writing, half of all UK car drivers are under the age of 35, and a seventh are over the age of 65. What fraction are between 35 and 65 years of age?

2.3 Multiplying and dividing fractions

Suppose that three-quarters of the three-year-olds in a village attend a nursery, and half of them attend full-time. What fraction of the toddlers attend nursery full-time? The answer is a half of three-quarters, and you can see from Figure 12 that this is three-eighths. That is,

$$\frac{1}{2} \times \frac{3}{4} = \frac{3}{8}.$$

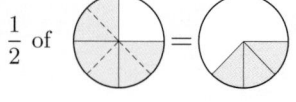

Figure 12 $\frac{1}{2} \times \frac{3}{4} = \frac{3}{8}$

This is an example of the following general rule.

Strategy *To multiply fractions*

Multiply the numerators together and multiply the denominators together.

For advice on multiplying fractions, see Maths Help Module 1, Subsection 3.12.

The next example illustrates some more things to remember when you multiply fractions.

Tutorial clip

Example 5 *Multiplying fractions*

Carry out the following fraction multiplications.

(a) $\frac{2}{5} \times \frac{4}{7}$ (b) $2 \times \frac{3}{7}$ (c) $\frac{2}{3} \times \frac{5}{6}$ (d) $3\frac{2}{3} \times \frac{5}{6}$

Solution

(a) $\frac{2}{5} \times \frac{4}{7} = \frac{8}{35}$

(b) Here you can either use the strategy, as is done below, or use the fact that 2 lots of 3 sevenths is 6 sevenths.

$$2 \times \frac{3}{7} = \frac{2}{1} \times \frac{3}{7} = \frac{6}{7}$$

(c) Here the number 2 is a factor of the numerator of the first fraction and also a factor of the denominator of the second fraction, so it is a factor of both the numerator and denominator of the product. It is easier to cancel factors like this *before* multiplying.

$$\frac{2}{3} \times \frac{5}{6} = \frac{\overset{1}{\cancel{2}}}{3} \times \frac{5}{\underset{3}{\cancel{6}}} = \frac{5}{9}$$

(d) To multiply by a mixed number, first convert it to a top-heavy fraction.

$$3\frac{2}{3} \times \frac{5}{6} = \frac{11}{3} \times \frac{5}{6} = \frac{55}{18} = 3\frac{1}{18}$$

The answer can be left as $\frac{55}{18}$ if you wish.

Here are some fraction multiplications for you to try.

Activity 20 *Multiplying fractions*

(a) Carry out the following fraction multiplications.

   (i) $\frac{5}{8} \times \frac{3}{10}$ (ii) $\frac{4}{5} \times 3$ (iii) $1\frac{1}{3} \times 2\frac{5}{6}$

(b) At a particular college, two-fifths of the students have jobs, and of these a quarter work for more than 35 hours per week. What fraction of the students work for more than 35 hours per week?

In the next activity you are asked to use your knowledge of fractions to spot a mistake in a newspaper article.

Activity 21 *Fractions in the media*

The newspaper clipping below is fictitious, but it contains a mistake similar to one that appeared in a real newspaper article. Can you find and correct the mistake? (Assume that half of teenagers are girls and half are boys.)

> **Teenage smoking rate still too high**
>
> A quarter of teenage girls and a sixth of teenage boys smoke regularly, research has shown. That's five-twelfths of the teenage population - nearly half of all teenagers.

Now let's look at how to divide fractions. The rule for doing this can be conveniently described using the idea of the *reciprocal* of a number.

A number and its **reciprocal** multiply together to give 1. So, for example,

$$0.25 \text{ is the reciprocal of } 4, \text{ since } 0.25 \times 4 = 1;$$

This line is labelled '(1)' because there is a reference to it further down the page. Labels like this are used occasionally throughout the course.

$$\tfrac{3}{2} \text{ is the reciprocal of } \tfrac{2}{3}, \text{ since } \tfrac{3}{2} \times \tfrac{2}{3} = 1. \tag{1}$$

Another way to think of the reciprocal of a number is that it is 1 divided by the number. For example,

$$\text{the reciprocal of } 5 \text{ is } \tfrac{1}{5} = 0.2.$$

As you can see from example (1), to find the reciprocal of a fraction, you just 'turn it upside down'. For example,

$$\text{the reciprocal of } \tfrac{3}{4} \text{ is } \tfrac{4}{3};$$
$$\text{the reciprocal of } \tfrac{1}{4} \text{ is } \tfrac{4}{1} = 4;$$
$$\text{the reciprocal of } 2 \text{ is } \tfrac{1}{2}, \text{ since } 2 = \tfrac{2}{1}.$$

Now suppose that you have a length of string, and you plan to cut it into two-metre pieces. How many pieces will you get? The answer is the length of the string in metres, divided by 2.

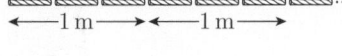

Next suppose that you want to cut the string into pieces one-third of a metre long. How many pieces will you get this time? The answer is the length of the string in metres, divided by $\tfrac{1}{3}$. But how do you divide by $\tfrac{1}{3}$?

Figure 13   A length of string cut into one-third metre pieces

Well, you get three pieces for every metre of string (Figure 13), so you need to multiply the length of the string by 3. So dividing by $\tfrac{1}{3}$ is the same as multiplying by 3, the reciprocal of $\tfrac{1}{3}$.

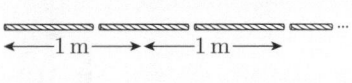

What if you want to cut the string into pieces two-thirds of a metre long – how many pieces will you get this time (Figure 14)? That is, how do you divide by $\tfrac{2}{3}$? Well, the number of pieces two-thirds of a metre long is half of the number of pieces one-third of a metre long. So to divide by $\tfrac{2}{3}$ you multiply by 3 and then by $\tfrac{1}{2}$, which is the same as multiplying by $\tfrac{3}{2}$. So dividing by $\tfrac{2}{3}$ is the same as multiplying by $\tfrac{3}{2}$, the reciprocal of $\tfrac{2}{3}$.

Figure 14   A length of string cut into two-third metre pieces

These are examples of the following general rule.

Strategy   *To divide by a fraction*

Multiply by its reciprocal.

Here are some more examples.

Tutorial clip

Example 6   *Dividing fractions*

Carry out the following fraction divisions.

(a) $\tfrac{4}{7} \div \tfrac{5}{6}$ (b) $\tfrac{5}{6} \div \tfrac{1}{4}$ (c) $\tfrac{3}{5} \div 2$

Solution

(a) $\tfrac{4}{7} \div \tfrac{5}{6} = \tfrac{4}{7} \times \tfrac{6}{5} = \tfrac{24}{35}$

(b) ☺ Here, once you have turned the second fraction upside down, there are factors that you can cancel before multiplying. ☺

$$\frac{5}{6} \div \frac{1}{4} = \frac{5}{6} \times \frac{4}{1} = \frac{5}{\underset{3}{6}} \times \frac{\overset{2}{4}}{1} = \frac{10}{3} = 3\tfrac{1}{3}$$

(c) $\frac{3}{5} \div 2 = \frac{3}{5} \div \frac{2}{1} = \frac{3}{5} \times \frac{1}{2} = \frac{3}{10}$

Here are some fraction divisions for you to try.

For advice on dividing fractions, see Maths Help Module 1, Subsections 3.13–3.14.

Activity 22 *Dividing fractions*

(a) Carry out the following fraction divisions without using your calculator.

   (i) $6 \div \frac{4}{3}$ (ii) $\frac{3}{8} \div \frac{11}{24}$ (iii) $1\frac{1}{3} \div 1\frac{7}{9}$

   Hint: In part (iii) you must turn the mixed numbers into top-heavy fractions before dividing.

(b) A factory worker makes a particular type of metal component. It takes him $1\frac{1}{4}$ hours to make each component, and he works a $37\frac{1}{2}$-hour week. How many components can he make in a week?

2.4 Negative indices

Consider the following powers of 2:

   $2^1,\ 2^2,\ 2^3,\ 2^4,\ 2^5,\ \ldots$.

You could extend this list as far to the right as you like. But does it also make sense to extend it to the left? That is, do all the powers in the following list mean something?

   $\ldots,\ 2^{-3},\ 2^{-2},\ 2^{-1},\ 2^0,\ 2^1,\ 2^2,\ 2^3,\ 2^4,\ 2^5,\ \ldots$

The powers with positive indices have the pattern shown below.

$$\ldots\ 2^{-3}\quad 2^{-2}\quad 2^{-1}\quad 2^0\quad 2^1\ \ 2^2\ \ 2^3\ \ 2^4\ \ 2^5\ \ldots$$
$$\div 2\ \ \div 2\ \ \div 2\ \ \div 2$$

If you assume that this pattern continues leftwards, then 2^0 must be the number that you get by dividing 2^1 by 2. That is,

   $2^0 = 2^1 \div 2 = 2 \div 2 = 1.$

Similarly, 2^{-1} must be the number that you get by dividing 2^0 by 2. That is,

   $2^{-1} = 2^0 \div 2 = 1 \div 2 = \frac{1}{2}.$

If the pattern continues in this way, then the zero and negative indices must have the meanings suggested in Table 2.

Table 2 Powers of 2

Power		2^{-3}	2^{-2}	2^{-1}	2^0	2^1	2^2	2^3	2^4	2^5	
Meaning	$\ldots$	$\frac{1}{2^3}$	$\frac{1}{2^2}$	$\frac{1}{2}$	1	2	2^2	2^3	2^4	2^5	$\ldots$

But do these meanings make sense? Do they work with the index laws that you met in Subsection 1.5? For example, one of the index laws is

   $$\frac{a^m}{a^n} = a^{m-n}.$$

If you use this rule and the meanings in Table 2 to work out 2^4 divided by 2^5, then you obtain

$$\frac{2^4}{2^5} = 2^{4-5} = 2^{-1} = \frac{1}{2}.$$

This makes sense, because

$$\frac{2^4}{2^5} = \frac{\overset{1}{\cancel{2}} \times \overset{1}{\cancel{2}} \times \overset{1}{\cancel{2}} \times \overset{1}{\cancel{2}}}{\underset{1}{\cancel{2}} \times \underset{1}{\cancel{2}} \times \underset{1}{\cancel{2}} \times \underset{1}{\cancel{2}} \times 2} = \frac{1}{2}.$$

Similarly, if you use the same rule and the meanings in Table 2 to work out 2^3 divided by 2^3, then you obtain

$$\frac{2^3}{2^3} = 2^{3-3} = 2^0 = 1,$$

which also makes sense, since 2^3 divided by 2^3 is 1.

It turns out that the meanings of negative and zero indices suggested in Table 2 do work with all the index laws you saw in Section 1. So, these are the meanings that are used. They are summarised below, and you can think of them as two further index laws.

Negative and zero indices

A non-zero number raised to the power zero is 1:
$$a^0 = 1.$$

A non-zero number raised to a negative power is the reciprocal of the number raised to the corresponding positive power:
$$a^{-n} = \frac{1}{a^n}.$$

The rules above hold for all appropriate numbers. So, for example, in the second rule a can be any number except 0; it cannot be 0 because you cannot divide by 0. The first rule also holds for all values of a except 0 (the power 0^0 has no meaning).

The second index law above tells you that, in particular,

$$a^{-1} = \frac{1}{a}.$$

So raising a number to the power -1 is the same as finding its reciprocal. For example,

$$\left(\tfrac{2}{3}\right)^{-1} = \tfrac{3}{2}.$$

Example 7 *Working with negative and zero indices*

Find the values of the following numbers.

(a) 17^0 (b) 3^{-2} (c) 0.4^{-3} (d) $\left(\tfrac{3}{4}\right)^{-1}$ (e) $\left(\tfrac{3}{4}\right)^{-2}$

Solution

(a) $17^0 = 1$

(b) $3^{-2} = \dfrac{1}{3^2} = \dfrac{1}{9}$

(c) $0.4^{-3} = \dfrac{1}{0.4^3} = \dfrac{1}{0.064} = 15.625$

(d) $\left(\dfrac{3}{4}\right)^{-1} = \dfrac{4}{3}$

(e) $\left(\dfrac{3}{4}\right)^{-2} = \dfrac{1}{\left(\dfrac{3}{4}\right)^2} = \dfrac{1}{\left(\dfrac{9}{16}\right)} = 1 \times \dfrac{16}{9} = \dfrac{16}{9}$

Alternatively, you can use the index law $(a^m)^n = a^{mn}$.

$\left(\dfrac{3}{4}\right)^{-2} = \left(\left(\dfrac{3}{4}\right)^{-1}\right)^2 = \left(\dfrac{4}{3}\right)^2 = \dfrac{4^2}{3^2} = \dfrac{16}{9}$

Activity 23   *Working with negative and zero indices*

Find the values of the following numbers, without using your calculator.

(a) $\left(\dfrac{1}{2}\right)^0$ (b) 7^{-1} (c) 7^{-2} (d) $\left(\dfrac{1}{3}\right)^{-1}$ (e) $\left(\dfrac{2}{5}\right)^{-1}$

(f) $\left(\dfrac{1}{3}\right)^{-2}$ (g) $\left(\dfrac{2}{5}\right)^{-2}$ (h) $\left(\dfrac{1}{3}\right)^{-3}$ (i) $(-2)^{-3}$

2.5   Scientific notation

In this subsection you will see one reason why negative and zero indices are useful. Some of the numbers used in mathematics, science, medicine and economics are very big or very small. For example, the population of the world at the time of writing is estimated to be about 6 770 000 000 people, and the mass of the Sun is about 1 990 000 000 000 000 000 000 000 000 000 kilograms. In contrast, the mass of an atom of hydrogen is about 0.000 000 000 000 000 000 000 000 001 674 kilograms. It's hard to tell how many zeros there are in these numbers without laboriously counting them.

Numbers like these are more usefully expressed in **scientific notation** (which is also called **standard form**). To write a number in scientific notation, you express it as a number between 1 and 10, multiplied by a power of 10. The number between 1 and 10 can be equal to 1 but not 10. Any number can be expressed in this form – here are some examples:

$$250 = 2.5 \times 10^2,$$
$$25 = 2.5 \times 10^1,$$
$$2.5 = 2.5 \times 10^0,$$
$$0.25 = 2.5 \times 10^{-1}.$$

Here is a strategy that you can use to express a number in scientific notation.

Strategy   *To express a number in scientific notation*

1. Place a decimal point between the first and second significant digits to give a number between 1 and 10.

2. Count to find the power of 10 by which this number should be multiplied (or divided) to restore it to the original number.

Tutorial clip

Example 8   *Converting numbers to scientific notation*

Express the following numbers in scientific notation.

(a) 523.4   (b) 0.006 71

Solution

(a) Place a decimal point between the first and second significant digits. This gives 5.234. To restore this number to the original number, you need to move the decimal point 2 places to the right. That is, you need to multiply by 10^2.

$$523.4 = 5.234 \times 10^2$$

(b) Place a decimal point between the first and second significant digits. This gives 6.71. To restore this number to the original number, you need to move the decimal point 3 places to the left. That is, you need to divide by 10^3, which is the same as multiplying by $\dfrac{1}{10^3}$, or 10^{-3}.

$$0.00671 = 6.71 \times 10^{-3}$$

I've told you, I don't work with small children, small animals or small numbers!

You might be wondering why scientific notation involves numbers between 1 and 10, rather than a different size of number. For example, why is it preferable to write 75 000 as 7.5×10^4 rather than, say, 75×10^3 or 0.75×10^5? The reason is simply that this notation has been agreed as the one that everyone will use. Using consistent notation makes it easy to compare numbers and carry out calculations. For example, you can tell immediately that 2.1×10^5 is greater than 7.5×10^4 by comparing the powers of ten. It is less easy to tell whether 2.1×10^5 is greater than 75×10^3.

To convert a number from scientific notation back to ordinary notation, you just need to carry out the multiplication or division. Since the multiplication or division is by a power of ten, this involves moving the decimal point. For example,

$$8.22 \times 10^4 = 82\,200,$$
$$1.7 \times 10^{-2} = 1.7 \div 10^2 = 0.017.$$

Activity 24   *Converting to and from scientific notation*

(a) Write the following numbers in scientific notation.

   (i) 7723   (ii) 50 007 000   (iii) 0.100 34   (iv) 0.000 208

(b) Write the following quantities in scientific notation, using the approximate values given at the start of this subsection:

   (i)   the population of the world

   (ii)   the mass of the Sun

   (iii) the mass of a hydrogen atom.

(c) Convert the following numbers from scientific notation to ordinary notation.

   (i) 7.04×10^3 (ii) 4.52×10^4 (iii) 7.3×10^{-2}

   (iv) 2.045×10^{-5}

Calculations using numbers in scientific notation

You will use your calculator to carry out most calculations involving numbers in scientific notation, and you will be asked to practise this in an activity at the end of this subsection. However, there may be occasions, perhaps when you are making a quick estimate, when it is more convenient to work out the answer by hand, using the index laws that you met earlier. The next example illustrates how to do this.

Example 9   *Calculating with numbers in scientific notation*

Carry out the following calculations without using your calculator.

(a) $(4 \times 10^9) \times (6 \times 10^{-7})$

(b) $\dfrac{4 \times 10^2}{8 \times 10^4}$

(c) $(8.2 \times 10^{-2}) - (5.4 \times 10^{-3})$

Give the answer to part (c) to two significant figures.

The brackets in parts (a) and (c) are included to help make the calculations clear. They are not essential because the calculations would mean the same without the brackets, by the BIDMAS rules.

Solution

(a) Use the index law $a^m \times a^n = a^{m+n}$ to multiply the powers of ten.

$$(4 \times 10^9) \times (6 \times 10^{-7}) = (4 \times 6) \times (10^9 \times 10^{-7}) = 24 \times 10^{9-7} = 24 \times 10^2$$

To write the answer in scientific notation, write the first number, 24, in scientific notation and use the same index law again.

$$24 \times 10^2 = 2.4 \times 10^1 \times 10^2 = 2.4 \times 10^3$$

(b) Use the index law $\dfrac{a^m}{a^n} = a^{m-n}$ to divide the powers of ten.

$$\frac{4 \times 10^2}{8 \times 10^4} = \frac{4}{8} \times \frac{10^2}{10^4} = 0.5 \times 10^{2-4} = 0.5 \times 10^{-2}$$

Write the answer in scientific notation.

$$0.5 \times 10^{-2} = 5 \times 10^{-1} \times 10^{-2} = 5 \times 10^{-3}$$

(c) To add or subtract numbers in scientific notation, first write the numbers so that the powers of 10 are the same.

$8.2 \times 10^{-2} = 8.2 \times 10 \times 10^{-3} = 82 \times 10^{-3}$, so

$$\left(8.2 \times 10^{-2}\right) - \left(5.4 \times 10^{-3}\right) = \left(82 \times 10^{-3}\right) - \left(5.4 \times 10^{-3}\right).$$

Now 82 lots of 10^{-3} subtract 5.4 lots of 10^{-3} is the same as $(82 - 5.4)$ lots of 10^{-3}.

$$\left(82 \times 10^{-3}\right) - \left(5.4 \times 10^{-3}\right) = (82 - 5.4) \times 10^{-3}$$
$$= 76.6 \times 10^{-3}$$
$$= 77 \times 10^{-3} \text{ (to 2 s.f.).}$$

Write the answer in scientific notation.

$$77 \times 10^{-3} = 7.7 \times 10 \times 10^{-3} = 7.7 \times 10^{-2}.$$

So $\left(8.2 \times 10^{-2}\right) - \left(5.4 \times 10^{-3}\right) = 7.7 \times 10^{-2}$ (to 2 s.f.).

You can use some of the methods illustrated in Example 9 to do the following two activities.

Activity 25   *Financial bailouts*

The following headline appeared in a British newspaper in February 2009, following the collapse of several banks.

A trillion is 10^{12}, and a million is 10^6.

> Bailouts add £1.5 trillion to Britain's public debt.

The British population in 2009 was approximately 61 million.

(a) Write both quantities quoted above in scientific notation.

(b) Work out the figure that should go in the gap in the extended headline below. (Give your answer to two significant figures.)

> Bailouts add £1.5 trillion to Britain's public debt – that's about [   ] for each person!

Activity 26   *The world's smallest guitar*

Figure 15 shows a scanning electron microscope image of a tiny 'nano guitar', made out of silicon at Cornell University in 1997. According to the press release, it is 10 micrometres long, and each of the six strings is about 50 nanometres wide. Use the conversion factors given in the margin to answer the following questions.

1 micrometre $= 10^{-6}$ metres.
1 nanometre $= 10^{-9}$ metres.

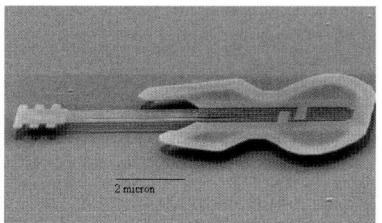

(a) An ordinary guitar is about 1 metre long. How many times smaller is the nano guitar?

(b) A human hair is about 100 micrometres wide. How many times smaller is the width of a string of the nano guitar?

Figure 15   The nano guitar

In the next activity you will learn how to use your calculator to carry out calculations involving scientific notation.

Activity 27   *Scientific notation on your calculator*

If you do not have the Course Guide to hand, then you can come back to this activity later.

Work through Subsection 4.5 of the Course Guide.

3   Irrational numbers and real numbers

3.1   What is an irrational number?

In the previous section you saw that many of the numbers that you use in everyday mathematics are *rational* numbers – they can be expressed in the form of an integer divided by an integer.

You saw that all rational numbers have decimal forms that are either terminating or recurring, and so the following number is not a rational number:

$$0.010\,010\,001\,000\,010\,000\,01\ldots.$$

But perhaps numbers like this are not 'proper' numbers? Perhaps the rational numbers form a sensible system of numbers that we can use for all the usual purposes, and we can ignore decimals like the one above? Let's consider whether this suggestion is workable.

One reason why we need numbers is so we can measure things, such as length. To measure length, you first need to decide on a unit of measure. The unit could be a centimetre, a metre, an inch or any other convenient length – it doesn't matter what it is, as long as it is used consistently.

Suppose that we decide to measure lengths in cm. Here are the lengths of some lines measured using this unit.

——   1 cm

————   2 cm

—————   3 cm

— $\frac{1}{2}$ cm

———— $1\frac{19}{27}$ cm

The numbers here, 1, 2, 3, $\frac{1}{2}$ and $1\frac{19}{27}$, are all rational numbers. But is the length of *every* line, measured in centimetres, a rational number?

Consider the diagonal lines in the tiling pattern in Figure 16. The pattern is made of four square tiles, each with sides 1 cm long, and each tile is half green and half yellow. The diagonal lines form the sides of a green square. Suppose that the length of these diagonal lines is d cm.

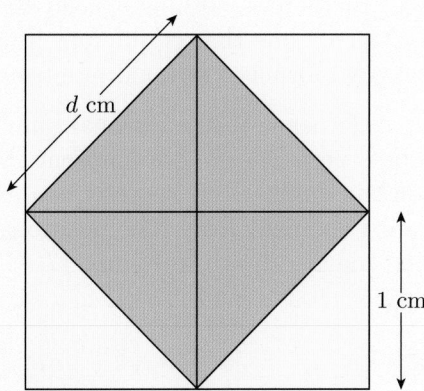

Figure 16   A tiling pattern

The whole pattern is a square with sides 2 cm long, so its area is $2 \times 2 = 4\,\text{cm}^2$. The green square covers half the total area, so its area is $\frac{1}{2} \times 4 = 2\,\text{cm}^2$. Therefore

$$d \times d = 2, \quad \text{that is,} \quad d^2 = 2.$$

For help with calculating areas, see Maths Help Module 7, Subsection 3.1.

So the length of the sides of the green square, measured in cm, is a number whose square is 2.

Now it turns out that there is no rational number whose square is 2. This is not obvious, but it can be proved in an argument that takes about half a page. So the length of the sides of the green square, measured in centimetres, is not a rational number.

A proof that there is no rational number whose square is 2 is available on the course website – take a look if you are interested.

Many other lines can be drawn, using similar patterns, that have lengths that are not rational numbers. This is true no matter what unit of measurement you choose. Of course, in practice you can approximate these lengths by rational numbers, but a sensible system of numbers should include the numbers that are the exact lengths of these lines.

So the rational numbers by themselves do not form a workable system of numbers. We must include many more numbers to obtain such a system, and the new numbers that we must include are the ones with decimal forms that are not terminating or recurring – that is, we must include the decimals with an infinite number of digits after the decimal point but no repeating block of digits. These numbers are called the **irrational numbers** – they are the numbers that are not rational.

One of these numbers is the number whose square is 2. This number is called the *square root* of 2, and is denoted by $\sqrt{2}$. Here it is to the first 120 decimal places:

> 1.414 213 562 373 095 048 801 688 724 209 698 078 569 671 875 376 948 073 176 679 737 990 732 478 462 107 038 850 387 534 327 641 572 735 013 846 230 912 297 024 . . . .

The irrational numbers also include the positive number whose square is 3, which is denoted by $\sqrt{3}$, and many other *roots* of rational numbers. You will learn more about these later in this section. Another irrational number is the number

$$\pi = 3.141\,592\,653\,589\,793\,238\,46\ldots,$$

which you encountered in Unit 2. This is an important number in mathematics, and you will see it used frequently in some of the later units of the course. You have also seen that

> $0.010\,010\,001\,000\,010\,000\,01\ldots$

is an irrational number, but there is nothing special about this one, except that its digits have a pattern – one that is different from the type of pattern found in the decimal forms of rational numbers.

The irrational numbers together with the rational numbers form the **real numbers**. These numbers are sufficient to represent the length of any line or curve. Each point on the number line represents a real number, so the number line is often called the **real line**. The positions of some real numbers on the number line are shown in Figure 17.

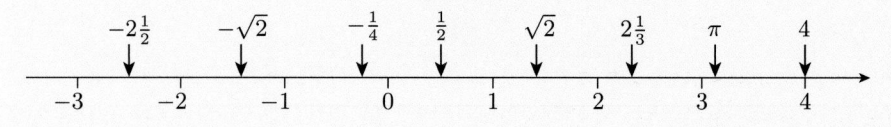

Figure 17   The real line

There are infinitely many rational numbers and infinitely many irrational numbers.

The Pythagoreans, who were followers of the philosophy of the Greek mathematician Pythagoras (c. 569 BC – c. 494 BC), one of the most elusive figures of antiquity, developed a theory of proportions between natural numbers. They believed in a harmony between the world and natural numbers and their theory can be considered to be an early version of our theory of rational numbers. However, they soon discovered that not all relations between quantities (such as lengths) can be expressed by such proportions. So the idea of irrational numbers dawned early in the history of mathematics, about two and a half thousand years ago.

Figure 18 shows a useful way to think about the types of numbers that you have learned about in this unit. It illustrates the facts that all of the natural numbers are also integers, all of the integers are also rational numbers and all of the rational numbers are also real numbers.

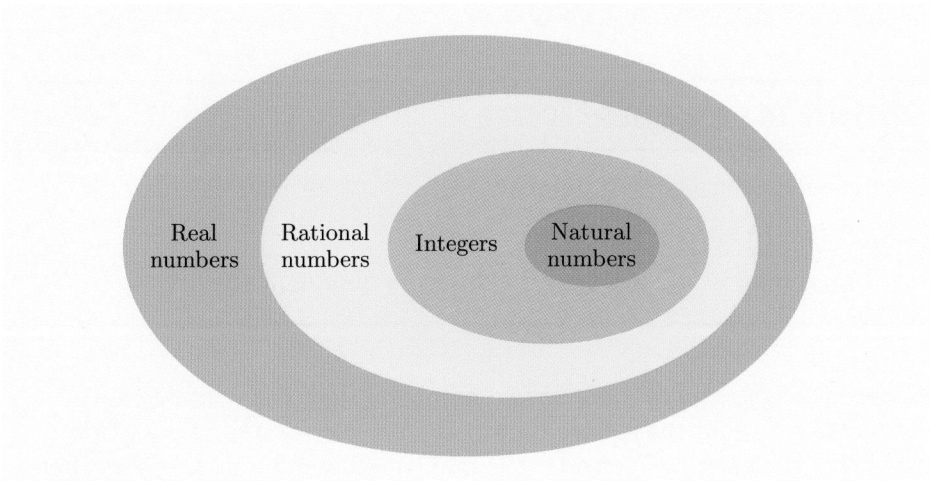

Figure 18 Types of numbers

If you go on to take further mathematics courses, then you can learn about yet another type of number. The *complex numbers* include all the numbers above, and also many 'imaginary' numbers, such as the square root of -1. The idea of imaginary numbers might seem strange, but the complex numbers have a huge number of useful practical applications.

3.2 Roots of numbers

As you have seen, the number whose square is 2 is called the *square root of 2*.

In general, a **square root** of a number is a number that when multiplied by itself gives the original number. For example, 6 is a square root of 36, since $6 \times 6 = 36$. The number -6 is also a square root of 36, since $(-6) \times (-6) = 36$.

Every positive number has two square roots – a positive one and a negative one. However, when we say *the* square root of a number, we mean the positive one. The symbol '$\pm$', which means 'plus or minus', can be useful when you are working with square roots; for example, you can write that the two square roots of 36 are ± 6.

The *positive* square root of a positive number is denoted by the symbol $\sqrt{}$. For example,
$$\sqrt{36} = 6.$$

There are other types of roots apart from square roots. A **cube root** of a number is a number such that if you multiply three 'copies' of it together, you get the original number. For example, 4 is a cube root of 64, because
$$4 \times 4 \times 4 = 64.$$
And -4 is a cube root of -64, because
$$(-4) \times (-4) \times (-4) = -64.$$
Similarly, a fourth root of a number is a number such that if you raise it to the power 4 you get the original number. For example, 5 and -5 are both

Because $\sqrt{}$ means the positive square root, it is incorrect to write, for example,
  'if $x^2 = 4$, then
  $x = \sqrt{4} = \pm 2$'.
What you should write is
  'if $x^2 = 4$, then
  $x = \pm\sqrt{4} = \pm 2$'.

The symbol $\sqrt{}$ for roots was introduced by René Descartes (see page 132).

fourth roots of 625, because $5^4 = 625$ and $(-5)^4 = 625$. Similarly, numbers can have fifth, sixth and seventh roots, and so on.

The (positive) cube root of a positive number is denoted by $\sqrt[3]{}$, the positive fourth root of a positive number is denoted by $\sqrt[4]{}$, and so on. So, for example, $\sqrt[3]{64} = 4$ and $\sqrt[4]{625} = 5$.

The symbols $\sqrt{}$, $\sqrt[3]{}$ and so on can also be used with zero under the root sign. Zero has just one square root, one cube root and so on, namely zero.

Activity 28 *Finding roots of numbers*

Find the following roots of numbers, without using your calculator.

(a) $\sqrt{9}$ (b) $\sqrt[3]{8}$ (c) $\sqrt[3]{27}$ (d) $\sqrt[4]{16}$

(e) Two square roots of 9   (f) Two fourth roots of 16

If you know the square roots of two numbers, then you can use this information to find the square root of the product or a quotient of the numbers. For example, consider the numbers 9 and 25, with square roots 3 and 5, respectively. By the index law $(a \times b)^n = a^n \times b^n$, we know that

$$(3 \times 5)^2 = 3^2 \times 5^2,$$

that is

$$(3 \times 5)^2 = 9 \times 25.$$

So the positive square root of 9×25 is 3×5. That is,

$$\sqrt{9 \times 25} = \sqrt{9} \times \sqrt{25}.$$

This is an example of the first rule in the box below. The second rule is similar, but it applies to quotients rather than products.

A square root of a product is the same as a product of square roots; a square root of a quotient is the same as a quotient of square roots:

$$\sqrt{a \times b} = \sqrt{a} \times \sqrt{b}, \qquad \sqrt{\frac{a}{b}} = \frac{\sqrt{a}}{\sqrt{b}}.$$

Analogous rules apply to cube roots, fourth roots, and so on.

Activity 29 *Finding more roots of numbers*

(a) Use the fact that $1764 = 36 \times 49$ to find $\sqrt{1764}$.

(b) Find the following square roots of fractions, without using your calculator.

   (i) $\sqrt{\dfrac{4}{9}}$ (ii) $\sqrt{\dfrac{36}{49}}$ (iii) $\sqrt{\dfrac{1}{4}}$

You can use your calculator to find square roots of numbers, and you will get a chance to practise this later in this section.

3.3 Surds

All the roots of numbers that you were asked to find in the last subsection were rational, but most numbers have irrational roots.

In particular, the square root of any natural number that is not a perfect square is irrational. So, for example, the following roots are irrational:

$$\sqrt{2},\ \sqrt{3},\ \sqrt{5},\ \sqrt{6}.$$

A *perfect square* is another name for a square number.

Because numbers like these cannot be written down exactly as terminating decimals or fractions, we often leave them just as they are in calculations and in the answers to calculations. For example, we might say that the two square roots of 2 are

$$\sqrt{2} \text{ and } -\sqrt{2}.$$

Or we might say that the answer to a calculation is

$$1 + \sqrt{5}.$$

The advantage of this approach is that it allows us to work with exact numbers, rather than approximations. This can help to simplify calculations.

Expressions like

$$\sqrt{2},\quad -\sqrt{2},\quad \sqrt[3]{2},\quad 1+\sqrt{5},\quad \frac{\sqrt{7}}{3},\quad 1-2\sqrt{5} \quad \text{and} \quad \sqrt{2}+\sqrt{3}$$

are called *surds*. That is, a **surd** is a numerical expression containing one or more irrational roots of numbers.

The word 'surd' is derived from the same Latin word as 'absurd'! The original Latin word is 'surdus', which means deaf or silent.

Surds are usually written concisely, in a similar way to formulas. Multiplication signs are usually omitted, though sometimes it is necessary or helpful to include them. Also, where a number and a root are multiplied together, it is conventional to write the number first. So the ~~last~~ *penultimate* surd in the list above is written as

$$1 - 2\sqrt{5}, \text{ rather than } 1 - \sqrt{5} \times 2, \text{ say.}$$

It is also usually helpful to write surds in the simplest form possible. In the rest of this subsection you will learn some ways to simplify surds.

First, you can sometimes use the rule

$$\sqrt{a \times b} = \sqrt{a} \times \sqrt{b}$$

to make the number under a square root sign smaller. For example,

$$\sqrt{12} = \sqrt{4 \times 3} = \sqrt{4} \times \sqrt{3} = 2\sqrt{3}.$$

You can simplify a square root in this way whenever the number under the square root sign has a factor that is a perfect square greater than 1.

The first ten perfect squares are 1, 4, 9, 16, 25, 36, 49, 64, 81, 100.

Here are some more examples.

Example 10 *Simplifying square roots*

 Tutorial clip

Simplify the following surds, where possible.

(a) $\sqrt{18}$ (b) $\sqrt{10}$ (c) $\sqrt{60}$ (d) $\sqrt{80}$

Solution

(a) Write 18 as the product of a perfect square and another number, then use the rule $\sqrt{a \times b} = \sqrt{a} \times \sqrt{b}$.

$$\sqrt{18} = \sqrt{9 \times 2} = \sqrt{9} \times \sqrt{2} = 3\sqrt{2}$$

(b) The factors of 10 are 1, 2, 5 and 10. None of the factors greater than 1 is a perfect square, so the surd $\sqrt{10}$ cannot be simplified. It is already in its simplest form.

(c) Write 60 as the product of a perfect square and another number.

$$\sqrt{60} = \sqrt{4 \times 15} = \sqrt{4} \times \sqrt{15} = 2\sqrt{15}$$

Now check whether 15 has any square factors. It doesn't, so the surd can't be simplified any further.

(d) Write 80 as the product of a perfect square and another number.

$$\sqrt{80} = \sqrt{4 \times 20} = \sqrt{4} \times \sqrt{20} = 2\sqrt{20}$$

The number 20 has a square factor, so the surd can be simplified further.

$$\sqrt{80} = 2\sqrt{20} = 2\sqrt{4 \times 5} = 2\sqrt{4} \times \sqrt{5} = 2 \times 2\sqrt{5} = 4\sqrt{5}$$

In Example 10(d) the square root of 80 was simplified by first using the fact that the perfect square 4 is a factor of 80. The working can be shortened by instead using the fact that the larger perfect square 16 is a factor of 80. This gives

$$\sqrt{80} = \sqrt{16 \times 5} = \sqrt{16} \times \sqrt{5} = 4\sqrt{5}.$$

So it's most efficient to begin with the largest square factor that you can spot, but if it turns out that there is a larger one, then you can simplify the root in stages, as in Example 10(d).

Activity 30   Simplifying square roots

Simplify the following surds, where possible, without using your calculator.

(a) $\sqrt{8}$ (b) $\sqrt{75}$ (c) $\sqrt{15}$ (d) $\sqrt{56}$ (e) $\sqrt{48}$

Another way in which you can sometimes simplify surds is to simplify products of two or more square roots. Where two identical square roots are multiplied together, this is easily done: for example, $\sqrt{2} \times \sqrt{2} = 2$. Where different square roots are multiplied together, you can use the rule

$$\sqrt{a \times b} = \sqrt{a} \times \sqrt{b}.$$

For example, $\sqrt{2} \times \sqrt{3} = \sqrt{2 \times 3} = \sqrt{6}$. Here are some more examples of multiplying square roots in surds.

Tutorial clip

Example 11   Multiplying roots

Simplify the following surds, where possible.

(a) $\left(\sqrt{3}\right)^2$ (b) $2\sqrt{5} \times 4\sqrt{5}$ (c) $\sqrt{6} \times \sqrt{3}$ (d) $5\sqrt{2} \times 3\sqrt{10}$

Solution

(a) $\left(\sqrt{3}\right)^2 = \sqrt{3} \times \sqrt{3} = 3$

(b) Multiply the numbers together, and multiply the roots together.

$$2\sqrt{5} \times 4\sqrt{5} = 8\sqrt{5}\sqrt{5} = 8 \times 5 = 40$$

(c) Use the rule $\sqrt{a \times b} = \sqrt{a} \times \sqrt{b}$ to multiply the roots. Simplify the result.

$$\sqrt{6} \times \sqrt{3} = \sqrt{6 \times 3} = \sqrt{18} = \sqrt{9 \times 2} = \sqrt{9} \times \sqrt{2} = 3\sqrt{2}$$

(d) Multiply the numbers together, and multiply the roots together using the rule $\sqrt{a \times b} = \sqrt{a} \times \sqrt{b}$. Simplify the result.

$$5\sqrt{2} \times 3\sqrt{10} = 15\sqrt{2 \times 10}$$
$$= 15\sqrt{20}$$
$$= 15\sqrt{4 \times 5}$$
$$= 15\sqrt{4}\sqrt{5}$$
$$= 15 \times 2\sqrt{5}$$
$$= 30\sqrt{5}$$

Activity 31   *Multiplying roots*

Simplify the following surds, where possible, without using your calculator.

(a) $(\sqrt{7})^2$ (b) $\sqrt{7} \times 3\sqrt{7}$ (c) $\sqrt{7} \times \sqrt{14}$ (d) $\sqrt{2} \times \sqrt{8}$
(e) $2\sqrt{3} \times 3\sqrt{2}$ (f) $2\sqrt{3} \times 2\sqrt{15}$

You can also sometimes simplify quotients of roots in surds. Both of the rules

$$\sqrt{a \times b} = \sqrt{a} \times \sqrt{b}, \qquad \sqrt{\frac{a}{b}} = \frac{\sqrt{a}}{\sqrt{b}},$$

can be useful.

Example 12   *Dividing roots*

 Tutorial clip

Simplify the following surds.

(a) $\dfrac{\sqrt{15}}{\sqrt{3}}$ (b) $\dfrac{2}{\sqrt{2}}$

Solution

(a) Use the rule $\sqrt{a \times b} = \sqrt{a} \times \sqrt{b}$.

$$\frac{\sqrt{15}}{\sqrt{3}} = \frac{\sqrt{3} \times \sqrt{5}}{\sqrt{3}} = \frac{\overset{1}{\cancel{\sqrt{3}}} \times \sqrt{5}}{\underset{1}{\cancel{\sqrt{3}}}} = \sqrt{5}$$

Alternatively, use the rule $\sqrt{\dfrac{a}{b}} = \dfrac{\sqrt{a}}{\sqrt{b}}$.

$$\frac{\sqrt{15}}{\sqrt{3}} = \sqrt{\frac{15}{3}} = \sqrt{5}$$

(b) Use the fact that $2 = \sqrt{2} \times \sqrt{2}$.

$$\frac{2}{\sqrt{2}} = \frac{\sqrt{2} \times \sqrt{2}}{\sqrt{2}} = \frac{\overset{1}{\cancel{\sqrt{2}}} \times \sqrt{2}}{\underset{1}{\cancel{\sqrt{2}}}} = \sqrt{2}$$

Alternatively, multiply top and bottom by $\sqrt{2}$.

$$\frac{2}{\sqrt{2}} = \frac{2 \times \sqrt{2}}{\sqrt{2} \times \sqrt{2}} = \frac{2\sqrt{2}}{2} = \sqrt{2}$$

Activity 32   Dividing roots

Simplify the following surds without using your calculator.

(a) $\dfrac{\sqrt{10}}{\sqrt{2}}$ (b) $\dfrac{5}{\sqrt{5}}$ (c) $\dfrac{\sqrt{8}}{\sqrt{2}}$ (d) $\dfrac{8}{\sqrt{2}}$

For example,
$$\sqrt{3}+\sqrt{5}=3.96\ldots,$$
whereas
$$\sqrt{3+5}=\sqrt{8}=2.82\ldots.$$

You cannot usually simplify a sum of two different roots, such as $\sqrt{3}+\sqrt{5}$, in a surd. In general,

$$\sqrt{a}+\sqrt{b}\ \text{ is } not \text{ equal to }\ \sqrt{a+b}.$$

However, you can add, or subtract, roots that are the same. This is illustrated in the next example.

 Tutorial clip

Example 13   Adding and subtracting roots

Simplify the following surds, where possible.

(a) $2\sqrt{3}+4\sqrt{3}$ (b) $5\sqrt{2}-\sqrt{2}$ (c) $\sqrt{3}+2\sqrt{5}$ (d) $\sqrt{12}-\sqrt{3}$

Solution

(a) Two lots of $\sqrt{3}$ plus four lots of $\sqrt{3}$ is six lots of $\sqrt{3}$.
$$2\sqrt{3}+4\sqrt{3}=6\sqrt{3}$$

(b) Five lots of $\sqrt{2}$ subtract one lot of $\sqrt{2}$ is four lots of $\sqrt{2}$.
$$5\sqrt{2}-\sqrt{2}=4\sqrt{2}$$

(c) The roots in the surd $\sqrt{3}+2\sqrt{5}$ are different (and are in their simplest forms), so the surd cannot be simplified.

(d) First write $\sqrt{12}$ in its simplest form. Then proceed as before.
$$\sqrt{12}-\sqrt{3}=\sqrt{4\times3}-\sqrt{3}=\sqrt{4}\sqrt{3}-\sqrt{3}=2\sqrt{3}-\sqrt{3}=\sqrt{3}$$

Activity 33   Adding and subtracting roots

Simplify the following surds, where possible, without using your calculator.

(a) $\sqrt{3}+\sqrt{3}$ (b) $\sqrt{2}+\sqrt{5}$ (c) $7\sqrt{3}-2\sqrt{3}$ (d) $5\sqrt{8}-2\sqrt{2}$

Here is a summary of some of the ways in which surds can be simplified.

To simplify surds

- Simplify roots of integers with square factors.
- Simplify products and quotients of roots.
- Add or subtract roots that are the same.

3.4 Fractional indices

Earlier in this unit you worked with powers that have negative and zero indices, such as 3^{-2} and 2^0. Meanings were given for these indices, and you saw that with these meanings the index laws work for negative and zero indices.

Meanings can also be given to *fractional* indices in such a way that the index laws work for these indices. For example, consider the power $5^{\frac{1}{2}}$. If this power has a meaning, then by the index law

$$a^m \times a^n = a^{m+n},$$

we have

$$5^{\frac{1}{2}} \times 5^{\frac{1}{2}} = 5^{\frac{1}{2}+\frac{1}{2}} = 5^1 = 5,$$

so you can see that a sensible meaning for $5^{\frac{1}{2}}$ is

$$5^{\frac{1}{2}} = \sqrt{5}.$$

(The meaning $5^{\frac{1}{2}} = \sqrt{5}$ is preferable to $5^{\frac{1}{2}} = -\sqrt{5}$ because you would expect $5^{\frac{1}{2}}$ to be positive. For example, you have seen that $5^0 = 1$ and $5^1 = 5$, so you would expect $5^{\frac{1}{2}}$ to be between 1 and 5.)

Similarly,

$$5^{\frac{1}{3}} \times 5^{\frac{1}{3}} \times 5^{\frac{1}{3}} = 5^{\frac{1}{3}+\frac{1}{3}+\frac{1}{3}} = 5^1 = 5,$$

so a sensible meaning for $5^{\frac{1}{3}}$ is

$$5^{\frac{1}{3}} = \sqrt[3]{5}.$$

By the index law
$a^m \times a^n = a^{m+n}$, we have
$$5^{\frac{1}{3}} \times 5^{\frac{1}{3}} \times 5^{\frac{1}{3}}$$
$$= 5^{\frac{1}{3}+\frac{1}{3}} \times 5^{\frac{1}{3}}$$
$$= 5^{\frac{1}{3}+\frac{1}{3}+\frac{1}{3}}.$$

We make the following definition, which you can think of as another index law.

> Raising a number to the power $\frac{1}{2}$ is the same as taking its square root, raising a number to the power $\frac{1}{3}$ is the same as taking its cube root, and so on:
> $$a^{\frac{1}{n}} = \sqrt[n]{a}.$$

This rule, together with the index laws that you have already met, can be used to give a meaning to any fractional index. For example, using the index law

$$(a^m)^n = a^{mn},$$

we obtain

$$5^{\frac{4}{3}} = 5^{\frac{1}{3} \times 4} = \left(5^{\frac{1}{3}}\right)^4 = \left(\sqrt[3]{5}\right)^4.$$

It is worth stating the general rule illustrated here as another index law.

> Raising a number to the power $\dfrac{m}{n}$ is the same as raising the nth root of the number to the power m:
> $$a^{\frac{m}{n}} = \left(\sqrt[n]{a}\right)^m.$$

The two rules in the boxes above hold for all appropriate numbers. For example, a must be positive, since the notation $\sqrt{}$ applies only to positive numbers.

Here are some more examples of fractional indices.

Example 14   Raising numbers to fractional indices

Find the values of the following powers.

(a) $9^{\frac{1}{2}}$ (b) $4^{\frac{3}{2}}$ (c) $4^{-\frac{3}{2}}$

Solution

(a) $9^{\frac{1}{2}} = \sqrt{9} = 3$

(b) $4^{\frac{3}{2}} = \left(\sqrt{4}\right)^3 = 2^3 = 8$

(c) Use the index law $a^{-n} = \dfrac{1}{a^n}$, then use the result of part (b).

$$4^{-\frac{3}{2}} = \frac{1}{4^{\frac{3}{2}}} = \frac{1}{8} \quad \text{(by part (b))}$$

Activity 34   Raising numbers to fractional indices

Find the values of the following powers, without using your calculator.

(a) $16^{\frac{1}{2}}$ (b) $9^{\frac{3}{2}}$ (c) $4^{-\frac{1}{2}}$ (d) $4^{\frac{5}{2}}$ (e) $27^{\frac{2}{3}}$

Now that you have met fractional indices, you can see that the two rules for square roots that you met earlier,

$$\sqrt{a \times b} = \sqrt{a} \times \sqrt{b} \quad \text{and} \quad \sqrt{\frac{a}{b}} = \frac{\sqrt{a}}{\sqrt{b}},$$

are really just index laws in disguise. They are obtained by taking $n = \frac{1}{2}$ in the index laws

$$(a \times b)^n = a^n \times b^n \quad \text{and} \quad \left(\frac{a}{b}\right)^n = \frac{a^n}{b^n},$$

which you met in Section 1.

You have seen that the index in a power can be any rational number. Perhaps you are now wondering whether an index can be irrational? For example, does $2^{\sqrt{2}}$ have a meaning? Powers like this do have precise meanings, which you can learn about in detail in more advanced mathematics courses. The basic idea is that since

$$\sqrt{2} = 1.414\,213\,562\,373\,09\ldots,$$

you can work out the value of $2^{\sqrt{2}}$ as accurately as you like by using as many decimal places of the decimal form of $\sqrt{2}$ as you like. For example, one approximation to $2^{\sqrt{2}}$ is

$$2^{1.414} = 2.664\,749\,650\,184\,04\ldots,$$

and a more accurate one is

$$2^{1.414\,213} = 2.665\,143\,103\,797\,72\ldots,$$

and so on. The indices here, 1.414 and $1.414\,213$, and so on, are rational, as they are terminating decimals.

So the index in a power can be any real number. All the index laws that you have seen in this unit hold for indices and base numbers that are any real numbers (except that the numbers must be appropriate for the operations – for example, you cannot divide by zero, or take a square root of a negative number). Here is a summary of the index laws.

Index laws

$$a^m \times a^n = a^{m+n} \qquad \frac{a^m}{a^n} = a^{m-n}$$

$$(a^m)^n = a^{mn}$$

$$(a \times b)^n = a^n \times b^n \qquad \left(\frac{a}{b}\right)^n = \frac{a^n}{b^n}$$

$$a^0 = 1 \qquad a^{-n} = \frac{1}{a^n}$$

$$a^{\frac{1}{n}} = \sqrt[n]{a} \qquad a^{\frac{m}{n}} = \left(\sqrt[n]{a}\right)^m$$

Powers and surds on your calculator

In the final activity of this section you can practise using your calculator for calculations involving powers, scientific notation and surds.

Activity 35 *Powers and surds on your calculator*

Work through Subsection 4.6 of the Course Guide.

If you do not have the Course Guide to hand, then you can come back to this activity later.

4 Ratios

4.1 What is a ratio?

If you have made vinaigrette salad dressing, then you may remember that the recipe is 3 parts oil to 1 part vinegar. So, for example, you could mix 30 ml oil and 10 ml vinegar, or 120 ml oil and 40 ml vinegar, or perhaps, if you need a lot of salad dressing, 1.5 l oil and 0.5 l vinegar.

We say that the **ratio** of oil to vinegar is

$3 : 1.$

This ratio is equivalent to

$30 : 10,$ and $120 : 40,$ and $1.5 : 0.5.$

The symbol ':' is a colon; it is read as 'to' when it is in a ratio.

Notice that ratios do not have units.

Ratios can contain more than two numbers. For example, to make a particular type of concrete, you need 1 part cement to 2 parts sand to 4 parts gravel. That is, the ratio of cement to sand to gravel is

$1 : 2 : 4.$

So, for example, you could mix 1 shovelful of cement with 2 shovelfuls of sand and 4 shovelfuls of gravel, or 5 shovelfuls of cement with 10 shovelfuls of sand and 20 shovelfuls of gravel, and so on, depending on how much concrete you need.

You met a particular type of ratio in Unit 2, when you looked at map scales. You saw that if the scale factor of a map is 500 000, say, then the map scale is often given in the form

$$1 : 500\,000.$$

This is the ratio between a distance on the map and the corresponding distance on the ground.

A ratio is changed to an **equivalent ratio** in the same way that a fraction is changed to an equivalent fraction.

> **To find a ratio equivalent to a given ratio**
>
> Multiply or divide each number in the ratio by the same non-zero number.

If the numbers in a ratio are rational, then the ratio has a simplest form in the same way that fractions do. A ratio is in its **simplest form** when each number in the ratio is a whole number, and these numbers are cancelled down as much as possible – that is, they have no common factors.

Example 15 *Simplifying ratios*

Express the following ratios in their simplest forms.

(a) $9 : 12 : 6$ (b) $0.5 : 1.25$

Solution

(a) Divide each number by 3.

$$9 : 12 : 6 = \frac{9}{3} : \frac{12}{3} : \frac{6}{3} = 3 : 4 : 2$$

The numbers 3, 4 and 2 have no common factors, so this ratio can't be cancelled down any further.

(b) Multiply by 100 to give integers, then cancel down.

$$0.5 : 1.25 = (100 \times 0.5) : (100 \times 1.25) = 50 : 125 = \frac{50}{25} : \frac{125}{25} = 2 : 5$$

Alternatively, you might spot that you can just multiply by 4.

$$0.5 : 1.25 = (4 \times 0.5) : (4 \times 1.25) = 2 : 5$$

Activity 36 *Simplifying ratios*

Express the following ratios in their simplest forms.

(a) $18 : 3$ (b) $12 : 60 : 18$ (c) $2 : 0.5 : 1.5$ (d) $6 : 12 : 7$

When you are working with ratios that contain just two numbers, it is sometimes helpful to convert them to the form 'number : 1'. For example, this can help you to compare different ratios. You can convert a ratio to this form by dividing both numbers by the second number. For example,

$$5 : 6 = \frac{5}{6} : \frac{6}{6} = 0.83 : 1 \quad \text{(to 2 d.p.)}.$$

Activity 37   *Comparing ratios*

A mother has the choice of two different after-school clubs for her child. Club A takes 46 children and has 6 staff, and club B takes 25 children and has 4 staff.

(a) Find the ratio of children to staff for each club in the form 'number : 1', rounding your answer to one decimal place.

(b) Which club has fewer children per member of staff?

Writing ratios in the form 'number : 1' can also help you to find approximate ratios, which can be useful when you want to compare quantities.

Example 16   *Finding an approximate ratio*

A secondary school has 823 boys and 534 girls on its roll. What is the approximate ratio of boys to girls at the school?

Solution

💭 Find the ratio in the form 'number : 1', approximate the number by a whole number or simple fraction, then simplify the ratio. 💭

The ratio of boys to girls is

$$823 : 534 = \frac{823}{534} : \frac{534}{534}$$
$$= 1.54\ldots : 1$$
$$\approx \tfrac{3}{2} : 1$$
$$= 3 : 2.$$

You can approximate $1.54\ldots$ by $1.5 = \tfrac{3}{2}$.

So there are about three boys for every two girls.

The next activity asks you to find two approximate ratios.

Activity 38   *Finding approximate ratios*

In 2007 the population of the UK was about 61.0 million. About 31.9 million of these people were taxpayers (paying income tax). About 3.9 million of the taxpayers paid tax at the higher rate, and the remainder paid tax at the basic rate or less. Calculate approximate values for the following ratios.

(a) The ratio of taxpayers to non-taxpayers

(b) The ratio of ordinary taxpayers to higher-rate taxpayers (where the ordinary taxpayers are those paying tax at the basic rate or less)

Sometimes you need to divide a quantity in a particular ratio. The next example illustrates how to do this.

Example 17   *Dividing a quantity in a ratio*

Three flatmates, Amy, Becky and Carol, have agreed to contribute to their joint budget in the ratio $5:2:3$. The flatmates' expenses amount to £1250 per month. How much does each flatmate contribute to this?

Solution

We have to divide £1250 in the ratio $5:2:3$.

The total number of parts in the ratio is $5+2+3=10$.

Amy contributes 5 of the 10 parts, so the amount that she contributes is

$$\frac{5}{10} \times £1250 = £625.$$

Similarly, Becky contributes

$$\frac{2}{10} \times £1250 = £250,$$

and Carol contributes

$$\frac{3}{10} \times £1250 = £375.$$

(Check: £625 + £250 + £375 = £1250.)

For every £5 Amy contributes, Becky contributes £2 and Carol contributes £3.

Activity 39   *Dividing a quantity in a ratio*

A bottle of screenwash for cars recommends the following ratios of screenwash to water.

Conditions	Ratio of screenwash to water
Summer	$1:20$
Winter	$1:4$
Severe winter	$2:1$

Calculate, to the nearest 100 ml, the volume of screenwash and the volume of water you would need to make 2 litres of diluted screenwash for your car in the following conditions.

(a) Winter   (b) Severe winter

Other forms of ratio

Ratios that contain just two numbers are sometimes written as fractions. For example, the ratio $3:2$ can be written as $\frac{3}{2}$. The first and second numbers in the ratio become the numerator and denominator of the fraction, respectively. The fraction representing a ratio can also be written as a decimal: for example,

$$3:2 = \tfrac{3}{2} = 1.5.$$

This is why you sometimes see ratios given as single numbers.

The single number that represents a ratio is just the number that is obtained when the ratio is written in the form 'number : 1'. For example,

The mathematical term 'rational' arises from the fact that a rational number is the *ratio* of two integers.

$3 : 2 = \frac{3}{2} : \frac{2}{2} = 1.5 : 1.$

You can use this fact to convert a ratio given as a single number into the usual colon form. For example, the ratio 1.4 is the same as

$1.4 : 1 = 14 : 10 = 7 : 5.$

Activity 40 *Converting forms of ratio*

Write the following ratios in colon form, and simplify them as much as possible.

(a) $\frac{3}{4}$ (b) 1.75   (c) 0.2

The fact that ratios can be written as single numbers also explains why you often see phrases such as 'the larger ratio'.

Activity 41 *Comparing more ratios*

In 2003 the United Kingdom had about 59.6 million people and 27.0 million cars, and Germany had 82.5 million people and 45.0 million cars.

(a) Calculate the ratio of cars to people for each of the two countries, to two significant figures.

(b) Which of the two countries had the larger ratio of cars to people?

4.2 Aspect ratios

Many forms of media involve rectangular shapes. For example, photographs, video images and sheets of paper are all usually rectangular. Some rectangles are long and thin, while others are closer to the shape of a square. The shape of a rectangle can be conveniently described using the idea of *aspect ratio*.

The **aspect ratio** of a rectangle is the ratio of its longer side to its shorter side. For example, the aspect ratio of the left-hand rectangle in Figure 19 is $25 : 15$, which simplifies to $5 : 3$. The aspect ratio of the right-hand rectangle is $10 : 6$, which also simplifies to $5 : 3$, so these two rectangles have the same aspect ratio. So the two rectangles have the same shape, though the second is smaller.

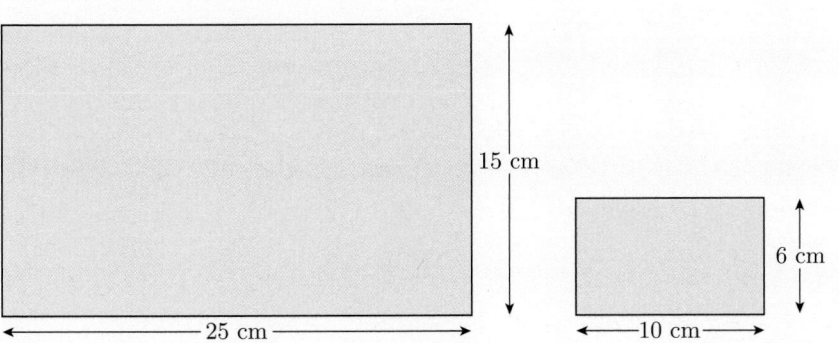

Figure 19 Two rectangles with aspect ratio $5 : 3$

Activity 42   *Finding aspect ratios*

Find the aspect ratios of the following rectangles, in their simplest forms.

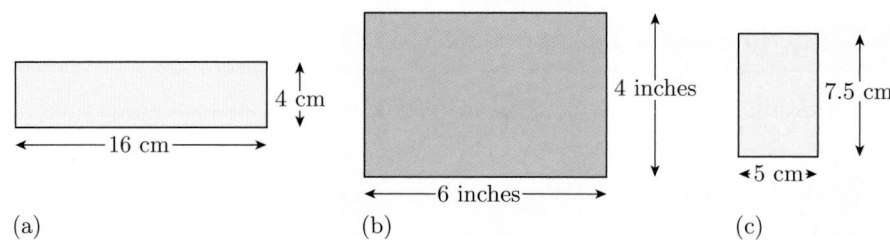

(a)   (b)   (c)

A rectangular image can be enlarged or reduced to any rectangle that has the same aspect ratio as the original image. If a different aspect ratio is required, then the image has to be cropped.

Photographs

Most digital cameras produce images with aspect ratio $3 : 2$ or $4 : 3$, depending on the camera. If your camera produces images with aspect ratio $4 : 3$, and you want a print of size $20 \, \text{cm} \times 15 \, \text{cm}$, then this can be made without losing any part of the picture, because $20 : 15 = 4 : 3$. However, if you want a $15 \, \text{cm} \times 10 \, \text{cm}$ print, which has an aspect ratio of $3 : 2$, then your photograph has to be cropped as illustrated in Figure 20(a). Similarly, if your camera produces images with aspect ratio $3 : 2$, and you want a print with aspect ratio $4 : 3$, then your photograph has to be cropped as illustrated in Figure 20(b).

(a)

(b)

Figure 20   (a) A crop of a $4 : 3$ image to give a $3 : 2$ image. (b) A crop of a $3 : 2$ image to give a $4 : 3$ image.

Activity 43 *Choosing photographic print sizes*

The first column of the table below contains some standard photographic print sizes, which are available from many photograph-processing shops and websites. The dimensions are in inches.

Print size	Aspect ratio in simplest form	Aspect ratio in form 'number : 1'
6×4		
7×5		
8×6		
9×6		
10×8		
12×8		

(a) Complete the second and third columns of the table, rounding the numbers in the third column to two decimal places.

(b) Which three print sizes are most appropriate for photographs taken with a camera that produces images with an aspect ratio of $3 : 2$? Which print size is the next most appropriate?

Scale factors

If an image that measures $3\,\text{cm} \times 2\,\text{cm}$ is enlarged to $9\,\text{cm} \times 6\,\text{cm}$, then the width and the height both triple. We say that the **scale factor** is 3. Similarly, if the same image is instead reduced to $1.5\,\text{cm} \times 1\,\text{cm}$, then the width and height both halve, and the scale factor is $\frac{1}{2}$. In general,

$$\text{scale factor} = \frac{\text{new length}}{\text{old length}},$$

where the length is the width or height of the image, or the length of anything that appears in the image.

The scale factors displayed on photocopiers are usually expressed as percentages. For example, if you want a photocopier to produce an image that is double the height of the original image, then you need a scale factor of 2, so you would set the copier to enlarge by 200%.

Activity 44 *Finding scale factors*

Find the scale factors of the following enlargements and reductions. Express each answer both as a number and as a percentage.

(a) An image measuring $4\,\text{cm} \times 3\,\text{cm}$ enlarged to $16\,\text{cm} \times 12\,\text{cm}$

(b) An image measuring $3\,\text{cm} \times 2\,\text{cm}$ enlarged to $7.5\,\text{cm} \times 5\,\text{cm}$

(c) An image measuring $20\,\text{cm} \times 10\,\text{cm}$ reduced to $4\,\text{cm} \times 2\,\text{cm}$

Videos

Aspect ratio is also an important issue for videos. Many older video programmes were made with an aspect ratio of $4 : 3$, but in recent years $16 : 9$ has become the most common video standard throughout the world. When a $4 : 3$ image is displayed on a $16 : 9$ screen, the image has to be *pillarboxed* (displayed with black bars on each side), stretched or cropped. Often a combination of these methods is used.

(a)   (b)   (c)

Figure 21   A $4 : 3$ image of Harold Wilson (a) pillarboxed, (b) stretched and (c) cropped to appear on a $16 : 9$ screen. The Open University was established by Harold Wilson's Government, and received its Charter on 23 April 1969.

Paper sizes

Finally in this subsection, we consider the aspect ratios of sheets of paper. You are probably familiar with the paper sizes A4, A3, and so on. The largest paper size in this series is A0, the next-largest is A1, and so on. This series of paper sizes is known as the ISO 216 standard.

The ISO (International Organization for Standardization) sets standards for a wide range of products, and 216 is the number assigned by this organisation to this particular standard.

The paper sizes in the series were designed so that they all have the same aspect ratio. This means that an A4 image, for example, can be scaled up to an A3 one with no need for cropping. They were also designed to have the additional property that each size of paper is exactly the same size and shape as two of the next-smaller sizes placed side by side. This is illustrated in Figure 22.

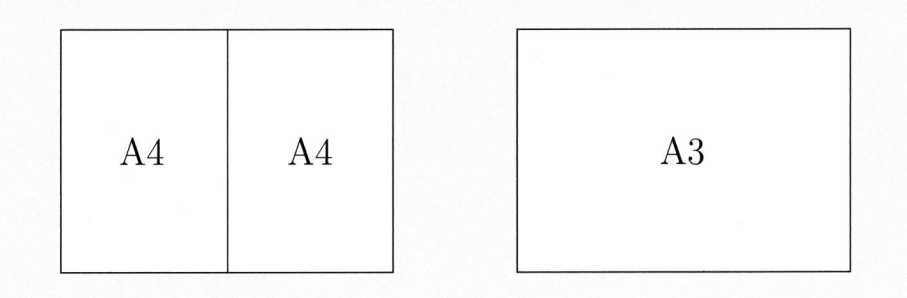

Figure 22 Two sheets of A4 make one sheet of A3

So, for example, if you fold an A3 sheet of paper in half, then it becomes the same size as a sheet of A4. There are various advantages of this property. For example, an envelope sized to fit an A5 sheet of paper will fit an A4 sheet folded in half, or an A3 sheet folded in quarters, and so on. You can see this property of the ISO paper sizes in the next activity.

This fact is illustrated by the pages of this book!

Activity 45 *ISO paper sizes*

 Animation

View the animated demonstration of the ISO paper sizes on the course website. Instructions are given within the animation.

The aspect ratio that is needed if the paper sizes are to have the properties described above can be worked out as follows. Suppose that the aspect ratio needed is $a : 1$, where a represents some number.

Consider a sheet of paper with this aspect ratio. If its shorter side has length w cm, say, then its longer side has length aw cm, since $aw : w = a : 1$. This is shown on the left of Figure 23.

You can see from the right of Figure 23 that since two smaller sheets of paper must make one larger sheet, the next-larger size of paper measures $2w$ cm by aw cm.

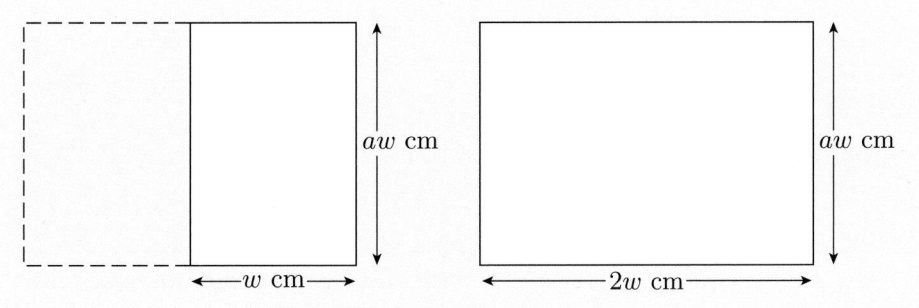

Figure 23 The dimensions of smaller and larger sheets of paper

So the aspect ratios of the two sizes of paper are

$aw : w$ and $2w : aw$.

These ratios can be simplified to

$a : 1$ and $2 : a$,

by dividing each number by w.

Remember that the aspect ratio of a rectangle is the ratio of the length of its *longer* side to the length of its *shorter* side.

Since the two paper sizes have the same aspect ratio, these ratios must be equal. So that we can compare them, let's make the first ratio have second number a, the same as the second ratio. To do this, we multiply both numbers in the first ratio by a. So the two ratios are now

$$a^2 : a \quad \text{and} \quad 2 : a.$$

Since these ratios are equal, you can see that

$$a^2 = 2.$$

The number a must be positive because $a : 1$ is an aspect ratio.

Therefore a must be $\sqrt{2}$. So the aspect ratio that is needed is $\sqrt{2} : 1$ – it involves an irrational number! Each size of paper in the ISO 216 standard has an aspect ratio of approximately $\sqrt{2} : 1$.

> The ISO 216 paper sizes were developed in Germany in the early 1900s. They were adopted as a standard there in 1922, and soon spread to other European countries. The UK adopted them in 1959, and they were adopted by the International Organization for Standardization in 1975. They are now used throughout the world: at the time of writing the only exceptions are the USA and Canada. The largest ISO 216 paper size, A0, has an area of $1\,\text{m}^2$.

Activity 46   *Scaling ISO paper sizes*

(a) Use the shorter sides of the rectangles in Figure 23 to work out the scale factor needed to enlarge from one ISO 216 paper size to the next-larger size.

(b) What scale factor is needed to reduce from one ISO 216 paper size to the next-smaller size?

(c) Explain why most photocopying machines offer the scale factors 141% and 71% as standard options for enlarging and reducing.

If you have not already done so, try the iCMA and TMA questions for this unit now.

Learning checklist

After studying this unit, you should be able to:

- understand multiples and factors of natural numbers
- find lowest common multiples and highest common factors
- begin to investigate some simple properties of numbers
- find prime factorisations of natural numbers
- carry out calculations with numbers in index form, including those with negative and fractional indices
- carry out calculations with fractions
- understand and use scientific notation
- understand the difference between rational and irrational numbers
- simplify surds
- understand and use the concepts of ratio and aspect ratio.

Solutions and comments on Activities

Activity 1

(a) The first five multiples of 7 are 7, 14, 21, 28 and 35, because

$1 \times 7 = 7,$

$2 \times 7 = 14,$

$3 \times 7 = 21,$

$4 \times 7 = 28,$

$5 \times 7 = 35.$

(b) Since $4183 \div 11 = 380.272\ldots$, the number 4183 is not a multiple of 11. So the amount of money in the cash box is not correct.

Activity 2

(a) The multiples of 2 are 2, 4, 6, 8, ...

The multiples of 3 are 3, 6, 9, 12, ...

The multiples of 4 are 4, 8, 12, 16, ...

The multiples of 6 are 6, 12, 18, 24, ...

The multiples of 8 are 8, 16, 24, 32, ...

(i) The LCM of 2 and 3 is 6.

(ii) The LCM of 4 and 6 is 12.

(iii) The LCM of 4 and 8 is 8.

(b) The LCM of 2, 3 and 8 is 24. (This is the smallest number that is a multiple of all of 2, 3 and 8.)

Activity 3

(a) The smallest number of chocolates is the LCM of 2, 3 and 4, which is 12.

(b) The next suitable number of chocolates is $2 \times 12 = 24$.

Activity 4

(a) The first factor pair is 1, 20.
The next is 2, 10.
The next is 4, 5.
The next is 5, 4, which is a repeat, so the factors of 20 are 1, 2, 4, 5, 10 and 20.

(b) The first factor pair is 1, 24.
The next is 2, 12.
The next is 3, 8.
The next is 4, 6.
The factors of 24 are 1, 2, 3, 4, 6, 8, 12 and 24.

(c) The first factor pair is 1, 45.
The next is 3, 15.
The next is 5, 9.
The factors of 45 are 1, 3, 5, 9, 15 and 45.

Activity 5

(a) The number 621 is divisible by 3, because the sum of its digits is $6 + 2 + 1 = 9$, which is divisible by 3.

(b) The number 273 is not divisible by 9, because the sum of its digits is $2 + 7 + 3 = 12$, which is not divisible by 9.

Activity 6

(a) The common factors of 20 and 24 are 1, 2 and 4. So their highest common factor is 4.

(b) The common factors of 12 and 24 are 1, 2, 3, 4, 6 and 12. So their highest common factor is 12.

(c) The common factors of 18, 20 and 24 are 1 and 2. So their highest common factor is 2.

Activity 7

A number ending in 0, 2, 4, 6 or 8 is even and so is divisible by 2. A number ending in 0 or 5 is divisible by 5. So if a number ends in 0, 2, 4, 5, 6 or 8, then it is divisible by either 2 or 5, and hence it is not prime, unless it is 2 or 5 itself. So every prime number except 2 and 5 ends with one of the other possible digits, 1, 3, 7 or 9. You can see from the list of prime numbers on page 124 that each of these possible digits occurs.

Activity 8

(a)

Prime number	3	5	7	11	13	17	19	23	29
Remainder	3	1	3	3	1	1	3	3	1

(b)

Prime number	3	5	7	11	13	17	19	23	29
Sum of two squares?	×	✓	×	×	✓	✓	×	×	✓

$(5 = 4 + 1, 13 = 9 + 4, 17 = 16 + 1$ and $29 = 25 + 4$.)

(c) It seems that the odd prime numbers that can be written as the sum of two square numbers are those that have remainder 1 when they are divided by 4.

To test this conjecture, you could consider the prime numbers 31 and 37, for example.

The first of these numbers, 31, has remainder 3 when it is divided by 4, and it cannot be written as the sum of two square numbers. To see this, notice that if 31 were the sum of two square numbers, then one of the square numbers would be greater than $31/2 = 15.5$, and the other square number would be less than this. So one of the square numbers must be either 16 or 25, and the other must be 1, 4 or 9. Also, one of the square numbers must be odd and the other must be even. So the only possibilities are $16 + 1$, $16 + 9$ and $25 + 4$, and none of these sums is equal to 31.

The second number, 37, has remainder 1 when it is divided by 4, and it can be written as the sum of two square numbers: $37 = 36 + 1$. So the two prime numbers 31 and 37 provide further evidence for the conjecture.

It has been proved that the conjecture above is true. That is, the odd prime numbers that can be written as a sum of two square numbers are those that have remainder 1 when they are divided by 4. This theorem is known as **Fermat's Christmas Theorem**, because the French mathematician Pierre de Fermat (1601–1665) announced it in a letter to Marin Mersenne dated 25 December 1640. Fermat's proof of the theorem was incomplete, however, and the missing steps were provided by the Swiss mathematician Leonhard Euler (1707–1783) about a hundred years later.

Activity 9

(a) $300 = 2^2 \times 3 \times 5^2$

(b) Any factor tree gives the same answer.

Activity 10

(a) $72 = 2 \times 2 \times 2 \times 3 \times 3 = 2^3 \times 3^2$

(b) $855 = 3 \times 3 \times 5 \times 19 = 3^2 \times 5 \times 19$

(c) $1000 = 2^3 \times 5^3$

(d) $847 = 7 \times 11^2$

Activity 11

$$9 = \qquad 3^2$$
$$18 = 2 \times 3^2$$
$$30 = 2 \times 3 \times 5$$

(a) The LCM of 18 and 30 is $2 \times 3^2 \times 5 = 90$. The HCF of 18 and 30 is $2 \times 3 = 6$.

(b) The LCM of 9, 18 and 30 is $2 \times 3^2 \times 5 = 90$. The HCF of 9, 18 and 30 is 3.

Activity 12

(a) The LCM is the product of all the numbers inside the circles, which is

$$3 \times 2 \times 2 \times 7 \times 2 \times 5 = 840,$$

and the HCF is the product of the numbers in the overlap, which is

$$2 \times 2 \times 7 = 28.$$

(b) The diagram is below.

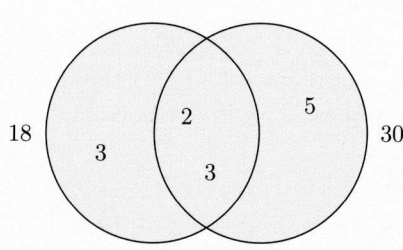

The LCM of 18 and 30 is the product of all the numbers inside the circles, which is

$$3 \times 2 \times 3 \times 5 = 90.$$

The HCF of 18 and 30 is the product of the numbers in the overlap, which is

$$2 \times 3 = 6.$$

Activity 13

(a) (i) $3^4 \times 3^3 = 3^{4+3} = 3^7$

(ii) $7^2 \times 7 = 7^{2+1} = 7^3$

(iii) $10^2 \times 10^3 \times 10^4 = 10^{2+3+4} = 10^9$

(iv) $3^4 \times 5^{12}$ cannot be written any more concisely in index form, because the base numbers are different.

(v) $8 \times 2^5 = 2^3 \times 2^5 = 2^{3+5} = 2^8$

(vi) $9 \times 3 = 3^2 \times 3 = 3^{2+1} = 3^3$

(b) $294 \times 441 = (2 \times 3 \times 7^2) \times (3^2 \times 7^2)$
$$= 2 \times 3^{1+2} \times 7^{2+2}$$
$$= 2 \times 3^3 \times 7^4$$

Activity 14

An estimate for the number of atoms in the observable universe, obtained using the figures in the question, is

$$10^{27} \times 10^{30} \times 10^{12} \times 10^{11} = 10^{27+30+12+11}$$
$$= 10^{80}.$$

This is much less than a googol, which is 10^{100}.

Activity 15

(a) (i) $7^6 \div 7^2 = \dfrac{7^6}{7^2} = 7^{6-2} = 7^4$

(ii) $\dfrac{2^{16}}{2^8} = 2^{16-8} = 2^8$

(iii) The quotient $\dfrac{5^{21}}{3^5}$ cannot be written any more concisely in index form, because the base numbers are different.

(iv) $\dfrac{3^7}{3} = 3^{7-1} = 3^6$

(b) $\dfrac{3456}{12} = \dfrac{2^7 \times 3^3}{2^2 \times 3} = 2^{7-2} \times 3^{3-1} = 2^5 \times 3^2$

Activity 16

(a) $(5^2)^4 = 5^8$

(b) $(7^3)^2 = 7^6$

(c) $(3^5)^3 \times 3^2 = 3^{15} \times 3^2 = 3^{17}$

(d) $\dfrac{(2^5)^2}{2^2} = \dfrac{2^{10}}{2^2} = 2^8$

(e) $\left(\dfrac{2^5}{2^2}\right)^2 = (2^3)^2 = 2^6$

Activity 17

(a) (i) $21^4 = (3 \times 7)^4 = 3^4 \times 7^4$

(ii) $24^3 = (2^3 \times 3)^3 = (2^3)^3 \times 3^3 = 2^9 \times 3^3$

(b) (i) $\left(\dfrac{2}{7}\right)^2 = \dfrac{2^2}{7^2} = \dfrac{4}{49}$

(ii) $\left(\dfrac{3}{4}\right)^3 = \dfrac{3^3}{4^3} = \dfrac{27}{64}$

Activity 18

(a) $(-3)^2 = (-3) \times (-3) = 9$

(b) $(-3)^3 = (-3) \times (-3) \times (-3)$
$\qquad = 9 \times (-3) = -27$

(c) $(-2)^4 = (-2) \times (-2) \times (-2) \times (-2)$
$\qquad = 4 \times 4 = 16$

(d) $(-1)^4 = (-1) \times (-1) \times (-1) \times (-1)$
$\qquad = 1 \times 1 = 1$

(e) $(-1)^5 = (-1)^4 \times (-1) = 1 \times (-1) = -1$

Activity 19

(a) (i) $\frac{2}{9} + \frac{4}{9} = \frac{6}{9} = \frac{2}{3}$

(ii) $\frac{7}{8} + \frac{9}{24} = \frac{21}{24} + \frac{9}{24} = \frac{30}{24} = \frac{5}{4} = 1\frac{1}{4}$

(iii) $\frac{11}{14} - \frac{3}{14} = \frac{8}{14} = \frac{4}{7}$

(iv) $\frac{5}{6} - \frac{1}{4} = \frac{10}{12} - \frac{3}{12} = \frac{7}{12}$

(v) $2\frac{1}{7} + 4\frac{2}{7} = 2 + 4 + \frac{1}{7} + \frac{2}{7} = 6\frac{3}{7}$

(vi) $3\frac{3}{4} - 1\frac{1}{5} = 3 - 1 + \frac{3}{4} - \frac{1}{5}$
$\qquad\qquad = 2 + \frac{15}{20} - \frac{4}{20} = 2\frac{11}{20}$

(vii) $\frac{1}{2} + \frac{1}{3} + \frac{1}{4} = \frac{6}{12} + \frac{4}{12} + \frac{3}{12} = \frac{13}{12} = 1\frac{1}{12}$

(b) Half of all drivers are under the age of 35, so half are aged 35 or over. One-seventh are over the age of 65, so the fraction of drivers who are between 35 and 65 years of age is

$$\tfrac{1}{2} - \tfrac{1}{7} = \tfrac{7}{14} - \tfrac{2}{14} = \tfrac{5}{14}.$$

So five-fourteenths of UK drivers are aged between 35 and 65. (This is slightly more than a third of UK drivers, since $\frac{5}{15} = \frac{1}{3}$.)

Activity 20

(a) (i) $\dfrac{5}{8} \times \dfrac{3}{10} = \dfrac{5}{8} \times \dfrac{3}{\overset{\underset{2}{}}{10}} = \dfrac{3}{16}$

(ii) $\frac{4}{5} \times 3 = \frac{4}{5} \times \frac{3}{1} = \frac{12}{5} = 2\frac{2}{5}$

(The answer can be left as a top-heavy fraction or written as a mixed number.)

(iii) $1\frac{1}{3} \times 2\frac{5}{6} = \frac{4}{3} \times \frac{17}{6}$
$\qquad\qquad = \dfrac{\overset{2}{\cancel{4}}}{3} \times \dfrac{17}{\underset{3}{\cancel{6}}} = \frac{34}{9} = 3\frac{7}{9}$

(b) The fraction of students who work for more than 35 hours per week is

$$\dfrac{2}{5} \times \dfrac{1}{4} = \dfrac{\overset{1}{\cancel{2}}}{5} \times \dfrac{1}{\underset{2}{\cancel{4}}} = \dfrac{1}{10}.$$

Activity 21

If a quarter of teenage girls and less than a quarter of teenage boys smoke, then less than a quarter of all teenagers smoke. The fraction five-twelfths is greater than a quarter, so it cannot be correct.

The fraction $\frac{5}{12}$ is obtained by adding $\frac{1}{4}$ and $\frac{1}{6}$, but this is not the correct calculation. The correct calculation is as follows.

About half of teenagers are girls, so the fraction of teenagers who are girls and smokers is

$$\tfrac{1}{2} \times \tfrac{1}{4} = \tfrac{1}{8}.$$

Similarly, the fraction of teenagers who are boys and smokers is

$$\tfrac{1}{2} \times \tfrac{1}{6} = \tfrac{1}{12}.$$

Therefore the fraction of all teenagers who smoke is

$$\tfrac{1}{8} + \tfrac{1}{12} = \tfrac{3}{24} + \tfrac{2}{24} = \tfrac{5}{24}.$$

(The fraction $\frac{5}{24}$ is halfway between $\frac{1}{4}$ and $\frac{1}{6}$.)

Activity 22

(a) (i) $6 \div \dfrac{4}{3} = \dfrac{6}{1} \times \dfrac{3}{4} = \dfrac{\overset{3}{\cancel{6}}}{1} \times \dfrac{3}{\underset{2}{\cancel{4}}} = \dfrac{9}{2} = 4\dfrac{1}{2}$

(ii) $\dfrac{3}{8} \div \dfrac{11}{24} = \dfrac{3}{8} \times \dfrac{24}{11} = \dfrac{3}{\underset{1}{\cancel{8}}} \times \dfrac{\overset{3}{\cancel{24}}}{11} = \dfrac{9}{11}$

(iii) $1\dfrac{1}{3} \div 1\dfrac{7}{9} = \dfrac{4}{3} \div \dfrac{16}{9} = \dfrac{4}{3} \times \dfrac{9}{16} = \dfrac{\overset{1}{\cancel{4}}}{\underset{1}{\cancel{3}}} \times \dfrac{\overset{3}{\cancel{9}}}{\underset{4}{\cancel{16}}} = \dfrac{3}{4}$

(b) The number of components that the factory worker can make in a week is

$$37\dfrac{1}{2} \div 1\dfrac{1}{4} = \dfrac{75}{2} \div \dfrac{5}{4} = \dfrac{75}{2} \times \dfrac{4}{5} = \dfrac{\overset{15}{\cancel{75}}}{\underset{1}{\cancel{2}}} \times \dfrac{\overset{2}{\cancel{4}}}{\underset{1}{\cancel{5}}} = 30.$$

Activity 23

(a) $\left(\dfrac{1}{2}\right)^{0} = 1$

(b) $7^{-1} = \dfrac{1}{7}$

(c) $7^{-2} = \dfrac{1}{7^2} = \dfrac{1}{49}$

(d) $\left(\dfrac{1}{3}\right)^{-1} = 3$

(e) $\left(\dfrac{2}{5}\right)^{-1} = \dfrac{5}{2}$

(f) $\left(\dfrac{1}{3}\right)^{-2} = 3^2 = 9$

(g) $\left(\dfrac{2}{5}\right)^{-2} = \left(\dfrac{5}{2}\right)^{2} = \dfrac{25}{4}$

(h) $\left(\dfrac{1}{3}\right)^{-3} = 3^3 = 27$

(i) $(-2)^{-3} = \dfrac{1}{(-2)^3} = \dfrac{1}{-8} = -\dfrac{1}{8}$

Activity 24

(a) (i) $7723 = 7.723 \times 10^3$

(ii) $50\,007\,000 = 5.0007 \times 10^7$

(iii) $0.100\,34 = 1.0034 \times 10^{-1}$

(iv) $0.000\,208 = 2.08 \times 10^{-4}$

(b) (i) The population of the world at the time of writing is about 6.77×10^9 people.

(ii) The mass of the Sun is about 1.99×10^{30} kg.

(iii) The mass of a hydrogen atom is about 1.674×10^{-27} kg.

(c) (i) $7.04 \times 10^3 = 7040$

(ii) $4.52 \times 10^4 = 45\,200$

(iii) $7.3 \times 10^{-2} = 0.073$

(iv) $2.045 \times 10^{-5} = 0.000\,020\,45$

Activity 25

(a) 1.5 trillion $= 1.5 \times 10^{12}$, which is in scientific notation, and 61 million $= 61 \times 10^6 = 6.1 \times 10^7$.

(b) The amount of public debt per person, in pounds, is

$$\dfrac{1.5 \times 10^{12}}{6.1 \times 10^7} = \dfrac{1.5}{6.1} \times \dfrac{10^{12}}{10^7}$$
$$= 0.25 \times 10^{12-7} \ \text{(to 2 s.f.)}$$
$$= 0.25 \times 10^5$$
$$= 25\,000$$

So the headline would be as follows.

> Bailouts add £1.5 trillion to Britain's public debt – that's about £25 000 for each person!

Activity 26

(a) The approximate length in metres of an ordinary guitar, divided by the length in metres of the nano guitar, is

$$\dfrac{1}{10 \times 10^{-6}} = \dfrac{1}{10^{1+(-6)}} = \dfrac{1}{10^{-5}} = 10^5 = 100\,000.$$

So the nano guitar is 100 000 times smaller than an ordinary guitar.

$\Bigg($ You can work out that $\dfrac{1}{10^{-5}} = 10^5$ in either of the following ways. You can use the index law $a^{-n} = \dfrac{1}{a^n}$:

$$\dfrac{1}{10^{-5}} = 10^{-(-5)} = 10^5.$$

Or you can use the index law $\dfrac{a^m}{a^n} = a^{m-n}$:

$$\dfrac{1}{10^{-5}} = \dfrac{10^0}{10^{-5}} = 10^{0-(-5)} = 10^5.\Bigg)$$

(b) The approximate width in metres of a human hair, divided by the width in metres of a string of the nano guitar, is

$$\dfrac{100 \times 10^{-6}}{50 \times 10^{-9}} = \dfrac{100}{50} \times \dfrac{10^{-6}}{10^{-9}}$$
$$= 2 \times 10^{-6-(-9)}$$
$$= 2 \times 10^3$$
$$= 2000.$$

So a string of the nano guitar is 2000 times less wide than a human hair.

Activity 28

(a) $\sqrt{9} = 3$

(b) $\sqrt[3]{8} = 2$

(c) $\sqrt[3]{27} = 3$

(d) $\sqrt[4]{16} = 2$

(e) Two square roots of 9 are ± 3.

(f) Two fourth roots of 16 are ± 2.

Activity 29

(a) $\sqrt{1764} = \sqrt{36} \times \sqrt{49} = 6 \times 7 = 42$

(b) **(i)** $\sqrt{\dfrac{4}{9}} = \dfrac{\sqrt{4}}{\sqrt{9}} = \dfrac{2}{3}$

(ii) $\sqrt{\dfrac{36}{49}} = \dfrac{\sqrt{36}}{\sqrt{49}} = \dfrac{6}{7}$

(iii) $\sqrt{\dfrac{1}{4}} = \dfrac{\sqrt{1}}{\sqrt{4}} = \dfrac{1}{2}$

Activity 30

(a) $\sqrt{8} = \sqrt{4 \times 2} = \sqrt{4}\sqrt{2} = 2\sqrt{2}$

(b) $\sqrt{75} = \sqrt{25 \times 3} = \sqrt{25}\sqrt{3} = 5\sqrt{3}$

(c) The surd $\sqrt{15}$ is already in its simplest form, since the factors of 15 greater than 1 are 3, 5 and 15, and none of these factors is a square number.

(d) $\sqrt{56} = \sqrt{4 \times 14} = \sqrt{4}\sqrt{14} = 2\sqrt{14}$

(The root $\sqrt{14}$ cannot be simplified.)

(e) $\sqrt{48} = \sqrt{16 \times 3} = \sqrt{16}\sqrt{3} = 4\sqrt{3}$

Activity 31

(a) $(\sqrt{7})^2 = \sqrt{7} \times \sqrt{7} = 7$

(b) $\sqrt{7} \times 3\sqrt{7} = 3 \times 7 = 21$

(c) $\sqrt{7} \times \sqrt{14} = \sqrt{7 \times 14}$
$$= \sqrt{7 \times 7 \times 2}$$
$$= \sqrt{7 \times 7} \times \sqrt{2}$$
$$= 7\sqrt{2}$$

(d) $\sqrt{2} \times \sqrt{8} = \sqrt{16} = 4$

(e) $2\sqrt{3} \times 3\sqrt{2} = 6\sqrt{6}$

(f) $2\sqrt{3} \times 2\sqrt{15} = 4\sqrt{3 \times 15}$
$$= 4\sqrt{3 \times 3 \times 5}$$
$$= 4\sqrt{3 \times 3} \times \sqrt{5}$$
$$= 4 \times 3\sqrt{5}$$
$$= 12\sqrt{5}$$

Activity 32

(a) $\dfrac{\sqrt{10}}{\sqrt{2}} = \dfrac{\sqrt{2} \times \sqrt{5}}{\sqrt{2}} = \sqrt{5}$

(b) $\dfrac{5}{\sqrt{5}} = \dfrac{\sqrt{5} \times \sqrt{5}}{\sqrt{5}} = \sqrt{5}$

(c) $\dfrac{\sqrt{8}}{\sqrt{2}} = \dfrac{\sqrt{4 \times 2}}{\sqrt{2}} = \dfrac{2\sqrt{2}}{\sqrt{2}} = 2$

(d) $\dfrac{8}{\sqrt{2}} = \dfrac{4 \times 2}{\sqrt{2}} = \dfrac{4 \times \sqrt{2} \times \sqrt{2}}{\sqrt{2}} = 4\sqrt{2}$

Activity 33

(a) $\sqrt{3} + \sqrt{3} = 2\sqrt{3}$

(b) The roots in the surd $\sqrt{2} + \sqrt{5}$ are different (and are in their simplest forms), so the surd cannot be simplified.

(c) $7\sqrt{3} - 2\sqrt{3} = 5\sqrt{3}$

(d) $5\sqrt{8} - 2\sqrt{2} = 5\sqrt{4 \times 2} - 2\sqrt{2}$
$$= 5 \times 2\sqrt{2} - 2\sqrt{2}$$
$$= 10\sqrt{2} - 2\sqrt{2}$$
$$= 8\sqrt{2}$$

Activity 34

(a) $16^{\frac{1}{2}} = \sqrt{16} = 4$

(b) $9^{\frac{3}{2}} = \left(\sqrt{9}\right)^3 = 3^3 = 27$

(c) $4^{-\frac{1}{2}} = \dfrac{1}{4^{\frac{1}{2}}} = \dfrac{1}{\sqrt{4}} = \dfrac{1}{2}$

(d) $4^{\frac{5}{2}} = \left(\sqrt{4}\right)^5 = 2^5 = 32$

(e) $27^{\frac{2}{3}} = \left(\sqrt[3]{27}\right)^2 = 3^2 = 9$

Activity 36

(a) $18 : 3 = 6 : 1$

(b) $12 : 60 : 18 = 2 : 10 : 3$

(c) $2 : 0.5 : 1.5 = 4 : 1 : 3$

(d) The ratio $6 : 12 : 7$ is already in its simplest form.

Activity 37

(a) The ratio of children to staff for club A is
$$46 : 6 = \dfrac{46}{6} : \dfrac{6}{6} \approx 7.7 : 1.$$

The ratio of children to staff for club B is
$$25 : 4 = \dfrac{25}{4} : \dfrac{4}{4} \approx 6.3 : 1.$$

(b) Club B has fewer children per member of staff.

Activity 38

(a) The number of non-taxpayers, in millions, was approximately
$$61.0 - 31.9 = 29.1.$$

So the ratio of taxpayers to non-taxpayers was approximately
$$31.9 : 29.1 = \dfrac{31.9}{29.1} : \dfrac{29.1}{29.1} = 1.096\ldots : 1 \approx 1 : 1.$$

So there was about one non-taxpayer for every taxpayer.

(b) The number of ordinary taxpayers, in millions, was approximately

$31.9 - 3.9 = 28.0.$

So the ratio of ordinary taxpayers to higher-rate taxpayers was approximately

$$28.0 : 3.9 = \frac{28.0}{3.9} : \frac{3.9}{3.9}$$
$$= 7.179\ldots : 1$$
$$\approx 7 : 1.$$

So there were about seven ordinary taxpayers for every higher-rate taxpayer.

Activity 39

(a) In winter conditions the recommended ratio of screenwash to water is $1 : 4$, so there are $1 + 4 = 5$ parts.

The volume of screenwash needed is

$\frac{1}{5} \times 2000\,\text{ml} = 400\,\text{ml},$

and the volume of water needed is

$\frac{4}{5} \times 2000\,\text{ml} = 1600\,\text{ml}.$

(Check: $400 + 1600 = 2000$.)

(b) In severe winter conditions the recommended ratio of screenwash to water is $2 : 1$, so there are $2 + 1 = 3$ parts.

The volume of screenwash needed is

$\frac{2}{3} \times 2000\,\text{ml} \approx 1300\,\text{ml},$

and the volume of water needed is

$\frac{1}{3} \times 2000\,\text{ml} \approx 700\,\text{ml}.$

(Check: $1300 + 700 = 2000$.)

Activity 40

(a) $\frac{3}{4} = 3 : 4$

(b) $1.75 = 1.75 : 1 = (1.75 \times 4) : 4 = 7 : 4$

(c) $0.2 = 0.2 : 1 = (0.2 \times 5) : 5 = 1 : 5$

Activity 41

(a) The ratio of cars to people in the United Kingdom was

$\frac{27.0}{59.6} \approx 0.45,$

and the ratio of cars to people in Germany was

$\frac{45.0}{82.5} \approx 0.55.$

(b) Germany had the larger ratio of cars to people. (It had about 55 cars for every 100 people, whereas the UK had about 45 cars for every 100 people.)

Activity 42

(a) The aspect ratio is $16 : 4 = 4 : 1$.

(b) The aspect ratio is $6 : 4 = 3 : 2$.

(c) The aspect ratio is $7.5 : 5 = 15 : 10 = 3 : 2$.

Remember that the aspect ratio of a rectangle is the ratio of its *longer* side to its *shorter* side.

Activity 43

(a)

Print size	Aspect ratio in simplest form	Aspect ratio in form 'number : 1'
6×4	$3 : 2$	$1.50 : 1$
7×5	$7 : 5$	$1.40 : 1$
8×6	$4 : 3$	$1.33 : 1$
9×6	$3 : 2$	$1.50 : 1$
10×8	$5 : 4$	$1.25 : 1$
12×8	$3 : 2$	$1.50 : 1$

(b) The three most appropriate print sizes for photographs taken with a camera that produces $3 : 2$ images are 6×4, 9×6 and 12×8, since all of these have aspect ratio $3 : 2$.

The next most appropriate print size is 7×5. This is because $3 : 2 = 1.50 : 1$, and the aspect ratio in the table closest to $1.50 : 1$ is $1.40 : 1 = 7 : 5$. So less of the picture will be lost in a print with aspect ratio $7 : 5$ than in a print with aspect ratio $4 : 3$, for example.

Activity 44

(a) The scale factor is $\frac{16}{4} = 4 = 400\%$.

(b) The scale factor is $\frac{7.5}{3} = 2.5 = 250\%$.

(c) The scale factor is $\frac{4}{20} = 0.2 = 20\%$.

Activity 46

(a) By looking at the shorter sides of the rectangles in Figure 23, you can see that a length of w cm must be scaled up to a length of aw cm. So the scale factor needed is $a = \sqrt{2}$.

(b) Similarly, from Figure 23 you can see that a length of aw cm must be scaled down to a length of w cm, so the scale factor needed is $\frac{1}{a} = \frac{1}{\sqrt{2}}$.

(c) $\sqrt{2} \approx 1.41 = 141\%$ and $\frac{1}{\sqrt{2}} \approx 0.71 = 71\%$, so

the given values are the scale factors needed for enlarging or reducing from one ISO 216 paper size to the next size.

Statistical summaries

Introduction

'Statistical thinking will one day be as necessary for efficient citizenship as the ability to read and write.'

Attributed to H.G. Wells, an English science fiction author.

This is the first of two units in the course that deal with statistical ideas. It looks first at some of the kinds of question that can be addressed by statistical methods and then at some issues that arise when appropriate data have been collected. It then provides an introduction to some important statistical techniques for finding numerical summaries (for example, calculating an average or a measure of spread) in order to see more clearly some of the useful information provided by the data.

This unit presents statistical techniques in the context of practical investigations. As you will see, in any purposeful statistical investigation, there are four useful stages that can help you to organise your planning of the tasks that need to be carried out. In fact, they make up a statistical version of the general mathematical modelling cycle that you met in Unit 2.

In this unit you will see how to use these four stages in the context of using calculations to reveal patterns in data. Then, in the second unit on statistics (Unit 11), you will look again at the four stages, this time in the context of statistical pictures (charts and graphs).

1 Questions, questions

You only need to glance at a newspaper, a magazine, television or the internet to see that statistical information is all around you. A key aim of this unit is to present statistical ideas as more than simply facts and techniques – statistical thinking is presented as a helpful way of seeing the world quantitatively (as opposed to qualitatively), and could become a valuable tool in your decision-making toolbox.

A quantitative view uses numbers such as measurements and counts. A qualitative view describes what something is like in words, for example, 'small, medium, large'.

Mathematical thinking can also be viewed in this way and, indeed, many of the remarks about statistics in this unit can be equally applied to mathematics in general.

'Statistics' can be used as either a singular or a plural word. Statistics in its plural form is probably more familiar to you: statistics are numerical facts. Statistics in its singular form – allowing the wording 'statistics is' – refers to statistics, like mathematics, as a scientific subject. The former are part of the concern of the latter!

Here are some of the ways in which statistics is unavoidable in our lives.

- *Numbers*: each person operates within a variety of key life roles, such as at work, at home, as a consumer and in the wider community. In each of these environments, you are presented with information, often in the form of numbers, that must be processed and interpreted if you are to be a successfully functioning worker, family member, consumer and citizen.

- *Graphs and charts*: statistical information often takes a visual form. You need to know how to interpret these 'data pictures', both in terms of the overall trends and patterns they suggest and also by knowing how to pull out and examine some of the relevant detail.

In fact, increasingly, almost every subject that you might wish to study has become more quantitative, making it ever more important to have a sound grasp of basic statistics.

Much of this statistical information arises as an attempt to *answer* questions of various kinds. For example, should people stop smoking? Should we drive more carefully? But they often end up *raising* just as many questions as they answer!

1.1 Types of statistical question

Before rushing into answering any question, it is always a good idea to ask: 'Have I seen one like this before?' Most of the questions and forms of investigation that occur in statistics can be categorised into one of the following three types.

Summarising: how can the information be reduced?

Looking at a lot of facts and figures does not always provide you with a clear picture of what is going on. To avoid data overload, it is often a good idea to find a way of summarising the information – perhaps by reducing the many figures to just one representative number.

For example, in many places, especially along a river, one town's waste water discharge may be part of the next town's water supply. It makes sense to monitor the water quality by taking regular measurements of the quality of the river water. This might require hourly measures of the number of milligrams per litre of solids in the water, sampled at many different points on the river. Quite quickly, such a mass of data is generated that it can become difficult to see any underlying patterns. What is needed is some way of reducing many figures into just a few representative ones. Computing a simple daily average, both globally for the entire stretch of the river and locally for each sample point, will provide a useful summary of the levels of pollution.

A second, and equally powerful, way of summarising data is to represent the numbers pictorially using statistical charts or plots – a central theme of Unit 11.

Here are some more examples of investigations of the form 'how many?' or 'how much?':

- How many people die from road accidents each day in the UK?
- What is the typical cost of a tube of toothpaste?
- How old are the students studying MU123?

These are the sorts of questions where a summary in the form of a simple average can really clarify things.

Comparing: is there a difference?

Many of the decisions that we make are based on deciding whether or not there is a difference between two things – does one thing perform better, last longer, or offer better value for money than another?

For example, suppose that in a particular town, some traffic-calming measures are introduced in order to reduce the speed of the vehicles. How would you know whether the initiative was successful? The relevant comparison here is between vehicle speeds before and after the initiative. Let's suppose that a sample of 20 vehicle speeds were recorded both before and after, and that the average speed did indeed fall slightly. What might be your conclusion? One possible explanation might be that the traffic-calming measures have worked. However, there are several problems with this conclusion. First, sample sizes of only 20 are too small to be reliable; one speeding car in the first sample may have made all the difference. Second, it is likely that the speeds of different vehicles vary quite a lot, so differences are to be expected anyway. Third, the difference between the two averages was small. And finally, the lower speeds might have been brought about by some other factor, such as a greater density of

Figure 1 Sampling water quality

Imagine being handed the hourly measurements over a whole month, for twenty different points along the river. For a 30-day month, this would consist of 14 400 numbers!

traffic in the 'after' phase of the experiment, perhaps because it was school term time. So an alternative explanation is that the result is just a matter of chance and that if the experiment were to be repeated, a different conclusion might be drawn. We'll return to this scenario in Activity 3, where you'll be asked to think about how we might perform a more formal statistical investigation into the effects of traffic-calming measures.

In general, investigations involving comparing two averages will depend on several factors, such as the sizes of the samples on which the averages are based, the degree of variation that one might reasonably expect to see in such values, and whether the size of the observed difference is sufficiently large to act upon.

Here are some examples of 'comparing' investigations following on from the previous three examples:

- Do more people, on average, die from road accidents on weekdays or at weekends?

- How does the cost of Brand X toothpaste compare with that of Brand Y?

- Are students studying MU123 older or younger than students on an introductory Arts course?

Seeking a relationship: what sort of relationship is there?

Sometimes a statistical question is not about differences between two or more sets of results but about investigating a possible relationship between quite separate things.

Sir Richard Doll, one of the scientists famous for establishing the link between smoking and lung cancer, originally suspected tarmac as the cause. Sir Ronald Fisher, an eminent statistician and leading sceptic about the link, suggested a genetic link between lung cancer and the propensity to smoke.

The first paper to propose the link between smoking and lung cancer was R. Doll and A.B. Hill (1950) 'Smoking and carcinoma of the lung. Preliminary report.', *British Medical Journal*, vol. 2, pp. 739–748.

For example, as far back as the 1950s, medical researchers were able to link the number of cigarettes smoked to the incidence of lung cancer. At the time they found that countries with relatively high smoking rates, like the UK, also showed high levels of lung cancer, whereas countries with low smoking levels, like Iceland and Norway, also had low rates of lung cancer. Of course, there were other factors at play that may have affected lung cancer rates, and it is part of the statistician's job to try to isolate and so take account of each of the relevant factors. It is important to remember that a statistical association between two measures does not prove a cause-and-effect relationship between them. For example, the changes in *both* measures may be caused by a *third* factor, such as (in the smoking example) that the citizens of some countries may experience a high level of general stress, which encourages smoking and also contributes to lung cancer.

If there appears to be a relationship between two factors, it is often useful to determine what that relationship is. That is, how much does one factor change relative to the other? Here are some more examples in which we might investigate whether there is a relationship between the factors under consideration:

- Are the numbers of road deaths in different countries linked to their respective maximum speed limits?

- How does the cost of tubes of toothpaste depend on their size?

- What is the connection between the numbers of hours that students work on a level 3 course in mathematics and their final grade?

Classifying statistical investigations

Three types of investigation have been described above:

- summarising
- comparing
- seeking a relationship.

Activity 1 asks you to distinguish between summarising investigations and those of other types.

It will be convenient to use the single word 'relationship' to point to the third type of investigation.

Activity 1 *Summarising or otherwise?*

Which of the following investigations are summarising investigations, and which belong to one of the other two categories – that is, either comparing or relationship investigations? Do not try to distinguish between the latter two categories just yet.

(a) How much does a typical loaf of bread cost?

(b) Do men earn more than women?

(c) How heavy is a typical bag of potato crisps?

(d) How do grades in an exam depend on the social backgrounds of the students who take the exam?

(e) Is there a link between income level and ill-health?

(f) Did the introduction of car seat-belts save lives?

(g) What proportion of MU123 students are female?

(h) Are people taller than they were 100 years ago?

I'm certainly taller than I was a hundred years ago!

While summarising investigations are fairly easy to pick out, it can be less easy to distinguish the other two. For example, suppose that an investigation was to be set up to look into the question: 'Do people with long legs tend to run faster than people with short legs?'

Depending on how the investigation was approached, this could be based either on comparing or on seeking a relationship. For example, one possible approach would be to identify two separate groups of people, those with long legs and those with short legs, and compare the running speeds of the two groups. This would be an investigation based on comparing. However, an alternative experimental design could be to choose a sample of people randomly, measure the running speed and leg length of each person, and see if there is a relationship between these two measures. This would be an investigation based on seeking a relationship.

Activity 2 asks you to revisit the five investigations in Activity 1 that were *not* based on summarising and try to classify them into one or other of the two remaining types.

Activity 2 *Comparing or seeking a relationship?*

Classify the investigations below into the 'comparing' and 'relationship' types.

(a) Do men earn more than women?

(b) How do grades in an exam depend on the social backgrounds of the students who take the exam?

(c) Is there a link between income level and ill-health?

(d) Did the introduction of car seat-belts save lives?

(e) Are people taller than they were 100 years ago?

Exploring questions like those above gives a purpose and a direction to statistical learning. In this unit and Unit 11, you will concentrate on questions of the first two types above – summarising and comparing. The third category of question, seeking a relationship between two things, is not explored in great detail in this course, although there is a little on this in Unit 6.

1.2 The statistical investigation cycle

As was mentioned in the Introduction to this unit, there are four clearly identifiable stages in most statistical investigations, which can be summarised as follows.

> ### The four stages of a statistical investigation
>
> Stage 1 **P**ose a question
> Stage 2 **C**ollect relevant data
> Stage 3 **A**nalyse the data
> Stage 4 **I**nterpret the results

It may be helpful to think of these stages set out as a cycle, the PCAI cycle, as illustrated in Figure 2. Here the problem starts in the real world and is resolved by making a journey into the statistical world and back again. Complete resolution of the problem might require several trips around the cycle.

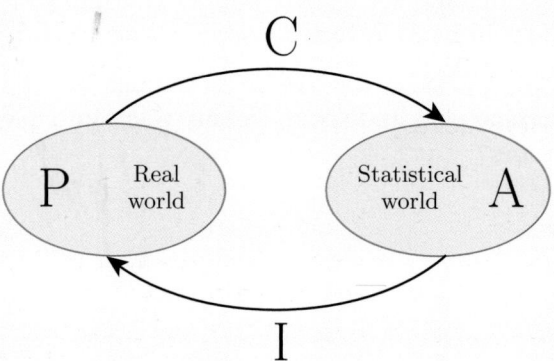

Figure 2 The PCAI statistical investigation cycle

Note that it is important to be as specific as possible in posing a statistical question. The more focused the question, the better the investigation can be attuned to the question, and the better the chance of obtaining a useful answer. The less focused the question, the wider the investigation and the greater the chance that nothing very informative will come out of it.

Not surprisingly, different statistical techniques apply to different stages of the statistical modelling cycle.

- P: Posing a clear question should normally be the first stage of any statistical work. The decision as to which techniques are to be used subsequently will depend on the sort of question that has been asked at the start of the investigation.

- C: Collecting relevant data will involve issues such as choosing samples and designing questionnaires.

- A: This stage, analysing the data, is where techniques like calculating averages and plotting graphs and charts will take place.

- I: The final stage, interpreting the results, takes the action back to the original context from which the initial question was posed. Does the data analysis help to answer the original question? If 'yes', then you can stop there. If 'no', then you may need to travel around the cycle once again, perhaps this time with a slightly modified question or using different analytical techniques.

Activity 3   *Applying the PCAI cycle to a traffic-calming investigation*

Consider a possible investigation, mentioned on page 177, into whether traffic-calming measures are successful in reducing vehicle speed. Spend a few minutes performing a 'back-of-an-envelope' design of this investigation, thinking about the various tasks involved. Then answer the questions below.

That is, jot down a few ideas. It's amazing how many useful things can be (and have been) written, drawn or scrawled on the back of an envelope!

(a) Try to write a description of how this investigation might be conducted, using the stages of the PCAI cycle set out above.

(b) This investigation was introduced as an example of a comparing investigation. What kind of statistical techniques do you think might be involved in the 'A' stage in this case?

The discussion in this subsection should all be rather reminiscent of the four-stage mathematical modelling cycle described in Unit 2; see Table 1 below.

Table I   A comparison of the four stages of statistical and mathematical modelling

Stage	Statistical modelling	Mathematical modelling (as in Unit 2)
1	P: pose question	Clarify question or problem
2	C: collect data	Make assumptions; collect data
3	A: analyse data	Use mathematics to describe the problem and obtain results
4	I: interpret results	Interpret and check results

Activity 4 asks you to think further about three of the four stages of the PCAI cycle and what sorts of statistical work might be linked to each one.

Activity 4   *Organising the tasks of an investigation*

Here are nine of the common types of task that tend to arise in the C, A and I stages of a statistical investigation. Try to match each task to one of these three stages and then fill in the table below.

- Calculate an average   *A*
- Calculate a percentage   *A*
- Choose a set of values, or sample   *C*
- Make a decision based on an observed, numerical difference   *I*
- Design a questionnaire   *C*
- Draw a conclusion   *I*
- Draw a helpful graph   *A*
- Key the data into a spreadsheet   *C*
- Make a prediction about the real world   *I*

C, A and I stages of a statistical investigation

Collect relevant data:

Analyse the data:

Interpret the results:

Activity 5   *Thinking through the stages of an investigation*

Conventional wisdom suggests that clouds tend to act as a warm blanket, keeping heat in at night and preventing the ground temperature from dropping too far. But is there any evidence, either way, with which to answer the question: 'Do clouds keep heat in?'

Spend up to ten minutes thinking about how you might investigate this question, and then use the four PCAI headings to organise your ideas. Note that you are not asked to carry out this investigation but just to think through the stages involved.

This section concerned two ways of thinking about and addressing statistical questions.

The first was the categorisation of statistical investigations into three types: summarising, comparing or seeking a relationship.

Second, the PCAI statistical investigation cycle was introduced. This cycle, which may be gone around more than once, consists of four stages: posing a question (P), collecting relevant data (C), analysing the data (A), and interpreting the results (I).

2 Dealing with data

This section looks at some issues to do with collecting data (stage 'C' of the PCAI cycle) as well as some important distinctions between different types of data, which have relevance when it comes to stage 'A', analysing the data.

2.1 Primary and secondary data

Having identified the question of interest in the 'P', pose a question, stage of the PCAI cycle, how might you go about the 'C' stage – collect relevant data?

You might consider collecting some data yourself. This might be particularly appropriate if the question of interest is one very specific to you and your surroundings or on which you can collect relevant data quite easily. Data that you collect yourself are called **primary data**. For more substantial research questions, this tends to be a reasonable approach only if 'yourself' refers to a research team in a university, company or other research unit.

As was mentioned at the start of Subsection 1.1, 'Types of statistical question', before rushing into collecting data about any question, it is always a good idea to ask: 'Has anyone collected data on this before?' The answer is often 'yes'! **Secondary data** are data that already exist and can be used or adapted for your purpose.

In this information age, secondary data are plentiful and often readily available through the internet, published literature and other sources. However, inevitably the quality of such data is highly variable. There are a number of consistently reliable sources such as UK government statistics, which are generally professionally collected and presented and free from bias. For example, a useful source of statistical data is *Social Trends*, an annual publication from the Office for National Statistics (ONS), which can be downloaded freely from its website (simply type 'social trends' into an internet search engine to find its site).

However, other sites are set up by organisations that may want to sell you some product or promote a particular set of ideas. In some cases, the data that they present may be subject to bias and distortion, and such sites are best avoided as sources of reliable secondary data.

Data are usually presented as 'datasets'. A **dataset** is a collection of data, usually presented in tabular form, or as a single row, or sometimes as a single column. In this unit you will see all three ways of presenting datasets.

An important convention when presenting any dataset, whether primary or secondary, is to provide an accurate reference to the data source (so that the reader can check the details if they so wish).

Backache in pregnancy

Table 2 contains an extract of data taken from a larger, secondary dataset collected at the London Hospital (now Royal London Hospital). It was designed to help answer questions concerning backache in pregnant women, including: How common is it and how severe? Which factors affect it? Which factors alleviate it?

' "Data! Data! Data!", he cried impatiently. "I can't make bricks without clay."

From *The Adventure of the Copper Beeches*, a Sherlock Holmes story by Sir Arthur Conan Doyle, first published in 1892.

Table 2 Backache in pregnancy dataset

	A	B	C	D	E	F	G	H	I	J	K	L	M
1	Patient number	Back pain severity	Month of pregnancy pain started	Age (years)	Height (m)	Weight at start of pregnancy (kg)	Weight at end of pregnancy (kg)	Weight of baby (kg)	Number of children	Relieved by aspirin?	Relieved by hot bath?	Aggravated by fatigue?	Aggravated by bending?
2	1	1	0	26	1.52	54.5	75	3.35	0	0	0	0	0
3	2	3	0	23	1.6	59.1	68.6	2.22	1	1	0	0	0
4	3	2	6	24	1.57	73.2	82.7	4.15	0	0	0	1	0
5	4	1	8	22	1.52	41.4	47.3	2.81	0	0	0	0	0
6	5	1	0	27	1.6	55.5	60	3.75	1	0	0	0	0
7	6	1	7	32	1.75	70.5	85.5	4.01	2	0	0	0	0
8	7	1	0	24	1.73	76.4	89.1	34	0	0	0	0	0
9	8	1	8	25	1.63	70	85	4.01	1	0	0	1	0
10	9	2	6	20	1.55	52.3	59.5	3.69	1	0	0	0	0
11	10	2	8	18	1.63	83.2	90.9	3.3	99	1	0	0	0
12	11	1	0	21	1.65	64.5	75.5	2.95	0	0	0	0	0
13	12	1	0	26	1.55	49.5	53.6	2.64	0	1	0	1	0
14	13	2	6	35	1.65	70	82.7	3.64	7	0	1	0	1
15	14	1	8	26	1.6	52.3	64.5	4.49	1	0	1	0	0
16	15	1	6	34	1.68	68.2	77.3	3.75	3	0	0	1	0
17	16	0	0	25	1.5	47.3	55	2.73	1	0	0	0	0
18	17	1	7	42	1.52	66.8	73.2	2.44	6	0	0	0	1
19	18	2	6	26	1.65	70	81.4	3.01	1	0	0	0	0
20	19	2	6	18	1.6	56.4	70	3.89	1	0	0	0	0
21	20	0	1	42	1.65	53.6		2.73	2	0	0	0	0
22	21	2	0	28	1.63	59.1	72.3	3.75	99	0	0	0	0
23	22	1	0	26	1.52	44.5	56.4	3.49	0	0	0	0	0
24	23	1	0	23	1.57	55.9	60.9	3.07	0	0	0	0	0
25	24	2	6	21	1.55	57.3	77.3	3.35	0	0	0	99	99
26	25	2	7	32	1.52	69.5	75.5	3.64	5	0	1	0	1
27	26	1	8	18	1.6	73.2	81.4	2.05	0	0	0	0	1
28	27	1	0	25	1.7			2.44	1	1	0	0	0
29	28	1	0	29.916666	1.63	62.7	72.3	3.07	4	0	0	0	0
30	29	1	0	19	1.92	73.6	92.7	3.35	0	0	0	0	0
31	30	2	7	26	1.65	70	89.1	3.21	1	0	0	1	1
32	31	1	8	28	1.68	56.69905	70.9	3.41	0	0	0	0	0
33	32	1	0	21	1.6	58.2	69.5	3.3	0	0	0	0	1
34	33	0	0	29	1.57	68.2	7.5	3.35	0	0	0	0	0

Source: M.J. Mantle et al. (1977) 'Backache in pregnancy', *Rheumatology and Rehabilitation*, no. 16, pp. 95–101, quoted in C. Chatfield (1988) *Problem solving: a statistician's guide*, London, Chapman and Hall.

In order to make the dataset manageable for your work in this unit, the number of respondents has been reduced from 180 women to 33, and the number of items of information reduced from 33 to 13. Note also that the data have been laid out in a spreadsheet format, with numbered rows (1, 2, 3, ...) and lettered columns (A, B, C, ...) which will facilitate identifying particular items of data by their column/row references.

In the remainder of the unit, this dataset will be referred to as the *backache dataset*.

This dataset will be used to illustrate most of the issues concerned with handling data in this section, and to that end, a few of the data values from the original source have been changed. Several of the columns in this table have been entered into the course software resource Dataplotter but, for reasons that will be explained shortly, a few of the data values from this table have been changed. (Also, you won't get around to directly considering the questions concerning backache here as we will focus on making sense of the numbers.)

Take a quick look at these data. The first thing to notice is that each row corresponds to results for one patient, and each column – except the first – to a specific item measured. The first column just contains patient reference numbers. (Notice that because there are column headings in row 1, the patient reference numbers are unfortunately not the same as the table row numbers – a common occurrence.)

Activity 6   *Scanning the data*

Look carefully at the 13 column headings in Table 2 and try to get a sense of what each is measuring. Then try to come up with a few impressions that strike you about the variations in the numbers in the table.

2.2   Discrete and continuous data

The distinction between 'discrete' and 'continuous' measures is important as it provides useful information about the nature of the data collected. As an introduction to these terms, here is a context that should help you get a sense of how they are used.

Look at the picture in Figure 3, which shows a route through a forest. The path itself is continuous, so any position on the path is possible, whereas the stepping-stones placed on the path are discrete; they represent distinct, separate positions with nothing in between any two consecutive steps. Using the path, you might mark your journey in terms of a measured distance, whereas taking the same journey on the stepping-stones involves counting out steps (first, second, third, and so on). In general, this distinction between measuring and counting is a useful way of identifying which measures are discrete and which are continuous.

When it comes to statistical data, the same distinction can be made. An example of discrete data is measurement of shoe size. You can talk about shoe sizes of, say, $7\frac{1}{2}$ or 9, but a shoe size of, say, 8.314 cannot occur in practice, since shoe sizes are restricted to either whole or half sizes. Foot length, on the other hand, has no such restriction – it is something that is measured on a continuous scale of measure and therefore produces continuous data.

Turn back to the data in Table 2. One of the clearest distinctions between the numbers in the columns is that in some columns, the numbers seem to be discrete values while in other columns, the numbers seem to come from a continuous scale. **Discrete data** are data that can take one of a particular set of values; such data typically, though not necessarily, take integer values.

Here are some examples of discrete data:

- the number of days in a week on which one takes exercise
- the number of times a particular website is visited in a day
- the quality of a person's recovery after a serious accident when coded 0 for full recovery, 1 for partial recovery, 2 for failure to recover.

Often, as in the first two examples, discrete data arise from a process of counting, sometimes over a limited range of possible integer outcomes (for example, up to a maximum of 7 days in a week), at other times over an unlimited range (for example, the number of 'hits' on a website, at least in principle!). Sometimes, as in the third example, discrete data arise as a convenient way of coding data whose outcome is really some non-numerical category. A widely-occurring example of this is when there are just two categories such as yes/no, pass/fail or true/false. Such data, coded by two numerical values, are said to be **binary data**. The two values are often taken to be 1 and 0.

Note that the word 'discrete' is not the same as 'discreet', which means 'unobtrusive and restrained'.

Figure 3   Discrete stepping stones on a continuous forest path

The 'bi' in binary means 'two' – as in bicycle (a cycle with two wheels).

Activity 7 *Identifying discrete data*

Examples of columns containing discrete data in the backache dataset are listed and explained below.

Columns	Values available	Explanation
Back pain severity	0, 1, 2, 3	0 = 'nil' 1 = 'nothing worth troubling about' 2 = 'troublesome but not severe' 3 = 'severe'
Relieved by aspirin?	0, 1	0 = no 1 = yes

Note that the 'Relieved by aspirin?' question is a binary measure (with just two outcomes).

Which other columns of data from the backache dataset do you think contain discrete data?

Unlike discrete data, **continuous data** can take all the in-between values on a number scale. In theory, and depending on the context, they may take any numerical value from the set of real numbers, either negative or positive. Alternatively, they may be constrained to be positive (e.g. the length of a particular manufactured item) or they may be limited to a finite interval (e.g. the percentage of active ingredient in a particular compound, which can be anywhere between 0 and 100). In Table 2, the columns not identified in Activity 7, namely 'Height', 'Weight at start of pregnancy', 'Weight at end of pregnancy' and 'Weight of baby', contain continuous data, as perhaps should 'Age'. Notice that all of these columns contain data that take positive values.

Mass and weight

Did you notice that the weights in Table 2 are given in kilograms, even though the kilogram is a unit of mass?

The mass of an object is a measure of the amount of matter that it contains, whereas its weight is a measure of the gravitational force acting on it. Weight, being a force, is measured in newtons. However, you will often see weights quoted in kilograms in everyday life and this informal approach will sometimes be used in MU123 too.

Now, with counts (such as the number of days in a week on which a person takes exercise) and other forms of discrete data, it is possible to give exact answers. With measurements (such as the length of a particular manufactured item), it is never possible to get an exact value, as the next activity illustrates.

Activity 8 *Investigating measurement precision: how exact is exact?*

Measure the width of a piece of A4 paper with a metric ruler and write down your answer. Please do this before reading any further. *20.8 cm*

But how will I know if I'm right? I mean, what degree of precision are we working to here?

You were deliberately not told in this activity what level of precision to use. You might have written down 21 cm and this would carry the implication that the page width was nearer 21 cm than 20 cm or 22 cm. Alternatively, you might have tried to be more precise and written down 21.1 cm or 211 mm. Again there would be an implication that the actual measurement was nearer 211 mm than 210 mm or 212 mm. If you had access to a more precise measuring device still, you might have been able to write down 211.0 mm or 211.03 mm, and so on.

However, no matter how good your measuring device, you would never be able to say what the *exact* width of the particular sheet of paper was.

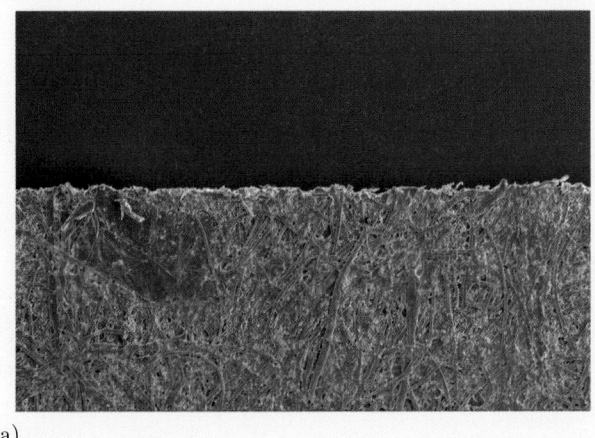

(a)

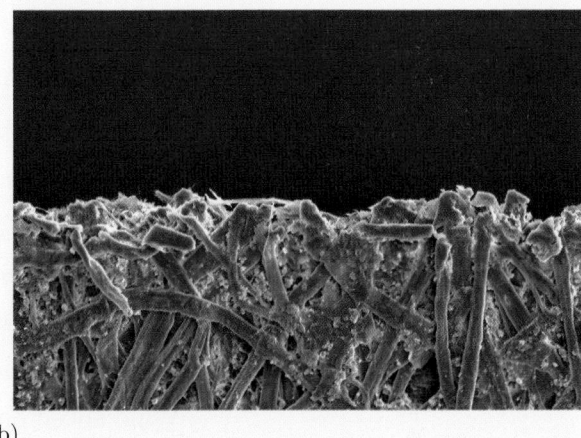

(b)

Figure 4   Images showing the ragged edge of a sheet of A4 paper magnified by a factor of (a) 40 and (b) 160

Indeed, as can be seen from Figure 4, at a microscopic level, the edge of a piece of paper is by no means straight and smooth – in fact, the closer we look, the rougher the edge appears to be! Clearly there is a limit to the precision with which is it meaningful to describe its width. However, for most practical purposes, there is no need for extreme precision, and recording the value of the width correct to, say, the nearest centimetre or the nearest millimetre may well suffice.

In practice, for all manufactured items there is a tolerance for the possible range of sizes that each item can be. For example, according to the ISO standard, the width of manufactured A4 paper should be 210 ± 2 mm (i.e. between 208 and 212 mm). This is despite the mathematical exactness suggested in Unit 3 of how ISO paper sizes relate to each other!

This argument about exact measurement applies to other continuous data too: time, age, weight, height, temperature, distance, area, volume or whatever. This is the sense in which each of the columns C to H in Table 2 can be considered to contain continuous data. It is just that the measurement and recording process has resulted in these columns of data being presented correct to the nearest month (when pain started), year (age), millimetre (height), tenth of a kilogram (mothers' weight measurements), and hundredth of a kilogram (babies' weights), respectively.

It follows that while the actual values of two items of continuous data can never strictly be identical, their stated values, given to a certain degree of precision, may well be. For example, patients numbered 15 and 31 in Table 2 are considered to be the same height, 1.68 m or 168 cm, correct to the level of precision measured and recorded.

Activity 9   *Discrete or continuous?*

Which of the following are examples of continuous values and which are discrete?

(a) Price of a loaf of bread, in pence

(b) Number of seagulls on a cliff face

(c) Time of an athlete running 1500 metres, in seconds

(d) Number of goals scored by a hockey team

(e) Distance between major cities, in miles

(f) TMA score achieved by a student

(g) Air temperature at midday at a weather station, in °C

(h) Wind speed measured in kilometres per hour

(i) Wind speed on the Beaufort scale (e.g. gale force 8)

You would be right to think that all measured data are actually discrete, but the idea of continuous data remains useful both conceptually and when creating mathematical and statistical models of the world.

2.3 Checking and cleaning data

In Activity 6, your inspection of the data in Table 2 probably came up with a number of apparent anomalies in the backache dataset. First, there are some blank cells in the spreadsheet where data are missing. Second, you probably also noticed the values of 99 appearing in columns that otherwise contain only small integer values. These must be wrong: those in cells I11 and I22 correspond to women having 99 children from previous pregnancies; those in cells L25 and M25 are given in answer to yes/no questions.

An explanation for these, other than a typing mistake, is that numbers such as 99 are sometimes used as codes that signal 'value missing'. (They can cause trouble: missing data codes might not always be so easy to spot and might even sometimes mistakenly correspond to reasonable actual values.) Good documentation of the data file should make the presence and value of a 'missing data' code clear, but with secondary data this information can get lost. Large datasets of real data inevitably contain plenty of missing data, and sophisticated statistical methodology has been developed to cope with these gaps.

Take another look at Table 2 on page 184. Are there any further outstandingly large (or small) values in the backache dataset?

Column H contains the weights of the babies, in kilograms. The minimum weight is 2.05 kg, which is not a great deal less than the next smallest weights, 2.22 kg and 2.44 kg. The largest baby's weight, however, appears to be 34 kg (as you might have spotted in Activity 6). This impossible value must surely be the result of a recording error. Most probably, the decimal point was missed out of a weight of 3.4 kg (but without confirmation from the original data collection source, there is no certainty that this is the explanation).

Activity 10   *Examining unusual values in columns of data*

Scan the following columns of the backache data in Table 2 and comment on whether or not you think there might be a problem with any of the most extreme values in each column.

(a) Column G, weights of the mothers at the end of their pregnancies (in kg).

(b) Column E, height (in m).

Outliers

One or more data values that are considerably smaller or larger than the other values in the same dataset are called **outliers**. Sometimes, outliers correspond to errors and it may be possible to correct them and thus remove the outliers. However, as in the case of the tallest mother mentioned in the solution to Activity 10, often there is no such obvious reason and the outlier may just be an unusual, but not unreasonable, observation. You might still wish to ignore or underplay the outlier to come to conclusions about the rest of the data without the outlier influencing results too strongly, or you might wish to embrace the outlier as an important aspect of the data. Either way, again, there are sophisticated statistical techniques available to deal with outliers but these are not explored here.

Figure 5   Spot the outlier!

2.4   Spurious precision

In the backache dataset, you probably noticed the values 29.916666 in cell D29 and 56.69905 in cell F32. These are given with five or six decimal places, whereas other entries in columns D and F are given with zero and one decimal places, respectively. These values are surely examples of **spurious precision**. In the first case, the data value seems to be a result of the person's age being given as 29 years and 11 months, and 11 months being $11/12 = 0.916666$ years (given to six decimal places). It is likely that this value was entered as '$= 29 + 11/12$', which would automatically be displayed in its decimal form. In the second case, the spurious precision has arisen by conversion, to kilograms, of data measured in different units (pounds).

The term 'spurious' means 'different from what it claims to be'.

Activity 11 *Converting spurious precision into appropriate precision*

(a) Given that 1 pound is equivalent to 0.45359237 kilograms, use a calculator to convert a weight of 125 pounds to kilograms. Express the answer correct to five decimal places.

(b) What should the values in cells D29 and F32 be when (appropriately) rounded to zero and one decimal places, respectively?

Spurious precision can arise in various ways. One way, which was illustrated in Activity 11, is in the conversion of units – particularly between metric and imperial measures. For example, a newspaper report may state: 'the flood water was 1 metre (3.2808 feet) deep …'. Another way is to imply that a quantity can be measured to a greater level of precision than is possible with the measuring instrument used. For instance, a household ruler may be used to measure lengths to the nearest millimetre, so it would be incorrect to state a measurement to the nearest tenth or hundredth of a millimetre, if the ruler is used.

Another way that spurious precision can arise is when figures are quoted to a greater number of significant figures than is warranted in the context. An example is contained in the following statement which appeared in a newspaper report of a court case in 2005:

> It was estimated that, over a nine-and-a-half year period, the defendant stole £557 327.11.

The accused was a council employee who regularly stole a portion of the money she was counting from the fees paid into machines by motorists in car parks. Think about the quotation for a moment. Do you believe it? Did she really keep a careful record of all the money taken and add it all up accurately? Ah, no, the figure was 'estimated' – but by whom and how?

Activity 12 *Where did the eleven pence come from?*

It is most implausible that the amount of money stolen was exactly £557 327.11.

(a) How do you think this figure might have been arrived at?

(b) In what sense is the figure spurious, and what might be a more reasonable estimate?

The point about using a rounded figure for the amount stolen, £550 000, is that it gives a fairer impression of the degree of precision of the data. Generally speaking it is customary, when analysing data gathered by others, to assume that the claimed precision is justified unless there is definite evidence to the contrary. Furthermore, in displaying data it is frequently unnecessary to retain their full precision. A key principle here is that displayed data should be just precise enough to reveal the key features – offering the reader an answer containing too many significant figures can easily obscure these patterns in a mass of numbers.

If you are collecting primary data, you should bear in mind the kinds of difficulty with data discussed above, and do your best to avoid them. In the case of secondary data, ideally you should be able to go back to the original data collector and check with them any suspicions you have about the data. Unfortunately, all too often this is not possible; with the passage of time, details concerning data collection tend to be forgotten or lost.

2.5 Single and paired data

Column H of the backache dataset in Table 2 contains 33 values of the weights of babies (in kg). This constitutes a single sample of weights of babies from mothers, many of whom suffered from backache in pregnancy. For the moment, ignore the remainder of the data in the table. Looking just at column H, these values are all based on a single measure (weight) and can be described as **single data**. These 33 numbers can be summarised and represented in a variety of ways. You could calculate an average: you will learn more about averages in Section 3, where two different types of average are explored (the mean and the median). Alternatively, you could measure how widely dispersed the values are – in other words, whether the values are tightly clustered together or widely spread. Three measures of spread are explained in Section 4. Finally, you could plot the values to discern the overall pattern visually, and you will be shown a number of useful statistical plots in Unit 11. The purpose of doing these things would be to try to gain an insight into baby weights in general.

Suppose now that there was a second sample, of birth weights from a different set of mothers, the babies in this second sample all being classed as premature. This is now a **two-sample**, as opposed to one-sample, dataset. Interest now is in comparing features of the birth weights of premature babies with those of full-term babies. Other examples of making statistical comparisons might include making a comparison between two medical treatments or two commercial products. Again, a sample of measures would be taken from each and the results compared. (When making such a statistical comparison, there is no requirement that the two samples contain the same number of values, although they could do.)

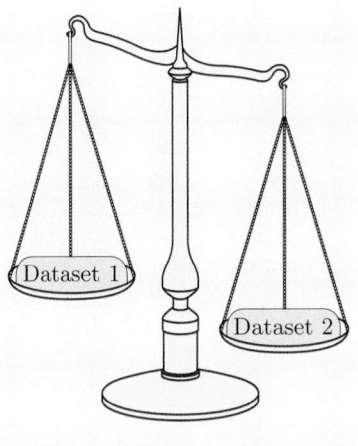

Figure 6 With two-sample data we are interested in comparing

Now return to the babies recorded in the backache dataset in Table 2. A statistical question of interest might be how the babies' weights (in column H) relate to the weights of their mothers at the start of their pregnancy (column F). This question links two pieces of information for each of the people in the study – a case of **paired data**. Interest centres on how one of these pieces of data (birth weight) relates to the other (mother's weight). In statistical investigation terms, this falls under the general heading of seeking a relationship. Although each measure can be explored individually, the main point of collecting paired data is to assess the relationship between the two variables in question.

A number of important statistical ideas are linked to exploring relationships to do with paired data (for example, regression and scatterplots), and some of these ideas are discussed in Unit 6.

To end this section on properties of data, tackle Activity 13, which asks you to think more deeply about the various data types and how they are typically used to draw sensible conclusions in a statistical investigation.

A characteristic feature of paired data is that the two data lists must contain the same number of values. Also, for each item in one list, there is a specific corresponding item in the other.

Activity 13   *Investigating mothers' weights*

Columns F and G of the backache dataset contain the weights at the beginning of pregnancy and at the end of pregnancy for the same set of mothers (ignoring the problem of missing data). Below are four descriptions of possible datasets.

- Weights of mothers and of their babies
- Weights of mothers at end of pregnancy
- Weights of two samples of babies, one in the UK and one in France
- Weights of mothers and average earnings in 20 EU countries

Classify each of these datasets as two-sample data, paired data, single data or two unrelated samples. Also, classify the relevance of each of these for statistical investigation. (One is of no direct interest; one is useful for summarising, one for comparing, and one for seeking a relationship.)

Lay out your solution in tabular form, by filling in the blank spaces below.

Datasets	Data type(s)	Relevance
Weights of mothers and of their babies		
Weights of mothers at end of pregnancy		
Weights of two samples of babies, one in the UK and one in France		
Weights of mothers and average earnings in 20 EU countries		

In this section you looked at dealing with data – in particular, how to classify and distinguish different types of data. Primary and secondary data are terms that identify the data source – primary data you collect yourself, whereas secondary data are taken from somewhere (or someone) else. Data can be discrete, like shoe sizes, or continuous, like the measurement of foot length. Subsection 2.3 explored questions to do with precision, and then introduced the important idea of spurious precision, where values are displayed to a greater-than-warranted number of significant figures. Finally, you looked at single and paired data. Single data are usually represented by a single set of values. Paired data, as the name suggests, involve two related datasets with each data value in one dataset corresponding to a data value in the other dataset. As you will see later in this unit, with single data, the aim is usually to summarise a set of values in order to get a handle on where they lie or to compare two sets of values to see whether one set is bigger or more widely spread than the other. With paired data there is usually a different aim – to investigate a possible relationship between the two measures.

In the next two sections, we will concentrate on single data and how to summarise the information that they contain.

3 Summarising data: location

In this section and the following one, you will take some first steps into stage 'A' of the PCAI cycle, analysing the data that have been collected. In particular, in this section you will look at simple summary measures of what statisticians often call the **location** of a dataset, that is, a single number that represents an 'average', 'typical' or 'central' value.

Activity 14 *Location, location, location*

A group of school students challenged their teachers to a speed-texting competition. The 12 participants (5 teachers and 7 students) each sent a short text message on a mobile phone. The times are given below, and for convenience, the data have been sorted in order of size.

Teacher times (seconds):	18	27	31	36	47			*31·8*
Student times (seconds):	19	19	21	24	25	27	29	*23·4*

Source: adapted from A. Graham (2006) *Developing thinking in statistics*, London, Paul Chapman Publishing, p. 82.

(a) If you had to summarise each set of times by a single number without doing any calculations, what might you say? (Please bear in mind that there is not a definitively correct answer here.)

(b) Can you make any general comparison of these datasets on the basis of your answer to part (a)?

A statement that describes whereabouts a dataset lies (e.g. 'about 25 seconds') is a way of describing the dataset's location. Activity 14 illustrated the two main purposes of measuring location:

- summarising a set of data values by a single number that might be thought of as an 'average' or 'typical' or 'central' value
- comparing sets of data values on the basis of their locations, to see which set tends to have bigger values.

Measuring language

In the following example, the context is investigating people's use of the language of chance.

At an Open University summer school, a group of 30 students were asked to investigate their understanding of various words used to describe degrees of likelihood (terms such as likely, impossible, nearly certain, fifty-fifty, and so on).

The students were studying the course 'Developing mathematical thinking at Key Stage 3'.

The task began with a consideration of just two such words, 'possible' and 'probable'. Each student was asked to make a personal, numerical estimate on a scale from 0 to 100 (where 0 means impossible and 100 means certain) of their interpretation of these two words as measures of likelihood. The question they were asked to investigate was:

This corresponds to the first stage of the PCAI cycle (discussed in Subsection 1.2): *posing a question.*

What do people understand by the words 'possible' and 'probable'?

Or, more specifically,

What numerical values do people attribute to the words 'possible' and 'probable'?

This is an example of a summarising investigation. Before looking at the student data, try this exercise for yourself in Activity 15.

Activity 15 *Investigating words for likelihood*

This task can be thought of as the second stage of the PCAI cycle: *collecting relevant data.*

(a) On a scale from 0 to 100, write down your estimates of the degree of likelihood suggested by the words 'possible' and 'probable'. (You might think of one or both of these words as describing a range of numerical values, but for the purposes of this activity please select a single number reflecting the 'centre' of such a range.)

(b) In your opinion, which of these words would most people rate as describing a higher level of likelihood?

(c) In your opinion, which of these words would generate scores that showed the greater measure of agreement among the respondents?

There are no comments on this activity.

The students' data are contained in the course resource Dataplotter (which you need not open on your computer yet) and shown in Table 3 below. Notice that these are paired data in the sense that each 'pair' corresponds to the response of a particular student. However, for the purposes of this unit, the values will be treated as two-sample data.

Table 3 Thirty students' interpretations of 'Possible' and 'Probable'

Student	Possible	Probable	Student	Possible	Probable
1	30	95	16	10	75
2	90	90	17	50	80
3	60	60	18	20	80
4	70	60	19	50	75
5	5	70	20	50	99
6	1	60	21	30	90
7	1	76	22	1	51
8	50	80	23	30	90
9	50	75	24	40	75
10	50	75	25	30	70
11	80	80	26	20	75
12	30	70	27	50	90
13	1	99	28	30	70
14	10	90	29	98	95
15	85	85	30	35	75

3.1 Scanning data

As you saw in Section 2, before performing a detailed analysis of any dataset, it is always a good idea to scan the data, looking closely at the numbers to see if any patterns or anomalies stand out.

Activity 16 *Scanning Table 3*

(a) Inspect the data in Table 3 and, referring back to the comments on Activity 6 for reminders of the kinds of things you might look for, comment on the presence or otherwise of each of the following:

(i) missing data

(ii) spurious precision

(iii) the constraint that the data lie between 0 and 100

(iv) the presence of outliers.

(b) Does any other feature of the numbers in Table 3 stand out?

Inspecting the data needn't stop there, however. In Activity 17 you are asked to get a first feel for the locations of these sets of data just by further inspection.

Activity 17 *Further inspection of Table 3*

(a) Look closely at the sets of 'Possible' and 'Probable' values in Table 3 and write down what you think would be a typical 'central value' for each one. Then think for a moment about how you came up with this figure – for example, did you do a rough calculation or did you try to pick out a typical value or use some other approach?

(b) Based on your estimates in part (a), which set of values shows the higher location?

3.2 Measuring location

The most important and useful summary of a dataset is a measure of its location, based on some sort of average or typical value. There is no single and universally most appropriate measure of location, but there are various useful measures that can be chosen, depending on the situation and on the nature of the data. Each measure has its own pros and cons. The three most common measures of location in statistics textbooks are the *mean*, the *mode* and the *median*. In this course we will mainly use the mean and the median. These are considered in detail below.

The mode of a dataset is the data value that occurs most frequently. Since there can be several 'most frequent' values, it is a rather problematic measure, which we shall not use in MU123.

You may find the diagram in Figure 7 a useful summary of the ideas set out in the previous paragraph. We will return to this diagram at the end of the next section, by which time a second important summary will have been added, namely the idea of spread and its associated measures: *range, interquartile range* and *standard deviation*.

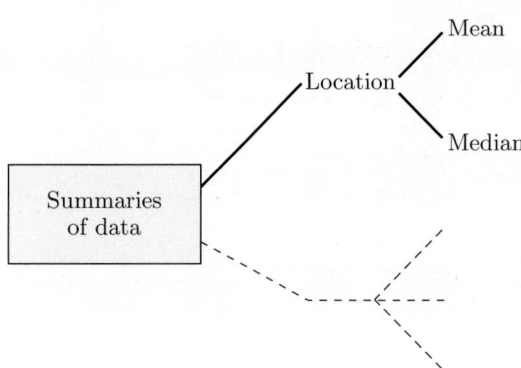

Figure 7   Summaries of data: the mean and median are useful measures of location

The **mean**, which is often just called the average, is probably quite familiar to you.

The mean is more specifically called the **arithmetic mean**, and when applied, as here, to data, it is often called the **sample mean**.

> **Strategy**   *To find the mean of a dataset*
>
> To find the mean of a set of numbers, add all the numbers together and divide by however many numbers there are in the set.

Let's look at a simple example, after which you can try a calculation for yourself.

Example 1   *Calculating the mean of a dataset*

Find the mean of the texting times of the five teachers given in Activity 14 (page 193).

Solution

Add together the numbers in the 'Teacher times' dataset and divide by however many numbers are in that dataset.

The mean is

$$(18 + 27 + 31 + 36 + 47)/5 = 159/5 = 31.8 \text{ seconds}.$$

Activity 18   *Finding means*

(a) Calculate the mean of the texting times for the seven students given in Activity 14 (remember to include units in your answer).

(b) Calculate the mean of the 'Possible' values given in Table 3, giving your answer correct to one decimal place.

In Activity 14(a), you may well have taken the approach of selecting the middle value from the five teacher times, which, as you may remember, were listed in increasing order of size. If so, you obtained a statistical average known as the **median**. Speaking roughly, the median is the data value that is in the middle when the data are arranged in order. A more precise definition is given in the following box.

Strategy   *To find the median of a dataset*

To find the median of a set of numbers:

- Sort the data into increasing or decreasing order.
- If there is an odd number of data values, the median is the middle value.
- If there is an even number of data values, the median is defined as the mean of the middle two values.

If the middle two values are equal, then the mean is just this common value.

Activity 19   *Finding medians*

(a) Calculate the median of the texting times for the seven students of Activity 14.

(b) How do the medians of the teacher and student texting times compare with the corresponding approximate values of location given in the Comment on Activity 14(a) and the means calculated above?

Activity 20   *More medians*

(a) Twelve sixteen-year-olds were asked to guess the size of the population of the UK and came up with the following estimates, in millions.

   60   100   25   60   60   100   80   160   58   23   60   200

   Order these numbers and then calculate the median.

(b) Here is an ordered list of the 30 'Possible' values given in Table 3:

   1   1   1   1   5   10   10   20   20   30   30   30   30   30   30
   35   40   50   50   50   50   50   50   50   60   70   80   85   90   98

   What is the median of these values?

Activity 21   *Calculating the 'Probable' mean and median*

Here is an ordered list of the 30 'Probable' values given in Table 3:

   51   60   60   60   70   70   70   70   75   75   75   75   75   75   75
   76   80   80   80   80   85   90   90   90   90   90   95   95   99   99

This activity, and the next one, represent the third stage of the PCAI cycle: *analysing the data.*

(a) What is the mean of these values?

(b) What is the median of these values?

(c) How do the mean and median compare?

As you are probably already thinking, calculating the mean by 'hand' or calculator becomes increasingly tedious and error-prone as the size of a dataset increases. Calculating the median is a lot easier *if* the data are already sorted. However, this too becomes a long calculation if you have to order a large set of values. So, for anything but the smallest sets of data, it seems appropriate to turn to a calculator, spreadsheet or other software to compute these summary values. Fortunately, these and similar summary calculations can also be easily carried out using the Dataplotter software.

Using Dataplotter to measure location

Using the instructions in Subsection 2.4 of the Course Guide, open Dataplotter, which is available on the MU123 website. You can see that four types of plot are available: Dotplot, Boxplot, Histogram and Scatterplot. Ensure that the first of these, Dotplot, is selected. With the 'Datasets' tab selected on the left of the screen, you will see two data lists. From the drop-down menu at the top of the first list, select the dataset '# Possible'. By a similar method, select the dataset '# Probable' from the second list. These two lists contain the data provided in Table 3.

As you can see, as soon as each dataset is selected, Dataplotter processes the information in two ways. First, the values are displayed visually as dotplots, a type of statistical plot where each data value is represented by the position of a dot along the number line below it. Dotplots are a useful way of seeing patterns in data at a glance.

The second main outcome of selecting these datasets is that a set of ~~nine~~ *ten* key summary values has been automatically calculated and displayed for each dataset. This is the feature that you are asked to look at now by tackling Activity 22.

 Dataplotter

---

Activity 22   *Summaries of location*

(a) By selecting appropriate values from the two summary lists, complete the table below.

Means and medians of students' values for 'Possible' and 'Probable'

Summary	'Possible' scores	'Probable' scores
Mean	38·6	78·5
Median	32·5	75·5

(b) Based on the information in the table in part (a), try to come to an initial conclusion about the original question: 'What numerical values do people attribute to the words "possible" and "probable"?' Which of the two datasets had the higher location? Were these results consistent with your previous impression?

The conclusions from using either measure of location in Activity 22 are the same: people tend to think that the word 'probable' indicates a higher degree of likelihood than the word 'possible'. This may not be surprising to you and may be in accordance with what you expected when you thought about the question for Activity 15. But that's not all there is to say about these data. So far you have looked at two summaries that concern measures of *location* from the 'Possible' and 'Probable' data – the calculation of mean and median. In Section 4 you will explore some measures of *spread*.

3.3   Mean versus median

You might be thinking that it's all very well being told how to calculate two different measures of location, but which should you use, and when? Well, it has already been suggested that there is no simple universally applicable answer to this question. But there are a few advantages and disadvantages of one measure compared with the other, and in Activity 23 you are asked to think what some of these might be.

Activity 23   *Mean versus median*

(a) Find the mean and the median of the following datasets.

> Dataset A: 3   4   5   6   7   8   9
>
> Dataset B: 3   4   5   6   7   8   99

(b) Which of these two averages seems a more appropriate summary for these datasets?

(c) List the advantages of using each location measure (mean and median).

With this question we are entering the fourth stage of the PCAI cycle: *interpreting the results.*

In practice, both the mean and the median are widely used. They often give similar results but can sometimes differ considerably. Typically, when the values of the dataset are bunched towards one or other end of the range of values, there are larger differences between the mean and the median. For example, with earnings data, it is often the case that the extremely high earnings of a small number of very wealthy individuals will drag up the value of the mean and so may give a rather distorted impression of the location of earnings. For this reason, the median rather than the mean tends to be used for summarising earnings. Where the values are symmetrically spread, there will be little difference between the values of the two summaries, in which case, it will not matter much which one is chosen.

To sum up this section, we have discussed summarising a dataset by measuring its location, that is, a number that might be thought of as an 'average', 'typical' or 'central' value. Two particular measures of location were looked at in detail: the mean and the median. The mean of a set of numbers is found by adding all the numbers together and dividing by however many numbers there are. To find the median, first sort the data in order of size. If there is an odd number of data values, the median is the middle value. If there is an even number of data values, the median is defined as the mean of the middle two values. The mean and median are two measures of location that were used as part of an initial study of the 'probability words' datasets. By comparing them, you were able to give support to the notion that the word 'probable' seems to indicate a higher degree of likelihood than the word 'possible'.

In the next section you will look at another important property of data that can be reduced to a single summary measure. It indicates how closely bunched or spread out the values are and is known as the *spread* of the dataset.

4 Summarising data: spread

In Section 3 you looked at the best known and most widely used summaries of a dataset, which provided information about the *location* of the numbers. These were the mean and median. A second basic property of data is how widely **spread** the values are. For example, here is a set of TMA marks of six students (sorted in increasing order):

   42   58   60   68   78   92

As you can see, there is a wide spread of marks here, from a minimum value of 42 to a maximum of 92. In the following TMA, the same students' marks were:

   60   65   72   74   75   80

This time the spread of marks is much narrower, ranging from a minimum of 60 to a maximum of 80.

In this section you will look at three of the most common measures of spread – the *range, interquartile range* and *standard deviation*.

If you go on to more advanced study of statistics, you will find that the measures of spread mentioned here continue to play an important role.

4.1 Range

As you have just seen, a simple way of estimating spread is to scan along the data to find the smallest (minimum, or 'min') and largest (maximum, or 'max') values. The **range** is the difference between these two values. In other words,

   range = max − min.

Let's try an example.

Example 2 *Calculating the range*

Look at the data below, which give the distances, in kilometres, travelled by eleven students to attend an Open University tutorial.

   Distances from home
   Distance (km):   12   40   26   4   2   18   66   30   45   12   15

Calculate the range of these data.

Solution

By inspecting the data, the maximum value is 66 km and the minimum value is 2 km.

So the range of these data is

   max − min = 66 km − 2 km = 64 km.

Now try Activity 24, which asks you to calculate the range for a different dataset and think about how useful it is as a measure of spread.

Activity 24 *Calculating the range*

Below are the earnings, for a particular week, of 15 staff (including the owner) working in a small business.

Earnings data from a small business

Weekly earnings (£): 280 370 305 285 480 1260 210 340
                      280 290 315 325 370   360 280

(a) Write down the minimum and maximum values in this dataset. Hence calculate the range of weekly earnings.

(b) Why might the range be an unhelpful measure of spread for these particular data?

As you saw in Activity 24, the range is sometimes a rather inadequate measure of spread, particularly where there are one or two extreme outliers in the dataset. In the jargon of statisticians, the range could be referred to as a 'quick-and-dirty' measure of spread – it is quick and easy to calculate, can sometimes give a useful overall impression, but lacks the subtlety and sophistication of other methods. You will now be introduced to two alternative measures of spread that overcome the basic weakness of the range, namely that it is too easily affected by outliers. These are the *interquartile range* and the *standard deviation*.

4.2 Quartiles and the interquartile range

The earnings data in Activity 24 are not very easy to absorb or interpret as presented. Figure 8 shows the same data displayed as a dotplot.

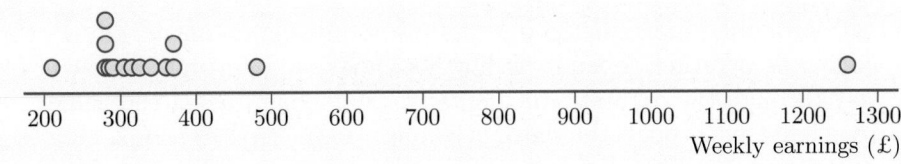

Figure 8 A dotplot showing the earnings data from Activity 24

The 15 dots have been placed above a number line, positioned to correspond to the weekly earnings of the 15 members of staff. Where values coincide (for example, there are three values of £280), the dots are placed vertically, one above another.

When you have a small number of values in a dataset, as is the case here, it is quick and easy to create a simple dotplot of the data like this. Usually it provides a useful, intuitive picture of where the values lie, whether there is some bunching of the data to one side or they are symmetrical, and whether there are clear outliers.

You will use dotplots again in Unit 11.

In this case, the extent to which the outlier is unrepresentative now shows up very clearly.

How then can the problem of the range being unduly affected by this outlier be solved? You might simply decide to ignore this particular untypical value, but that is a somewhat arbitrary decision and not one that can be called a general method, although it is sometimes done.

Alternatively, you might choose to omit, say, the largest and smallest values and take the range of the remaining 13 values. This is a better solution, and one that works well in this particular instance, but if there were several outliers at either end, the problem would not be solved. In order to be confident that you have dealt with the outlier problem, you really need to exclude a greater number of values at either end. The question is, how many?

Introducing the quartiles

The conventional solution, and the one described now, is to exclude the top quarter and bottom quarter of the values and create a new measure of spread that measures the 'range' of the middle 50% of the values. There are two such points that mark the cut-off points of the top and bottom quarters of the data. They are known as the **quartiles** – in particular, the **lower quartile** (Q1) and **upper quartile** (Q3).

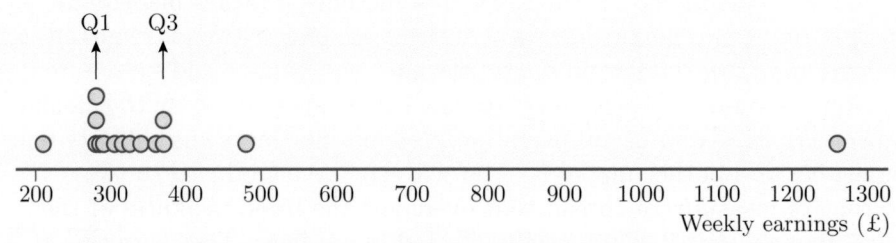

Figure 9   A dotplot of the earnings data from Activity 24 with the quartile positions marked

These quartiles are marked on a dotplot of the earnings data in Figure 9. Take a few moments to satisfy yourself that these values do lie, respectively, roughly one-quarter (Q1) and three-quarters (Q3) of the way through the data.

You will probably find that the description of quartiles is not totally convincing as it rather depends on how we choose to interpret 'a quarter of the way through the dataset'. Incidentally, the median, being the value that lies halfway through the data, is sometimes referred to as Q2, as it is the second quartile.

The convention when defining which quartile is Q1 and which is Q3 is that the data should be presented in increasing order of size. Then, even and odd sample sizes need slightly different approaches, and there are various ways of coping with this. The method for finding the quartiles described in the following two examples is used on some graphical calculators – it is straightforward and quite easy to perform. These examples also show you how to find the measure of spread known as the **interquartile range**, or IQR. The interquartile range is the difference between the upper and lower quartiles, that is, it is the value Q3 − Q1.

Example 3   *Finding the lower and upper quartiles: even sample size*

Find the lower quartile (Q1), the median and the upper quartile (Q3) of the following dataset.

    8 3 2 6 4 1 5 7

Then find the interquartile range.

Solution

Sort the data into increasing order. Find the median.

In increasing order, the dataset is

    1 2 3 4 5 6 7 8.

The median is the mean of the two middle data values, 4 and 5.

Median = 4.5.

To find the lower quartile, focus on the lower half of the dataset and find the median of this smaller dataset.

The lower half of the dataset is   1 2 3 4.

Its median is 2.5.

So Q1 = 2.5.

To find the upper quartile, focus on the upper half of the dataset and find the median of this smaller dataset.

The upper half of the dataset is   5 6 7 8.

Its median is 6.5.

So Q3 = 6.5.

The interquartile range is the difference between the upper and lower quartiles.

The interquartile range is thus

    $6.5 - 2.5 = 4$.

Example 4   *Finding the lower and upper quartiles: odd sample size*

Find the lower quartile (Q1), the median and the upper quartile (Q3) of the following dataset:

    1 2 3 4 5 6 7

Then find the interquartile range.

Solution

First find the median.

The median is the middle value of the ordered dataset.

Median = 4.

To find the lower quartile, ignore the middle data value and find the median of the lower 'half' of the dataset.

The lower half of the dataset is   1   2   3.

Its median is 2.

So Q1 = 2.

To find the upper quartile, ignore the middle data value and find the median of the upper 'half' of the dataset.

The upper half of the dataset is   5   6   7.

Its median is 6.

So Q3 = 6.

The interquartile range is the difference between the upper and lower quartiles.

The interquartile range is thus

$$6 - 2 = 4.$$

These examples lead to the following strategy for finding the quartiles and interquartile range.

Strategy *To find the quartiles and the interquartile range of a dataset*

1. Arrange the dataset in increasing order.

2. Next:

    (a) If there is an even number of data values, then the lower quartile (Q1) is the median of the lower half of the dataset, and the upper quartile (Q3) is the median of the upper half of the dataset.

    (b) If there is an odd number of data values, throw out the middle data point (which of course has the median value of the dataset). Then the lower quartile (Q1) is the median of the lower half of the new dataset, and the upper quartile (Q3) is the median of the upper half of the new dataset.

3. The interquartile range (IQR) is Q3 − Q1.

As you have seen, when there is an even number of data values, the dataset breaks neatly in half and the quartiles are simply the medians of these two half-sets. The procedure is slightly more complicated if the original dataset contains an odd number of values, as a decision needs to be made about what constitutes these half-sets. In the strategy above, the data value in the middle is excluded from these half-sets, and this is the convention used on this course. However, the choice of whether or not to include the middle data value is quite arbitrary – some authors include it and others, as we have done here, exclude it. Indeed, there are yet other methods of calculation that are different again and all of these may give slightly different answers for the values of the quartiles. With very small datasets like the ones you have been using, these differences may be noticeable, but in a real investigation, where the sizes would be larger, these small differences tend to disappear.

Activity 25 *Calculating the lower and upper quartiles*

Here again are the earnings data of 15 employees, first introduced in
Activity 24. This time, for your convenience, they have been sorted by size.

Weekly earnings (£): 210 280 280 280 285 290 305 | 315
325 340 360 370 370 480 1260

(a) What are the lower and upper quartiles of these values?

(b) Hence find the value of the interquartile range.

4.3 Standard deviation

The best known measure of spread is the **standard deviation**, or SD.
The bad news is that, using pencil and paper, it is hard work to calculate
the standard deviation, particularly with large datasets. The good news is
that, these days, once the data have been keyed in, a calculator or
computer can work out the standard deviation in a flash. But before
becoming totally reliant on a machine, it is a good idea to perform one or
two pencil and paper calculations of the standard deviation using very
simple datasets.

An alternative name for the standard deviation is the *RMS deviation* – in
full, the **root mean squared deviation**. Literally, it is the (square) root
of the mean of the squared deviations. This complicated name will make
more sense when you follow through the steps involved in the calculation.

Strategy *To find the standard deviation of a dataset*

1. Find the mean of the dataset.

2. Find the difference of each value from the mean – these are the
   'deviations', often labelled as the d values.

3. Square each deviation – this gives the d^2 values.

4. Find the mean of these squared deviations – this number is the
   'mean squared deviation', better known as the **variance**.

5. Find the square root of the variance to get the 'root mean squared
   deviation' – that is, the standard deviation.

There are in fact two different
versions of the standard
deviation – the method used
here involves the mean found in
the usual way of adding together
all the numbers in a dataset and
dividing by n, the size of the
dataset. In the other technique
for finding the standard
deviation,* the mean is found by
dividing by $n - 1$ rather than n.
These two methods are used in
different circumstances, but a
discussion of when it is
appropriate to use each one is
beyond the scope of MU123. In
this course, the divisor n will
always be used when calculating
the standard deviation.

Example 5 *Finding a standard deviation*

Find the standard deviation of the following dataset.

1 2 4 6 7

Solution

◌ Find the mean. ◌

Mean $= (1 + 2 + 4 + 6 + 7)/5 = 20/5 = 4$.

◌ Subtract the mean from each data value to find the deviations. ◌

The deviations are $-3, -2, 0, 2, 3$.

⟲ Square the deviations. ⟳

The squared deviations are 9, 4, 0, 4, 9.

⟲ Calculate the mean of the squared deviations to find the variance. ⟳

The variance is $(9 + 4 + 0 + 4 + 9)/5 = 26/5 = 5.2$.

⟲ The standard deviation is the square root of the variance. ⟳

So, the standard deviation is

$$\sqrt{5.2} = 2.3 \quad \text{(to 1 d.p.)}.$$

The steps of the calculation may be easier to see when laid out using a table such as the one in Figure 10.

Data values	Deviations (d)	d^2
1	$1 - 4 = -3$	$(-3)^2 = 9$
2	$2 - 4 = -2$	$(-2)^2 = 4$
4	$4 - 4 = -0$	$(0)^2 = 0$
6	$6 - 4 = 2$	$(2)^2 = 4$
7	$7 - 4 = 3$	$(3)^2 = 9$

Mean $= 4$ Mean $= 5.2$ SD $= \sqrt{5.2} = 2.3$ (to 1 d.p.)

Step 1: Find the mean   **Step 2:** Find the deviations   **Step 3:** Square the deviations   **Step 4:** Find the variance   **Step 5:** Find the standard deviation

Figure 10   The calculation of standard deviation (SD)

Students often find the calculation of standard deviation rather complicated and the steps hard to remember. It can be helpful to think about some of the ideas visually. Look at Figure 11, which shows these same five data values, 1, 2, 4, 6, 7, in a dotplot. As you can see, the mean, 4, is shown with a vertical line, while the deviations from the mean are represented by horizontal arrows.

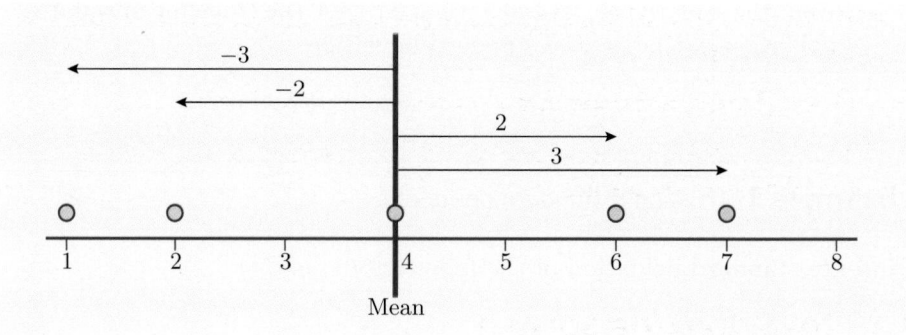

Figure 11   Deviations from the mean

You may have wondered why it is necessary to square the deviations in Step 3 of the calculation. In order to see the point of this, consider what would have happened if you had not squared them. For example, why not just find the mean of these deviations? This would be calculated as follows:

$$\text{mean deviation} = (-3 + (-2) + 0 + 2 + 3)/5 = 0/5 = 0.$$

As you can see, the positive and negative deviations have cancelled each other out and we are left with a numerator of zero. So the value of the mean deviation is zero. In fact, this will always be true of the mean deviation; the positive and negative deviations will always cancel each other out, leaving an answer of zero for the mean deviation. You may like to try this yourself with some other simple numerical examples. For example, take the dataset 3, 4, 6, 11, which has a mean of 6. This produces deviations -3, -2, 0, 5, and again these add to zero.

It is to avoid this problem that the deviations are squared in Step 3 (making them positive), and this is then 'undone' by taking the square root in Step 5.

Now tackle Activity 26, which will give you practice at performing standard deviation calculations using simple datasets.

Activity 26 *Calculating the standard deviation*

Calculate the standard deviations of the following simple datasets.

(a) 1   2   6   11

(b) 2   3   5   6   9

Although calculating standard deviation by pencil and paper is quite hard work, rest assured that these days it is normally done on a calculator or computer; as you will see later, the course resource Dataplotter calculates and displays it and other statistical summaries automatically. There are a number of reasons why the standard deviation is a useful measure of spread, and here are two of the main ones.

> ### Reasons for using the standard deviation as a measure of spread
>
> The standard deviation is the best known and most commonly used measure of spread.
>
> All the values in a dataset are included in its calculation.
>
> (However, unlike the interquartile range, its value can be to some extent distorted by outliers.)

4.4 Investigating spread

Just as Dataplotter provided instant summary measures of location (the mean and the median), it also provides the three summaries of spread introduced in this section: range, interquartile range and standard deviation. To end this section, you are asked to return to the two datasets concerning the words 'possible' and 'probable'. But this time you will explore what these three summaries reveal about the *spread* of these two datasets and how this can be interpreted.

Dataplotter

Activity 27   *Summaries of spread*

Return to Dataplotter and choose the same settings that you used in Activity 22, namely with the Dotplot option checked and the datasets '# Possible' and '# Probable' selected.

(a) By selecting appropriate values from the two summary lists on the screen, complete the table below.

Range, interquartile range and standard deviation of students' values for 'Possible' and 'Probable'

Summary	'Possible' scores	'Probable' scores
Range		
Interquartile range (IQR)		
Standard deviation (SD)		

(b) Based on the information in the table in part (a), which of the two datasets had the wider spread? How would you interpret this?

We should now be able to reach a conclusion about the original question: 'What do people understand by the words "possible" and "probable"?' For reference, Table 4 provides you with a handy list of all of the summaries from Dataplotter associated with the 'Possible' and 'Probable' datasets given earlier.

Table 4   Summaries of the 'Possible' and 'Probable' data

Summary	'Possible' scores	'Probable' scores
Min	1	51
Q1	20	70
Median	32.5	75.5
Q3	50	90
Max	98	99
Mean	38.6	78.5
SD	27.1	11.9
IQR	30	20
Range	97	48
n (size of dataset)	30	30

So, taking the mean and median (found in Activity 22) together with the range, interquartile range and standard deviation (calculated in Activity 27), two conclusions can be drawn. There is evidence that:

- people tend to think that the word 'probable' indicates a higher degree of likelihood than the word 'possible' (a conclusion based on comparing locations)

- there is a greater degree of agreement on the meaning of the word 'probable' than on the meaning of the word 'possible' (a conclusion based on comparing spreads).

As a footnote to this investigation, one of the students who carried out the study commented that the meaning of the word 'possible' rather depends on the tone of voice used when saying it and also on the context. Another said that there was so much variation in its interpretation that 'possible' really seemed to be a useless word for conveying meaning and should be dropped from the vocabulary!

In Activity 28, the final activity of Section 4, you are invited to enter data directly into Dataplotter to explore the properties of the five summary values that have been introduced in Sections 3 and 4.

 Dataplotter

Activity 28   *Investigating small datasets*

Open Dataplotter and clear both datasets by clicking on 'New'.

(a) Enter the four numbers $3, 4, 6, 7$ into the first column (press Enter after each data entry). From the displayed list summaries, you will see that the mean and median of this dataset are both equal to 5.

See Section 2 of the Course Guide for more information on using Dataplotter.

Now think about entering a fifth number that will raise the overall mean from 5 to 6; what must this number be, and what will be the value of the median of the new dataset? Enter this number to see if you are correct.

(b) Now change the number you entered to 10, if necessary. With the five numbers $3, 4, 6, 7, 10$ entered in the dataset, the range is 7 (that is, $10 - 3$) and the interquartile range is 5 (that is, $8.5 - 3.5$). Alter one of these five numbers to a different whole number so that the range remains unchanged but the value of the interquartile range increases to 6.

To edit a cell entry, click on the cell, type the new value and press Enter.

(c) Click on 'Clear' in the first column. The title of the dataset is displayed under the drop-down box. Click on the title, type 'SD1' into the box and press Enter. Then enter the six numbers $3, 4, 6, 6, 7, 10$ into the list. The value of the standard deviation is 2.2 (to 1 d.p.).

Next, in the drop-down menu of the second data column, select the dataset 'SD1' that you have just created, click on its title below the drop-down box, change its name to 'SD2' and press Enter. In this second dataset, alter the two 6s by the same amount in opposite directions, that is, by adding some non-zero number to one and subtracting the same number from the other.

Compare the displayed summaries of the two datasets: what effect does this change have on the value of the standard deviation? Can you explain why?

Following on from Section 3, where you looked at summarising a dataset by measuring its location, this section looked at measures of spread. Three particular measures of spread were looked at in detail.

- The *range* of a set of numbers is found by calculating max − min.

- The *interquartile range* (IQR) is the range of the middle half of the data and is calculated as $Q3 - Q1$ (where Q3 is the upper quartile and Q1 is the lower quartile).

- The *standard deviation* (SD) is the square root of the mean of the squares of the deviations of each data value from the mean. (You were also briefly introduced to a fourth measure of spread, the *variance*, which is the square of the standard deviation.)

These three main measures of spread (range, interquartile range and standard deviation) were used as part of the investigation of the 'Possible' and 'Probable' datasets to demonstrate that there seems to be a greater measure of agreement on the meaning of the word 'probable' than on the meaning of the word 'possible'.

Figure 12 is a development of the figure introduced in Subsection 3.2. As you can see, it sets out some of the main ideas of this unit, namely that location and spread are the two key forms of data summary, that two measures of location are the mean and median, and that three measures of spread are the range, the interquartile range and the standard deviation.

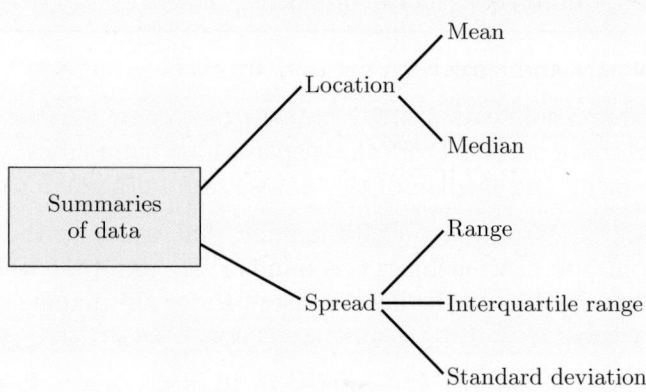

Figure 12   The completed summaries diagram

5 Measuring with accuracy and precision

This unit has looked at some important statistical questions. First, types of statistical questions were categorised (summarising, comparing, seeking a relationship), after which came the idea of a framework for investigating statistical questions (the 'PCAI' framework) – both these notions were explored in Section 1. In Section 2 you saw how to classify and distinguish different types of data (for example, primary and secondary data, discrete and continuous data). Sections 3 and 4 looked at the sorts of measures of location and spread that typically crop up in the 'A' (analyse the data) stage of most statistical investigations. It is these sorts of summary values that really help you to make decisions about data. The second statistical unit of the course, Unit 11, will extend this set of techniques to include a variety of statistical representations in the form of charts and plots.

To end this unit, we look at datasets of a particular kind. It is often useful or necessary to measure the size of a quantity, and this can be done in different ways, depending on the quantity – for example, a length or weight could be measured by using a measuring device, the amount of unemployment in a country or the viewing figures for a television programme could be measured by using surveys, and the strength of gravity could be measured by carrying out an experiment (as you will see shortly). No matter how a measurement is made, it is important to think about how good the measurement is. One way to do that is to consider datasets of *repeated* measurements, and this is the topic of this final section.

First, you are invited to use your own initiative to explore a small dataset created as part of a science investigation. The unit ends with an examination of two important terms that are often misused and confused: *precision* and *accuracy*, with reference to the statistical summaries *location* and *spread*.

5.1   Summarising a set of scientific measurements

Gravity on the Earth's surface is the downward force exerted on an object by the mass of the Earth. The size of this force varies slightly at different parts of the Earth, in particular at different altitudes and latitudes. When an object is dropped, and if no other forces except gravity are acting on it, its speed increases at a constant rate as it falls to the ground. At sea level, the speed increases by approximately 9.81 m/s every second. This increase in the speed each second is known as the acceleration due to gravity and it is denoted by the letter g. In SI units, g is measured in 'metres per second per second' which is written as m/s^2, so $g \approx 9.81\,m/s^2$.

The unit m/s^2 can also be written as $m\,s^{-2}$.

A group of experimenters tried to measure g, based on the following two different methods:

- 'free fall', where a ball bearing is dropped, and the time taken for it to fall through a known height is measured

- 'pendulum', where the period of swing of a pendulum (which is affected by the strength of gravity) is timed.

An interesting question arising out of this experiment is: which of these two methods gives the better estimate for g? You are asked to investigate this, using the data that the experimenters collected.

Posing the question

The data from the two experiments are given in Table 5 and are also available in Dataplotter. The numbers represent the researchers' results for g, measured in units of m/s^2, based on 16 'free fall' trials and 14 'pendulum' trials.

Collecting the data

Table 5   Estimates of g from two experiments

Free fall (m/s^2)	Pendulum (m/s^2)
9.97	10.18
9.84	10.08
9.80	9.78
9.81	9.83
9.80	10.13
9.80	9.95
9.81	9.82
9.81	10.12
9.88	9.96
9.97	9.97
9.78	9.80
9.81	9.81
9.78	9.83
9.80	9.73
9.87	
9.81	

Source: C. Maher and J. Pancari (1990) 'Statistics in high school science', *Teaching Statistics*, vol. 12, pp. 34–7.

At first glance, you may have noticed that there are some subtle variations in the measured values of g shown in Table 5. These variations are not necessarily associated with any geographical differences in g; we can assume that each experiment took place in the same location, so in theory the results should all be the same.

In fact, the differences that we observe in the data can be ascribed to what is known as *experimental error*. All experiments involve a degree of inherent error – inaccuracy in a measurement can arise from a number of sources, for example, poor experimental design, limitations of the measuring equipment, inconsistent application of techniques or even simple human error when reading a measurement. Statistical analysis of repeated measurements, such as calculating the mean of a dataset of repeated trials, is an important method for minimising the effects of experimental error in scientific experiments.

Activity 29   Scanning the data

Run your eye down both columns of figures. What general impressions do you have of these figures and what clues do they give about the success of the two experiments?

 Dataplotter

Activity 30   Analysing the data

Return to Dataplotter. Using the drop-down menus at the top of each list, select dataset '# Free fall' for the first list and '# Pendulum' for the second list.

Use suitable measures of location and spread to decide which of these two experiments produced a better estimate for g. It will suffice to consider all summary measures rounded to two decimal places.

Analysing the data

As was done in Sections 3 and 4 with the 'Possible' and 'Probable' datasets, a variety of measures of location and spread are instantly calculated and displayed in Dataplotter. Table 6 gives the various location and spread summary measures (rounded to 2 decimal places) for these two datasets.

Table 6   Summaries of the 'Free fall' and 'Pendulum' datasets

	Free fall	Pendulum
Min	9.78	9.73
Q1	9.80	9.81
Median	9.81	9.89
Q3	9.86	10.08
Max	9.97	10.18
Mean	9.83	9.93
SD	0.06	0.14
IQR	0.06	0.27
Range	0.19	0.45
n (size of dataset)	16	14

Two features stand out from these summaries.

In terms of location, the averages (i.e. mean and median) of the 'free fall' data lie closer to the 'true' value for g of $9.81 \, \mathrm{m/s^2}$ than do the 'pendulum' averages.

In terms of spread, there is a much narrower spread for the 'free fall' than for the 'pendulum' data as calculated by any of the measures.

Interpreting the results

So, on the evidence of these summaries, the 'free fall' experiment produced better results, since the average of the experimental values was closer to the true value and the results were more closely clustered together.

5.2   Accuracy and precision

A word often used in this unit is 'precision'. Elsewhere in the course it is used in the context of a number being stated to so many decimal places or a certain number of significant figures. Its meaning will be extended here. It is a term that can easily be confused with 'accuracy', but in fact these two terms have a subtle difference in meaning.

Imagine that you have been asked to audition for Robin Hood's 'merry men' and you have passed all the necessary merriment tests. The final set of tests requires you to demonstrate prowess with the bow and arrow. On your first run, with the sun glinting through the old oak tree, your five arrows land as shown in Figure 13.

Figure 13   First run: accurate but not precise

How would you describe this performance? The answer is that this shows *accuracy* but not precision. You can be described as accurate, because the average of the five shots is close to the centre. You are not precise, because the shots are widely spread.

Robin wasn't too impressed with your first effort, but he agrees to give you five more shots. This time, there is greater consistency, as shown in Figure 14.

'More consistent, yes,' says Robin, who was known throughout Sherwood Forest for his wit and repartee, 'but you are consistently missing!'

What Robin meant to say was that your shooting shows greater *precision* (the shots now cluster together) but the accuracy is actually worse than before (they are off-centre).

Figure 14   Second run: precise but not accurate

You beg for one last chance – and this time you really show that you have got to grips with the accuracy and precision issues in your archery skills, as shown in Figure 15. The tight clustering on this final run shows that you have lost none of the precision of Run 2, while the centring on the bull's-eye shows that your accuracy from Run 1 has returned.

Welcome to Sherwood Forest!

The first moral of this little tale is that accuracy is a statement about the location of a set of measurements: the closer the *average* of the measurements to the true value of what is being measured, the more *accurate* your estimation of that value. The second message is that precision tells you about the spread of that set of measurements: the more tightly *packed* your values, the more *precise* your measurements are.

> **Accuracy versus precision**
>
> For a set of (repeated) measurements:
>
> - **Accuracy** describes how close the average is to the true value.
> - **Precision** describes how close the measurements are to each other.

Figure 15   Third run: both accurate and precise

Ideally, when making measurements, you would like to have both accuracy and precision! In Subsection 5.1, the measurements from the 'free fall' experiment were both more accurate and more precise than the measurements from the 'pendulum' experiment.

Activity 31 *Distinguishing between precision and accuracy*

Two kitchen weighing scales are being tested to see if they measure accurately. A 100 g test weight is weighed five times on each set of scales and the results are shown below.

Scales A: 102 g   101 g   102 g   100 g   100 g

Scales B: 98 g   100 g   99 g   99 g   103 g

(a) Calculate the mean and range of each dataset.

(b) Use the measures in (a) to decide which set of scales is more accurate and which is more precise.

This final short section began by asking you to apply your skills in calculating summaries (both of location and spread) to a scientific investigation for estimating the value of g, the acceleration due to gravity. The final subsection looked at two words, accuracy and precision. It suggested that accuracy is a statement about the location of a set of measures, whereas precision tells you about their spread.

To review the ideas in this unit, have a go at the practice quiz for Unit 4 and then try the iCMA and TMA questions.

Learning checklist

After studying this unit, you should be able to:

- distinguish between different types of data, such as: primary and secondary data; discrete and continuous data; single and paired data

- use the PCAI cycle and appreciate how the various statistical skills and techniques fit into the PCAI stages of a statistical investigation

- gain a rough-and-ready, but sensible, overview of a dataset by just scanning the data (inspecting the values by eye)

- check and, if justified, clean data where there are numerical discrepancies such as outliers

- summarise a dataset in terms of measures of location and spread, select suitable data summaries for the context and use them as evidence to draw a conclusion

- appreciate the differences between accuracy, precision and spurious precision and use appropriate rounding in numerical summaries.

Solutions and comments on Activities

Activity 1

Investigations (a), (c) and (g) are in the summarising category. All the remaining investigations are in either the comparing or the relationship category.

Activity 2

The cases (a), (d) and (e) are 'comparing' investigations. Case (c) is a 'relationship' investigation. In case (b), the social backgrounds can be measured on a numerical scale and a relationship investigation carried out. However, the social backgrounds can also be used to split the students into two groups so that a comparing investigation can be carried out.

Activity 3

(a) Although this is a hypothetical example, the potential stages should be fairly easy to identify. Here is one possible answer (yours may be different in several respects).

Stage P: The general question here is: 'Did the traffic-calming measures slow the traffic?' A more focused question might be: 'Were vehicle speeds slower, on average, after the measures were introduced?'

Stage C: A suitable sample of vehicle speeds would be collected before and after the traffic-calming measures were introduced. Care would need to be taken to ensure that the sample sizes were sufficiently large, that the vehicles were chosen randomly, and that the circumstances of the sampling (e.g. time of day) were similar between the two samples.

Stage A: A simple technique for analysing these figures is to calculate and compare the two average speeds. (You haven't seen these yet, but useful techniques at the 'A' stage could include drawing a variety of different charts and plots: for example, dotplots, boxplots and histograms, all of which are covered in Unit 11.)

Stage I: The trickiest stage is relating the data analysis to the original problem. In simple terms, if the average speed is lower after traffic-calming measures are in place, then we might conclude that they have been successful. However, although average traffic speeds may have fallen slightly, how do we know that this was *because* of the traffic-calming measures? There might be some other explanation for these results, such as that the 'after' measurements were conducted in very different weather conditions when traffic conditions

could be expected to be slower anyway. Also, the difference may not be sufficiently large to allow us to draw any firm conclusions. It is worth pointing out that although more focused questions are usually easier to answer, they may contain certain in-built assumptions that compromise the original question that you asked. So, as has already been indicated, it is one thing to show that the average speeds after the traffic-calming measures were introduced had fallen, but it is another to prove cause-and-effect.

Furthermore, it is conceivable (though perhaps unlikely) that average speeds are indeed reduced but that this makes no difference to the number and severity of accidents. (Reducing accidents and their severity was probably the purpose of the exercise in the first place.)

(b) Calculating averages and plotting data graphically are very useful statistical techniques, particularly for investigations of comparing.

Activity 4

Collect relevant data:
    Choose a sample ✓
    Design a questionnaire ✓
    Key the data into a spreadsheet ✓

Analyse the data:
    Calculate an average ✓
    Calculate a percentage ✓
    Draw a helpful graph ✓

Interpret the results:
    Make a decision based on a difference ✓
    Draw a conclusion ✓
    Make a prediction about the real world ✓

Activity 5

Clearly there are no uniquely correct answers to this activity, but you might like to compare your notes with the suggestions below.

Stage P: A suitable question might be: 'Do clouds keep heat in?' A more focused question might be something like: 'Do night temperatures drop less when it is cloudy?'

Stage C: Various newspapers publish daily lists of the highest and lowest temperatures recorded on the previous day across a number of towns in the UK, and also whether the weather had been sunny, cloudy, raining, and so on. For a particular town or region, collect this information for 30 consecutive days, noting whether each day was cloudy or clear.

Stage A: Separate the 30 days' data into two groups, labelled cloudy and clear. For each of the 30 days, calculate the 'temperature swing', that is, the difference between the highest and lowest temperatures. Calculate the average temperature swing for the cloudy data and the clear data.

Stage I: Observe which average temperature swing was greater. If the answer was the 'clear' data, this would provide evidence to suggest that clouds do tend to retain heat. However, a weakness with the design of this investigation is that we are not strictly comparing like with like. Since sunny days are generally warmer than cloudy days, an alternative explanation might be that temperature swings are larger on warmer days (as opposed to sunny days, which are not necessarily the same thing).

Activity 6

Probably the most striking features are the following.

- Some columns (such as E to H) seem to contain 'detailed' decimal numbers taking a wide range of values, while all the others seem to contain many fewer integers, some (such as J to M) containing a lot of zeros.

- Some cells (G21, F28, G28) that might be expected to contain data are blank.

- Some individual numbers stand out as being much larger than the rest of the numbers in the same column. For example, the values of 99 in cells I11, I22, L25 and M25 are enormous compared with other numbers in those columns, as is (rather less obviously) the value in cell H8 which corresponds to a baby weighing 34 kg!

- Some individual numbers stand out as being given in a rather different form from the rest of the numbers in the same column. The values in cells D29 and F32 are given to many more decimal places than the other values in their columns.

Activity 7

Discrete data can be found in the columns 'Month of pregnancy pain started', 'Number of children', 'Relieved by hot bath?', 'Aggravated by fatigue?' and 'Aggravated by bending?'. The last three of these contain binary data (except for the values of '99'). You may have added 'Age' to the list – the column contains (mostly) integer values between 18 and 42 – but you may have had a nagging doubt that surely age is measured on a continuous scale; more on this very soon!

Activity 8

Comments on this activity are included in the text.

Activity 9

Discrete:

(a) Price of loaf

(b) Number of seagulls

(d) Number of goals scored

(f) TMA score

(i) Wind speed on the Beaufort scale

Continuous:

(c) Athlete's time

(e) Distance between cities

(g) Air temperature

(h) Wind speed measured in kilometres per hour

In cases (c), (e), (g) and (h) the underlying measures (time, distance, temperature and wind speed) are continuous, but in practice values are measured and recorded on what is effectively a discrete scale.

Activity 10

(a) Column G has a maximum weight of 92.7 kg, which is both a realistic value and in line with the next largest weights, and a minimum of 7.5 kg ... which is not realistic and wholly out of line with other mothers' weights! A possible explanation here is that a decimal point has been erroneously introduced into a true value of 75 kg.

(b) The data in cells E2 to E34 range from 1.5 m to 1.92 m. The latter is very much greater than any other height in this column. However, is it necessarily in error? Such a woman would be unusually tall, but such a height is by no means impossible.

Activity 11

(a) 125 pounds, in kg, is
$125 \times 0.45359237 = 56.699046\ldots$ kg, which is 56.69905 kg when given correct to five decimal places, as in cell F32.

(b) 29.916666 years becomes 30 years, and 56.69905 kg becomes 56.7 kg.

Activity 12

(a) The likelihood is that this estimate involved 'scaling up' daily or weekly data. For example, suppose on a particular day the accused was found to have stolen, say, £266.65. Let us assume that the employee worked roughly 220 days per year (44 weeks at 5 days per week). Over 9.5 years, the number of days worked would be $9.5 \times 220 = 2090$

days. Based on the assumption that £266.65 was a typical day's 'takings', a rough estimate of the total theft could be made by calculating £266.65 × 2090 = £557 298.50.

(b) One wonders where the spare 11p or, more particularly, the final 1p would have come from. This is the sort of spurious precision that makes one smell a statistical rat! It seems unlikely that car park pay-and-display machines were accepting pennies in 1996. It would be much more reasonable to accept, say, £550 000 as a rough estimate of the amount of money stolen.

Activity 13

Datasets	Data type(s)	Relevance
Weights of mothers and weights of their babies	Paired data	Seeking a relationship
Weights of mothers at end of pregnancy	Single data	Summarising
Weights of two samples of babies, one in the UK and one in France	Two-sample data	Comparing
Weights of mothers and average earnings in 20 EU countries	Two unrelated samples	No direct interest

Activity 14

(a) You might say that the teacher times were all about 30 seconds, while the student times were all about 25 seconds.

(b) On the basis of the answer to part (a), student times were generally faster than teacher times.

Activity 16

(a) **(i)** There are no missing data.

(ii) There do not appear to be any numbers given to spurious levels of precision in the sense of too many decimal places.

(iii) All the data values lie between 0 and 100.

(iv) You might or might not think of labelling some values as outliers (e.g. the single-figure values for 'Possible' stand out ... but there are several of them). All told, the data seem to be pretty 'clean'.

(b) An interesting observation of human behaviour is that, when asked to make an estimate of something, most people have a tendency to round their answers to, say, the nearest 5 or 10. There seems to be considerable evidence of such a tendency here since a large number of values in both columns are divisible by 5 or 10. (You might particularly have noticed the many numbers ending with a zero. These represent respondents who have applied an appropriate degree of precision to the question asked.)

Activity 17

(a) You might have tried to identify the values that tended to crop up most often, or maybe disregarded the very large and very small values and identified a value that lies in the middle of the remaining items.

(b) Based on inspecting the data and perhaps your own response to Activity 16(b), you may have thought that the 'Probable' values were a bit higher than the 'Possible' values.

Activity 18

(a) The mean texting time for the seven students is

$$(19 + 19 + 21 + 24 + 25 + 27 + 29)/7$$
$$= 164/7 = 23.4 \text{ seconds (to 1 d.p.)}.$$

(b) The mean of the 'Possible' values in Table 3 is

$$(30 + 90 + 60 + \cdots + 35)/30$$
$$= 1157/30 = 38.6 \text{ (to 1 d.p.)}.$$

Activity 19

(a) Where there are seven values sorted in order of size, the median is the fourth value. So the median of the seven student texting times is 24 seconds.

(b) The table below shows the three sets of summaries already used for these data. (The 'Estimate' column refers to the estimated values in the solution to Activity 14(a).)

	Estimate	Mean	Median
Teacher times (s)	30	31.8	31
Student times (s)	25	23.4	24

As you can see, all three teacher averages are fairly similar, as are the three student averages.

Activity 20

(a) In increasing order, the data become:

23 25 58 60 60 60

60 80 100 100 160 200

The median is the mean of the 6th and 7th values in the ordered list, i.e. $(60 + 60)/2 = 60$. As these estimates are millions, the median estimate is therefore 60 million.

Alternatively, in decreasing order, the data values (in millions) are:

200 160 100 100 80 60

60 60 60 58 25 23

The two middle values are still 60 and 60, so again the median estimate is 60 million.

(b) The median is the mean of the 15th and 16th values in the ordered list, namely $(30 + 35)/2 = 32.5$.

Activity 21

(a) The mean is

$(51 + 60 + 60 + \cdots + 99)/30 = 78.5.$

(b) The median is the mean of the 15th and 16th values in the ordered dataset, namely $(75 + 76)/2 = 75.5.$

(c) The mean is larger than the median for this dataset.

Activity 22

(a) *Means and medians of students' values for 'Possible' and 'Probable'*

Summary	'Possible' scores	'Probable' scores
Mean	38.6	78.5
Median	32.5	75.5

(These values have been rounded to 1 d.p.)

(b) There are two pairs of summary values here, each of which gives a direct answer to the question posed.

Means: the 'Possible' mean of 38.6 is well below the 'Probable' mean of 78.5.

Medians: the 'Possible' median of 32.5 is well below the 'Probable' median of 75.5.

Further comments on this activity can be found in the text following the activity.

Activity 23

(a) For Dataset A, mean $= 6$ and median $= 6$.

For Dataset B, mean $= 18.9$ (to 1 d.p.) and median $= 6$.

(b) Dataset A is perfectly symmetrical – i.e. the values are not bunched together on one side or the other but are located in a way that is evenly balanced around the middle value of 6. Where datasets are highly symmetrical, the values of the mean and the median are very similar, so it really doesn't matter which you choose.

With Dataset B, the outlier 99 has a big impact on the value of the mean, but has no effect on the value of the median. There is no easy answer to which is the better choice of summary value in this case, as it all depends on the context from which the numbers were taken. If you feel that the 99 is a freak value and should effectively be disregarded, then choose the median. However, if the 99 is important and needs to be recognised in the summary, then choose the mean.

(c) Several advantages of the mean and the median are listed below, in no particular order. Please note that what seem to be advantages to some people might seem to be disadvantages to others! Also, you are not expected to have thought of all the pros and cons listed here.

Possible advantages of the mean:

- The mean, or average, is familiar to most people and widely used.

- There is often a button on a simple scientific calculator for calculating the mean, but not one for calculating the median.

- The mean includes every value in its calculation. (This, in particular, may or may not be an advantage!)

Possible advantages of the median:

- When there is an odd number of values in the dataset, the median is one of the values from the dataset and so can be thought of as being a 'representative' of the complete dataset.

- Following on from the point above, you might think that the median is a more intuitive summary (see also the way Activity 14 was approached).

- With reference to small datasets, the median is easier to calculate in your head than is the mean.

- As you saw in part (a) of this activity, an important property of the median is that it isn't affected by outliers: even if, say, the largest value in a dataset is made very much larger than the other values in the dataset, the median, being the 'middle value', doesn't change.

- You can identify the median item even in situations where there are no actual figures. For example, if you want to choose a soldier of average height, simply ask all the soldiers under consideration to line up in order of size and choose the one in the middle.

Activity 24

(a) min = £210, max = £1260, so
range = £1260 − £210 = £1050.

(b) The max value (£1260) is clearly very far out of line with the rest of the data. (It is likely that this figure represents the weekly earnings of the owner.) In fact, most of the values are bunched between £200 and £400, so for this particular dataset, the range does not give a useful impression of the spread of the main part of the data.

Activity 25

(a) The median is the 8th value when placed in order, i.e. £315.

Q1 is the median of the bottom half of the data (excluding the median data value), i.e. the median of
210   280   280   280   285   290   305
So Q1 = £280.

Q3 is the median of the upper half of the data (excluding the median data value), i.e. the median of
325   340   360   370   370   480   1260
So Q3 = £370.

(b) Interquartile range = £370 − £280 = £90.

Activity 26

(a) Mean = $(1 + 2 + 6 + 11)/4 = 20/4 = 5$.

The deviations are found by subtracting the mean from each data value in turn, giving $-4, -3, 1, 6$.

The squared deviations are $16, 9, 1, 36$.

The variance is the mean of these squared deviations:

$(16 + 9 + 1 + 36)/4 = 62/4 = 15.5.$

The standard deviation is the square root of the variance:

$\sqrt{15.5} = 3.9$ (to 1 d.p.).

(b) Mean = $(2 + 3 + 5 + 6 + 9)/5 = 5$.

The deviations are found by subtracting the mean from each data value in turn, giving $-3, -2, 0, 1, 4$.

The squared deviations are $9, 4, 0, 1, 16$.

The variance is the mean of these squared deviations:

$(9 + 4 + 0 + 1 + 16)/5 = 30/5 = 6.$

The standard deviation is the square root of the variance:

$\sqrt{6} = 2.4$ (to 1 d.p.).

Activity 27

(a) *Range, IQR and SD of students' values for 'Possible' and 'Probable'*

Summary	'Possible' scores	'Probable' scores
Range	97	48
IQR	30	20
SD	27.1	11.9

(b) There are three pairs of summary values here, each of which gives a direct answer to the question posed.

Ranges: the 'Possible' range of 97 is much wider than the 'Probable' range of 48.

IQRs: the 'Possible' interquartile range of 30 is much wider than the 'Probable' interquartile range of 20.

SDs: the 'Possible' standard deviation of 27.1 is much wider than the 'Probable' standard deviation of 11.9.

So, in general, the spread of estimates for the 'Possible' data is considerably wider than that for the 'Probable' data. What this suggests is that, if this sample is typical, when people use the word 'possible', it is difficult to know what sort of level of likelihood they are referring to since numerical estimates for defining this word are so widely spread.

Activity 28

(a) The fifth number is 10. This will also raise the value of the median from 5 to 6.

(b) Change the 7 to 9. The min and max values are unchanged, so the range remains at 7. The upper quartile, Q3, increases from 8.5 to 9.5, which increases the interquartile range to 6 (i.e. $9.5 - 3.5$).

(c) Changing the 6s as described should have the effect of increasing the value of the standard deviation. The reason is that 6 happens to be equal to the value of the sample mean, so the two data items 6 each have a deviation of zero. Changing the 6s as described to any other values will produce non-zero deviations for these data values (without changing the mean), which will increase the value of the standard deviation.

Activity 29

At first glance, you can see that there don't seem to be any outliers or examples of spurious precision. A closer look might suggest that the 'free fall' values seem to be slightly lower and less widely spread than the 'pendulum' data.

Activity 30

Comments on this activity are included in the text.

Activity 31

(a) For the Scales A, the mean (in g) is $(102 + 101 + 102 + 100 + 100)/5 = 505/5 = 101$.

The range is $102\,\text{g} - 100\,\text{g} = 2\,\text{g}$.

For the Scales B, the mean (in g) is $(98 + 100 + 99 + 99 + 103)/5 = 499/5 = 99.8$.

The range is $103\,\text{g} - 98\,\text{g} = 5\,\text{g}$.

(b) The mean weight from Scales B ($99.8\,\text{g}$) is closer to the true weight of 100g than the mean weight from Scales A ($101\,\text{g}$), so the Scales B are more accurate.

The range of the weights from Scales A ($2\,\text{g}$) is smaller than the range of the weights from Scales B ($5\,\text{g}$), so the Scales A are more precise.

Acknowledgements

Grateful acknowledgement is made to the following sources for permission to reproduce material in this book.

Unit 1

Figure 1 © The Science Museum of Brussels, www.wikipedia.org; Figure 2 © The Italian Post Office; Figure 24 © Bloomsbury Publishing; Figure 30(a): Institute of Anatomy, University of Bern, Switzerland, Prof. Ewald R. Weibel; Figure 30(b): *Romanesco broccoli* www.wikipedia.org; Figure 30(c): *Leaf of fern*, www.wikipedia.org; Figure 31: *Full tiling dragon* and *Full tiling dragon 2*, www.wikipedia.org; Figure 32 © The French Post Office.

Unit 2

Cartoon on page 66 © CartoonStock Ltd; Cartoon on page 67 © CartoonStock Ltd; Figure 4: Department for Transport; Cartoon on page 78 © CartoonStock Ltd; Highway Code extract and Figure 6 on page 80: Crown copyright material reproduced under Class Licence Number C01W0000065 with the permission of the Controller of HMSO and the Queen's Printer for Scotland; Cartoon on page 98 © Sidney Harris.

Unit 3

Figure 2: *Marin Mersenne*, www-history.mcs.st-andrews.ac.uk; Figure 6: *C.F. Gauss*, www-history.mcs.st-andrews.ac.uk; Cartoon on page 130 © R. Munroe, xkcd.com; Figure 15 © Oddmusic 1999-2008; Figure 20 © Photos by Tom Hustler (Getty Images).

Unit 4

Figure 1 © University of Kentucky; Figure 3: *Forest path* www.seacology.org/project_photos/large/INDON87.htm (accessed 23/9/08); Figure 4: These photos of a magnified sheet of paper were taken on a Zeiss Supra 55VP Field Emission Gun Scanning Electron Microscope (FEGSEM), courtesy of Interfaculty Electron Microscope Suite, Open University.

INDEX